J. J. Connington and The Murder Room

››› This title is part of The Murder Room, our series dedicated to making available out-of-print or hard-to-find titles by classic crime writers.

Crime fiction has always held up a mirror to society. The Victorians were fascinated by sensational murder and the emerging science of detection; now we are obsessed with the forensic detail of violent death. And no other genre has so captivated and enthralled readers.

Vast troves of classic crime writing have for a long time been unavailable to all but the most dedicated frequenters of second-hand bookshops. The advent of digital publishing means that we are now able to bring you the backlists of a huge range of titles by classic and contemporary crime writers, some of which have been out of print for decades.

From the genteel amateur private eyes of the Golden Age and the femmes fatales of pulp fiction, to the morally ambiguous hard-boiled detectives of mid twentieth-century America and their descendants who walk our twenty-first century streets, The Murder Room has it all. ›››

The Murder Room
Where Criminal Minds Meet

themurderroom.com

J. J. Connington (1880–1947)

Alfred Walter Stewart, who wrote under the pen name J. J. Connington, was born in Glasgow, the youngest of three sons of Reverend Dr Stewart. He graduated from Glasgow University and pursued an academic career as a chemistry professor, working for the Admiralty during the First World War. Known for his ingenious and carefully worked-out puzzles and in-depth character development, he was admired by a host of his better-known contemporaries, including Dorothy L. Sayers and John Dickson Carr, who both paid tribute to his influence on their work. He married Jessie Lily Courts in 1916 and they had one daughter.

By J. J. Connington

Sir Clinton Driffield Mysteries

Murder in the Maze (1927)
Tragedy at Ravensthorpe (1927)
The Case with Nine Solutions (1928)
Mystery at Lynden Sands (1928)
Nemesis at Raynham Parva (1929)
(a.k.a. Grim Vengenace)
The Boathouse Riddle (1931)
The Sweepstake Murders (1931)
The Castleford Conundrum (1932)
The Ha-Ha Case (1934)
(a.k.a. The Brandon Case)
In Whose Dim Shadow (1935)
(a.k.a. The Tau Cross Mystery)
A Minor Operation (1937)
Murder Will Speak (1938)
Truth Comes Limping (1938)
The Twenty-One Clues (1941)
No Past is Dead (1942)
Jack-in-the-Box (1944)
Common Sense Is All You Need (1947)

Supt Ross Mysteries

The Eye in the Museum (1929)
The Two Tickets Puzzle (1930)

Novels

Death at Swaythling Court (1926)
The Dangerfield Talisman (1926)
Tom Tiddler's Island (1933)
(a.k.a. Gold Brick Island)
The Counsellor (1939)
The Four Defences (1940)

The Twenty-One Clues

J. J. Connington

An Orion book

This edition published by
The Orion Publishing Group Ltd
Orion House
5 Upper St Martin's Lane
London WC2H 9EA

An Hachette UK company
A CIP catalogue record for this book is available from the British Library

ISBN 978 1 4719 0619 0

www.orionbooks.co.uk

CONTENTS

Introduction by Curtis Evans i

CHAPTER PAGE

I. THE ALVINGTON DIVORCE CASE . . . 1
II. SUICIDE PACT 13
III. IDENTIFICATION 27
IV. THE TELEGRAM 34
V. THE BLACK BAG 56
VI. THE YELLOW DWARF 72
VII. THE SUIT-CASES 86
VIII. THE BULLETS 104
IX. THE CAR 119
X. THE TWENTY-ONE CLUES 133
XI. THE SHOOTER OF CATS 151
XII. AN ORGANIST AND SOME OTHERS . . 164
XIII. THE DOUBLE-FLORIN 187
XIV. DEATH CALLS AGAIN 205
XV. JUGGERNAUT 222
XVI. THE FOUR CARTRIDGE-CASES . . . 238
XVII. "THEY ARE SO GRATEFUL" . . . 254

Introduction by Curtis Evans

During the Golden Age of the detective novel, in the 1920s and 1930s, J. J. Connington stood with fellow crime writers R. Austin Freeman, Cecil John Charles Street and Freeman Wills Crofts as the foremost practitioner in British mystery fiction of the science of pure detection. I use the word 'science' advisedly, for the man behind J. J. Connington, Alfred Walter Stewart, was an esteemed Scottish-born scientist. A 'small, unassuming, moustached polymath', Stewart was 'a strikingly effective lecturer with an excellent sense of humor, fertile imagination and fantastically retentive memory', qualities that also served him well in his fiction. He held the Chair of Chemistry at Queens University, Belfast for twenty-five years, from 1919 until his retirement in 1944.

During roughly this period, the busy Professor Stewart found time to author a remarkable apocalyptic science fiction tale, *Nordenholt's Million* (1923), a mainstream novel, *Almighty Gold* (1924), a collection of essays, *Alias J. J. Connington* (1947), and, between 1926 and 1947, twenty-four mysteries (all but one tales of detection), many of them sterling examples of the Golden Age puzzle-oriented detective novel at its considerable best. 'For those who ask first of all in a detective story for exact and mathematical accuracy in the construction of the plot', avowed a contemporary *London Daily Mail* reviewer, 'there is no author to equal the distinguished scientist who writes under the name of J. J. Connington.'[1]

Alfred Stewart's background as a man of science is reflected in his fiction, not only in the impressive puzzle plot mechanics he devised for his mysteries but in his choices of themes and depictions of characters. Along with Stanley Nordenholt of *Nordenholt's Million*, a novel about a plutocrat's pitiless efforts to preserve a ruthlessly remolded remnant of human life after a global environmental calamity, Stewart's most notable character is Chief Constable Sir Clinton Driffield, the detective in seventeen of the twenty-four Connington crime novels. Driffield is one of crime fiction's most highhanded investigators, occasionally taking on the functions of judge and jury as well as chief of police.

Absent from Stewart's fiction is the hail-fellow-well-met quality found in John Street's works or the religious ethos suffusing those of Freeman Wills Crofts, not to mention the effervescent novel-of-manners style of the British Golden Age Crime Queens Dorothy L. Sayers, Margery Allingham and Ngaio Marsh. Instead we see an often disdainful cynicism about the human animal and a marked admiration for detached supermen with superior intellects. For this reason, reading a Connington novel can be a challenging experience for modern readers inculcated in gentler social beliefs. Yet Alfred Stewart produced a classic apocalyptic science fiction tale in *Nordenholt's Million* (justly dubbed 'exciting and terrifying reading' by the *Spectator*) as well as superb detective novels boasting well-wrought puzzles, bracing characterization and an occasional leavening of dry humor. Not long after Stewart's death in 1947, the Connington novels fell entirely out of print. The recent embrace of Stewart's fiction by Orion's Murder Room imprint is a welcome event indeed, correcting as it does over sixty years of underserved neglect of an accomplished genre writer.

Born in Glasgow on 5 September 1880, Alfred Stewart had significant exposure to religion in his earlier life. His father was William Stewart, longtime Professor of Divinity and Biblical Criticism at Glasgow University, and he married Lily Coats, a daughter of the Reverend Jervis Coats and member of one of

Scotland's preeminent Baptist families. Religious sensibility is entirely absent from the Connington corpus, however. A confirmed secularist, Stewart once referred to one of his wife's brothers, the Reverend William Holms Coats (1881–1954), principal of the Scottish Baptist College, as his 'mental and spiritual antithesis', bemusedly adding: 'It's quite an education to see what one would look like if one were turned into one's mirror-image.'

Stewart's J. J. Connington pseudonym was derived from a nineteenth-century Oxford Professor of Latin and translator of Horace, indicating that Stewart's literary interests lay not in pietistic writing but rather in the pre-Christian classics ('I prefer the *Odyssey* to *Paradise Lost*,' the author once avowed). Possessing an inquisitive and expansive mind, Stewart was in fact an uncommonly well-read individual, freely ranging over a variety of literary genres. His deep immersion in French literature and supernatural horror fiction, for example, is documented in his lively correspondence with the noted horologist Rupert Thomas Gould.[2]

It thus is not surprising that in the 1920s the intellectually restless Stewart, having achieved a distinguished middle age as a highly regarded man of science, decided to apply his creative energy to a new endeavor, the writing of fiction. After several years he settled, like other gifted men and women of his generation, on the wildly popular mystery genre. Stewart was modest about his accomplishments in this particular field of light fiction, telling Rupert Gould later in life that 'I write these things [what Stewart called tec yarns] because they amuse me in parts when I am putting them together and because they are the only writings of mine that the public will look at. Also, in a minor degree, because I like to think some people get pleasure out of them.' No doubt Stewart's single most impressive literary accomplishment is *Nordenholt's Million*, yet in their time the two dozen J. J. Connington mysteries did indeed give readers in Great Britain, the United States and other countries much diversionary reading pleasure. Today these works constitute an estimable addition to British crime fiction.

After his 'prentice pastiche mystery, *Death at Swaythling Court* (1926), a rural English country-house tale set in the highly traditional village of Fernhurst Parva, Stewart published another, superior country-house affair, *The Dangerfield Talisman* (1926), a novel about the baffling theft of a precious family heirloom, an ancient, jewel-encrusted armlet. This clever, murderless tale, which likely is the one that the author told Rupert Gould he wrote in under six weeks, was praised in *The Bookman* as 'continuously exciting and interesting' and in the *New York Times Book Review* as 'ingeniously fitted together and, what is more, written with a deal of real literary charm'. Despite its virtues, however, *The Dangerfield Talisman* is not fully characteristic of mature Connington detective fiction. The author needed a memorable series sleuth, more representative of his own forceful personality.

It was the next year, 1927, that saw J. J. Connington make his break to the front of the murdermongerer's pack with a third country-house mystery, *Murder in the Maze*, wherein debuted as the author's great series detective the assertive and acerbic Sir Clinton Driffield, along with Sir Clinton's neighbor and 'Watson', the more genial (if much less astute) Squire Wendover. In this much-praised novel, Stewart's detective duo confronts some truly diabolical doings, including slayings by means of curare-tipped darts in the double-centered hedge maze at a country estate, Whistlefield. No less a fan of the genre than T. S. Eliot praised *Murder in the Maze* for its construction ('we are provided early in the story with all the clues which guide the detective') and its liveliness ('The very idea of murder in a box-hedge labyrinth does the author great credit, and he makes full use of its possibilities'). The delighted Eliot concluded that

Murder in the Maze was 'a really first-rate detective story'. For his part, the critic H. C. Harwood declared in *The Outlook* that with the publication of *Murder in the Maze* Connington demanded and deserved 'comparison with the masters'. 'Buy, borrow, or – anyhow – get hold of it', he amusingly advised. Two decades later, in his 1946 critical essay 'The Grandest Game in the World', the great locked-room detective novelist John Dickson Carr echoed Eliot's assessment of the novel's virtuoso setting, writing: 'These 1920s [. . .] thronged with sheer brains. What would be one of the best possible settings for violent death? J. J. Connington found the answer, with *Murder in the Maze*.' Certainly in retrospect *Murder in the Maze* stands as one of the finest English country-house mysteries of the 1920s, cleverly yet fairly clued, imaginatively detailed and often grimly suspenseful. As the great American true-crime writer Edmund Lester Pearson noted in his review of *Murder in the Maze* in *The Outlook*, this Connington novel had everything that one could desire in a detective story: 'A shrubbery maze, a hot day, and somebody potting at you with an air gun loaded with darts covered with a deadly South-American arrow-poison – *there* is a situation to wheedle two dollars out of anybody's pocket.'[3]

Staying with what had worked so well for him to date, Stewart the same year produced yet another country-house mystery, *Tragedy at Ravensthorpe*, an ingenious tale of murders and thefts at the ancestral home of the Chacewaters, old family friends of Sir Clinton Driffield. There is much clever matter in *Ravensthorpe*. Especially fascinating is the author's inspired integration of faerie folklore into his plot. Stewart, who had a lifelong – though skeptical – interest in paranormal phenomena, probably was inspired in this instance by the recent hubbub over the Cottingly Faeries photographs that in the early 1920s had famously duped, among other individuals, Arthur Conan Doyle.[4] As with *Murder in the Maze*, critics raved about this new Connington mystery. In the *Spectator*, for example, a reviewer hailed *Tragedy at Ravensthorpe* in the strongest terms, declaring of the novel: 'This is more than a good detective tale. Alike in plot, characterization, and literary style, it is a work of art.'

In 1928 there appeared two additional Sir Clinton Driffield detective novels, *Mystery at Lynden Sands* and *The Case with Nine Solutions*. Once again there was great praise for the latest Conningtons. H. C. Harwood, the critic who had so much admired *Murder in the Maze*, opined of *Mystery at Lynden Sands* that it 'may just fail of being the detective story of the century', while in the United States author and book reviewer Frederic F. Van de Water expressed nearly as high an opinion of *The Case with Nine Solutions*. 'This book is a thoroughbred of a distinguished lineage that runs back to "The Gold Bug" of [Edgar Allan] Poe,' he avowed. 'It represents the highest type of detective fiction.' In both of these Connington novels, Stewart moved away from his customary country-house milieu, setting *Lynden Sands* at a fashionable beach resort and *Nine Solutions* at a scientific research institute. *Nine Solutions* is of particular interest today, I think, for its relatively frank sexual subject matter and its modern urban setting among science professionals, which rather resembles the locales found in P. D. James' classic detective novels *A Mind to Murder* (1963) and *Shroud for a Nightingale* (1971).

By the end of the 1920s, J. J. Connington's critical reputation had achieved enviable heights indeed. At this time Stewart became one of the charter members of the Detection Club, an assemblage of the finest writers of British detective fiction that included, among other distinguished individuals, Agatha Christie, Dorothy L. Sayers and G. K. Chesterton. Certainly Victor Gollancz, the British publisher of the J. J. Connington mysteries, did not stint praise for the author, informing readers that 'J. J. Connington is now established as, in the opinion of many, the greatest living master of the story of pure detection. He is one of those who, discarding all the superfluities, has made of deductive fiction a genuine minor art, with its own laws and its own conventions.'

Such warm praise for J. J. Connington makes it all the more surprising that at this juncture the esteemed author tinkered with his successful formula by dispensing with his original series detective. In the fifth Clinton Driffield detective novel, *Nemesis at Raynham Parva* (1929), Alfred Walter Stewart, rather like Arthur Conan Doyle before him, seemed with a dramatic dénouement to have devised his popular series detective's permanent exit from the fictional stage (read it and see for yourself). The next two Connington detective novels, *The Eye in the Museum* (1929) and *The Two Tickets Puzzle* (1930), have a different series detective, Superintendent Ross, a rather dull dog of a policeman. While both these mysteries are competently done – the railway material in *The Two Tickets Puzzle* is particularly effective and should have appeal today – the presence of Sir Clinton Driffield (no superfluity he!) is missed.

Probably Stewart detected that the public minded the absence of the brilliant and biting Sir Clinton, for the Chief Constable – accompanied, naturally, by his friend Squire Wendover – triumphantly returned in 1931 in *The Boathouse Riddle*, another well-constructed criminous country-house affair. Later in the year came *The Sweepstake Murders*, which boasts the perennially popular tontine multiple-murder plot, in this case a rapid succession of puzzling suspicious deaths afflicting the members of a sweepstake syndicate that has just won nearly £250,000.[5] Adding piquancy to this plot is the fact that Wendover is one of the imperiled syndicate members. Altogether the novel is, as the late Jacques Barzun and his colleague Wendell Hertig Taylor put it in *A Catalogue of Crime* (1971, 1989), their magisterial survey of detective fiction, 'one of Connington's best conceptions'.

Stewart's productivity as a fiction writer slowed in the 1930s, so that, barring the year 1938, at most only one new Connington appeared annually. However, in 1932 Stewart produced one of the best Connington mysteries, *The Castleford Conundrum*. A classic country-house detective novel, Castleford introduces to readers Stewart's most delightfully unpleasant set of greedy relations and one of his most deserving murderees, Winifred Castleford. Stewart also fashions a wonderfully rich puzzle plot, full of meaty material clues for the reader's delectation. *Castleford* presented critics with no conundrum over its quality. 'In *The Castleford Conundrum* Mr Connington goes to work like an accomplished chess player. The moves in the games his detectives are called on to play are a delight to watch,' raved the reviewer for the *Sunday Times*, adding that 'the clues would have rejoiced Mr. Holmes' heart.' For its part, the *Spectator* concurred in the *Sunday Times*' assessment of the novel's masterfully constructed plot: 'Few detective stories show such sound reasoning as that by which the Chief Constable brings the crime home to the culprit.' Additionally, E. C. Bentley, much admired himself as the author of the landmark detective novel *Trent's Last Case*, took time to praise Connington's purely literary virtues, noting: 'Mr Connington has never written better, or drawn characters more full of life.'

With *Tom Tiddler's Island* in 1933 Stewart produced a different sort of Connington, a criminal-gang mystery in the rather more breathless style of such hugely popular English thriller writers as Sapper, Sax Rohmer, John Buchan and Edgar Wallace (in violation of the strict detective fiction rules of Ronald Knox, there is even a secret passage in the novel). Detailing the startling discoveries made by a newlywed couple honeymooning on a remote Scottish island, *Tom Tiddler's Island* is an atmospheric and entertaining tale, though it is not as mentally stimulating for armchair sleuths as Stewart's true detective novels. The title, incidentally, refers to an ancient British children's game, 'Tom Tiddler's Ground', in which one child tries to hold a height against other children.

After his fictional Scottish excursion into thrillerdom, Stewart returned the next year to his English country-house roots with *The Ha-Ha Case* (1934), his last masterwork in this classicmystery setting (for elucidation of non-British readers, a ha-ha is a sunken wall, placed so as to delineate property boundaries while not obstructing views). Although *The Ha-Ha Case* is not set in Scotland, Stewart drew inspiration for the novel from a notorious Scottish true crime, the 1893 Ardlamont murder case. From the facts of the Ardlamont affair Stewart drew several of the key characters in *The Ha-Ha Case*, as well as the circumstances of the novel's murder (a shooting 'accident' while hunting), though he added complications that take the tale in a new direction.[6]

In newspaper reviews both Dorothy L. Sayers and 'Francis Iles' (crime novelist Anthony Berkeley Cox) highly praised this latest mystery by 'The Clever Mr Connington', as he was now dubbed on book jackets by his new English publisher, Hodder & Stoughton. Sayers particularly noted the effective characterisation in *The Ha-Ha Case*: 'There is no need to say that Mr Connington has given us a sound and interesting plot, very carefully and ingeniously worked out. In addition, there are the three portraits of the three brothers, cleverly and rather subtly characterised, of the [governess], and of Inspector Hinton, whose admirable qualities are counteracted by that besetting sin of the man who has made his own way: a jealousy of delegating responsibility.' The reviewer for the *Times Literary Supplement* detected signs that the sardonic Sir Clinton Driffield had begun mellowing with age: 'Those who have never really liked Sir Clinton's perhaps excessively soldierly manner will be surprised to find that he makes his discovery not only by the pure light of intelligence, but partly as a reward for amiability and tact, qualities in which the Inspector [Hinton] was strikingly deficient.' This is true enough, although the classic Sir Clinton emerges a number of times in the novel, as in his subtly sarcastic recurrent backhanded praise of Inspector Hinton: 'He writes a first class report.'

Clinton Driffield returned the next year in the detective novel *In Whose Dim Shadow* (1935), a tale set in a recently erected English suburb, the denizens of which seem to have committed an impressive number of indiscretions, including sexual ones. The intriguing title of the British edition of the novel is drawn from a poem by the British historian Thomas Babington Macaulay: 'Those trees in whose dim shadow/The ghastly priest doth reign/The priest who slew the slayer/And shall himself be slain.' Stewart's puzzle plot in *In Whose Dim Shadow* is well clued and compelling, the kicker of a closing paragraph is a classic of its kind and, additionally, the author paints some excellent character portraits. I fully concur with the *Sunday Times*' assessment of the tale: 'Quiet domestic murder, full of the neatest detective points [. . .] These are not the detective's stock figures, but fully realised human beings.'[7]

Uncharacteristically for Stewart, nearly twenty months elapsed between the publication of *In Whose Dim Shadow* and his next book, *A Minor Operation* (1937). The reason for the author's delay in production was the onset in 1935–36 of the afflictions of cataracts and heart disease (Stewart ultimately succumbed to heart disease in 1947). Despite these grave health complications, Stewart in late 1936 was able to complete *A Minor Operation*, a first-rate Clinton Driffield story of murder and a most baffling disappearance. A *Times Literary Supplement* reviewer found that *A Minor Operation* treated the reader 'to exactly the right mixture of mystification and clue' and that, in addition to its impressive construction, the novel boasted 'character-drawing above the average' for a detective novel.

Alfred Stewart's final eight mysteries, which appeared between 1938 and 1947, the year of the author's death, are, on the whole, a somewhat weaker group of tales than the sixteen that appeared between 1926 and 1937, yet they are not without interest. In 1938 Stewart for the last time managed to publish two detective novels, *Truth Comes Limping* and *For Murder Will Speak* (also published as *Murder Will Speak*). The latter tale is much the superior of the two, having an interesting suburban setting and a bevy of female characters found to have motives when a contemptible philandering businessman meets with foul play. Sexual neurosis plays a major role in *For Murder Will Speak*, the ever-thorough Stewart obviously having made a study of the subject when writing the novel. The somewhat squeamish reviewer for *Scribner's Magazine* considered the subject matter of *For Murder Will Speak* 'rather unsavory at times', yet this individual conceded that the novel nevertheless made 'first-class reading for those who enjoy a good puzzle intricately worked out'. 'Judge Lynch' in the *Saturday Review* apparently had no such moral reservations about the latest Clinton Driffield murder case, avowing simply of the novel: 'They don't come any better'.

Over the next couple of years Stewart again sent Sir Clinton Driffield temporarily packing, replacing him with a new series detective, a brash radio personality named Mark Brand, in *The Counsellor* (1939) and *The Four Defences* (1940). The better of these two novels is *The Four Defences*, which Stewart based on another notorious British true-crime case, the Alfred Rouse blazing-car murder. (Rouse is believed to have fabricated his death by murdering an unknown man, placing the dead man's body in his car and setting the car on fire, in the hope that the murdered man's body would be taken for his.) Though admittedly a thinly characterised academic exercise in ratiocination, Stewart's *Four Defences* surely is also one of the most complexly plotted Golden Age detective novels and should delight devotees of classical detection. Taking the Rouse blazing-car affair as his theme, Stewart composes from it a stunning set of diabolically ingenious criminal variations. 'This is in the cold-blooded category which [. . .] excites a crossword puzzle kind of interest,' the reviewer for the *Times Literary Supplement* acutely noted of the novel. 'Nothing in the Rouse case would prepare you for these complications upon complications [. . .] What they prove is that Mr Connington has the power of penetrating into the puzzle-corner of the brain. He leaves it dazedly wondering whether in the records of actual crime there can be any dark deed to equal this in its planned convolutions.'

Sir Clinton Driffield returned to action in the remaining four detective novels in the Connington oeuvre, *The Twenty-One Clues* (1941), *No Past is Dead* (1942), *Jack-in-the-Box* (1944) and *Commonsense is All You Need* (1947), all of which were written as Stewart's heart disease steadily worsened and reflect to some extent his diminishing physical and mental energy. Although *The Twenty-One Clues* was inspired by the notorious Hall-Mills double murder case – probably the most publicised murder case in the United States in the 1920s – and the American critic and novelist Anthony Boucher commended *Jack-in-the-Box*, I believe the best of these later mysteries is *No Past Is Dead*, which Stewart partly based on a bizarre French true-crime affair, the 1891 Achet-Lepine murder case.[8] Besides providing an interesting background for the tale, the ailing author managed some virtuoso plot twists, of the sort most associated today with that ingenious Golden Age Queen of Crime, Agatha Christie.

What Stewart with characteristic bluntness referred to as 'my complete crack-up' forced his retirement from Queen's University in 1944. 'I am afraid,' Stewart wrote a friend, the chemist and forensic scientist F. Gerald Tryhorn, in August 1946, eleven months before his death, 'that I shall never be much use again. Very stupidly, I tried for a session to combine a full course of lecturing with angina pectoris; and ended up by establishing that the two are immiscible.' He added that since retiring in 1944, he had been physically 'limited to my house, since even a fifty-yard crawl brings on the usual cramps'. Stewart completed his essay collection and a final novel before he died at his study desk in his Belfast home on 1 July 1947, at the age of sixty-six. When death came to the author he was busy at work, writing.

More than six decades after Alfred Walter Stewart's death, his J. J. Connington fiction is again available to a wider audience of classic-mystery fans, rather than strictly limited to a select company of rare-book collectors with deep pockets. This is fitting for an individual who was one of the finest writers of British genre fiction between the two world wars. 'Heaven forfend that you should imagine I take myself for anything out of the common in the tec yarn stuff,' Stewart once self-deprecatingly declared in a letter to Rupert Gould. Yet, as contemporary critics recognised, as a writer of detective and science fiction Stewart indeed was something out of the common. Now more modern readers can find this out for themselves. They have much good sleuthing in store.

1. For more on Street, Crofts and particularly Stewart, see Curtis Evans, *Masters of the 'Humdrum' Mystery: Cecil John Charles Street, Freeman Wills Crofts, Alfred Walter Stewart and the British Detective Novel, 1920–1961* (Jefferson, NC: McFarland, 2012). On the academic career of Alfred Walter Stewart, see his entry in *Oxford Dictionary of National Biography* (London and New York: Oxford University Press, 2004), vol. 52, 627–628.
2. The Gould-Stewart correspondence is discussed in considerable detail in *Masters of the 'Humdrum' Mystery*. For more on the life of the fascinating Rupert Thomas Gould, see Jonathan Betts, *Time Restored: The Harrison Timekeepers and R. T. Gould, the*

Man Who Knew (Almost) Everything (London and New York: Oxford University Press, 2006) and *Longitude,* the 2000 British film adaptation of Dava Sobel's book *Longitude:The True Story of a Lone Genius Who Solved the Greatest Scientific Problem of His Time* (London: Harper Collins, 1995), which details Gould's restoration of the marine chronometers built by in the eighteenth century by the clockmaker John Harrison.

3. Potential purchasers of *Murder in the Maze* should keep in mind that $2 in 1927 is worth over $26 today.
4. In a 1920 article in *The Strand Magazine,* Arthur Conan Doyle endorsed as real prank photographs of purported fairies taken by two English girls in the garden of a house in the village of Cottingley. In the aftermath of the Great War Doyle had become a fervent believer in Spiritualism and other paranormal phenomena. Especially embarrassing to Doyle's admirers today, he also published *The Coming of the Faeries* (1922), wherein he argued that these mystical creatures genuinely existed. 'When the spirits came in, the common sense oozed out,' Stewart once wrote bluntly to his friend Rupert Gould of the creator of Sherlock Holmes. Like Gould, however, Stewart had an intense interest in the subject of the Loch Ness Monster, believing that he, his wife and daughter had sighted a large marine creature of some sort in Loch Ness in 1935. A year earlier Gould had authored *The Loch Ness Monster and Others,* and it was this book that led Stewart, after he made his 'Nessie' sighting, to initiate correspondence with Gould.
5. A tontine is a financial arrangement wherein shareowners in a common fund receive annuities that increase in value with the death of each participant, with the entire amount of the fund going to the last survivor. The impetus that the tontine provided to the deadly creative imaginations of Golden Age mystery writers should be sufficiently obvious.
6. At Ardlamont, a large country estate in Argyll, Cecil Hambrough died from a gunshot wound while hunting. Cecil's tutor, Alfred John Monson, and another man, both of whom were out hunting with Cecil, claimed that Cecil had accidentally shot himself, but Monson was arrested and tried for Cecil's murder. The verdict delivered was 'not proven', but Monson was then – and is today – considered almost certain to have been guilty of the murder. On the Ardlamont case, see William Roughead, *Classic Crimes* (1951; repr., New York: New York Review Books Classics, 2000), 378–464.
7. For the genesis of the title, see Macaulay's 'The Battle of the Lake

Regillus', from his narrative poem collection *Lays of Ancient Rome*. In this poem Macaulay alludes to the ancient cult of Diana Nemorensis, which elevated its priests through trial by combat. Study of the practices of the Diana Nemorensis cult influenced Sir James George Frazer's cultural interpretation of religion in his most renowned work, *The Golden Bough: A Study in Magic and Religion*. As with *Tom Tiddler's Island* and *The Ha-Ha Case* the title *In Whose Dim Shadow* proved too esoteric for Connington's American publishers, Little, Brown and Co., who altered it to the more prosaic *The Tau Cross Mystery*.

8. Stewart analysed the Achet-Lepine case in detail in 'The Mystery of Chantelle', one of the best essays in his 1947 collection *Alias J. J. Connington*.

CHAPTER I

THE ALVINGTON DIVORCE CASE

AT eighty-seven, Mrs. Victoria Alvington was beginning to break up. After a long life of robust health, during which she had ruled her children and grandchild with unsparing severity, she was taking her decline badly; and it was only after prolonged argument that her son Arthur had been allowed to call in a specialist to report upon her symptoms. The result of the consultation that afternoon had not been wholly satisfactory from Arthur's point of view. He had put one or two questions to Dr. Dungarvan which had surprised the physician, who was unaware that Mrs. Alvington ruled more by the power of the purse than by any filial affection in her family.

After he had got Dr. Dungarvan off his hands, Arthur Alvington rang up his niece Helen to give her the specialist's verdict. Her husband, the Rev. John Barratt, answered the phone and intimated, not too courteously, that Mrs. Barratt was going that evening to a meeting in the hall of the Church of Awakened Israel, and would thus not be home until half-past nine.

Arthur Alvington was a little surprised. In the first years of her married life, Helen had taken a keen interest in church work; but this had died down, and now it was only when Barratt insisted on her attendance that she ever went near such functions. Some of the congregation were deeply offended by this laxity, Arthur knew; but he himself rather sympathised with it, having little enthusiasm for such affairs. Besides, as he recognised, Helen was a fish out of water amongst the congregation, most of whom were decent lower-middle-class people with whom she had nothing in common. Her own friends were drawn from a different social stratum, and the narrowness of the Awakened Israelites had long been irksome to her.

Arthur decided to go to the church hall and intercept her as she came out. Barratt would probably be detained in conversation after the meeting. He was a hearty fellow, ever eager to be genial to any of the congregation. Arthur disliked that kind of heartiness. There was always a hint of superiority about it, which he thought uncalled-for in a person of Barratt's humble extraction. If Helen came out of the hall first, her uncle meant to pick her up and drive her home without waiting for her husband. As Barratt had no car, he would have to walk, and Arthur could count on a few minutes uninterrupted talk with Helen before they were disturbed.

He stopped his car by the pavement and got out, so as to be able to pounce on his niece as soon as she appeared. He had timed his arrival neatly, for the meeting broke up almost as he reached the hall door. He passed on, glancing up at the façade of the hall and reflecting sourly that most of the money spent on the building had been subscribed by his mother, who was one of the few rich members of the congregation. His thin lips tightened involuntarily at this disagreeable recollection. They had done their best to dissuade her—himself, his brother Edward, and even Helen—but the stubborn old woman took her own line and handed over the cash. "So much less for us eventually," Arthur reflected angrily. He passed on, and then turned back to keep an eye on the emerging stream of people. As he did so, he almost collided with a tall, gaunt man who had just come down the steps.

"Sorry, Kerrison!" Arthur apologised.

"No matter, no matter," Kerrison assured him ungraciously and then paused as though he intended to fall into conversation.

Like old Mrs. Alvington, Stephen Kerrison was a strong supporter of the Church of Awakened Israel; and, unlike Arthur, he took his religion seriously so far as church meetings were concerned. Arthur, who had a good figure and prided himself on being a man of the world, looked on Kerrison with a sort of compassionate contempt. Kerrison was ungainly, short-bodied and long-legged, with big splay feet which seemed incapable of haste. He was seldom well-shaven; his tie was usually crooked; and he invariably carried an umbrella which he used as a walking-stick to help himself along. Unmarried at fifty, he lived at the apron-strings of a mother whom he adored and who adored him in return. Of all his lineaments, his eyes were the most striking: dark, deep-sunken, surrounded by black rings and burning with a fanatical fire.

"You weren't at the meeting?" he asked, in a tone which carried both criticism and reproach.

Arthur Alvington shook his head impatiently.

"I've just come to have a word or two with my niece—on business," he explained curtly, intending to make it clear to Kerrison that he was not wanted.

"Mrs. Barratt?" said Kerrison with a touch of acidity in his tone. "Yes, she was at the meeting. She doesn't come often, nowadays. It seems rather a pity. She used to take such an interest in church affairs, and she might do so much good among the younger people, if she chose."

"She has her own friends," Arthur retorted sharply.

Kerrison had no right to criticise his niece, he felt; and if the fellow talked like this to him, one could be sure that he said harsher things to other people. No wonder that Helen had lost interest in church affairs, if this sort of nagging was the kind of thing she had to suffer. Kerrison was a nice person to set up as a critic, with two slander actions to his discredit. Lucky that some people had made him pay for his loose tongue.

At that moment, Helen Barratt emerged from the door of

the hall and Arthur, with a nod of farewell to Kerrison, stepped forward to attract her attention. Arthur had an eye for a good-looking woman, and he glanced at his niece with æsthetic approval. She had worn remarkably well, he reflected. Though she was actually thirty-five, no stranger would take her for more than twenty-six or twenty-seven. She had lost girlishness without falling into matronliness. Arthur liked to see a woman with a straight back and her chin well up. "Still enough there to make a man turn and look after her in the street," was his crude but contented conclusion. "No children, of course. That may have helped her to keep that slim figure." She dressed well, too. Not expensively, of course, because Barratt's miserable salary would not run to that; but even if the materials were cheapish, her taste made them look well enough. She came towards him, light-stepping, with a smile of recognition.

"Well, uncle, I'm sorry I put you to the trouble of coming to meet me. I wanted to stay at home to-night, but John insisted on my going to that meeting, and he got so disagreeable over it that it was cheaper to let him have his way."

"Yes, it gave him a chance of annoying me," said Arthur. "I expected something of the sort when he answered the phone. He seems to dislike me, I can't think why. Is he busy inside there?" he ended, with a nod towards the door of the hall.

"I left him talking to Mrs. Callis," Mrs. Barratt answered indifferently. "She had some arrangements to make with him, so I left them. They seem to have plenty to discuss. She's always hanging about him, nowadays. Not that I care."

"She's full of zeal for church affairs, I hear," Arthur commented with a smile. "Just as you used to be yourself, a good many years ago."

"She's a bossy little creature," Helen Barratt said, without malice. "She likes to be *in* everything, and running it, if possible. I don't mind. The more she does, the less need there is for me to take a hand. That's always something.

She seems quite keen on John," she added unconcernedly. "Some people have been good enough to remark on that to me."

"Get into the car before he comes out," Arthur directed. "I'll drive you home and we can have a few minutes' private talk before the Reverend John turns up."

He refrained from saying anything more until they reached her house and could talk comfortably. Then he began.

"Dungarvan had a look at the old lady this afternoon. She's breaking up; there's no doubt about that. What can you expect, at eighty-seven. When I got him to myself, I asked him a question or two. Was she fit to make a will? In his opinion, she was. Even a lunatic can make a will, apparently, so long as he does it in a lucid interval. Any will or codicil that she's executed lately will stand, certainly."

"So there's no hope for Uncle Edward, then," commented Helen Barratt.

"Not a shadow of one," her uncle admitted, "unless the old lady changes her mind. And she won't do that. She's as bitter as ever on the subject of that divorce of his—more mid-Victorian than usual, if one gets on to the question. No, she's cut him out of her will and out he stays. The amount of talk I've listened to about the sacredness of the marriage bond. . . . If Ted wants to see her again, he'll have to wait till she's in her coffin; she'll never let him cross her doorstep as long as she has life in her. Not that he's pressing for an interview. He's completely fed with what's happened. And he doesn't love your good husband much, over it."

"I did my best," said Helen. "But you know what John's like."

"I do," said Arthur, caustically. "All the same, it was indecent of him to lead the hue and cry against Ted over that divorce business. I dare say he had some grounds for insisting on kicking Ted out of his deaconship—not that Ted was much grieved over that part. But Barratt did more than a little to stiffen the old lady in her decision to cut Ted out of her will. I know that, from some things she's dropped. Ted's pretty bitter over it, and I don't blame him there."

"Neither do I," Helen concurred. "I did my best to dissuade him, but you know how it is; one might as well talk to a stone wall, once he's made up his mind. I suppose if I want to see Uncle Ted after this I'll have to pay him a visit. He'd hardly come to see me, if there was a chance of John being on the premises. And there's someone else who was almost as bad as John, and that's Mr. Kerrison. I saw you talking to him at the hall door. He helped John to work up feeling against Uncle Ted amongst the church people. I think he might have left that to somebody else after his own doings in these slander actions."

"He seems to have his knife in you," said Arthur, thinking of what Kerrison had said to him. "And he's a bit of a talker, you know."

"I *do* know it," said Helen Barratt. "But I'm not worrying about him just now. From what you've told me, Granny might change her will at any moment and cut you and me out, just as she cut Uncle Ted, if it crossed her mind to do it. And the new will would hold?"

"So it seems, according to Dungarvan. She may live for years yet. She's doddering badly," Arthur declared, brutally, "but she's sane enough to execute a valid will or make an extra codicil. That's the unfortunate fact, Helen. We'll need to watch our step, in case she gets her back up some fine morning. If I were you, I'd display a little more enthusiasm for church affairs. It would do no harm. . . ."

"I hate the lot of them," Helen retorted, with equal directness. "It's granny's fault from start to finish. After father and mother died and I went to live with her, she brought me up in that atmosphere and when I was in my teens I thought it was all right. One's like that before one gets any experience. Then John came along, and I married him before I knew what I was letting myself in for. It seemed rather fine in those days to marry a minister and be made much of by the congregation, and all that sort of thing. I suppose I was quite genuine about it while the enthusiasm lasted."

Arthur looked at her angry expression with some surprise. He had suspected for some years that Helen had changed markedly in her outlook, but she had never before put her views so plainly into words.

"I suppose you were," he admitted.

"Oh, I was, undoubtedly, at that time. I was so young, and I'd no real ideas about things. It seemed grand, marrying on next to nothing with a career of good works and so on in front of one. But it all bores me stiff nowadays, uncle. They're so frightfully narrow-minded, not like an ordinary church, somehow. And they're not my sort. I can't make friends amongst them. They're not my class, and they think differently from me on almost everything one can talk about to them."

"I know, I know," Arthur agreed sympathetically. "You were caught young and you made a mess of it when you married Barratt. He may be all right for some people, but he's not my sort, I quite admit. Too hearty, altogether, for my taste; and not quite It. Still, it's done now, unfortunately. You can't get out of it, poor thing."

"Not by Uncle Ted's way, certainly," said Helen.

"No, I shouldn't advise that," said Arthur, with a wintry smile. "By the way, that husband of yours goes to see your granny regularly, doesn't he?"

"Once a week at least—oftener, if she asks him."

"I suppose he reports on my attendance at church," said Arthur, sourly. "She's sure to ask him about that. Has he any influence over her, do you think?"

"He's proved it," retorted Helen glumly. "Uncle Ted could tell you that. What's worrying you, uncle?"

"Well, you know what he is," responded Arthur morosely. "All for the church being supported, and people living a simple life of contentment. It goes down with her.

Remember how he persuaded her to put up that cash to build the church hall? That was money which ought to have come to us, eventually. What troubles me is that he might put more silly notions into her head. I've got a feeling that he might come it over her and suggest that she should leave her whole packet to the church instead of to us. And where should we be, then? He's keen enough on his church to do a thing of that sort. He didn't marry you for money, you know."

Helen's face showed that she was aghast at her uncle's surmise.

"You don't imagine he'd do anything of that kind, really?" she demanded in a startled tone.

"He's capable of it," said Arthur grimly. "It occurred to me not long ago, and it's been bothering me ever since. One or two things she let drop . . . they made me prick up my ears. Nothing definite, and I may be just imagining it all. . . . It may not have crossed his mind yet. But if it does, he'd never give us a thought. We'd be in Queer Street, so far as her cash goes. If she did a thing like that, she'd never change her will back again; you can be sure of that."

He glanced at his watch.

"I think I'll go before he turns up," he went on. "He and I never hit it off, somehow; and I don't feel too friendly just now. You don't mind?"

"I quite understand," Helen assured him. "So, good night, uncle. You'd better go. He may be here any moment now."

She saw Arthur Alvington start off in his car; then she went upstairs to take off her hat. While she was there, she heard her husband's key in the front door. When she came downstairs again, she found him in the sitting-room, staring blankly out of the window. He ignored her for a moment or two; then he turned and spoke in a rather strained voice.

"Not a very good meeting, to-night."

"No," Helen agreed, indifferently.

"I had to stay and talk to Mrs. Callis. She wanted to ask me something."

"Did she?" asked Helen, in an incurious tone. "I didn't see Mr. Callis there."

"No, he wasn't there."

John Barratt evidently had something on his mind; but he seemed to have difficulty in bringing it out. She saw no reason for helping him. Usually he was fluent enough, even boringly loquacious, for he loved to hear his own voice. She stepped over to the mantelpiece, took a cigarette from a box, lighted it, and then sat down in an arm-chair. Her action seemed to annoy her husband.

"I wish you wouldn't smoke, Helen. I don't like it."

Helen Barratt looked up at him under her brows.

"Mrs. Callis smokes, and yet you never say anything about that," she pointed out coolly. "She's practically a chain-smoker. I only take a cigarette now and again. If you're starting an anti-smoking campaign, John, you'd better begin with her."

Barratt's annoyance at this counter betrayed itself in a heavy frown.

"I've no right to object in her case," he declared, weightily. "She's different. She's not a minister's wife like you. It's your business to set a good example."

Helen Barratt blew a cloud of smoke and watched it dissipate itself in the air. The action seemed to rasp her husband's temper, as if it had been a defiance of his authority.

"There are other things besides smoking," he said with a harsh note in his voice. "This gambling of yours . . ."

"I don't call bridge at threepence a hundred very heavy gambling," retorted Helen, acidly. "It doesn't cost you anything. I keep a note of my winnings and losings, and I've come out a winner every year yet. Are you suggesting that I should drop playing bridge with my own friends and take to 'old maid' or 'snap' amongst the congregation?"

"You know I hate people playing cards for money," said Barratt.

"And you dislike my going to dances, too, don't you?" said Helen, determined to throw everything into the discussion, now that it had begun. "You never learned to dance, yourself; and you don't care for my doing something which you can't do. If my own friends ask me to a dance, I don't see why I shouldn't go."

"Some of the congregation don't like it," said Barratt, heavily. "Mr. Kerrison said something to me about it, just the other day."

"Kerrison!" echoed Helen contemptuously. "Of course he's just the sort of man who's fitted to sit in judgement on me. Now let us have this perfectly clear, John, since you've raised the matter. I didn't marry you for money. But it's the plain fact that because I married you with your poor salary I've had to go without a good many things which a girl of my class looks on as necessities. We've no maid, and I have to act as one. You can't afford a car, and there isn't a girl I know who hasn't got one. And now you want me to give up the few amusements that I've got left. I don't feel inclined to. I've given up a good deal by marrying you. You might think of that side of the matter for a change."

Barratt made no immediate answer to this. Possibly he had never guessed that she had been thinking along these lines, for he seldom gave much time to other people's thoughts. After a minute or two, he made an impatient gesture as though dismissing the subject, and then he opened a fresh topic in a tone which betrayed some perplexity.

"Rather a nasty thing's happened, Helen. I've had an anonymous letter. A most disturbing affair, though of course there's nothing in it. Still, it's worrying. . . . I'd better show it to you."

He fumbled in his pocket and produced a crumpled envelope from which he drew a single sheet of note-paper.

"Just read that, will you?" he said, as he passed it across to her.

Helen Barratt unfolded the letter and glanced at its few lines. She knitted her brows as she read, but she showed far less surprise and discomposure than her husband had expected.

"Not very nice," was her comment.

"Not very nice!" ejaculated John Barratt. "Is that all you've got to say about it? Just see what it hints at. I wonder you can read it without . . ."

"It doesn't surprise me so much as you'd expect," she explained dispassionately, "because I've had a letter of the same sort myself. Only, mine was full of tales about *you* and your doings."

"Me and my doings?" said Barratt, raising his voice. "What doings? Let me see it. I insist on seeing it."

"I'm afraid you can't," Helen replied in a level voice. "The proper way to treat things of that sort is to burn them and say nothing about them to anyone. That's what I did. That's what you ought to have done."

"My doings!" Barratt was a slow thinker. "What sort of doings of mine could anyone find fault with?"

"It hinted—or rather, it said bluntly that you and Mrs. Callis were too friendly with each other. You do let her fuss round you a good deal, you know. People notice these things more than you'd think, and some of the eyes on you aren't friendly, it seems. I'm not in the least jealous; don't imagine that for a moment. It's nothing to me. . . ."

"But there's nothing in it to make you jealous," protested Barratt angrily. "I've never said a word to her that couldn't be heard by anyone. I'm not in love with her, nor she with me. You know that perfectly well, Helen. I meet her and talk to her as I talk to anyone else. There's not a word of truth in it, not a single one. You don't believe it, surely?"

"No more than you believed all this stuff about me," his wife answered. "I don't suppose you believed it, did you?"

Barratt flushed painfully under her steady scrutiny. From

boyhood onwards, he had been troubled by a tendency to blush when in an awkward position.

"No, of course I didn't believe it," he asserted.

"Then why get so red?" she retorted, adding to Barratt's discomfort by the remark. "It's not worth bothering about, really. Someone had evidently turned spiteful, that's all. Have you been treading on any corns lately? I wonder.... Has Mrs. Callis been put in charge of anything when somebody else was looking for the job? That's perhaps at the root of the trouble. You know how easily some people take offence; and you're not very tactful, John, even at your best. Think it over; perhaps you'll see light. In the meantime, I'll pitch this precious production into the waste-basket."

She suited the action to the word.

"It's safe enough there. I'll use it in lighting the kitchen stove in the morning. There are advantages in having no maid, after all," she added, ironically.

"But..." Barratt began.

"I shouldn't worry over it," his wife advised him seriously. "That sort of person isn't worth thinking about. Still... I wish I knew who wrote it."

CHAPTER II

SUICIDE PACT

AMONG his colleagues and subordinates, Inspector Rufford had the reputation of being "a good starter, but a poor stayer." When a case was presented to him, he threw himself into it with all his energy, spared himself no labour to secure all available evidence, collated his results with considerable care, and, if a solution was attainable within a few days, he generally succeeded in discovering it. But if the case dragged on for some time without apparent progress, he was apt to lose interest; and thereafter his investigation was inclined to be mechanical rather than eager. As one of his colleagues put it: "Rufford's top-hole as a hundred-yards' sprinter, but no earthly good as a miler." But the crimes which come to the notice of the police are generally simple, so Inspector Rufford had many successes to his credit.

In addition, he had some rarer qualities. He kept excellent notes of his cases, and he drilled his subordinates into something like his own efficiency in this respect. The note-books of his constables were models of their class. He took a keen interest in criminological methods in general, and had acquired a considerable library on that subject, so that he was able at times to utilise methods usually reserved for experts. While his initial zeal lasted, he was untiring in his search for clues, even of the most obscure types, for he was by no means devoid of the imaginative gift for seeing behind the surface of events. Even a carping critic had admitted that "Rufford can see the obvious quicker than most people." Which was his peculiar way of saying that the inspector sometimes saw things which were obvious to the critic after they had been pointed out to him.

The inspector was an even-tempered man; and although he was busy with routine work when a constable entered the room, he merely looked up from his papers without a trace of annoyance at the interruption.

"Two railwaymen outside, sir," reported the constable. "Asking to see you. They say it's urgent."

"Send them in," ordered Rufford concisely, putting his documents aside for the moment.

Almost at once, the two callers were ushered into the room by the constable. One was a short, square-built, keen-eyed man in his early forties; the other was a burly fellow, rather younger, with a humorous face.

"Off duty?" queried the inspector, with a glance at their working clothes.

"No," explained the older man, "but the next train we take out is the eleven-fifty-seven an' we've got permission to come across here an' make a report. I'm a driver. Jack Gage is my name an' I live at 33 Cranborne Street. This is my fireman, Tom Handen, 72 Rugby Street."

Rufford jotted down the names and addresses and then looked up inquiringly.

"This is the way of it," began the engine-driver in response. "Me an' Handen took out the seven-forty-seven from here this morning as usual: the Aldred train. Stops at every station an' gets to Aldred at eight-thirty-six. Maybe you know the line."

"I've been over it often," Rufford admitted.

"Right! Then likely enough you'll remember the high embankment about five miles out o' town. The line takes a bend there, round a sort of spur o' high ground on the left-hand side. There's a fairly steep slope, covered with high bracken, with a rough sort of road at the foot, between the slope an' the line. The road runs under a bridge that stands just about the tip o' this spur, this high ground I'm talkin' about. Can you remember the place I mean, or have I got to go on?"

"I remember it well enough," Rufford assured him.

"You do? That's fine! Now I'll tell you somethin' more. That stretch of bracken's quite popular with courtin' couples, an' some couples as *ought* to be courtin' anyhow, by the way they go on. They can get up the hillside among the bracken-stems an' do all the kissin' an' cuddlin' they have a mind to. The bracken hides them from anyone chancin' to pass along the road at the bottom. O' course, they're in plain sight from trains passin' on the line, it bein' high up an' more or less over-lookin' 'em. But they don't seem to mind that. At least not judgin' by some queer sights Tom an' me sees there from time to time as we happen along."

"You can kiss the Book on that!" interjected the fireman, with a reminiscent chuckle.

"Now, if you remember," went on the engine-driver, "there's a distant signal about a hundred yards before you come to the bridge, on the down line; an' the home signal's round the corner, about two hundred yards beyond the bridge. When me an' Tom took out the seven-forty-seven this mornin', the distant signal was against us, so I slowed down a bit; an' when we got round that bend, the home signal was up, an' I had to stop. Tom, here, happened to give a glance up at the bracken, an' then he turned to me an' said ... What was it you said, Tom?"

"What I said was: 'Them two must be keen, startin' as early in the day as this.' It was just three minutes past eight."

"So I had a look myself," continued the engine-driver, "an' there they were, the two of 'em, up among the bracken. The girl was lyin' on her back, so far's we could see; she was wearin' a dark green dress. The man was in a dark suit o' togs an' he was lyin' on his face just alongside or near-by. We hadn't much of a chance to take more than a glint at 'em, for the home signal went down just then an' off we had to toot. Still, it seemed a bit funny; an' Tom he said to me . . . What was it you said, Tom?"

"I said: 'They must ha' rocked themselves to sleep, last night, them two, an' forgot to wake up in time to take the milk in. It's a rum go, that is,' I said, 'for the dew's heavy this mornin' an' they must be fair soaked with it, lyin' out all night that way,' I said. 'But there's no accountin' for tastes. Some folks like their pleasures wet,' I said, 'an' I'm much in the same way of thinkin' when there's any beer about,' I said."

The engine-driver took up the tale again.

"We thought no more about it, an' we got to Aldred at eight-thirty-eight—just two minutes late. We bring the nine-sixteen from Aldred back here. When we got near here again, I remembered them two up on the hillside, an' I says to Tom, here: 'You keep your eyes skinned as we pass, an' see if they've woke up an' gone away.' So when we was passin' that slope, we both of us 'ad a good dekko. An' there, sure 'nough, was the pair lyin' just as we'd seen 'em two hours before. That didn't seem somehow natural, seein' as it was close on ten o'clock in the mornin' by then. We're due in here at ten-two, an' we was on time. So Tom and me talked it over a bit; an', come to think o' it, it seemed to us that these two 'adn't seemed to be lyin' there in a comfortable sort o' way. I can't just tell you what it was about 'em, but . . . What do you say, Tom?"

"Same as what you say," confirmed the fireman. "The man 'ad 'is arm—'is right arm, if I remembers proper—flung straight out, an' it looked to me a kind o' uncomfortable sort o' way to lie, if you see what I mean—face down and arm out like that. I'd 'appened to note that partic'lar the first time, an' I was more surprised nor a bit to see 'im a-lying just that same way, after a couple o' hours. Puzzled by that, I was."

"Just a moment," interrupted the inspector. "Were they tramps, or that kind of people?"

The engine-driver shook his head, and the fireman put the matter beyond doubt.

"Tramps? No, they was *not* tramps. It's a fair distance, but my eyes is good, an' I knows a tramp when I sees one. They was middle-class people, by the look of 'em. Not but what their clo'es wasn't a bit ruffled. But they looked good clo'es; no rags about 'em an' all o' one piece, if you see what I mean. No, they wasn't tramps. If they 'ad 'ave been tramps, we'd a' spotted it. There's plenty o' tramps about. Now I come to think, there's a sort o' place among some rocks near-by there where a tramp sometimes settles for the night an' lights a fire for to boil 'is tin o' tea. We see 'em sometimes, in passin'."

"Very good," said Rufford, making a note. "And then?"

"Well, as I said," the engine-driver resumed, "we talked it over, me an' Tom, an' we thought we'd be as well just to step across an' put you wise about what we'd seen. I'm not sayin' there's anythin' wrong. I don't know as there *is* anythin' wrong. But I said to Tom, here: 'If there's been any funny business goin' on down there, then we'd better report it an' be done with it. Then it'll be off *our* hands, anyway.' An' Tom, here, he agrees with me that it was a bit rum, look 'ow you choose. So we steps across. An' now there's no more as we can tell you, mister. You've 'ad it all, an' it's up to you to carry on or to drop it, just as you please."

Rufford had been taking notes as the two men gave their evidence. He read over his précis to them, got their signatures, and then, as they seemed anxious to be off, he let them go. When they had left the room, he reconsidered what he had heard. The evidence amounted to little enough, so far as the actual statements went; but the men's manner of giving it had betrayed a genuine uneasiness in both of them. Plainly they were convinced that there was something suspicious about those two figures among the bracken, though they had not been able to convey the full force of their suspicions in words. In any case, these two railwaymen had pulled the string to set him in motion. He could not take the risk of disregarding their statement. The thing would have to be looked into. Luckily the scene was within easy range. His superintendent was ill just then, so Rufford was free to make his own arrangements. He had a car outside the police station; and after a moment or two's consideration he decided to take a couple of constables with him.

When the car reached the road between the railway embankment and the bracken-covered slope, the inspector pulled up and got out, followed by his men.

"You wait here," he ordered. "We can't afford to go trampling among that bracken at random, and there's nothing to be seen from here. Wait a bit until I get up the embankment and see what I can see. I can direct you better from there."

Leaving them by the car, he vaulted the low fence separating the road from the railway, and scrambled up the steep embankment to the level of the line. From this point of vantage, he could see down among the bracken-stems, and his first glance assured him that he had not come on a wild-goose chase. Two figures were lying on the upper part of the slope before him; and the attitude of the male body, face downward with its right arm outstretched, tallied wholly with the railwaymen's description of what they had seen nearly three hours earlier. No living man was likely to have stayed in that position all that time. Even asleep, he would have shifted unconsciously to some extent. The woman's figure was partly concealed by intervening bracken fronds; but from what he could see of it, the inspector inferred that she could hardly have fallen asleep in such an uncomfortable attitude.

Rufford ran his eyes over the rest of the slope. Here and there, he could detect places where the bracken had been crushed down; and this confirmed the railwaymen's hint about courting couples frequenting the place. Closer inspection revealed trails of disturbance in the bracken which indicated the routes to the various spots where the couples had sat or lain down. The inspector noted that two such tracks led up from the road to the spot where the bodies lay.

"So they came there independently," he inferred, "and the one that came first must have called to the other to let him or her know where to go. Or else the first one stood up so as to be seen by the second one. To judge by the number of snuggeries, people do come here for peace and quiet. But it's not a crowded resort. Too far out of town for that, except for a car; and people with cars generally prefer to do their cuddling inside."

He jotted a note in his pocket-book, with a rough sketch of the scene before him. Then he descended the embankment again and gave instructions to his men. He had noted where the two tracks emerged on the road, but it seemed inadvisable to trample over either of them until he knew more of the facts. Instead, he and his subordinates fetched a compass around the bodies and approached them from the top of the slope.

At close range, no doubt remained, for a quantity of blood had oozed from the head of the male body, staining the turf among the bracken-stems. As he came within a few feet of the dead man, one of the constables checked himself abruptly in his stride and exclaimed:

"Here, sir! A pistol! I almost trod on it."

"Don't touch it, Loman!" ordered the inspector, as the constable stooped as though to pick up the weapon.

"It looks as if he'd shot himself, sir, and when he fell flat, the pistol jerked out of his hand," suggested the constable. "It's here, you see, and there's his hand, half open, quite close by."

"Maybe," conceded the inspector. "Leave it for the present."

He turned to examine the body, snapping out disjointed comments for the benefit of his subordinates.

"His hat's fallen off. . . . Black felt, semi-clerical pattern.

. . . Ah! there's some blood on it, so he must have had it on his head when the shot went in. . . . Bullet's gone through his right temple, rather low down. . . . His togs have a semi-clerical look about them, too. . . ."

Very gently he insinuated his hand under the body and felt the clothes and the turf.

"Grass under the body's a bit moist. . . . So's his waistcoat. . . . There was heavy dew last night. . . . His back's covered with it and the grass all round is dewy. . . . I don't want to shift him till we get a photograph taken. . . . No exit wound on the left side of the head, so the bullet must still be inside his skull. . . ."

He rose to his feet again and looked about him. Then a fresh aspect of the affair seemed to strike him. He turned to the second constable.

"Tatnell! You go back to the car. Keep in the track you made, coming up here. Take the car back to the station and pick up Sergeant Ilford and another constable. Bring them here, after the sergeant has ordered the ambulance to follow on. You'd better bring a photographer as well. But don't go spreading the news of this affair. We want some peace and quietness, if we can get it, until we've seen to things here. Until we've got the bodies away, anyhow. Hurry up."

Constable Tatnell was not pleased at being thus ordered off, but he had no choice in the matter. When he had gone, Rufford turned to the second body, continuing his abrupt comments as he pursued his investigation.

"By the position's she's in, she must have been sitting up when the shot was fired, and then fell over to her right. . . . And the bracken on her left's crushed down, as if somebody had been sitting there with her. . . . Shot in the left temple, rather high up. . . . It missed her hat, for she's wearing one that cants down on the right-hand side so that her left temple's been completely exposed. . . . No exit wound here either. . . . Looks as if she might have been a pretty girl, before the shot. . . . Quite good class, too, judging by her clothes, and the smell of verbena bath salts. . . . H'm! wedding-ring on her finger, but no others. . . . Wrist-watch, still going. . . . The grass under her's quite dry, or almost dry. . . . So's her dress, on the ground side. . . . Dew's all over the top of her, of course. . . . No use moving her till we get a photo taken. . . . But here's her handbag beside her."

He picked up the bag, a morocco pochette with a fancy twist clasp, and after opening it gingerly, examined the contents.

"Not much help here. . . . Lipstick, powder compact, comb, handkerchief. . . . No laundry-mark or initials on that . . . a couple of notes, some silver and coppers in the purse section. . . . No visiting-cards or papers. . . . Some cigarettes and paper matches. That's all. . . ."

A thought seemed to strike him and he gently slipped the wedding-ring from the dead woman's finger.

"They sometimes engrave initials inside these things. . . . Just so! Here they are, Loman. 'E.C. and J.B.' H'm! Better than nothing, but not much use at the moment."

He slipped the ring back into place and rose to his feet again. The bracken was the next thing which caught his attention; and he glanced at the four tracks which converged upon the space where the bodies lay.

"Let's see, now," he said reflectively to the constable. "You and Tatnell came in that way"—indicating the track with a nod as he spoke—"and you came side by side, didn't you?"

"Yes, sir," confirmed the constable.

"I came along that track there," continued Rufford, with another nod. "Mine's a narrow track; your one's double width or more, with two of you abreast. Now, let's see about the other trails. One of them's like mine—a single person's track. The other one's like the one that you and Tatnell made, double width; so two people must have come up abreast there. . . . That looks funny."

He reflected for a moment or two before hitting upon a possible explanation.

"They may have come in a car and climbed up here together. That would account for the double track. Then perhaps one of them went back to the car for something, and came back along the same route without trampling it down any wider. It's what I'd have done myself if I had to go through these bracken-stems. H'm! That seems to fit?"

"It does, sir," agreed Loman, evidently impressed by the ingenuity of the inspector. "It looks just like that to me, now you've pointed it out."

"There's no use looking for foot-prints in this turf," said Rufford regretfully, after some examination of the ground. "Grass sometimes holds them; but not here, so far as I can see. No, no good. Now that pistol."

He knelt down and examined it as it lay.

"It's a Colt .38 automatic. There seem to be some finger-prints on the smooth part of the slide. We may get something definite there. The rest of the metal's all corrugated and wouldn't take prints of much use to us. Don't touch the thing, Loman, whatever you do; and mind you don't tramp on it by accident."

"Oh, no, sir," the constable protested, as if shocked at the mere suggestion.

"And now these bits of paper strewed about the ground," Rufford went on. "They may have nothing to do with the case, but we'd better gather them up. Wait a moment, first!"

He bent down and examined some of the fragments, picking them up for closer inspection.

"They're all damp with the dew and need careful handling, or the writing may get smudged. Two kinds of letter-paper, plain white and a bluish shade. . . . There's what looks like a man's writing on the white stuff, and a woman's writing on the bluish paper. . . . They've been fairly well torn up and scattered about. . . . Was there much of a wind last night?"

"Not much, sir. I happened to speak about it to Worsley when he came off duty this morning, and he said it was starry, with no wind to speak of."

"Then this stuff can't have blown far. Pick up every scrap you see, Loman. Don't finger-print it more than you can help, though I don't suppose there'll be much left in that line, after all this soaking in the dew. Some of the paper's quite flabby with moisture."

They set to work and soon collected a number of scraps of the torn paper. Rufford placed the bluish fragments in one envelope and the white ones in a second. He made no attempt to piece them together at that moment; but one scrap caught his eye as he picked it up. It held a complete printed address in neat Roman type;

FERN LODGE

HAYDOCK AVENUE

Rufford recalled that Haydock Avenue was a quiet residential street in a middle-class neighbourhood, with detached villas and small gardens.

"Haydock Avenue's on your beat, isn't it?" he asked Loman as he stowed the scrap of paper in the appropriate envelope. "Who lives in Fern Lodge?"

The constable hesitated for a moment or two before answering.

"I've just been shifted on to that beat in the last day or two, sir, and I haven't got the lie of the land, yet. Fern Lodge has a big shady bank of ferns in the garden. Perhaps that's why they called the house Fern Lodge. Or else they called it Fern Lodge and planted the ferns on account of the name. The name of the people is Callis, I know that much; but I haven't been long enough on the beat to tell you much about them. I don't know that I've even seen them—not to recognise anyway."

"Callis?" mused the inspector. "That tallies with those

initials E.C. on that wedding-ring. E. Callis might be the husband's name, and the J.B. might be the wife's maiden initials. It's a fairly new ring by the look of it. Are they a young couple?"

"I really don't know, sir, but I've an idea that they are, though how I picked it up I can't say. Perhaps somebody may have mentioned them to me in a casual way, maybe. I can't remember exactly how I got the notion."

"Well, we'll soon find out," returned the inspector. "By the way, when I was up on the embankment yonder I noticed an old house just beyond the crest of this slope. You don't know whose it is, I suppose?"

"Well, sir, as a matter of fact, I do. I lived round about here when I was a boy. It's the Kerrisons' house, the Hermitage, they call it. Mrs. Kerrison, she owns it: an old lady she must be by this time, seventy-odd or so, from what I remember of her when I was a lad."

"A widow? Anybody living there with her?"

"She's been a widow all the time I've known of her, sir. She has a son that lives with her; Stephen his name is. She's a strong-minded old lady, sir, or at least she was when I used to be about here, and she wasn't the sort to change much as time went on, so I expect she's much the same as ever. Brought up young Master Stephen very strict, she did. Very religious old lady, I remember; and he took after her in that, too. You could have set your watch by seeing them pass our door every Sunday, thrice a day, on the way to church. She kept young Master Stephen well tied to her apron strings. Never mixed with girls, I remember. She made him a bit goody-goody when he was young, and he just adored her, I remember from one little thing and another that's stuck in my mind."

"What's his line in business?" asked Rufford out of idle curiosity.

"He never was in business that I know of," Loman answered. "He's twenty years or more older nor me, sir, and he'd have been shaping for business when I was a boy, in the ordinary run of things. But she had enough to live on comfortably, if all talk's true, and she kept him out of work, just living with her up there. It suited her, and it seemed to suit him, he being a solitary kind of creature anyhow."

"What kind of place is it, up there?"

"A sort of old farm-house, you might call it, sir, with a yard and some stables, and outhouses, mostly gone to rack and ruin, even in my day."

"You don't know what staff they keep? How many maids?"

Loman shook his head.

"I haven't been near the place for years, sir. They used to keep two. Likely they do with one, now. People live simpler, nowadays."

"Quite likely," admitted Rufford.

The constable glanced compassionately at the two bodies lying in the disarray of death.

"This is the first murder case I've been mixed up in, sir," he ventured. "It's worse than I thought. If there had been a fight, or something like that, it would have seemed more what one looks for. But it seems kind of sad to see this sort of thing happening to a fine-looking young girl like her. Nice brown hair, she has. She can't be more than twenty-five by the looks of her. All her life before her, so to say; and she ends up like this—snuffed out, just snuffed out. And a good class, too. I just can't imagine how it can have happened."

"No more can I," said Rufford, who was no sentimentalist. "But it's our job to clear that up. Obviously they got into a scrape and took this way out of it."

"A suicide pact, sir? I read about 'em in the papers, but I never rightly understood why they do that sort of thing. Why not face it out, whatever it is?"

"Why not?" echoed the inspector. "Heaven alone knows. But they don't seem able to, sometimes. A rum problem,

Loman. I suppose they must be terrified of scandal, since usually a divorce would put the thing right without suicide. I can't get inside the heads of people like that, and I don't suppose you can, either."

They stood for a moment or two in silence, gazing down at the bodies. Loman, moved by some obscure feeling, broke off a stem of bracken and drove off some flies which had come to settle on the blood.

"Now, let's see," said the inspector, in a business-like tone. "There's an entrance wound in each skull and no exit wounds; so the bullets will turn up at the P.M. That's that. The pistol's there, with finger-prints on it. That's that. Now what we still need are the spent cartridge-cases. They must be amongst the bracken somewhere. It's no good hunting for them now. We'll need to cut down the whole patch before we can see to find them. You'll stay here to watch the place, after we get the bodies away; and I'll send up someone with a couple of pairs of garden shears. Your job will be to clip away this bracken and hunt for these cartridge-cases; and if you come across any more bits of paper, collect them also. And be sure to take measurements of the places where you find anything, so that we can draw a plan of the spot."

"Yes, sir," said Loman obediently.

The inspector turned to look across the railway.

"Nice bit of countryside, this," he commented. "One gets a fine view over that rolling country, with the woods, yonder. And that's a pretty little spinney just along the slope, there."

The sound of an approaching motor caught his ear and interrupted his æsthetic reflections.

"Ah! This'll be the photographer and the ambulance. Lucky that no one has come along to see us and spread the glad news. Our people will be able to work without a crowd jostling around and getting in the road."

CHAPTER III

IDENTIFICATION

WHEN the two bodies had been placed in the mortuary and, as Loman put it, "tidied up a bit," the inspector ordered the photographer to take pictures of the two heads, and then prepare rough prints as quickly as possible. While this was being done, Rufford occupied himself with other factors in the case.

An examination of the Colt automatic disclosed two or three very clear finger-prints on its slide. Those on the roughened parts of the weapon were, as the inspector had foreseen, useless for identification purposes. The cartridges still left in the magazine were two less than the full capacity, tallying with the two fatal shots. Rufford wasted no time over examining the fouling in the barrel, beyond ascertaining that fouling was present. He knew well enough that it is impossible to ascertain with any accuracy the time which has elapsed since a weapon has been fired.

Leaving the matter there for the moment, Rufford rang up the local coroner and gave him particulars of the discovery of the bodies. He next rang up the police surgeon, and was lucky enough to find him at home. Arrangements were made for a post-mortem examination.

"There's just one thing, doctor," Rufford concluded, before ringing off. "In each case there's an entrance wound, but no exit one; so you'll probably find the bullets inside the skulls. I want you to be careful with them, please. Don't scratch them with your instruments or anything like that. It may be important for all I can tell. You'll see to it? Right! Then good-bye."

Armed with a few necessary utensils, Rufford next went to the mortuary along with a constable, to make a further examination of the bodies. The "tidying up" process had been confined to the unwounded sides of the heads. Rufford began his task by expanding his earlier rough notes on the powder-blackening caused by the shots. Taking the woman's body first, he found some blackening around the wound, though much less than would have been produced if black powder had been used. There were signs of scorching on the hair at the temple.

"That shot was fired at fairly close range, evidently," he reflected. "Eight inches, say. A foot at the outside. That fits well enough with the notion that the man was sitting beside her, where the bracken was crushed down; and that he shot her from that position. Some of her blood might have spurted over his right side, then. But there's no help in that, because when he shot himself in his own right temple, he got blood from his own wound over him on that side."

He turned to examine the male body. Here, the signs of powder-blackening were much less conspicuous, showing that in this case the pistol must have been further from the skin when fired. This was confirmed by the absence of any scorching of the hair on the man's temple.

"I wonder, now," mused the inspector. "It almost looks as if she had done the shooting: close range in her case, and the pistol not so near when the shot was fired into him. Well, the finger-prints will settle that."

He took a complete record of the finger-prints from both bodies. Then he made a few measurements with an inch-tape, finding that the man was about five feet eight in height whilst the woman was five feet six.

A search of the pockets followed. In the man's case, rather to the inspector's surprise, he found no engagement-book and no papers which furnished any clue to the owner's identity. There was a pair of reading spectacles; but the case had evidently been bought from a chain store and bore no maker's name. A fountain-pen of a well-known make was too common in type to be helpful. Nor did a cheap note-case with a couple of notes in it furnish any clue, though Rufford took the precaution of jotting down the numbers. He found a Yale latch-key; but that also was useless for his present purpose, as were the few coins which he fished out of the trouser pockets. There were no smoking materials or matches. The man's handkerchief had two minute punctures at one corner; but the aluminium laundry-tag which caused them had been removed, either purposely or by accident.

It was in the ticket-pocket of the man's jacket that he made his first promising discovery: two railway tickets and a piece of paper which he unfolded and examined. It proved to be a left-luggage office voucher for two suit-cases, issued at the local main line station and dated on the previous day, the day on which the shooting had occurred.

"Two suit-cases," Rufford pondered. "That looks as if they'd made some plan for travelling, yesterday."

He turned to the tickets.

"Two third class singles for London, dated yesterday, with consecutive numbers, which looks as if they'd been bought by the same person. That would be the man, of course. So they'd planned to go up to town together, evidently. Then what made them change their minds and go in for the shooting business? That's a rum start."

He cogitated for a moment or two before finding a possible solution.

"One of them must have weakened at the last moment. The girl, most likely. A girl has usually got more to lose than a man has, in an affair of this sort. But against that, the pistol looks like premeditation. The man in the street doesn't go about armed, not in this country. A very rum start. I wish I knew just when that shooting happened."

He fished a penny local time-table from his pocket and

consulted it. An up train left for London at 8.9 p.m., arriving at 10.8 p.m. The next one left at 8.55 p.m. and, being a slow one, did not reach town till 11.46 p.m. The final train, leaving at 11 p.m. and getting to London at 3.55 a.m. was obviously an unlikely one, for passengers reaching London at that hour in the morning would probably have difficulty in getting into an hotel without attracting attention; and notice was the last thing which an eloping couple would wish to attract. He put the matter aside for the moment, promising himself to make inquiries at the station later on.

The girl's coat had two pockets, but they were empty.

Each body had a watch on its wrist. Rufford examined them and found both watches still going. Knowing that wearers of wristlet-watches are apt from time to time to wind them up before they have run down, he did not think it worth while to meddle with them.

"Not much of a catch here," he grumbled to himself as he completed his search. "If it weren't for that address on the note-paper, I'd probably have had to wait till these two were reported missing, before I got much further. What beats me is how they laid their hands on a pistol. It's not the sort of thing one expects, somehow."

He examined finally the shoes in both cases. The girl's were smart town walking-shoes, size five; the man's were serviceable articles, size eight, which had obviously been re-soled a month or two previously.

Returning to the police station, he questioned his staff, all of whom by now had inspected the bodies. None of them had recognised either the man or the woman. The constable who had experience of the beat including Haydock Avenue was off duty at the moment and it did not seem worth while disturbing him, since it was just as easy to make inquiries at Fern Bank itself. But before going there, Rufford wanted the photographs which had been taken in the mortuary, and they were not yet available. To fill in his time, he took out the two envelopes in which the fragments of letter-paper had been stowed and began to piece together the torn documents, handling the moist scraps gingerly for fear of tearing them or leaving his own finger-prints upon them.

Without fitting them completely together, he made out the tenor of the two notes. They were ardent love-letters. For the moment, he went no further, since it would be safer to wait for the paper to dry before handling it too much. The letter in the woman's handwriting bore only the name of a weekday, Tuesday, instead of the ordinary date. In the case of the man's letter, the right-hand upper corner of the first page was missing; but the remainder bore an embossed heading which was incomplete: "38, GRA . . ." Rufford was glad that he had cautioned Loman to collect any further scraps which might have drifted among the bracken. But even failing these, he felt certain of being able to identify the complete address if it were a local one. There could not be many streets with names beginning with the letters GRA.

He turned to the signatures. The woman had signed with a mere initial: "E," which reminded the inspector of the "E.C." in the inscription inside the wedding-ring. Her letter began: "Dearest John." The letter in the man's handwriting opened with: "My darling," and was signed: "John," which seemed to tally with the "J.B." on the wedding-ring. Rufford realised that there was a misfit amongst these facts. If a woman "E.C." had married a man "J.B.," then her name would change to "B." In that case, how did she come to be staying at Fern Bank, whose owner was called Callis? Then the obvious solution struck him. Her maiden name must have been Callis, and at Fern Bank she had been staying with some relation of hers, a brother, possibly. There was no need at the moment for Rufford to speculate further. He would soon learn the facts.

He cautiously gathered up the moist fragments and placed them between two sheets of glass, so that they would dry flat and be easy to piece together later on.

A glance at his watch showed that he had still a short time in hand before he could receive the photographs, and he decided to spend this in making a rough examination of the finger-prints on the Colt automatic. The pistol had been brought in carefully strapped to a board so that the prints had been preserved intact during transit; and, as it chanced, there was a very clear print on the exposed smooth surface of the slide, so clear that powder was unnecessary to bring out the lines. Rufford noted that it was a "whorl" pattern—that is, one which has a central core to its maze. By using a magnifying glass, he counted the number of ridges which intervened between the core and the nearest "delta"—a point where the ridges eddied away into subsidiary patterns—and found fourteen of them. There were two fairly prominent "islands" in the pattern, and he counted the number of the ridges between each of them and the "core," noting the relative positions of the three features.

He next took up the prints which he had made from the fingers of the two bodies. The designs on the woman's finger-tips were all of the "loop" type, so he was able to discard them immediately. The right thumb of the male body showed a "whorl" pattern, however; and a repetition of the counting process proved that here also there were fourteen ridges between the core and the nearest delta. Rufford was able to pick out the two islands, also; and the numbers for them were identical with those which he had found on the pistol-print. The relative positions of the various features were alike in both patterns.

"Not much need to go further for the present," Rufford assured himself thankfully. "I can get the rest of the prints checked carefully by and by. It's plain enough from this that the man must have had the pistol in his hand."

He had hardly put the pistol into a place of safety, and given some orders to his subordinates, when the photographer brought in the rough bromide prints of the photographs he had taken.

"You'd better go easy in handling them, sir," he pointed out. "I dried them with alcohol, but it may be a little while yet before they can stand rough treatment."

The inspector glanced at the prints. By his orders, the pictures had been taken in profile, from the uninjured sides of the faces, so that they showed no trace of the damage done by the bullets. Dismissing the photographer, he put the prints carefully into a folder and then glanced at his watch. A good many business men in the town lunched at home; and it seemed possible that he might catch Callis—whoever he was—at Fern Bank. That, for many reasons, would be better than interviewing him at his office, Rufford decided.

He consulted the telephone directory, found the Fern Bank number, and in the line below he noted a repetition of the name Callis in the title of a firm of chartered accountants: Callis, Frensham & Olney, with offices in South Street. Callis was an uncommon name, so it was likely that Callis of Fern Bank and Callis of South Street were identical. Rufford dialled the Fern Bank number, and was relieved to find Callis at home, though just preparing to leave again for his office. The inspector reflected sourly that he himself would have to go luncheonless, for by the time he had paid his visit, it would not be worth while to trouble about food. He fixed an immediate appointment at Fern Bank, picked up his folder, and made his way to Haydock Avenue.

CHAPTER IV

THE TELEGRAM

INSPECTOR RUFFORD had a predilection for guessing the financial status of householders from the general appearance of the streets in which they lived. In many cases, his estimate was probably far astray, but on the average he came near the mark. Mr. Smith, living in Acacia Drive, was a five-hundred pounder; Mr. Jones, in Laurel Grove, probably just reached the thousand pound-level. And so on. Haydock Avenue, he judged when he came to it, was probably an eight-hundred-a-year street; and this conclusion was reinforced in his mind by the number of perambulators which he noted in the front gardens. Evidently this was a street where young couples started married life without actually having to pinch. Then, if they got on in the world, they moved to quarters better suited to their increased incomes and growing families, leaving a house vacant for a pair of new recruits.

At Fern Bank he was shown into a comfortable sitting-room; and almost immediately the door opened and a frank-looking young man came in, with a faintly puzzled expression on his face as he greeted the inspector.

"Well, Mr. Rufford," he began in a pleasant voice, "I hope you won't keep me long. I want to get back to my office. What's the trouble? Nothing serious, I hope. Leaving my car unattended, perhaps?"

"I'm afraid it's more serious than that, sir," the inspector explained soberly.

His tone seemed to take Callis by surprise. He looked at

Rufford in obvious doubt, and his rather amused expression changed to a much graver one.

"More serious?" he echoed. "Then what is it? I can't think of anything."

It was no part of the inspector's business to enter into the feelings of people with whom he had to deal in the course of his duty; but he had his human side as well as his official one; and this human side now said very plainly: "Another damned disagreeable job here." Without answering directly, he produced his folder, extracted the print of the woman's face, and handed it across to Callis.

"Do you recognise her, sir?"

The accountant took it in his hand, gave it one startled glance, and then broke into counter-questions:

"What's happened, man? Has she been in a motor smash? Is she badly hurt? Answer man, answer! It's my wife. Where is she? In hospital?"

Long experience had made Rufford apt in the breaking of ill news, but this was a much worse task than usual. It was no business of his to tell all that he had discovered until it suited him to do so. With as much kindness as he could summon up, he gave Callis the main lines of the affair, stopping short at the discovery of the bodies. The tale, even toned down as it was, could not but be terrible. As the inspector proceeded, Callis seemed to lose his normal physical tautness. He listened with head bent, his hands clasped between his knees, and his eyes fixed on the floor. Once, an unintentionally vivid touch in Rufford's narrative seemed to flick him almost like the stroke of a whip, and he flinched under it. When the inspector had finished his story, Callis sat for some seconds without making a sign. At last he pulled himself together with an obvious effort and, in a toneless voice, he put another question:

"Who was this man? Have you found out yet?"

The inspector shook his head, opened his folder again, and produced his second print.

"Perhaps you recognise him yourself, sir?"

Callis took it from his hand, gazed at it for a moment or two in silence, then passed it back again. He seemed completely stunned by what had been shown to him. Rufford waited patiently.

"I recognise it," Callis said at length in a monotone. "Of course I recognise Barratt. But I can't understand it. He's been hanging about her skirts for long enough. He's the minister of our church. People have been talking, I know, about her and him, but I paid no attention to all that. I can swear she was quite straight, Mr. Rufford. She'd never have . . . Why, she kissed me good-bye, when she went off yesterday, and I . . . I can't realise it. I can't."

His voice ran up a tone or two in the scale and then broke off. For some reason or other, the sight of Barratt's portrait seemed to have hit him very hard. He bent his shoulders again and stared at the carpet, the picture of a broken man. The inspector made no attempt to intrude on his sorrow. He had been through scenes of this kind before, in connection with deaths on the road; and he thought it well to let Callis have time to pull himself together after the shock. In a few moments the accountant managed to collect himself, but his voice still showed the effect which these revelations had made on him.

"I can't make head or tail of this business," he confessed. "But one thing I'm sure of: she would never have been unfaithful to me."

Rufford knew the ring of a true statement when he heard it; and there was no doubt in his mind that Callis really believed in his wife's fidelity. It would be a nasty knock for him when all the facts came out, the inspector reflected with a certain amount of unprofessional pity.

"No, I can't make it out at all," Callis continued in that toneless voice. "Do you think he lured her away into this out-of-the-way place, and then, when she wouldn't fall in with his ideas, he . . . he killed her?"

"That's what we've got to find out, Mr. Callis," Rufford pointed out in a judicial tone. "And it's up to you to help us, there. The best thing you can do is to pull yourself together—I know it's a terrible shock to you, coming out of the blue like this—and tell me anything that'll help to make things clearer."

The business-like tone in the inspector's voice seemed to brace the accountant, as Rufford meant it to do. He lifted his head and stared at his visitor, though there was still a dazed expression in his eyes.

"You're quite right," he agreed, with an obvious effort to bring himself under full control. "I'm sorry. But you can guess what a shock this has been. I'm all right now—or nearly. Tell me what you want. I'll not go off the handle again."

He glanced away; and Rufford, following his eyes, found that he was gazing across the room to the mantelpiece on which stood a photograph of Mrs. Callis. Touched by the misery of Callis's expression, the inspector hastened to distract his attention: and out of kindness he began by putting questions which bore less directly on the tragedy than those which he intended to ask later on.

"You see, Mr. Callis," he began. "I know nothing about your affairs; and it's essential that I should learn something about them. The coroner will probably expect me to be able to give him any facts which may come up at the inquest. . . ."

"Good Lord!" ejaculated Callis, evidently revolted at the idea. "Will there be an inquest?"

Rufford recognised the tone. It was the old story which he had heard so often before. "An inquest? But inquests don't have to be held on people like *us*, surely."

"Do you mean to say," Callis went on heatedly, "that some miserable jurymen will go and look at her body?"

"The coroner may dispense with a jury, nowadays," Rufford explained. "That is, if he sees fit to do so. And the the more he learns about the case beforehand, the more inclined he might be to handle it himself. I can't guarantee anything, you understand. I'm merely telling you this."

"I see," said Callis, dully. "I'll tell you anything you want. I hadn't thought of an inquest, somehow. . . ."

His voice tailed off into silence. Rufford guessed what he was thinking. A beastly business, having someone dear to you turned into a public show for an odd lot of jurymen. But time was flying, and the inspector had no desire to see more of it go past unused. He spoke again in a brisker tone.

"I'll begin at the beginning, Mr. Callis. When were you married?"

"Two years ago."

"You must have been young then?"

"I was twenty-three; and my wife was twenty-two."

Rufford was glad to notice that under this matter-of-fact examination, Callis was recovering fuller control of himself.

"What was her maiden name, please? Did she come of a local family or from elsewhere?"

"Esther was her name, Esther Prestage," Callis explained. "Her family were townspeople here. In fact, this was their house. They died before she grew up, and she stayed on here with an aunt to look after her. When we married, the aunt moved out. It's my wife's house."

"Had she a private income?" inquired the inspector.

"What on earth do you want to know that for?" asked Callis, obviously surprised by the question. "She had, as a matter of fact, or we couldn't have got married as early as we did. It wasn't much—just three or four hundred a year; but we could make a start on it, together with what I get from my firm. I'm only a very junior partner."

Rufford ignored the question. But he noted the fact that Mrs. Callis had control of enough money to live upon if she had left her husband. That certainly made an elopement easier.

"Any children?" he inquired casually.

Callis shook his head. Rufford noted that this was another

factor which would make it simpler for a wife to leave her husband in the lurch.

"And, by the way, what about yourself?" he demanded. "Your Christian name, and so on. I don't know them, you see."

Callis had apparently pulled himself together completely now, under the inspector's matter-of-fact treatment.

"John Callis," he replied to the question. "I'm a C.A., and junior partner in Callis, Frensham, and Olney, of South Street. My uncle was the senior partner until his death. That's why our name comes first on the list."

"I know the firm," Rufford volunteered. "Now, Mr. Callis, I want to hear something about your doings yesterday. You mentioned saying good-bye to your wife, I think. When was that?"

Callis made a movement as though to rise from his chair. Then he changed his mind, leaned back, and answered the question.

"My wife sometimes used to go and spend a day or two with one of her relations, a Mrs. Longnor. I'm not sure what the relationship is, exactly. Something pretty far-distant, anyhow, second cousin once removed or that kind of thing. Mrs. Longnor's a few years older than my wife, but they've always been close friends."

"Yes?" prompted Rufford, as Callis paused for a moment.

"I come home here for luncheon every day," the accountant went on. "Yesterday, when I got back, my wife was out. She'd gone down town to do some shopping. I remember she mentioned at breakfast-time that she meant to do that, and I asked her to get me one or two things. When I came in, there was a telegram on the hall table, addressed to me, as I thought—just 'Callis' and the address on the envelope. I opened it. Just a moment. . . ."

He rose from his chair, walked over to a gimcrack little escritoire, searched for a moment or two amongst the pigeon-holes, and came back with a telegram in its envelope, which he handed to the inspector. Rufford opened it and read the wire.

"Callis, Fern Bank, Haydock Avenue. Am in town unexpectedly. If you can, meet me for tea at Robinson's, drive me back home, and stay for a day or two. Edith."

"Edith is Mrs. Longnor?" asked Rufford.

Callis nodded in confirmation.

"Robinson's?" continued the inspector. "That would be the big drapery place in Victoria Street; they have a tea-room in the shop, of course. H'm! Wire handed in at eleven-fifty-five a.m. and sent out from Maxwell Park post office at twelve-ten. Have you a phone, Mr. Callis?"

"Oh, yes," Callis replied. "I see what you mean. Why didn't Mrs. Longnor ring up, instead of wiring? That's funny. . . ."

He reflected for a moment or two over this problem. Then a solution seemed to occur to him.

"The Longnors have no phone in their house, I remember, so Mrs. Longnor might not think of ringing up from a call-office, as you or I would do, being accustomed to the phone. She's rather feather-headed. You can see the number of words wasted in that wire; you or I could have got it much shorter. Probably she was passing a post office and thought wiring was the easiset way of doing it. My wife might have been out, as she actually was, you see. The wire made it certain that she'd get the message when she came home to luncheon."

"I see," said Rufford. "Likely enough you're right, since you know the lady. Now, when Mrs. Callis got this wire, did she say anything about it?"

"She showed it to me—of course I'd seen it already when I opened it—and she told me she felt she'd like a little change so she'd go to the Longnors for a day or two. It's not much of a change of air, really, for they live at Toynton Lacey, only an hour's drive away. But my wife and Mrs. Longnor always get on together and it's not a bad thing to get a change of company now and again."

"Then when you went back to the office in the afternoon you said good-bye to your wife, I suppose, in view of this visit she was making to Mrs. Longnor. Did she seem quite as usual? No agitation? Nothing to suggest that it wasn't just an ordinary visit to an old friend?"

"Nothing whatever," Callis said, decidedly. "Why should she have been upset? It was a perfectly ordinary affair. She's stayed with the Longnors often and often. If you're suggesting that my wife had any other plans in her mind, then I'll say as plainly as I can that you're wholly mistaken. My wife was absolutely straight. I'm sure of it. Absolutely certain of it. I'm not going to be persuaded into thinking anything else, Mr. Rufford. I knew her, through and through."

"You should know, sir," Rufford agreed. "Now, another matter. You were at your office when she set out from here, weren't you? But your maid must know when your wife left the house. I'd like to ask her about that, later on. That, and one or two other points. But they'll keep, for the moment. Here's something else. Have you a specimen of your wife's handwriting that you could give me? Anything will do."

Callis got up from his chair again and walked over to the escritoire, where he hunted about for a time in search of something which would satisfy the inspector. At last he returned with a sheet of letter-paper in his hand, and Rufford noted that it had the same heading and was of the same bluish shade as the fragments which he had collected beside the bodies.

"Will this do?" asked the accountant. "It's just a list of members of some church committee that she had to summon to a meeting next week."

"She took an interest in church work?" queried the inspector.

"Oh, yes," Callis explained. "She took a strong interest in them. More than I did, I'm afraid, though I'm treasurer. But she was very busy amongst committees and so forth, really interested. She was head of the Guides and Brownies contingent amongst the girls of the congregation and very enthusiastic over them."

"What church is that?" demanded Rufford, seeing in this an easy transition to questions about Barratt.

"Oh, none that you ever heard of, Mr. Rufford," said Callis in a tone which almost suggested that he was half ashamed of the denomination. "It's a very small sect: the Church of Awakened Israel. My wife and I were brought up in it by our parents, and we went on attending when we grew up, more by force of habit than anything else. One gets into a rut and it's a bother to get out of it. I don't suppose there are a dozen churches altogether of the Awakened Israelities. Most of the congregation are uneducated people. It's a very small affair, and dying out gradually, at that. I'd have dropped out myself, if they hadn't made me treasurer. I could hardly leave them, after that. And my wife's always been interested in the church's affairs, so we stayed on."

Rufford had never heard of the Awakened Israelites and had no interest in them now.

"This interest in church work would bring her into contact with Mr. Barratt, evidently," he suggested, watching Callis closely. "But you weren't in any way suspicious of their relations, obviously. Still, you said a few minutes ago that people had been talking about them. How did that come to *your* ears?"

Callis moved uneasily in his chair, as though this question made him uncomfortable.

"Is it *really* necessary to go into that?" he demanded, in obvious bitterness.

"I'm afraid it is, sir," said Rufford, relentlessly.

Callis hesitated for a moment, as though loath to fall in with the inspector's wishes. Then he went over to the escritoire and unlocked one of its drawers with a key on his chain. After searching for a time, he came back with a sheet of paper which he handed to Rufford.

"I got that through the post, a day or two back," he said, with an angry frown. "After you've looked at it, you'll admit that some people have been doing more than talk. I had a good mind to put you people on the track of the writer, whoever it is; but on second thoughts I concluded that there was no use stirring up mud and making more gossip by dragging the affair into publicity. I kept the letter, though, in case any more came; for if there had been a number of them I'd made up my mind to put a stop to the business, cost what it might. And, of course, if I had to do that, then the more of these precious productions I could hand over to you, the better chance you'd have of tracing the writing."

"You didn't keep the envelope?" queried the inspector.

Callis made a gesture of vexation.

"No, I didn't," he confessed. "Now that you mention it, I see that it was stupid of me to throw it away. It might have given some clue, I suppose. Still, it's too late now. The fact is, when I got this production, my first impulse was to destroy it and put it out of my mind—forget it, if possible. And I destroyed the envelope while I was in that way of thinking. When I changed my mind, I forgot all about the envelope and didn't think of fishing the fragments of it out of the waste-paper basket."

"A pity, that," commented Rufford.

The average man, he reflected, never seemed to think of taking the most obvious precautions. Something might have been gleaned from the postal marks on that envelope. However, Callis had at any rate kept this letter, and that was better than nothing. He unfolded the sheet and glanced at the straggling printed capitals which made up the message:

"YOU MUST BE VERY BLIND IF YOU DONT SEE WHAT GOES ON UNDER YOUR NOSE. WATCH YOUR WIFE AND YOULL SEE WHAT OTHER PEOPLE HAVE SEEN LONG AGO. A PREACHER OUGHT TO SET A BETTER EXAMPLE. THERES A PLAIN HINT TO YOU. AND READ PROVERBS, VII."

"I'll keep this," said Rufford, folding up the paper and stowing it away in his pocket.

Callis made a movement as though to take back the document, but apparently resigned himself, after a glance at the inspector's face.

"You won't go reading that stuff out in public at the inquest, I hope," he said protestingly. "It's not evidence, really; and it would just set a lot of ill-natured people gossiping on the strength of it. I want to keep my wife's name clear. I *know* she was perfectly straight, and I won't have people thinking she was anything else but straight. This has been a sore business, Mr. Rufford, as you can well guess. I don't understand it. But at least I want her name kept clear of lies and slurs. I owe that to her."

He almost broke down as his own reference brought up the matter of his wife's fate. Rufford hastened to switch the conversation to less painful subjects.

"In that wire of hers, Mrs. Longnor asked your wife to drive her home to Toynton Lacey," he reminded Callis. "Have you one car only, or two?"

"Just one."

"It isn't in your garage now, I noticed as I came in. The garage door was open and the place was empty."

Callis nodded.

"It wasn't there when I came home last night," he said, and then with a change of tone he added: "I see what you're after. If she took our car to meet Mrs. Longnor, then the car must be somewhere; and that ought to throw some light on things."

He broke off, apparently perplexed by following this idea further.

"But if she met Mrs. Longnor, why didn't she carry on and drive to Toynton Lacey? I don't see my way through it."

Again he fell silent and his face showed that he was thinking hard. Rufford himself was in no better case at the moment. But, he assured himself, the car was bound to be identified, and when it *was* found, its position could not but help to carry things a stage further towards elucidation. And, besides, he had Mrs. Longnor still in hand, with her evidence.

"Just a question or two more, Mr. Callis. You can tell me something about this man Barratt. Where did he live?"

"At 38 Granville Road."

"Was he married or single?"

"Married, been married for years."

"A man of between thirty-five and forty, by the look of him. Any children?"

Callis shook his head, and this seemed to give the inspector a fresh idea.

"What's his wife like?—in appearance, I mean."

Callis seemed rather taken aback by a question of this kind.

"Oh, I don't know—how to describe her, I mean. About medium height for a woman. Dark-haired. Some people think she's very good-looking. She probably is, but not in my style. She's got a nice voice. I really can't think of anything else."

"Is she much younger than Barratt?"

"I don't really know. She looks it, but you never can tell, can you, nowadays?"

Rufford reflected that the average person had no notion whatever of giving a useful description, even of a friend. The man in the street didn't even know what were important details, like eye-colour. All he could do for you was to make a guess at height, hair-colour, and possibly good looks or bad—factors which depended purely on his own personal likes and dislikes.

"When did you last see Barratt?" he inquired.

"I saw him at church last Sunday, in the morning," Callis replied. "But I didn't speak to him then. But here's something which may be important, Mr. Rufford. I told you I'm treasurer of the church, didn't I? As it happened, I'd some points I wanted to discuss with Barratt this week. Nothing important, just about some organ repairs. So, after a cold supper, I walked round to his house last night to talk them over. He wasn't in. Mrs. Barratt told me he'd gone to a meeting of some committee in the church hall and would probably be back soon, when it was over. I waited for a good while, till about a quarter-past ten or so, but he didn't turn up; and I didn't like to be keeping Mrs. Barratt talking any longer, so I came away without seeing him. Mrs. Barratt thought that he must have gone to pay a sick-call after the meeting was over, so there was no telling when he'd get home again."

The inspector did not press for details. He could get them from Mrs. Barratt, who would know more about Barratt's normal routine than Callis did.

"That finishes my business with you, Mr. Callis. For the present, at least, for if anything fresh turns up that you know about, I may have to see you again."

He added a word or two of sympathy, which Callis received gratefully, though he was obviously still stunned by the tragedy.

"Just one thing more," Rufford added as he rose to his feet. "I'd like to see your maid for a moment or two. Would you send her in, please?"

"I'll ring," said Callis obligingly.

Rufford had meant to interview the maid alone, but he did not object when Callis reseated himself after ringing the bell. It would be easy to summon the girl to the police station if he needed to ask any questions about the relations between husband and wife. She would probably be more communicative in strange surroundings. In about a minute she came into the room: a neat, smartly-dressed girl.

"Not bad-looking," mused the inspector, committing the very fault he had attributed to the man in the street.

Callis saw the girl's hesitation as she glanced from one face to the other, and he hastened to reassure her.

"Inspector Rufford wants to ask you a question or two; but they have nothing to do with your own affairs, so you needn't be frightened."

"First of all, I'd like to know your name," said Rufford with a smile which put the girl more at her ease.

"Maud Endell."

"No need to get flurried," Rufford told her. "Now just cast your mind back to yesterday. You were in the house during the morning. Can you remember when Mrs. Callis went out?"

"It would be about half-past ten, or between that and eleven. She told me she was going out shopping and I reminded her to call at the greengrocer's."

"That's the way I wish most people would answer," praised Rufford. "Now, during the morning, do you remember any phone calls, either before or after Mrs. Callis went out?"

"I remember one. I'm sure there were no more. That one came about eleven o'clock. Mrs. Barratt rang up and wanted to speak to Mrs. Callis; and when I told her Mrs. Callis was out, she said 'Never mind' and then she explained it was some message from Mr. Barratt about some church business, but it didn't matter, for she could ring up later on in the day. That's the only phone call I can remember, except that one of my own friends rang up to make an appointment with me in the afternoon, since it was my afternoon off."

"That's just what I want," said Rufford, encouragingly. "Now can you tell me anything about a telegram?"

"There was a telegram came yesterday morning, about half-past twelve, as near as I can remember. I put it on the hall table, and Mr. Callis picked it up when he came in."

She glanced at Callis as she spoke, as though doubtful whether he would be pleased or not by this. His nod evidently reassured her.

"You didn't see the actual contents of the wire?"

"Oh, no, sir. Mr. Callis put it in his pocket after he'd opened it."

"That's all right. Mr. Callis has shown it to me himself," Rufford explained, apparently to the girl's relief. "Now can you remember when Mr. Callis came in at midday?"

"It would be close on one o'clock, I think. He usually comes at between ten and a quarter past—don't you, sir?—and lunch is at half-past. Mrs. Callis came in about twenty past and went straight upstairs to take her hat off."

"Does Mrs. Callis usually go out shopping in the morning?"

"Not regularly, not every day, I mean. Just from time to time. I heard her yesterday telling Mr. Callis that she'd call at Winterwell's and get something he'd asked her to buy there, so I knew she was going out and that was why I reminded her about the greengrocer."

"And she usually comes back just in time for luncheon, when she does go out shopping?"

"Oh, yes. At least, generally. Mostly, I'd say."

"It was your afternoon off, you said. When did you leave the house yesterday afternoon?"

"About three o'clock, same as usual."

"Had Mrs. Callis gone out again before you left?"

"Oh, no. She was in the drawing-room, reading, I think."

"You didn't see her packing a suit-case, did you?"

The maid shook her head decidedly.

"And you didn't see a suit-case left in the hall, or anywhere about the premises?"

"Oh, no. I'd have noticed it, if it had been in the hall."

"Do you know the look of Mrs. Callis's suit-cases? I suppose you see them when you clean out the box-room or wherever they're kept?"

"Oh, yes, I know them quite well. There's a small leather one, and an expanding one, and another bigger leather one, a bit old and used, but it's one that Mr. Callis generally uses himself, and then there's a cabin trunk. . . ."

"Never mind about trunks," interrupted the inspector. "I want to know about the suit-cases. Suppose you take me to this box-room and show me them, please."

Again the maid consulted Callis with a glance and seemed relieved by the expression on his face.

"If you'll come with me, sir, I'll show you them now," she agreed, leading the way to the door.

They went upstairs, with Callis following in the rear, and the maid opened the box-room door.

"Oh!" she exclaimed, in evident surprise. "The small leather one isn't there."

Then she recollected, apparently, that Mrs. Callis had not returned home, and drew the natural conclusion:

"Mrs. Callis was away last night. She must have taken it with her. It's the one she usually takes away for a day or two, when she goes."

"Can you describe it?" demanded the inspector.

"Well, it's pretty new, hardly scratched, and it's about this length and that deep."

She illustrated the dimensions with her arms.

"Any labels on it that you remember?"

"I do remember one, because the name on it was funny: 'Strathpeffer'."

The inspector turned to Callis, who explained.

"That's quite right. My wife and I were up at Strathpeffer at Easter."

The inspector seemed satisfied by this, but as they turned away from the box-room he put another question to the girl:

"I suppose you know what dresses Mrs. Callis had? I want to know what she took away with her in that suit-case."

By this time, it was plain, Maud Endell's original coolness was wearing off, despite Rufford's matter-of-fact methods. She had begun to see that there was something more than odd about all this inquiry, and her expression showed this more and more clearly. Finally, her curiosity grew too much for her.

"Has anything happened, sir?" she demanded, turning to Callis. "There's nothing happened to Mrs. Callis, has there . . . ?"

"Never mind about that just now," intervened the inspector, a shade brusquely. "Just answer any questions first."

"But *has* anything happened to her?" the girl persisted stubbornly. "She's always been very nice to me, Mrs. Callis; and I hope nothing's gone wrong. She wasn't home last night, I know that. She'd gone to stay at Mrs. Longnor's, Mr. Callis told me, same as she often does."

"There's been a mishap," Callis intervened. "Just tell Mr. Rufford what he wants to know."

The inspector was not pleased by this intervention. However, in a way it simplified his task. But before he could ask another question, Maud Endell supplied him with some unsolicited information.

"That's funny," she said, doubtfully. "When I went into the bath-room yesterday morning I just noticed a box of bath salts, verbena, the kind she always uses; and it was full except for one cube, same as it was in the morning; and she always takes some cubes with her when she goes away to stay with anyone. There's only two cubes missing now."

Rufford pricked up his ears at this. Evidently this girl was sharper than he had imagined.

"Did you notice anything else?" he demanded.

"Not last night, because then I didn't know she was going away. But this morning, knowing she was gone, I did notice that she'd left her tooth-brush behind."

"People often forget a tooth-brush in packing. You can always buy a new one at the nearest druggist's," said the inspector, unimpressed.

"Yes, but it's not many people forget a brush and comb," retorted the maid triumphantly. "And her brush and comb are on her dressing-table."

"They are, are they?"

"I'll let you see them, if you'll come along here," said Maud, leading the way. "This is her bedroom. There they are, on the dressing-table."

There they were, undoubtedly: a silver-backed brush and a silver comb, lying beside a hand-mirror. Rufford's opinion of the maid went up several points.

"Now we are here," he said, with less asperity in his tone, "perhaps you can tell us something more. I want to know what Mrs. Callis packed in that suit-case she took away with her: handkerchiefs, stockings, evening shoes, and all that kind of thing. You must have some idea of what she had, and you can tell us what's missing, I suppose?"

"Not handkerchiefs, nor stockings, nor anything like that, I couldn't," Maud declared flatly. "I'm not one to go prying amongst a mistress's things and counting her handkerchiefs. But if she was going away for a night or two, she'd need some sort of frock for the evenings, and I *do* know what dresses she had. Do you want me to look?"

Rufford nodded, and without more ado Maud threw open the door of a large cupboard, recessed in the wall, which served as a wardrobe. On a shelf below the dresses stood a row of shoes, each with its tree inside. The girl began a systematic search amongst the dresses, and in a few seconds had discovered what was required; but the result seemed to puzzle her a little, as the inspector inferred from her expression as she turned round again.

"There's just one dress missing," she explained. "It's a black silk one, with a bunch of some sort of flowers on it, to relieve the black. Artificial flowers, I mean. And it had a belt to match, with one of these diamantée clasps. The belt would be in this drawer here."

She opened the drawer as she spoke, and showed a number of belts of different types.

"Here's the one I mean," she said, pointing to it.

Rufford, thinking of something else, did not notice the puzzled look on her face. Women's clothes were not a subject of much interest to him.

"Have a look at the shoes, will you?" he suggested. "See if you can tell what she took away with her."

Maud closed the belt-drawer and went back to the wardrobe.

"She's taken just one pair," she announced, after a glance along the row. "Glacé, they were, with Louie Kangz heels. I remember them quite well."

Rufford was jotting down some notes in his book.

"Black silk dress, with bunch of flowers . . ." he murmured as he wrote.

"Yes, that's it," Maud confirmed. "It wasn't one she wore often. I got the idea, somehow, that she didn't like it much; but maybe I was wrong, there. You can see by the empty hanger how it was put away behind the others, the ones she was more likely to be wearing."

"Anything else missing, that you can think of?" demanded the inspector.

Maud considered for a moment or two, pinching her lower lip in a pose of perplexity. Then her face brightened; and she went over to the tallboy, pulled out a drawer and took from it a pair of pyjamas.

"These are what she wore last night," she explained. "If she's gone away and left these behind, she must have taken another pair with her. I do know how many sets of pyjamas she had. Just a moment. . . ."

She pulled out another drawer, made a rapid search, and then turned to the waiting inspector:

"Yes, there's a pair missing. Nearly new, they are: white silk ones with coral facings. They ought to be here, but they aren't."

Rufford went through the drawer himself to confirm her statement. Then, after making a note, he turned again to the girl with a further question:

"When did you come in last night?"

Maud considered for a moment or two before answering.

"I caught the last tram. It would be about twenty past eleven when I got back here."

"Mr. Callis was in, then, was he?"

"Oh, yes. I saw him in the sitting-room as I passed the window, going to the front door. He hadn't drawn the curtains. You were reading a book, weren't you, sir?"

Callis confirmed this with a nod, and Rufford put another question.

"Have you a latch-key?" he asked the girl.

"No, I don't need one. The front door's always on the latch till the last person happens to go to bed. I just came in and went straight upstairs."

"You didn't wash up the supper things?" demanded the inspector.

"Oh, no. I left them till the morning. There was only Mr. Callis's dishes, and he'd had only some cold fowl, salad, and an apple pie. It wasn't worth while washing up four or five dishes at that time of night. I just left them, and washed them up with the breakfast things this morning. I didn't even go into the kitchen last night."

The inspector glanced at Callis, who nodded again in confirmation.

"I heard her come in," he said. "I sat up until about midnight, myself, and I released the catch on the Yale lock before I went to bed. That's all right."

"Very well," said Rufford, turning back to the maid.

"I suppose you'd recognise that dress and these shoes, if I happened to show them to you, by and by?"

"Oh, easily," she declared, confidently. "I couldn't mistake them if I saw them."

"Well, say nothing to anyone about what I've been speaking about," Rufford cautioned her. "Don't go chattering, see? Mrs. Callis has come by a mishap, and the less said about it the better, till we get hold of the right party."

"A motor smash, is it?" asked Maud, obviously much concerned at the idea that her mistress had been hurt. "I do hope it ain't serious. I mean, I hope she's not crippled or disfigured, or anything; for she was always very kind to me, she was, and very nice-looking, too. I couldn't bear to think she was badly hurt."

"She's had a nasty knock," Rufford admitted, with apparent candour. "We'll just hope for the best."

Maud turned to Callis.

"Indeed I *am* sorry to hear that, sir," she said, with genuine feeling. "I'm sorry for her and for you, too."

Rufford felt that this was none of his business. He dismissed the maid with a gesture and, going downstairs, led Callis into the sitting-room.

"Mrs. Callis wore a wedding-ring, of course. A plain gold one?" he asked.

Callis shook his head decidedly.

"No, no. When we were married, I gave her a platinum one," he explained. "What they call an Eternity ring, with some sort of pattern chased on it, inside and outside."

"And initials, perhaps?" hazarded the inspector.

"No, no initials. Just this chased pattern. People noticed it, I know, when she was a bride"—he gulped slightly, and the inspector guessed that this subject had touched a raw spot—"and she used to make a little joke about keeping a score of the people who asked to be allowed to look at it each day when we came back from our honeymoon. Why do you ask?"

"Well . . ." the inspector hesitated before inflicting the stab, "when we found her, she had a plain gold ring on her wedding finger. I'll let you see it, later on."

This piece of information seemed to perplex Callis more than anything else had done throughout the interview.

"I don't understand that," he said, almost plaintively.

As the inspector turned while closing the garden gate, he saw Callis still on the doorstep, his head down-bent, with an expression on his face as if he had been completely puzzled by what he had just been told.

CHAPTER V

THE BLACK BAG

AFTER leaving Fern Bank, the inspector stopped at the first telephone-box on his way, rang up one of his subordinates, and gave an order. He knew the Longnors had no phone. Callis had mentioned that. But the Toynton Lacey constabulary could get him the information he needed, and it would be waiting for him when he got back to the police station. He was not in the best of tempers. The loss of his luncheon had begun to rankle in his mind, for even the keenest detective has his human side.

"Round about £400 to £450 a year," was his automatic estimate of the average yearly income of the residents in Granville Road when he reached it. "Some of them don't keep a maid."

The Barratts apparently fell into this category, for when he rang the bell the door was opened by the obvious mistress of the house. At the first glance, she surprised Rufford, for instead of the household drudge he had expected, he found himself confronted by an attractive, dark-haired, grey-eyed young woman, with lips whose fine modelling owed their lines to nature and not to lipstick.

"Might be anywhere between twenty-eight and thirty-odd," he decided as he glanced at her. "And she's a real lady, by her looks. A bit of a fish out of water in this neighbourhood."

This comment was not intended as a depreciation of the inhabitants of Granville Road. It was extracted from the inspector by his feeling that a woman of this type must have been born and brought up in quite other surroundings, an environment more spacious and leisurely than a suburban street of the Granville Road level.

Mrs. Barratt did not wait for him to introduce himself.

"You are Inspector Rufford, aren't you?" she asked in a low, clear voice which Rufford found very attractive. "I've been expecting you. Mr. Callis rang me up a few minutes ago and explained matters. Won't you come in?"

Rufford was confirmed in his conclusions by this opening. Callis had evidently saved him the trouble of breaking the news to her. She must have learned of her husband's death only a few minutes before, but she had pulled herself together and was able to face a stranger with a cool collected manner as if she was receiving a formal caller. That showed the results of early training and a certain standard of behaviour. "Never show a wound." If she could keep it up, his task would be less uncomfortable than he had expected.

She led the way into a room which was obviously her husband's study, with its desk and some shelves of theological works round the walls. Taking a chair herself, she invited the inspector to sit down and then she seemed to leave the next move to him.

"Mr. Callis has told you what's happened?" he queried.

"Yes, he told me about my husband and Mrs. Callis. You've come to ask some questions, I suppose. I'm quite ready to tell you anything you wish."

Rufford could guess that her composure was not being easily maintained. She was sitting with her knees pressed together, her feet side by side, her hands clasped in her lap, and there was a stiffness in her whole attitude which suggested that she was holding herself in by a strong effort, though her voice remained as level as it had been when she met him at the door.

"You can imagine how sorry I am to trouble you at this moment," Rufford went on. "It's no choice of mine, Mrs.

Barratt. But we have to do these things, whether we like them or not."

"I quite understand," Mrs. Barratt assured him, evidently with the intention of being helpful. "You mustn't mind my feelings. Please ask any questions you wish to put."

"Very well, then," the inspector continued. "I think you rang up Mrs. Callis about eleven o'clock yesterday morning?"

"That's quite correct," said Mrs. Barratt frankly. "My husband asked me to do that. He'd something he wanted to talk to her about, I believe, something in connection with the Guides; but he didn't tell me exactly what it was. When I rang up, the Callis's maid told me that Mrs. Callis had gone down town. I told my husband that when he came in to dinner. We have dinner at half-past one and supper at seven. He'd gone out after breakfast and had been at our church all morning. The organist wants the organ overhauled, and they had an expert in, to discuss the matter and give them an estimate. That was why he asked me to ring up Mrs. Callis for him, instead of doing it himself."

"I see," said Rufford. "Now can you tell me what you and Mr. Barratt did in the afternoon, yesterday?"

"I can tell you what I did myself. I went out, after I'd washed up our dinner dishes, and I spent the afternoon at a picture-house. I did some shopping, too. It was about half-past five when I got home again. My husband went out before me. He had calls to make on a few of the congregation, he said. He came back again shortly after I did, before six o'clock it was, for I remember he switched on the wireless for the six o'clock news."

"Did you see him go out after dinner? I mean, did you actually see him leave the house?" demanded Rufford, thinking of the second suit-case mentioned on the left-luggage office receipt which he had found in Barratt's pocket.

"No," answered Mrs. Barratt promptly. "I was in the scullery at the moment. But I heard the front door close after him."

"You had supper with Mr. Barratt at seven o'clock, as usual? When did he go out to his church meeting?"

"The meeting was at eight, and he left here about a quarter to."

"That was the last time you saw him, was it?"

"I'm afraid I didn't actually see him leave the house," Mrs. Barratt explained carefully. "I was busy washing up the supper dishes. We keep no maid, you see, Mr. Rufford."

"Ah, that reminds me of another question," said the inspector. "Had Mr. Barratt any private means? Had he any income apart from his salary from the church, I mean?"

Mrs. Barratt seemed faintly amused by this question.

"Oh, dear, no. I thought you'd guessed that we have to live very simply. Neither of us has any private means."

So when Barratt planned his elopement with Mrs. Callis, he must have meant to sponge on her, since he had no funds of his own. Evidently a despicable creature, Rufford decided, and far from scrupulous.

"Had your husband any sum of money immediately available to him in the last week or two?" he asked, as a fresh idea occurred to him. "I mean something in the neighbourhood of twenty or thirty pounds."

Obviously, even if Barratt meant to live on Mrs. Callis in the future, they would need some ready money to go on with.

"Oh, no," Mrs. Barratt answered promptly. "We never have as much as that in the house. You can see for yourself, Mr. Rufford, that we don't live on a lavish scale. So far as money goes, it's rather a hand-to-mouth business with us, I'm afraid. My husband's salary just covered our outgoings and no more. I know exactly what we spent, because I take charge of that side of things. My husband has—had, I mean—no money-sense whatever. I took all that off his hands, paid outstanding bills, and kept our household accounts. . . . Ah! that reminds me of something. I was wrong, a moment ago. We pay some of our bills quarterly, when my husband's cheque for his salary comes in. I made out a list of the outstanding ones, the day before yesterday, and gave it to him, so that he could draw a cheque and get the cash required from his bank. He gives me the money and I pay the bills myself."

"How much did you require, this time?" demanded Rufford.

"I can remember it. It was over twenty-four pounds—twenty-four pounds eighteen shillings and sixpence, I think. He was to draw out twenty-five pounds. But he forgot to hand me the cash."

"So he must have had twenty-five pounds actual cash in hand, yesterday, if he cashed a cheque? What bank did he deal with?"

"The Burlington and Industrial, the branch in Kandahar Street."

So evidently Barratt had £25 at least, in hand, when he made his break-away, the inspector inferred. He had drawn his cheque, stuck to the cash instead of handing it over to his wife in the normal manner. That would set him up with enough money to carry him on for a week or so, perhaps. After that, Mrs. Callis would pay. But it was never safe to take things for granted, so he put another question.

"Do you know where your husband kept his cheque-book?"

"In his desk, usually." She rose, went over to the desk and searched in one of the drawers. "Yes, here it is," she added, offering it to the inspector.

Rufford opened the book, glanced at the last counterfoil, and made a jotting in his notes.

"Apparently he drew a cheque for twenty-five pounds," he commented. "There's a counterfoil filled in with 'Self, £25', dated the day before yesterday. And as he didn't give you the money, he must have had at least that sum in hand."

But although this cleared up one point, it raised a fresh

difficulty at once. Barratt's body had been carefully searched, and only a small sum had been found upon his person. He had, perhaps, spent a certain amount on the railway tickets and other items, but nothing like the full £25. Where had the balance gone? Had someone found the bodies and gone through Barratt's pockets before the police arrived? The engine-driver had made a casual mention of tramps frequenting that district. Twenty-five pounds would be a windfall to a tramp. And, if the money was in pound notes, even a tramp could use it without exciting much suspicion, so long as he was sensible enough not to spend it lavishly in one place. Rufford decided that he would have inquiries made amongst the public-houses in the district. In the meantime, he switched over to a fresh line.

"By the way," he pursued, "can you tell me if Mr. Barratt took anything with him when he went to the meeting—a case with papers, or something like that?"

It was the second suit-case he had in his mind, but Mrs. Barratt's answer put him on a fresh trail.

"Usually he carried a very small black bag with him. A collection is taken up, and he brings the money home with him in this bag."

"Have you seen the bag about the house to-day?"

Mrs. Barratt shook her head and rose to her feet.

"I'll look for it now," she suggested.

"I wish you would," replied Rufford, rising also. "And at the same time, would you mind examining your box-room to see if all your suit-cases are there."

Mrs. Barratt seemed surprised at this demand, but she contented herself with a nod of agreement. After a perfunctory search round the study, she left the room. In a very few minutes she returned again, looking puzzled.

"I can't find the black bag," she explained as she sat down again opposite Rufford. "Usually it's left in our cloak-room. But it's gone. And a suit-case is missing also, though I can't imagine how you guessed that."

"Can you describe the suit-case?" asked the inspector.

"Oh, yes. It's an old one, compressed cane, with rows of brass nails on its top, and three locks. It has a big initial 'B' on the top, in white paint. That's really all I can remember about it."

"Now let's go back to yesterday," Rufford suggested, after making a note in his pocket-book. "You didn't join Mr. Barratt at this meeting? How did you spend the evening?"

"I finished washing the supper dishes. After that, I rang up a friend, Mrs. Stacey, about a bridge engagement. Then I switched on the wireless after a time. While the nine o'clock news was running, the front door bell rang and I found Mr. Callis when I went to open the door. He had called to consult my husband about church affairs—something to do with the organ, I think, I invited him in, as I expected my husband back very shortly, once the meeting was over; but when it came to about a quarter-past ten, Mr. Callis said he would see my husband some other time, and he went away."

"Did he come in his car?" asked the inspector casually.

"Oh, no," Mrs. Barratt replied without hesitation. "It was a fine night. He must have walked here. I saw no car at the gate when I went to the front door with him."

"Did anything more happen after Mr. Callis had gone?" asked Rufford. "I mean, had you any other visitors?"

"Oh, no," Mrs. Barratt answered. Then after a second or two she remembered something. "Now I think of it, at about a quarter-past ten, there was a phone call from a Miss Legard which puzzled me. She's a member of our congregation. She told me some long tale about a Jubilee double-florin, whatever that is. She'd put it in the collection or something. But the wires were crossed or there was some interference on the line, and I couldn't make head or tail of what she was talking about. I said I'd tell my husband about it when he came in; and she rang off."

"Were you not surprised when Mr. Barratt didn't come home at all last night?" demanded Rufford, who had reserved this question until he had dealt with less disturbing subjects.

Mrs. Barratt, rather to his surprise, shook her head.

"Oh, no," she said calmly, as if the absence of a husband overnight was of no importance. Then at the sight of the inspector's expression, she smiled rather cynically. "My husband and I use different bedrooms, you see. After I finished talking to Miss Legard, I went upstairs to bed. I fall asleep very quickly; and naturally I didn't lie awake, waiting for my husband to come in. Why should I?"

She had relaxed her tense attitude by this time, and now she leaned back in her chair and crossed one knee over the other in an easy pose. Rufford judged that she had grown accustomed to his questioning and was no longer on edge as she had been at the beginning of the interview.

"So it wasn't until this morning that you realised that Mr. Barratt hadn't come back?" he pursued.

"No, not until breakfast-time. When he didn't come down as usual, I went up to his room and found the bed hadn't been slept in. Of course *then* I was anxious; I thought he'd met with an accident, and I rang up the hospital to ask if he'd been brought in, hurt. But they knew nothing about him. I thought of ringing up the police; but you can guess that in our position one doesn't want even the suspicion of a scandal, and to ring up the police would have started a lot of talk. . . . He might have been detained all night, if one of our congregation had fallen suddenly ill and he'd been called in. That's happened before now, more than once. So I wasn't in the least anxious about him, on that account. I didn't want to start a hue and cry after him which would start people chattering. Some people are always eager to gossip, Mr. Rufford, even when there's nothing to gossip about. Especially in a church like ours," she ended, with a touch of bitterness in her tone.

Putting two and two together, the inspector was able to

guess the cause of that bitterness easily enough. Callis had given him the impression of a narrow little sect with ultra-rigid ideas. No doubt some of the women were jealous of Mrs. Barratt, who obviously came from a higher social level than themselves; and they would be glad to find some gossip which would be disagreeable to her. Callis, he remembered, had the same fear of ill-natured tittle-tattle about his wife.

"There's another question I must ask," he went on. "Had Mr. Barratt a pistol, an automatic?"

Mrs. Barratt seemed completely taken aback by this. She sat up in her chair and stared at Rufford with an expression of extreme surprise.

"A pistol? No. What on earth would he need a pistol for?"

Evidently Callis had not given her full details, Rufford inferred, and she knew nothing about how the deaths had been brought about.

"Mr. Barratt and Mrs. Callis were killed by a pistol," he explained hurriedly, "and I found his finger-prints on it. So he must have had one, although you knew nothing about it. You've never seen one about the house?"

"No, never," Mrs. Barratt answered in a tone of complete certainty. "What would we need a pistol for? There's nothing in this house to attract a burglar," she added, rather contemptuously.

Rufford had kept his eyes open, and he wholly concurred with her; but it might not have been tactful to agree in words. He contented himself with an understanding nod.

"Now, I'm sorry; but I must ask a question or two which may be painful," he continued. "Can you tell me anything—anything at all—about Mrs. Callis which seems to throw light on this affair?"

"I don't quite understand what you mean," Mrs. Barratt replied, looking him straight in the eye. "Perhaps it would be better if you asked questions. Then I could see what you wanted, exactly."

This was precisely what Rufford had been trying to avoid. He had meant to lure her into general talk about Mrs. Callis, hoping that some fresh facet in the case might show itself unexpectedly. But it was clear that he would have to fall back upon plain questioning now.

"Very well, then," he said, "since you prefer it, I'll ask one or two questions. Now, I'm told that your husband and Mrs. Callis saw a good deal of each other. Some people seem to have disapproved of their association. Did you yourself feel suspicious about it?"

Before answering, Mrs. Barratt hesitated for a few seconds, and a curious expression flitted across her face which gave Rufford an uncomfortable feeling that she was amused by what he had said.

"Suspicious?" she replied at last. "I suppose you really mean jealous, Mr. Rufford? No, I saw nothing to make me feel jealous. It's true that Mrs. Callis and my husband saw a good deal of each other and seemed to like each other's company. Why not? I had no objection. Mrs. Callis was a friend of mine. I liked her. Most people did. Some people *were* jealous, I suspect. I had a nasty letter . . . but of course I put it in the fire at once. A minister, you know, is a target for all sorts of ill-wishers. Someone thinks she's been slighted in the distribution of church work, somebody else dislikes to see another woman getting a bigger share of the minister's attention than she's been able to secure for herself, and another is just spiteful, and vents her spite on the handiest mark. One comes to disregard that kind of thing, in time."

"I see," said Rufford. "You believe that the association was entirely innocent. But that fails to throw any light on what's happened. A double tragedy of this sort doesn't arise out of nothing, you know."

"You asked your question, Mr. Rufford, and I've answered

it. I'll go further, if you like. I knew Mrs. Callis well. I simply don't believe, not for a moment, that she was the kind of woman who'd indulge in . . . what shall I say . . . an underhand intrigue."

Rufford thought of the love-letter which he had pieced together, but it was no part of his game to refer to that. Then it occurred to him that Mrs. Barratt, while doing her best to exculpate Mrs. Callis, had said nothing about her own husband. And that brought back to his mind what she had told him incidentally about the domestic arrangements of the Barratts. They had occupied separate rooms. That might mean something. Or it might have no importance. He resolved to risk a plain question.

"I'm afraid I must ask an awkward question," he said. "What were relations between yourself and Mr. Barratt?"

Mrs. Barratt was obviously amazed by the bluntness of this question. She raised her finely-arched eyebrows in unfeigned surprise.

"We were quite friendly," she began, coldly.

Then, evidently, she decided to leave no grounds for misunderstanding.

"We've been married for about fourteen years now. You don't expect the enthusiasm of a honeymoon to last through fourteen years, do you? It doesn't. Nor do one's illusions, either."

There was a touch of bitterness in her voice which did not escape the inspector. And he thought he detected a spice of contempt as well. Neither of them, he guessed, was directed at himself. He glanced at the mantelpiece on which stood a silver-framed photograph of Barratt: full-blooded, self-satisfied, handsome in a coarse way, and with a faint suggestion of commonness in the expression. How would a man of that type run in double harness with the woman before him? She obviously came from a higher social grade, with tenets and training wholly different from his. There must have been a good deal of disillusionment on her side, at least, after "the enthusiasm" had worn off. But evidently she had no intention of giving much away. Except for its tone, her statement had been the merest platitude.

"Quite friendly," Rufford echoed. "I see what you mean."

Her answering glance suggested that she was grateful to him for not pursuing the matter further. Quite plainly she had no wish to pose as a *femme incomprise* or to seek sympathy from the first comer. Rufford switched to another subject.

"You don't keep a maid, do you?"

Mrs. Barratt shook her head.

"I don't think I need trouble you with any further questions at the moment," Rufford said, after a few moments' reflection. "But I'll have to look about now, if you have no objections, and see if I can spot anything which might throw more light on the matter. There may be some papers, or diaries, in that desk which I ought to see."

"I've no objections," Mrs. Barratt assured him. "Do whatever you think necessary."

She remained in her chair, showing no great interest in his doings. Rufford went to the dead man's desk; and the first thing which caught his eye was a small pile of quarto paper with some writing on the top sheet. Rufford glanced at the heading: "Exodus, XXIII, I." Evidently the few further lines of manuscript were the beginning of a sermon which Barratt had been composing. There was a Bible alongside the sermon paper, and Rufford had the curiosity to pick it up and refer to the text: *Thou shalt not raise a false report: put not thine hand with the wicked to be an unrighteous witness.* The choice of that particular passage might have some significance, the inspector reflected. Possibly Barratt had some inkling of the gossip about him and Mrs. Callis, and had decided to hit back in this indirect manner. Rufford was in search of a specimen of Barratt's handwriting, so, after showing the sheet of paper to Mrs. Barratt, he placed it in his folder.

Two deep drawers in the desk contained papers which Rufford found to be sermons, each dated to mark the day on which they had been preached. The other drawers contained odd papers, envelopes, and unused stationery. The letter-paper was inexpensive and had no printed heading. Rufford, from a cursory examination, thought it identical with the torn-up white paper which he had found beside the bodies. He secured two sheets for comparison later; and then, as his eye caught an embossing press on the desk, he slipped one of the sheets into it and stamped the house address upon the paper. Apart from this, all that the desk furnished was evidence that Barratt had been a tidy person with a place for everything, and everything in its place.

Behind the desk was a series of bookshelves. Rufford glanced incuriously at the titles of some of the volumes. Dull stuff, he decided. Theology was not one of his hobbies. But all at once, as his glance ran along the rows, it rested on several books standing together at the end of a shelf, and his interest brightened. He took down one or two of the books, leafed over a few pages, and then turned back to the front where, in each case, he found Barratt's name inscribed. He replaced the volumes on the shelf and turned to Mrs. Barratt with a fresh question:

"Your husband seems to have taken some interest in hypnotism? Did he go in for it practically, or did he just read about it?"

Mrs. Barratt had apparently not been watching him, for she seemed surprised by his inquiry. The inspector put out his hand and tapped the volumes, whereat her face cleared.

"Oh, that was how you found out, was it?" she said, with a faint smile. "I couldn't imagine how you'd hit on it. Well, he did make some attempts to hypnotise a few people amongst our friends, but I don't know that he made much of a success with his experiments. He tried me, of course; but that was a complete failure. He seemed to get some results with my uncle, Mr. Alvington; but my uncle has a queer sense of humour, and it's just possible that he was pulling my husband's leg by merely pretending to be influenced. I shouldn't be surprised at that. He tried the Callises, too. Mr. Callis seemed to be influenced to some extent. With Mrs. Callis he was fairly successful. But the best results he got with a Miss Spencer, one of the congregation. She really did seem to be quite under his control and did the most astonishing things without seeming to remember anything about them afterwards. But, taking it over all, I don't think you could say that he made much of a success of it."

"You didn't quite care about these experiments?" asked Rufford, judging by the tone she had used in speaking about them.

"I didn't," Mrs. Barratt declared, quite frankly. "I don't take any interest in hypnotism, so I know very little about it. But it seems to me that either you get no results, or else it's a dangerous business and best left alone. I didn't encourage my husband to go on with it. Nor did the members of his congregation as a whole, when they got to hear about it."

As her ideas were almost identical with Rufford's own ones upon the subject, the inspector gave her a good mark for common sense. He dropped this line of examination and went back to his search of the study, without finding anything likely to be of the slightest value, until his eye fell upon an ash-tray containing the stub of a cigarette.

"Mr. Barratt was a non-smoker, wasn't he?" he asked.

"Yes, he was. But I smoke myself a little, just now and again."

"Mrs. Callis smoked, I think?" Rufford pursued.

"Yes," Mrs. Barratt confirmed. "She was almost a chain-smoker."

"Now there's another thing," the inspector went on. "You must know what suits your husband had. I want to find out if any of them are missing."

"I can look and see," said Mrs. Barratt, rising. "Perhaps you'd like to come upstairs and go over his wardrobe with me. I can't guarantee to tell you much about underclothing, handkerchiefs, collars, and those kinds of things. I never keep count of these. But I know what suits he had."

An inspection of Barratt's wardrobe proved that a plus-four suit was missing, and Rufford jotted down a note about the cloth. Mindful of what the Callis' maid had noticed, the inspector glanced at Barratt's dressing-table and saw on it a pair of well-worn military hair-brushes. This suggested something which he had overlooked in his search.

"I suppose you can't tell me anything about pyjamas?"

Mrs. Barratt seemed rather doubtful; but after opening a drawer and examining several pairs, she told Rufford that one set seemed to be missing, rayon, with slate-tinted stripes. Again the inspector recalled something further, and she was able to tell him that Barratt owned a Saxe bath gown, which had apparently disappeared.

"Now I'd like to have a look at your bath-room," Rufford suggested.

The inspector found there the usual mirror-fronted wall-cabinet; and inside this a tooth-brush rack from which hung two brushes. Two tubes of tooth-paste, Vinolia and Euthymol, were also in the cabinet along with some other toilet requisites.

"He didn't take away either tooth-brush or tooth-paste," Rufford pointed out. "Which brand of tooth-paste did he use?"

"Euthymol," Mrs. Barratt explained. "I use Vinolia."

She glanced round the room and her eyes lighted on the bath-tray.

"He's taken his bath-sponge with him," she pointed out to Rufford. "It's always kept in the tray, there."

While she was speaking, Rufford noticed a safety-razor case in the cabinet. He took it out, opened it, found the razor and blade-case inside, and put the case back into the cabinet again.

"Now just one last point," he said, turning to Mrs. Barratt. "What sort of slippers did your husband wear?"

"A pair of rather shabby ones, glacé kid," Mrs. Barratt told him. "I'll let you see them, if you'll come downstairs."

They proved to be a pair of well-worn Grecian slippers.

"He wore these always when he was in the house," she explained. "I remember that before he went out last night to his meeting, he took these off and put on his shoes."

"How many pairs of shoes had he?" inquired the inspector.

"Three, altogether. One pair he was wearing; another pair which is being re-soled, just now; and this third pair."

Rufford picked up a shoe and a slipper and glanced at the soles to satisfy himself that they were eight's, like those on Barratt's feet.

"Now I needn't trouble you any longer, Mrs. Barratt," he said, moving towards the front door as he spoke. "I hope I shan't have to bother you again. Oh, that reminds me, though. We shall need to get someone to identify him. It's a mere formality. I don't wish to ask you to do it. Can you suggest someone else?"

"My uncle could do that for you," Mrs. Barratt suggested, after a momentary consideration. "Mr. Arthur J. Alvington, Crest Hill, Windsor Drive. I'll ring him up, if you like."

"Don't trouble, please," said Rufford, jotting down the address. "We can easily ring him up ourselves. And now, I must be off. Thanks for giving me all this information."

CHAPTER VI

THE YELLOW DWARF

PETER DIAMOND was a reporter on the staff of a local paper. Young enough to be cynical and old enough to be disillusioned, he had a whole-hearted contempt for the caution of his editor, whom he regarded as lacking in pep, especially in the matter of headlines. Donnington hated yellow journalism and, having run the paper with financial success for twenty years, preferred the old tried methods which Peter despised. He listened to all Peter's suggestions with kindly interest, and then did something entirely different and much less sensational. He was a tolerant man. He could afford to be, knowing that he had the last word in matters of policy. He contented himself with nicknaming Peter "The Yellow Dwarf." Peter was five feet four in height, rather tubby in figure, with a pleasantly ugly face and a compellingly friendly smile. He accepted the sobriquet in good part, and used it as a pen-name for signing any special articles he wrote, thus robbing it of its sting.

Peter was a good mixer; and when he was put in charge of the crime-news section of the *Gazette*, he made it his business to become hail-fellow-well-met with any of the local constabulary who were likely to be useful to him journalistically. Between him and Inspector Rufford in particular a close relationship had sprung up. Each of them believed that he could use the other without betraying the fact and so incurring an obligation. Rufford could give Peter early information. Peter could sometimes fish essential facts from sources which would have dried up immediately at the sight of an official. Rufford was often inclined to discuss current cases with Peter. The inspector liked to think aloud, at times; and he found an auditor stimulating to his mental processes. It was a safe enough practice with Peter, who never divulged Rufford's opinions without first obtaining permission to do so.

As the inspector swung round a corner and sighted the police station, he saw Peter sitting on the doorstep, smoking, and apparently at peace with the world. Peter was naturally unconventional in his habits, and the inspector was not in the least surprised. He paused at the foot of the steps and looked at the reporter.

"What are you doing here?" he demanded.

"Waiting for the Coming of the Cocklicranes," said Peter, placidly. He loved to puzzle the inspector by semi-recondite references. "But they seem a bit behind time. You'll do instead. Sit down, Rufford. It's a nice sunny afternoon and this step's warm."

"Glad you find it comfortable. It's the best we have. But we've got some very nice cells inside, suitable for reporters, loiterers, and suspected persons. You've got a holiday this afternoon, have you?"

"No-o-o," drawled Peter. "I've come out for a breath of fresh air, after going through your staff with a case-opener in search of the latest news. You seem to have struck it lucky up the line, I gather."

He rose reluctantly to his feet.

"I see you're burning to spill the beans—or vouchsafe some information, as my esteemed chief would put it. Since you won't sit here, let's go inside. Not that your chairs are any softer than your doorstep. Still, it's always a change of attitude."

Rufford considered for a moment before making up his mind. Peter had a store of information about even obscure people in the town; and it was possible that he might be able to throw fresh light upon the persons mixed up in the

Barratt case. This decided the inspector, who made a curt gesture of invitation. Peter gave him a shrewd glance.

"I recognise the symptoms," he said, blandly. "You want to pick my brains? Right! Then we pick turn about, as in the game of spillikins. That gives you a considerable handicap, my brains being better than yours and therefore more likely to be worth picking. . . . Now, don't let's have any vulgar altercation on that subject. We know what we know."

"Well, what do *you* know?" demanded Rufford.

"About as much as your staff know, I think. I turned 'em inside out while I was waiting for you. Blood on the Bracken; Minister Murders Mistress; Intelligent Inspector Investigates. That seems to cover it, up to the present moment," said Peter, who occasionally spoke in headlines. "I've collected most of the horrible details, I think. More than my chief will let me get into print, I'm sure, curse him!"

"Do you know anything about a Rev. John Barratt?"

"Barratt? Let's see. Oh, yes, I've come across him. My chief once made me do a series of articles on local churches and preachers. He thought it would calm me, so he said. Much to his annoyance, I found it quite interesting. Now, Barratt. . . . Oh, yes. A red-faced fellow, not quite It, but rather pleased with himself nevertheless. Just the kind that does go down with some types of women. He's a rather good-looking wife. What *you*'d call 'a real lady'."

Rufford winced imperceptibly at this thrust, since it exactly voiced the impression Mrs. Barratt had made upon him.

"Who was she, before she married Barratt?" he asked.

"She's a grand-daughter of an old Mrs. Alvington. The grandma lives in a big house, Oaklands, out the Templedown road a bit. An old-fashioned dame, very straight-laced, with a fair amount of the ready. Mrs. Barrett's an orphan."

"Nothing extraordinary in that," said Rufford. "I was an orphan myself at her age."

"No doubt. But she began younger than you did. About ten years of age. Brought up by grandma. Very strictly. Married Barratt quite young. Owns two uncles: Arthur John for one and Edward for another. Surname Alvington in both cases."

"How the devil do you know all this?" demanded Rufford, suspiciously. "Are you bluffing, or are you one of the family?"

Peter made a gesture of commiseration.

"Terrible, the spread of de-education among the criminal classes and their associates. Don't you bobbies ever read the newspapers, except to see your own names in print? You don't mean to say you never heard of the Alvington divorce case, a few weeks ago? That was Uncle Ted, that was. Deacon Debauches Domestic. Pursues Pretty Parlourmaid. And now we come to Parson Plugs Paramour. A lively home circle, that. The old matriarch at Oaklands will be vexed. Rumour goes that she was more than a little peevish over Uncle Ted's divorce case."

"He was a deacon, was he?"

"He was. In Barratt's church."

"That's the Church of Awakened Israel, isn't it?"

"Bull's-eye. And a very strict denomination they are. They ex-communicated Uncle Ted forthright as soon as his wife got her decree *nisi*. I was in their midst about that time, writing up my article on them. Grandma was the power behind the throne there. She's one of their financial mainstays and what she says, goes. Though I think they'd have jettisoned Uncle Ted without that. Puritan virtue, deaconship, and divorce don't make a sound team."

"Did you come across a man Callis amongst them? He's their treasurer."

"Let's see. Young chap with flashing eyes and teeth to match? And a rather bossy young wife. . . . By Jove! *That*'s the Mrs. Callis of this case, is it? I hadn't linked them up. H'm! Well, she was a nice-looking wench; but

Barratt had a handsomer one at home, so far as my taste goes. He'd no need to cross his own doorstep in search of beauty."

Peter's further reflections were interrupted by the entry of a constable, who addressed the inspector.

"I've gone through the list, sir, as you told me; and I can't find that any permit for a pistol was issued to John Barratt."

"Very good," said Rufford, dismissing his subordinate at once.

Peter had listened to this brief dialogue with a puzzled expression on his face.

"Pistol, eh?" he said slowly. "Now that reminds me of something, but I can't think what it is, just at the moment. It's at the back of my mind. Pistol? . . . No, it's slipped my memory. It'll come back, by and by. So Barratt had no permit for a pistol, eh? But he had a pistol, hadn't he?"

"He had. His finger-prints were on it," the inspector volunteered. "We'll just see about that now. I gave orders for a fuller examination to be made."

He left the room for a few moments and came back with a satisfied look on his face.

"Yes, that's O.K.," he announced. "Our finger-print expert has examined that automatic, and he finds several of Barratt's finger-prints on it and no prints belonging to anyone else."

"I've heard of the Church Militant somewhere," commented Peter, "but this seems to be carrying the notion a shade too far, if they go about armed like gangsters. Why did he shoot the woman? That's what I can't make out."

"It looks like a suicide pact," said Rufford. "I found some torn-up love-letters beside the two of them. One letter, in her handwriting, was on bluish paper with her address printed on it as a heading. I've got a sample of exactly the same note-paper with her writing on it. There's no doubt she wrote that love-letter. The other letter I found was in Barratt's writing, and I've checked that up also."

"Guilty Glamour, eh? Barratt's Baleful Bewitchment? No, that's a rotten headline. Delete it. But why suicide, Rufford? Why weren't they content to jog along quietly on the sly?"

"Perhaps because people had begun to talk," suggested Rufford curtly. "But against that, I've evidence that they were thinking of making a bolt together. And she had an income of her own that would have kept them going, though it wouldn't have spelt luxury. What I can't see is why they should change their minds at the last moment. And it was the very last moment, for they had tickets for London all bought and everything ready."

At this moment there was another interruption. The inspector was called to the telephone.

"That was the Toynton Lacey inspector—Fowler—ringing up," he explained, when he came back again. "Here's what happened. Yesterday morning, a wire came to the Callis's house about lunch-time. The maid saw it; Callis read it. It was to his wife from a Mrs. Longnor of Toynton Lacey, an old friend of Mrs. Callis, who happened to be in town that morning. The wire invited Mrs. Callis to pick up Mrs. Longnor at Robinson's tea-room, drive her home to Toynton Lacey, and stay there for a day or two. Mrs. Callis packed a suit-case and went off in her car that afternoon. I put Fowler on to inquire about this from Mrs. Longnor. He says that Mrs. Longnor sent no such wire. She wasn't in town yesterday at all, and she hadn't invited Mrs. Callis to stay with her just now. But the wire came, for all that. I saw it myself."

"Then someone else must have sent it, obviously."

"I saw that myself, without your help," said Rufford, crossly. "It stares you in the face. But I'll tell you something you don't know. Mrs. Callis was down town when that wire was despatched. And it doesn't take much brains to see what that means. She sent it herself to cover up this proposed elopement as long as possible. She and Barratt were vamoosing together that afternoon, probably, according to plan. That meant that when she didn't get back home, Callis would be perturbed. So she sent this wire, inviting herself to the Longnors for a day or two. She knew Callis would see it, or she could show it to him when she got back for lunch. Then he wouldn't worry over her disappearance. She and Barratt would get at least a couple of days' start, before Callis made any inquiries about her; and that would be quite enough to cover the trail."

"Something in that, perhaps," Peter admitted. "But it still leaves an explanation due. Why did she and Barratt change their minds at the last moment? And why did they suicide? Puzzling problems, these."

Another summons to the telephone interrupted the inspector as he was about to answer. He was absent rather longer this time.

"That was Callis ringing up," he explained to Peter on his return. "He wanted to know about the pistol found beside the bodies. I described it to him—I'd noticed a scratch on the butt—whereupon he claimed it as belonging to him. He says he's got a perfect young arsenal of firearms. . . ."

Peter brought his palm down on his knee with a smack.

"Of course! I knew there was something at the back of my mind. Now I remember. I wrote a three-line paragraph about Callis a year or more ago. Time he did pretty well in the revolver-shooting competition at Bisley. That's it! I remember all about it. He's by way of being quite a good marksman with small arms. He makes a regular hobby of it. Unless I'm mistaken, he has a range, of sorts, in his back garden, and he got up a kind of club for pistol and revolver shooting amongst his neighbours."

"Ah!" said Rufford, with relief. "That accounts for the pistol, then. I couldn't make out how that Barratt man had got hold of one without a permit. Now I see it, it's obvious that Mrs. Callis must have helped herself to one from Callis's arsenal and given it to Barratt. But that means this suicide business was prearranged, surely. She must have grabbed it from stock before she left the house. Or maybe she'd given it to Barratt days beforehand."

"That's not likely," interrupted Peter. "If she'd taken it days ahead, Callis might have missed it, if he happened to take a fancy to do some practising. He's the sort of man who would know just what he had in the way of weapons and he'd spot at once that one was amissing. No, obviously she must have lifted it at the last moment."

The inspector picked up a pen and jabbed viciously at the blotting-pad on the table before him.

"But that doesn't make sense, if they had their get-away all fixed up. Suicide won't fit in with that side of the affair," he asserted.

"Oh, yes, it will," said Peter, coolly. "Here's the solution, by our crime expert. Meaning me. They meant to go off together. That's plain on the facts. But they didn't reckon it as a permanency, if you see what I mean."

"I don't," said Rufford bluntly.

"Put it this way, then," Peter amplified. "What they aimed at was a Week's Wild Whirl of Bliss, or Carnival of Concupiscence. But it was to be a real carnival, meaning Farewell to the Flesh. In other words, they meant to have a short orgy and then . . . Pong! Thus cutting loose from all future complexities and complications and saving themselves from possible regrets and repinings. It's not an uncommon plan. See Sunday papers, *passim.*"

"I wonder, now," said Rufford, musingly. "Put in the way you put it, it sounds just possible. And as you say, it's not uncommon. Most of these suicide pacts run on rails just like that. But it leaves things still obscure, if you ask me. I can understand the notion of having a real riot for a week or so and then, as you say. . . . Pong! But I can't see the point of cutting out the riot and going straight to the shooting. It's like paying for something and not taking delivery of the goods. And that's not according to human nature as I understand it."

"Perhaps human nature's more complicated than you suppose," Peter suggested. "Or else your understanding's not so deep as you imagine. Let's take the plain facts of the case and see what they suggest. First of all, how long has this game been going on between Barratt and Mrs. C.? What's the evidence there?"

"It must have been going on for quite a while," declared Rufford confidently. "Callis showed me an anonymous letter he'd received. That pointed to someone having suspicions. And people don't usually get suspicious about an affair of that kind until it's lasted for a good while. Then these love-letters we found in the bracken. They were all wet with the dew, but the ink hadn't run. That means they weren't written in the last day or two. What's more, a guilty couple don't usually get worked up to the pitch of bolting together, unless the intrigue's been going on for some time."

"I'm with you there," Peter agreed promptly. "Imaginary dialogue: 'Darling, I've just discovered I adore you. Let's fly together instanter.' 'Beloved, this is so sudden. Make it next Tuesday.' No, that doesn't ring true, somehow. The process must be more drawn-out, one would think. Pass that. Next question is, can we assume the worst, or had they not got that length?"

"When a woman discards her own wedding-ring and wears another one with her initials and a man's inside it, she's got herself to blame if people *do* assume the worst," said the inspector.

"Meaning that she was kidding herself that this intrigue was a new marriage, made in heaven without the intervention of mere registrars and such-like? Well, it's not improbable. Some people can persuade themselves that anything's straight, so long as they want it badly enough. You're going to hunt round to find when this ring was bought? The initials should make that an easy job."

"If it was bought locally, yes. But it may have been bought anywhere for all one can tell," said Rufford, doubtfully.

"Now let's take the rest of the evidence," Peter continued. "This bolt by the two of them was prearranged, obviously. And pretty well thought out too. Witness the telegram and the railway tickets."

"And the suit-cases packed and dumped in a left-luggage office," amplified the inspector. "You don't know about them yet. One belongs to Mrs. Callis and one to Barratt. I've got the left-luggage office receipt for them, and I've sent a man down to collect them. There's not a shadow of doubt that this affair was planned ahead."

"And yet it goes flop at the last moment. All these preparations wasted. Funny, that is. But turn to a fresh facet. How did they get out to that place up the line where you found the bodies?"

"In the Callis's car," explained Rufford. "The telegram I told you about made that clear. It asked Mrs. Callis to bring her car down town. The car's not in the Callis garage now. Obviously she used it to take Barratt out to the bracken-patch."

"In company with the pistol? But why go near the bracken-patch at all, at that stage of the game? See what I'm trying after? I'd like to guess just when they changed their minds—or one of them did. It was a change in somebody's mind that prevented them from going off by train, obviously. Then whose mind? And why?"

"I bank on the woman," said Rufford without hesitation. "She'd most to lose."

"Well, if she did change her mind about bolting, why couldn't she just come back home and jog along with the old clandestine intrigue? Nothing to prevent that, was there? Then why all this bloody drama? I can't make sense of it," Peter confessed, in a tone of perplexity. "But leave that now. Next point is, what's become of the car? If they went up there to shoot themselves, they must have left the car near-by. They couldn't drive it away after they'd suicided, now could they?"

"I've given instructions to have the car traced," said Rufford, "but that may take time. I've no more notion than you have, about where it is just now. And there's another thing that's amissing. Barratt's last appearance before vanishing was when he attended a meeting at his church. A collection was to be taken there. He had a small black bag with him, to park the dibs in. That bag's gone also. It may be in the car, of course; and we'll see about that when we track down the car. But before I forget, I want to ask you about somebody else. The nearest house to the bracken-slope belongs to some people Kerrison. Do you know anything about them, by any chance?"

He had regarded this question as a forlorn hope; but to his surprise, Peter pricked up his ears at it.

"Kerrison?" he said at once. "That would be Stephen Kerrison. He lives there. I know the house; I've been there, once. Oh, yes, I can tell you something about Stephen Kerrison. He's one of the Awakened Israelites. Likewise a religious maniac, in a sort of way."

"How d'you know that?" demanded Rufford, surprised.

"Well, he wrote a book. It was printed locally, by Simonds and Yabsley, the jobbing printers in Topsfield Street. Whence I infer that no publisher would look at it, and he had to bring it out at his own expense. I got it to review for the *Gazette*. 'Local author. Let him down lightly.' So my chief desired. I read it; which is always a good thing to do when you're reviewing a book. Love's Labour Lost, I regret to say. I did my best, but no one could have understood that book. Wild stuff. All about Seven Seals, and Beasts, and the Scarlet Woman—he seemed to have a special down on the Scarlet Woman, I gathered—and the Great

Pyramid and how the British were the Lost Ten Tribes, and a lot more besides. Made my head spin, trying to make head or tail of it. The only bit I did seem to understand clearly was a chapter on Hawthorne. How *that* crept in, Heaven alone knows. But he dealt at some length with *The Scarlet Letter*—red seems to act on him as if he was a bull—and I gathered that he thought Hester Prynne got off much too lightly. He'd have sent her to the stake, just to l'arn her better. And boiling oil treatment was his prescription for the Reverend Arthur. Frailty of the flesh got no sympathy from Stephen, I can tell you. One got the notion that he had ideas. But what the ideas were, on the whole, I frankly couldn't make out, though he seemed to get very worked up about them. Anyhow, I reviewed it briefly. Let him down lightly, as Donnington ordered. Did that content him? Far from it. He said I'd misrepresented him. I may have, for all I know. I did my best, I give you my word; but apparently it wasn't good enough for him. These young authors are very touchy. Donnington ordered me to go and see him. Smooth him down, and all that sort of thing. So I did. Crawled in the dust before him and left him happy in his victory. All saved except honesty. There were moments when I thought he might hit me on the jaw in defence of his ideas. A violent fellow, I fear, when you touch him on that side. There's a nasty fanatical look in his eye. However, we parted friends; and he told me a lot more about the measurements of the Great Pyramid and how the English were the Lost Ten Tribes. One lives and learns."

"One lives, certainly," conceded the inspector.

A fresh thought seemed to strike Peter.

"Your Chief's on holiday at the moment, isn't he?" he inquired.

"Yes, he is. He's due back shortly, if you want to interview him."

Peter shook his head rather despondently at the suggestion.

"No one ever gets much change out of Driffield. If he ever wants a coat of arms sketched out, the Heralds' College ought to give him supporters: a tin-opener on one side and an oyster on the other. One to symbolise his methods of investigation and the other his attitude towards inquirers. It's true that supporters ought to be pairs; and a tin-opener isn't a living creature; but Driffield's original enough not to mind a trifle like that. Motto: *On les aura*!"

Rufford hastened to defend his Chief Constable.

"Well, anyhow, he generally does 'get 'em' when it comes to the pinch," he pointed out. "And I'll say this for him. He never grabs any subordinate's credit and often he gives subordinates the credit of his own brains."

"His brand of brains is too scientifico-mathematical for me, altogether," grumbled Peter. "At school, the only way I could get over the Pons Asinorum was to tear the page out of my Euclid, pin it on the back of a pal at the desk in front of me, and read it off for the delectation of my revered teacher. I don't lay claim to a logical mind. I'm a literary cove. But I know how Driffield would set about this Barratt case."

"Do you?" said the inspector, interested.

"Oh, bless you, yes," retorted Peter. "He'd say as follows: 'Here we have two dead people. The possibilities are these. First, it may be accident. Second, it may be suicide. Third, it may be murder. Or it may be accident *and* suicide, or accident and murder, or suicide and murder . . . and so on, with a neat little mathematical formula to put the thing in a nutshell. Then, after going over the evidence, he'd begin to discard from strength—chuck out the absolutely impossible cases, one by one. And finally he'd be left with the real solution staring him in the face, Lord bless you! It's as easy as winking, the Driffield method."

"I've seen worse, all the same," said the inspector. "Surprising how often he gets there, once he takes a thing up. Suppose you go and give it a run yourself. I've nothing more to tell you at the moment and I've got a lot to do myself. And there's one thing *you* might do, if you've the fancy. Go and pick up some opinions amongst the Awakened Israelites. Some of them might know a thing or two about the doings of their late pastor and Mrs. Callis. They'd probably shut up like clams if I sent a man to interview them. But you're got a soapy way with you, and you might chance on something useful."

Peter considered for a few seconds before replying.

"Might be something in that," he conceded, finally. "I'll have a dash at it, anyhow."

CHAPTER VII

THE SUIT-CASES

PETER had hardly left the room when Constable Loman presented himself to make his report to the inspector. He saluted, advanced to the table and produced various envelopes which he put down before Rufford.

"We carried out your instructions, sir, and clipped away the bracken carefully. Amongst it, we found four more bits of paper. They're in this envelope here."

Rufford picked up the envelope, shuffled the scraps of paper out on to the table, and examined them. Three of them were bluish, the other one was white. Each of them had some words on it, but Rufford found no trace of address on these additional white fragments. He replaced them in the envelope without comment, promising himself to fit the two letters together later on, now that he had all the available material.

"What else?" he demanded.

"We've found some empty brass cartridge-cases, sir. Four of them."

"Four?" interjected the inspector, taken aback.

"Four, sir," said Loman. "It surprised me, too, sir. But there they are. I've put each in a separate envelope, with a number on it, just to have everything according to Cocker. And I've drawn a rough sketch, sir, to show where they lay. Here it is, sir."

He drew from his pocket a piece of paper bearing a rough diagram, which he spread out on the table.

"I've got the measurements in my note-book, sir; but this

gives you the general lay-out of the position, so that you can see the thing at a glance."

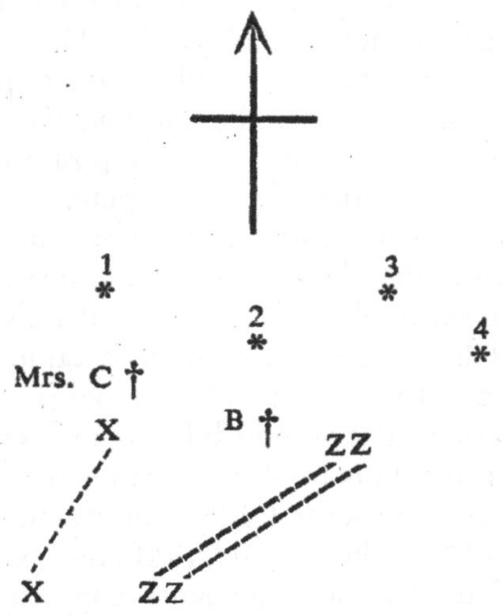

"I see," commented Rufford, with his eyes on the diagram. "The dagger signs represent the two bodies: Mrs. Callis's and Barratt's. The stars show the positions where you found the cartridge-cases, and the numbers correspond to these figures on the envelopes. That's it? And I suppose the dotted line X to X represents the single track we found going up through the bracken. And the other line, ZZ to ZZ, corresponds to the double trail we noticed. That's it?"

"That's it, sir, as you say. Tatnell and me, we measured out the tracks down to the road, before we started cutting away the bracken, so as not to be destroying any evidence if such was needed, by and by. I've got all the figures in my note-book, sir."

"Excellent," commended Rufford, who now remembered that he had omitted to give instructions on this point and who was only too relieved to find that his subordinates had wiped his eye in the matter. He gave them mentally a good mark for their thoroughness.

He bent over the table, scanning the diagram thoughtfully and trying to make some meaning out of it. Four shots? He had expected two at the most, one for each head wound. Could there be two bullets in each skull? He dismissed that idea almost at once, from his recollection of the character of the wounds. In any case, the surgeon would find the actual bullets when he carried out his post mortem, and that would settle the matter beyond dispute.

He examined the contents of the envelopes in turn. Each of them contained the shell of a .38 automatic cartridge. Four shots had been fired, undoubtedly. Peter's caricatured account of the Chief Constable's methods came back to his mind, and influenced the trend of his thoughts. Treating it mathematically, one had five possibilities: four shots fired by one person, A; three shots by A and one by B; two shots by A and two by B; two shots by A, one by B, and one by C; and finally, all four shots fired by different persons, A, B, C, and D. These five arrangements covered the whole ground, and the truth must lie somewhere amongst them.

Then a complementary piece of evidence drifted out to the front of his mind. Up to that moment he had put it aside, engrossed as he had been in collecting fresh facts from his interviews. He recalled those tracks in the bracken: the single track and the double width track which had crossed the other lower down the slope and which, by the bending of the bracken-stems, had appeared to be made later than the single trail. That seemed to suggest that three people had been on the spot: two coming up together, side by side, whilst the third had been made independently. The two who came up together would probably be Barratt and Mrs. Callis. But who could this third party be? Someone who had surprised the couple? A moment's reflection led Rufford to discard this idea. Since the double track had been made later than the single trail, obviously the third party must have been on the spot first, and was waiting for the other two when they came up. In other words, there had been prearrangement between the trio, and they had an appointment to meet on the scene of the tragedy.

"I wonder, now," mused the inspector. "Three people on the spot. One of them was a woman. She was hardly likely to play any part in the shooting, except to get shot. *She* was shot; Barratt was shot; and that leaves two bullets unaccounted for. Suppose these two shots were fired by Barratt at this third party. He must either have hit or missed. If he missed his mark, these two bullets will be out in the wide world somewhere, and there's not much chance of finding them. If he hit and wounded this third party, then the missing pair of bullets will be somewhere inside the third party's skin—perhaps—and we've got to hunt for somebody who's been seeking medical assistance for a shot-wound."

Feeling the need of an auditor to clarify his ideas, he turned to Loman.

"Look here, Loman," he said. "Just let's work this business out on the basis of your diagram."

"Yes, sir," answered the constable, eager enough to listen, but chary of suggesting any ideas of his own.

"After you fire an automatic," said the inspector, "it ejects the spent cartridge from the breech and brings up a fresh cartridge to the barrel. The case of the spent cartridge is jerked out backwards and a little to the right. Generally it goes over your right shoulder or thereabouts."

"Yes, sir," repeated Loman, obviously waiting for a lead.

"When Mrs. Callis was shot," Rufford expounded, "she must have been sitting among the bracken, facing south; and she was shot in the left temple. Barratt seems to have been standing up, facing her. He fell face downwards, shot in the right temple. Obviously the case of the cartridge which shot Barratt would be ejected eastwards and a bit to the north. So that must have been the empty shell which you found at position 4. That's right?"

"That's right, sir," agreed the constable. "And the one

I found at position 3 would be the one that shot Mrs. Callis, wouldn't it?"

"I imagine so," agreed the inspector. "Now that leaves us to see what we can make out of the remaining two shells. Allow for the same jump before the shell caught in the bracken and number 1 shell might have come from a pistol fired by someone standing about where the ZZ is in your diagram and firing southwards. And number 2 might have been fired in the same way by somebody standing a bit to the east of your ZZ point. But that doesn't make much sense, does it? Why should anyone turn his back on Barratt and Mrs. Callis when he was firing? And what could he be firing at? That notion doesn't seem to fit in."

"No, sir, it does not," agreed Loman, evidently relieved at knowing just what was expected from him.

"These shots couldn't have been fired from anywhere north of 1 and 2," the inspector proceeded, "because in that region the bracken was quite untrodden until we ourselves came along."

"That's true, sir, I noticed that myself."

"But if they were fired from south of 1 and 2, then the gunman must have had his back to the two victims. That's right? And the same's true if the man firing had stood either east or west of Barratt and Mrs. Callis."

"Yes, sir, that's plain enough," said Loman, staring at the diagram on the table.

Rufford saw that he was making very little of this puzzle. He put up his hand and rubbed the back of his head in perplexity.

"This wants a bit more thinking out," he said, in an attempt to cover his failure.

"It does indeed, sir," agreed Loman unhelpfully.

"Well, think over it and see what you make of it," ordered Rufford. "There's a screw loose somewhere; but there's no getting over the facts, is there? We'll need more information before we can put this jigsaw together. By the way, have these suit-cases been brought up from the left-luggage office yet?"

"Yes, sir, Sergeant Quilter has them outside. Shall I tell him you want them now?"

"Yes. Ask him to trot them along."

Loman left the room and within a few seconds Sergeant Quilter came in, carrying the suit-cases, which he placed on the table before the inspector. The sergeant was a methodical man, and had gained his promotion by thoroughness. No one could accuse him of any imaginative powers. "Facts are facts," was his favourite apophthegm. He dumped the two cases on the table, retreated one pace, and waited for the inspector to make the next move. A glance showed Rufford that he had got what he had hoped for. One suit-case was an oldish one, of compressed cane, with three locks, and bearing a white-painted letter "B" on it, exactly as Mrs. Barratt had described. The other was a fairly new leather case, with an L. M. & S. Strathpeffer label stuck on it, which tallied with the account given by Callis's maid. Rufford leaned over to examine the outsides, and his eye was caught by the two tie-on labels attached to the handles of the cases: "Barratt, Alcazar Hotel, Leicester Square, London." He recognised the handwriting as Barratt's.

Rufford knew the Alcazar. It was an enormous caravanserai, popular with visitors of a certain class, since it supplied bed and breakfast for a very moderate sum, while its amenities and central position made it the ideal of country cousins unaccustomed to such garish splendours. Rufford himself invariably stayed there when on a visit to the metropolis.

"The Alcazar?" he said, musingly, with a glance at the sergeant. "They get a mixed lot of guests there. All sorts. I remember I once went there with Mrs. Rufford; and the clerk at the desk asked me point-blank if she and I were married. They must get a lot of divorce business, I expect, or they wouldn't ask that kind of question."

Amongst the "facts" docketed in the sergeant's mind was his impression that Mrs. Rufford was a strikingly pretty young woman with rather go-as-you-please manners, and what Quilter described to his own wife as "an R.S.V.P. eye." This seemed hardly the occasion for mentioning such matters, however, so he made no comment upon his superior's remarks.

The inspector lifted the leather case on to the floor to make more room on the table. Then he tried the fastenings of the other, and, finding them unlocked, he opened the cane suit-case and began to go through its contents, dictating a list to the sergeant as he did so.

"Man's pyjamas, rayon, slaty-blue stripes. They were gone from his house when I asked about his things. No slippers or pumps here. His wife told me he'd only one pair of slippers and they were a bit shabby. I saw them myself, well-worn and hardly what one would take on a honeymoon. Bath-sponge. That's right. It's missing from his home. Saxe bath-gown, ditto. No shoes. He must have been depending on the ones he was wearing, for there was another pair at his house. Pair of military hair-brushes, split new. He left his old ones behind him. Grey plus-four suit. One complete change of underclothing. Two pairs socks. Split new tooth-brush and an unopened tube of Euthymol tooth-paste. That's right. I saw the old brush and a half-used tube of Euthymol in his bath-room. He evidently meant to start afresh with a new set. That's the lot."

The sergeant pondered for a moment; then rubbing his chin, apparently by force of suggestion, he inquired:

"No shaving tackle, sir?"

Rufford shook his head.

"No, he left a safety razor, shaving-brush, and a stick of soap behind in his bath-room. Forgot them, apparently. I did the same thing myself, once, though never again. That wouldn't have hampered him. You can buy 'em in any druggist's or at a chain store. Well, that's that."

He repacked and closed the case, swung it off the table and replaced it by the leather one, which also proved to be unlocked.

"A bit more stuff here," commented the inspector, as he began to unpack the contents. "Pair of silk pyjamas, white with coral facings. Half-dozen handkerchiefs, various. Slacks, navy. Jumper, one. Blouse, one. Black evening frock—make a note that the belt's missing. Pair of evening shoes, glacé, with trees in them. That's right. Silk stockings, three pairs, various. Change of underclothing complete, as far as I can see. Note 'em down for yourself. Packet of cigarettes. Book of paper matches. A cheque-book. No sign of brush and comb: I know about them, she left them behind. Small morocco jewel box with . . . let's see . . . a blue zircon brooch with some diamonds round the zircon in a platinum setting. A sapphire and diamond ring, the ring's gold, the setting's platinum. Another ring, gold with diamonds only. Another gold ring, with twin diamonds. An emerald pendant, or something of that sort, anyhow. And a pearl necklet with diamond snap. Must be a fake by the size of it, but I'm no judge. That's the lot. By the way, make a note that we found no bath-salts."

The sergeant nodded as he jotted this down and then looked up inquiringly.

"I found a box of bath-salts at her house," Rufford explained. "She must have packed in something of a hurry if she forgot them, not to speak of her face-cloth."

"Perhaps she didn't use a face-cloth," objected the sergeant.

"She did. I saw it in her bath-room," retorted Rufford. "Now we're done with these things."

He repacked the suit-case, closed it, and placed it on the floor beside Barratt's one.

"What about the wire in the name of Mrs. Longnor?"

"It was handed in at the G.P.O., just as you said. I made inquiries there, and managed to get hold of the clerk who took it in. He couldn't remember anything definite about it; they're kept pretty busy at the telegrams counter and he paid no particular attention to who handed it in. He did seem to remember, after a bit, that it was handed over the counter by a woman. I didn't prompt him there. But I wouldn't put too much weight on his recollections. He'd seen the signature and the address on the back of the form, and probably they gave him the hint that it was a woman that sent it."

"Likely enough," agreed the inspector. "You got the form?"

"It's here," explained Quilter, pulling out his note-book and taking the telegraph form from among the pages.

"H'm! All written in block letters," commented Rufford, after a glance at the paper. "I'd been hoping it was in her ordinary handwriting. That would have clinched things, seeing that it was supposed to be written by Mrs. Longnor. It doesn't matter much. We've got Mrs. Longnor's evidence that *she* didn't write it. Now another thing. Did you inquire at the booking-office about the buying of these tickets?"

"Yes, sir. All the booking-clerk could tell me was that likely they were bought between eleven and twelve, yesterday morning; and he wasn't too sure about the time. But he does remember, queerly enough, that the fellow who bought them had a soft black felt hat on—the sort of thing——"

"That parsons sometimes wear?" Rufford completed the sentence to hasten the sergeant's rather slow discourse. "I saw one of the sort on Barratt's hat-stand at his house. Did you show him a copy of the photo of Barratt?"

"I did, sir. He didn't recognise it at once, but after a bit he thought it was like the man who came to his window."

"A fat lot of good that kind of identification would be in

court," said Rufford impatiently. "If you'd shown him a photo of the Grand Mogul, he'd probably remember seeing him last Friday week."

"There isn't any Grand Mogul nowadays, sir," said Quilter firmly. "That's a matter of fact."

"Oh, call him the Shah of Persia, if you like it better."

"I'm not sure if there's a Shah either, nowadays, sir; and I read in the paper, not long ago, that they've been changing the name of Persia into Iran or something like that. I'm not just sure how a country changes its name, sir, whether it's by deed poll or how——"

"Never mind," said Rufford, hastily, lest Quilter should put him in a difficulty by asking a question which he could not answer. "Did you inquire at the left-luggage office about the person who left these suit-cases?"

"I did, sir. They were just as vague as the ticket-office fellow. All they could remember was that perhaps, or probably, they were left by a man in darkish clothes."

"Semi-clerical, like the hat?" Rufford surmised.

He glanced at his watch.

"Here's another job for you," he ordered. "Ring up this Alcazar hotel in Leicester Square and ask them if any room was booked for last night in the name of Barratt or Callis. And if none was booked in either of these names, ask if anyone from this town booked a room or rooms and get particulars. I want to know when and how the booking was done, in any case. Make sure they're careful about it. Then, if a room was booked by phone, get the date and see if the post office can give you any information. If it was done by wire, get the original form, if possible. And if the room was booked by letter, tell the Alcazar to send on the letter, if they still have it. Now I'm going to get some grub, and then I'm going on to see Callis again, about this armoury of his. He'll be home again by the time I get to his house, probably, but you'd better ring him up, anyhow, and tell him I'm going to call. And please tell Dr. Fanthorpe that I specially want the bullets he finds in those two bodies, as soon as he can conveniently give me them."

"He's working at the P.M. now, sir."

"Very good. Oh, and another thing. Ring up Arthur Alvington, Crest Hill, Windsor Drive, and ask him if he'll kindly come down here at . . . oh, say nine o'clock, if it suits him, or any time round about then that suits him better. You can say Mrs. Barratt gave me his name. It's the identification of Barratt. You can explain that I don't want to put Mrs. B. to trouble over an unpleasant job like that, and so on. You understand how to put it."

"I'll fix it, sir," said Quilter, confidently. "Nine o'clock or any time round about then. Very good."

"Nothing come in yet about that missing car? Callis's, I mean."

"Nothing reported so far, sir. But we've warned all stations about it, and something ought to come in very soon, surely."

"Good. Then I'm off. I'll be at Short's first of all for some grub. After that, you can phone me at Callis's if you want me. I'm coming straight back here after I've seen him."

"I'll note that, sir."

"Then I'll go now. I'm infernally hungry after missing my lunch."

Rufford picked up his hat and went out. At Short's restaurant, he was faced with the problem of whether to make a light meal and wait for his dinner later, or to make sure of food when he could get it, since quite possibly he might not have a chance of any more that evening. He finally opted for a square meal, thus ensuring that Callis would be home from his office before the inspector called. When Rufford reached Fern Bank, he noticed that Callis seemed to have got over the first shock of his wife's death, though he was still obviously distressed. Rufford had been rather surprised to learn, over the phone, that Callis had gone back to his office in the normal way, that afternoon; but the routine of his work there had apparently been the best treatment for his troubles. It must have prevented him from dwelling continuously on the tragedy; and that was always some gain, the inspector admitted to himself.

"I want to see these fire-arms of yours, Mr. Callis," he explained when the accountant came into the room. "I have a list of those mentioned on your certificate and I just want to check the details, so as to have everything ship-shape, in case any questions are asked."

"Certainly," agreed Callis, at once. "If you'll come this way, I'll show you them. And my shooting-range in the garden, if you like, as well. It's an old long greenhouse, put up in my father-in-law's day for growing tomatoes. I merely had to modify it a bit to make it safe for shooting in."

"Another day, perhaps," said Rufford politely. "All I want at the moment is to check up these fire-arms."

Callis nodded and led the inspector along a passage to the back of the house where there was a small pantry which Callis had fitted up as a store. He pulled open a long drawer and displayed a number of weapons lying on a bed of cotton-wool.

"Here they are," he announced with a gesture towards them. "I'd better name them to you, perhaps, for one or two of them are a bit out of the way, and you might not recognise them. Here's a Webley, Mark IV target revolver, .22. This is a Smith and Wesson pistol, also .22. This one I'm sure you haven't seen before: it's a German one, a Walther .22 automatic. Another .22; this is a Stevens No. 10 target pistol. Here's something heavier; you'll know it well."

"Oh, yes," Rufford confirmed. "Service model Mark VI, isn't it?"

"Correct," said Callis. "And here's another .455; it's a Webley W.S. Bisley target model. And, finally, here's a .38 Colt automatic. That's the lot."

"Is it?" said Rufford, with sudden suspicion. "Surely not, Mr. Callis. There are three .38 Colts noted on your certificate. Where are the other two?"

"One of them's in your own hands," Callis pointed out.

"Yes, yes. But what about the third one? Where's it got to?"

Callis seemed faintly amused by the inspector's eagerness.

"I lent the third one to a Mr. Kerrison a week or two ago," he explained. "Kerrison of The Hermitage."

"I know who you mean," Rufford admitted. "What did he want with a pistol?"

"He told me he'd been bothered by some stray cats and wanted to shoot them. He's one of these people who have a positive horror of cats. I never can understand it, myself; but some people undoubtedly are afflicted in that way. Kerrison's rather a bad case of it. If you shut him in a room with a cat, I believe he'd either kill it or go into a nerve-storm. Besides, he keeps chickens up there, and it seems these stray cats have managed to get into the runs and kill some of his stock. Naturally he wanted to discourage them."

Rufford looked grave at Callis's answer.

"Has he a fire-arms certificate, do you know?" he demanded.

"He's a member of my little pistol-shooting club," explained Callis, "so I take it he ought to have a certificate. I assumed that he had one when I lent him the thing."

"Hasn't he got any fire-arms of his own?"

"I don't think so," Callis declared. "He uses mine, when he comes here to shoot. A good many of my little club do that, and I don't mind their doing so. All except my .455's. I can't afford to have them deteriorated."

"You use them at Bisley?" said Rufford. "Naturally you want to keep them in good condition."

"Exactly. I don't care about lending them to all and sundry. But the rest of the stuff's different. I don't mind who uses that."

"Is Mr. Kerrison a good shot?" queried the inspector.

Callis shook his head in a very decided fashion.

"Good Lord, no!" he declared. "He's only a beginner, remember. He shapes well enough, though, and might do better in time; but all he wants is to kill those cats that bother him. He's got no real interest in firearms or markmanship. He doesn't know enough about a pistol to dismantle it for cleaning. I have to do that for him, after he's been using my Colt."

The inspector considered for a moment or two before speaking again.

"You might give me a list of the people you have in this shooting club of yours, Mr. Callis."

The accountant received this proposal rather doubtfully.

"Why do you want that?" he asked. "Are you going to snoop round and find out if any of them haven't got licences and get them fined? You can hardly expect me to supply evidence for use against friends of mine; and I don't believe you can force me to give you their names."

"The law's the law," retorted Rufford. "If people break it, they have to pay. But all I really want is to warn your friends to take the proper steps. I'm not very keen on petty prosecutions for technical offences, Mr. Callis, I may tell you without prejudice. If your friends will take my tip, there'll be no trouble."

Callis looked the inspector in the eye, apparently attempting to gauge his earnestness in this matter. He seemed satisfied.

"Very well, then," he conceded, "I'll give you a list of them."

"Please write it here," requested Rufford, pulling out a note-book and opening it at a blank page.

Callis took the book from him and, with intervals for reflection, wrote down a list of about a dozen names and addresses.

"That's the lot," he declared, handing back the note-book.

Rufford glanced down the list. Most of the names were unfamiliar, and he fastened upon those which chanced to be known to him.

"Kerrison—you've told me about him already. . . . Barratt? Did he go on for this sort of thing?"

"I only put him in to make the list complete," Callis explained with a wry expression, as though Barratt's name had wakened painful memories. "He came only once, and I showed him how to load and fire an automatic. I don't think he took much interest, really, for he never came back again."

This explanation solved one of Rufford's problems. An ignoramus would hardly have tumbled to the necessity of pulling back the slide of an automatic in order to bring the first cartridge up from the magazine into the barrel. Now he knew how Barrett had come by that knowledge.

"Arthur Alvington," he read out, as he went down the list.

"That's Mrs. Barratt's uncle," Callis explained. "He was one of the first to join. He's always been interested in target shooting; and it's cheaper to practise in my place than to go to a gunsmith's. He has a couple of pistols of his own: a Colt .38, like mine, and a Belgian thing, a .32 Bayard, I think it is."

"A good shot, is he?" Rufford inquired casually.

"Fair," said Callis, judicially. "It was he who brought Barratt along, that day, I remember."

"Did your wife know anything about fire-arms?" said the inspector, unexpectedly.

Callis shook his head very definitely.

"Not the beginnings of it, so far as actual shooting went. She was always nervous of guns, wouldn't touch one even if you told her it was unloaded. In fact, when we had a meeting here, she preferred to go out for the afternoon, if she could. She disliked even the sound of the shots. When we were married first, I tried to get her to take an interest in shooting, taught her how to load a pistol and so on. But when it came to firing, she was so nervous that it obviously wasn't worth while to go on with it."

Rufford understood that. Some women had a terror of fire-arms. He turned back to the drawer which still remained open and idly picked out the .38 Colt automatic for examination, slipped the catch, and pulled out the magazine, which he found empty. Callis had been watching the operation.

"None of them's loaded," he explained. "If a burglar came along, he'd find me quite harmless, in spite of all this, unless he gave me time to load up. The ammunition's here."

He opened a cupboard and showed the inspector a few stacks of boxes containing cartridges of various makes and calibres. Some of the boxes had been opened, others were still intact.

"I keep a stock, you see," he pointed out. "When my friends come here to shoot, they use my stuff and pay for what they fire off. It saves carrying ammunition about."

Rufford made no immediate comment. Here was a possible explanation of another matter which had been puzzling him. Callis kept his pistols unloaded in this drawer, open to anyone. Mrs. Callis thus had easy access to both weapons and ammunition; and although she had a horror of actual shooting, she had learned how to fill and insert a magazine. Thus it had been simple enough for her to secure a fully-loaded pistol, which she had apparently handed on to Barratt. But there was yet another point still left mysterious. The .38 Colt found beside the bodies was two cartridges short of its full load, and yet four empty shells had been found by Loman beside the bodies. That implied that she had filled the magazine from the cartridge store in the cupboard and had taken away two extra cartridges as well. And these two extra cartridges had been used to reload the pistol after two shots at least had been fired from it. But why reload at all, when the magazine still contained unused cartridges? The inspector puzzled over that for a moment or two and then added this mystery to the earlier one: why two extra shots had been fired at all, since apparently they had found no detectable billets. He dismissed the subject from his mind at the moment, and replaced the Colt on its cotton-wool bed in the drawer.

"Kerrison isn't much of a marksman, you told me," he said, turning back to the accountant. "Had he any luck with his cat-shooting?"

"Better than he deserved," Callis said, with a faint grimace. "He killed two poor brutes, he told me. But he'd fired away four or five bobs' worth of ammunition in doing it. A trap would have been cheaper, at that rate."

"I hope he killed them outright, anyhow," commented Rufford. "Pity if the poor brutes struggled away to die slowly in some odd corner."

"He seems to have been lucky," Callis declared. "He told me he'd buried both bodies, so they must have been shot dead or else he finished them off, after crippling them. I don't think any got away. He didn't say anything about that, anyhow."

"It's rather a lonely place, that house of his," said Rufford. "Not a neighbourhood where you'd expect to find many stray cats, surely. Not much food in sight except Kerrison's chickens, surely?"

"Wherever you have chickens, you usually have rats," Callis pointed out. "The rats may have attracted the strays. Besides, there's a spinney quite close to the house, on the other slope of the hill from the railway. You probably didn't notice it if you keep on the railway side of the crest-line. There are birds there, and some rabbits as well. Cats could find quite enough provender round about Kerrison's, without raiding his chicken-runs."

"Something in that," admitted the inspector.

He glanced at his watch.

"Well, thanks for showing me all this," he said. "I shan't make things awkward for your friends. Just give them a tip that they must get certificates if they haven't got them already."

Callis acknowledged this with a nod of appreciation.

He accompanied the inspector to the door and as he opened it, he paused to make a final statement.

"Just one thing, Mr. Rufford," he said with complete sincerity. "I know things look very black against my wife. That's obvious. But there's one thing I'm absolutely convinced about in my own mind: she never was unfaithful to me. She may have been incautious in some ways, I'm not going to deny that. It was her way, to go her own road and not mind what people said about her. But she was absolutely straight. I'm not afraid of the truth so far as she's concerned; and that's a great help to me in this trouble. I know it isn't your affair to establish her innocence. But bear it in mind, please, will you? And if any evidence turns up to clear her character, do please bring it out publicly so that everyone will know the truth. I owe that to her. I've done my best to be matter-of-fact with you; but it's been a strain, I don't mind admitting that. And you're not the only one. I've been rung up half a dozen times by reporters and other people to-day, all asking questions and hinting plainly enough what they think about the business. One of the hardest things to bear has been this slur on my wife's character, when there's been no chance of clearing it away at once. All the town gossips—I know them!—will fasten on this affair and put the poor girl's doings in the worst light, just for their own amusement. Do what you can to end that, as soon as it's possible."

From Callis's manner, Rufford feared that the accountant's nerve was beginning to weaken and that he might break down if the strain were prolonged. The inspector had secured all the evidence he needed at the moment, so he hastily took his leave, thinking it best to give Callis a chance to recover his self-possession in peace.

On the way back to the police-station, Rufford went into a stationer's shop, where he purchased some sticks of plasticine and a few sheets of pasteboard; and he also paid a call at the shop of a gunsmith with whom he had dealings in the past.

CHAPTER VIII

THE BULLETS

WHEN Rufford returned to the police station, he found Sergeant Quilter waiting for him with a report.

"I've got that cotton waste and the boxes, sir. They're out in the yard. Will you be wanting them to-night? It looks as if there might be rain, and they might get wet if it comes on."

"I'll be using them later on," said Rufford. "Just leave them there for the present unless a shower starts. Anything else fresh?"

"Dr. Fanthorpe left this for you, sir. It's an envelope with two bullets that he found in the skulls. Each of them's labelled. He said to tell you he found only the two, one in each skull."

"Right. I'll take them," said the inspector, holding out his hand for the envelope, which he locked away in a drawer without examining the contents at that moment. "Anything else?"

"Dr. Fanthorpe hasn't finished his examination, sir. Not yet. But he wrote an interim report. Here it is, sir."

"Very good."

Rufford took the report from the sergeant and stowed it away in his pocket.

"Any word about that car of Callis's yet?" he demanded.

"No, sir, not yet. It can't be on the roads, or we'd have had word of it before now."

"Probably it's in some garage—a private garage. You warned all the public garages?"

"We did, sir. None of them's seen it."

"Very good. Let me know at once as soon as any news comes in. And when Mr. Alvington turns up, take him over to the mortuary, show him the bodies, and then bring him to me."

While Rufford had been busy with the Barratt case, his routine work had, perforce, been set aside. He now sat down to overtake the day's arrears, and in this task the time passed unnoticed until he was interrupted by the sergeant ushering Arthur Alvington into the room.

"I'm sorry to give you such an unpleasant job," said Rufford, after he had greeted his visitor. "But it was hardly the kind of thing for Mrs. Barratt to do. You've seen the bodies? And you can identify Mr. John Barratt, of 38 Granville Road?"

"Oh, it's Barratt, all right," Alvington answered, with no sign of emotion. "And the other's Mrs. Callis. I knew her quite well."

Rufford had not hitherto encountered Alvington in person, but his name was familiar enough to the inspector since it appeared on many notice-boards scattered about the town. Alvington was a speculative builder in a small way of business and not altogether prosperous, if local gossip were to be trusted.

"We didn't find much in his pockets," the inspector explained, "but you'd better see what he had in them. It may suggest something to you which we haven't spotted."

He opened a drawer and laid the pathetic little collection of odds and ends on his desk for Alvington's examination. The builder bent over and inspected each article in turn. The note-case attracted his attention and, with a gesture to ask permission, he picked it up and seemed surprised by finding so few notes in it.

"This is curious," he said, in his usual suave tone. "There seems to be only a couple of notes here, and yet my niece told me that Barratt cashed a cheque for twenty-five pounds yesterday morning. He didn't give the cash to her. I wonder what's happened to the balance. Twenty-five pounds is a fair sum and one would like to know where it's gone."

"You can't suggest anything?" inquired Rufford. "There were one or two newly-bought articles in a suit-case he left at the station, and he may have used some of this money in buying two tickets to London; but that would leave him with a fair balance in hand. More than's here, certainly. And he had an hotel bill to face in London, I suppose."

"Very curious," Alvington said in a neutral tone. "I can't account for it at all. Unless . . . perhaps someone robbed the body before you arrived on the scene."

In a flash, Rufford's memory went back to the third trail which he had noticed among the bracken, and he seemed to see a glimmer of light in the mystery. Then he remembered that the single trail had been made before the double one, and he abandoned the solution which he had begun to sketch out.

"I doubt it, Mr. Alvington," he declared. "Any chance thief would probably have taken the whole of the notes *en bloc.*"

"Unless he foresaw your line of reasoning and left a couple behind on purpose," Alvington pointed out with his thin-lipped smile. "As he might well have done."

"Something in that, possibly," the inspector conceded. "I'll admit that it's queer to find these notes gone. There's not much chance of getting anything from inquiries at the bank, I'm afraid. These are old notes, pretty worn. The bank isn't likely to have kept a record of their numbers."

Alvington nodded rather absent-mindedly and picked up the two railway tickets.

"Singles?" he commented. "Evidently he didn't mean to come back in a hurry—if at all. I never cared for him much," he added, with apparent irrelevance. "He wasn't my sort and I was against my niece ever marrying him.

Obviously I was right in that, but it's a bit late for her to find it out now."

The inspector seized on the chance which this offered him.

"You can tell me something about him," he said. "Naturally I didn't care to put too many awkward questions to Mrs. Barratt when she was in such trouble. I knew I could get what I wanted from you. What sort of man was Barratt?"

"Barratt?" echoed Alvington. "Oh, a very worthy fellow, on the surface. Started from small beginnings and made his own way in the world. Though he hadn't got very far, after all, when one comes to think of it. His salary was nothing to write home about, you know. He'd got so far and no further. Reached a blank end. Still, he *had* got on, by his modest standards, and he wasn't inclined to under-rate the feat. A little self-satisfied, perhaps, and rather apt to imagine he was invariably right; but that's a failing we all have, I'm afraid."

From this carefully-diluted praise, Rufford saw how the land lay. Alvington's dislike for Barratt was of longer standing than yesterday; for, so far as this interview had gone, he had not even referred to the liaison and the tragedy which ended it. They seemed to have left him quite indifferent. Rufford inferred that Alvington's susceptibilities would not be ruffled by plain speaking about this nephew-in-law; and plain speaking might be necessary to extract the information he wanted. He decided to risk it, under the guise of blundering frankness.

"I was a bit surprised when I met Mrs. Barratt," he confessed. "She didn't, somehow, seem to fit into the picture."

Alvington rose to the bait at once.

"I don't wonder," he declared. "She isn't quite the sort of woman to be altogether happy as the wife of a minister with a lower-class congregation in a narrow little sect.

I'm not saying anything against them, remember. Quite decent people, no doubt, and very earnest, I'm sure. But it's a pity she ever landed herself where she is."

"I can't understand it," Rufford admitted, to draw him out further.

"There's a lot in environment," Alvington continued in a thoughtful tone. "My brother George and his wife died of typhoid when my niece was just a baby. She was brought up by my mother. In those days, my mother was a widow. She's changed a lot, but at that time she was a big Junoesque figure, something in the style of Tenniel's cartoons of France and Germany in the old volumes of *Punch*, very dominating and impressive, you know. What you might call a kind of human steam-roller. Very effective in squashing opposition, but working within restricted limits. She has a lot of good points, my mother. She was very religious then. She is so still, though her health keeps her away from church services nowadays. She's very generous along certain lines, always ready to shell out a subscription to help the organ-bellows, or anything of that sort, though I don't know that she d cough up much for an honest beggar in a hard case. You see what I mean by restricted limits."

"Many people are like that," commented Rufford.

"My niece was brought up strictly by her grandmother," Alvington went on. "When she was twenty or so, she was very enthusiastic about church matters. Some young girls pass through that phase. It was about that time that Barratt began to take an interest in her. I suppose she was flattered by that, on account of the church connection; she hadn't seen much of the world, then, and no doubt it seemed a wonderful prospect to be a minister's wife, doing good, being looked up to, and all that sort of thing. She didn't know enough to see the snags in the fairway. Most minister's wives must know them well, I imagine. It's a position like the old pillory: very prominent and defenceless. But my mother rather encouraged Barratt in his suit; and as I told you, she's rather apt to get her own way. Anyhow, my niece was Mrs. Barratt by the time she was twenty-one."

"What age is she now?" asked the inspector.

"Thirty-four or thirty-five," answered Alvington, rather to the surprise of Rufford, who had judged from her looks that Mrs. Barratt was several years younger than this. "She doesn't look it, does she? But that's neither here nor there. I'll go on. My mother has a fair amount of capital at her disposal. Barratt knew that, well enough. I don't say he married for money; but he took the advice of Tennyson's *Northern Farmer* and went where money was. Not that I blame him for that; it's a sensible policy and I'd follow it myself, if I were a marrying man. But if he was counting on immediate cash, he made a mistake. My mother doesn't part easily; and she's got strong ideas about the fine moral discipline furnished by being hard up. She's never been hard up herself, of course, or she might think differently. But anyway she made no allowance to my niece when she got spliced to Barratt. I see no harm in that. Why should my mother set Barratt up in Easy Street when she won't part with a stiver to her own sons, even to get them out of temporary financial difficulties? When you've got the cash, it's a sound policy to hang on to it; then you know it won't be wasted."

"Quite true," agreed the inspector. "I'd do it myself, if I had any capital to hang on to. Was Barratt disappointed, do you think?"

"He may have been. I don't know if he was. What I do know is that he's been working to establish a certain influence over my mother, as time goes on. She liked people to pay her attentions, and he danced attendance on her pretty assiduously. I thought there was something behind that, for she's none too amiable nowadays or easy to get on with; and from some things she dropped from time to time I have an idea he was doing his best to persuade her to leave her money to the church. That would be a nice disappointment to the rest of us," he concluded crudely, "after we've put up with her tantrums and domination all these years."

Rufford was merely bored by this recital of grievances.

"I quite understand," he interrupted, as Alvington showed signs of resuming his tale of woe. "You mean that after your niece married, she lost the enthusiasm she'd shown in her teens?"

"Yes, just so," Alvington confirmed. "She'd got herself into a false position by that marriage: saddled herself with a husband who came from a lower class and who had no . . . no . . . Well, call it culture, or intellectual interests, or whatever you like. She had next to nothing in common with Barratt's congregation—decent people, no doubt, but not her sort; and Barratt's pittance of a salary kept her from mixing freely with people in her own grade of society. You've got to entertain a bit if you want to keep in the swim; and the cash didn't run to that. And these Awakened Israelites are a strict lot. They don't approve of dances, for instance. Barratt didn't dance. So she wasn't invited to many dances in her old circle, after a while. She just dropped out. Cocktail parties, of course, were anathema to that congregation."

"They sound a bit prehistoric," commented the inspector.

"It's what they are," said Alvington. "I don't know how they manage it, but they're just survivals from the mid-Victorian times, with all the prejudices intact. Decent people, I admit, but living in a groove that never gets any wider, generation after generation. There was that divorce case of my brother's lately. They turned him out of the church on account of that. And my mother got her solicitor in at once and cut him out of her will. It leaves more for the rest of us, of course, but still I didn't quite like that move of hers. She made quite a public ceremony of it, she was so furious; for she's got very strong views about marriage and fidelity and all that sort of thing."

The inspector had heard more than enough about the Alvington family. He made a determined effort to switch the interview on to more useful lines.

"What about this Mrs. Callis?" he asked. "Can you tell me anything about her?"

"Esther Callis? H'm! If she'd been born ten years earlier, she might have married Barratt and no great harm done. She had an income of her own; not a fortune, you know, but enough to keep the wheels greased. And she took a lot of interest in church affairs: Girl Guides and that sort of stuff, she'd always been keen on. A very alert young woman, and always got value for her money, from what I saw of her."

"Did you notice that she saw much of Barratt?"

"I didn't bother much about her, to tell you the truth," Alvington explained. "But some of the congregation certainly thought she was always hanging round him on the excuse of church business. She was a very capable sort of girl, always ready to dash in and manage things if she thought they weren't being run properly; and of course that brought her into contact with Barratt a good deal. I thought nothing of it myself, until this business came along."

A thought crossed the inspector's mind at this moment and prompted a fresh question.

"Was Barratt's life insured?" he demanded.

"He had some sort of policy, I believe," Alvington answered. "I remember he consulted me about various insurance companies when he took it out. It was a beggarly little thing—five hundred pounds or something like that. He hadn't enough income, you know, to pay a decent premium."

"What was the company, do you remember?"

"Let's see. . . . Oh, yes, I recommended him to go to the Eaglesham and Exeter Union. I'm insured with them myself and I've gone into the bonuses and all the rest of it carefully."

"You didn't chance to see any of the people involved in this case last night, I suppose?"

"No, I didn't," said Alvington without hesitation. "It's my housekeeper's day out, so I had dinner at the Regal down town. Then I went home and spent the evening with my brother going over our business accounts."

"There's just one thing more," said Rufford. "Callis says you're a member of this pistol-shooting club that he got up amongst his friends. You've got a .38 Colt pistol, I think? Have you a fire-arms certificate for it."

"Oh, yes, of course I have," said Alvington at once. "I haven't it with me, but you'll find it noted in your books."

"So I expected," Rufford declared, not quite truthfully. "Well, Mr. Alvington, that's all I want at the moment. Thanks for giving me your help. You'll get your summons to the inquest in due course."

After ridding himself of the builder, the inspector sat down and made a full note of the salient points of the interview, which he added to his increasingly bulky folder. Then he leaned back in his chair and pondered for a moment or two on the impression which Alvington had left upon his mind. A phrase from Edgar Wallace put the thing in a nutshell:

"That fellow spells Life with an £."

He had no further time to spend on Alvington's psychology just then. Going into the next room, he singled out Sergeant Quilter.

"That box and the cotton waste are out in the yard, you said?"

"Yes, sir. I cut the hole in the end, as you ordered. Do you want them now?"

"I do. You'd better come out and give me a hand."

Rufford returned to his room, took the fatal pistol from a drawer, felt in his pocket for another Colt pistol which he had borrowed and a packet of ammunition which he had bought at the gunsmith's on his way from Callis's house.

He loaded the magazines of both pistols, picked up some cleaning materials, and went out into the yard, where Quilter was awaiting him.

With the help of the sergeant, he packed the box with cotton waste, interleaving this with vertical pasteboard sheets at six-inch intervals. Then from a short distance he fired a shot from the borrowed pistol through the hole in the end of the box. Withdrawing the sheets of pasteboard, he ascertained exactly where the bullet lay, in front of the first unpierced sheet; and this simplified his search for the projectile among the waste. His first two shots were unsatisfactory, as he had initially packed the waste too tightly; but his third shot gave better results, and he fired four more under the same conditions, cleaning the pistol-barrel between each pair of shots and recovering the bullets at the end of the trials. Then, with the same precautions, he fired five shots from the fatal pistol. Quilter observed the operations with obvious interest.

"Ever seen this done before?" asked the inspector. "No? Then you'd better come along and see it through. One lives and learns, as Mr. Peter Diamond was good enough to tell me this afternoon."

He led the way back into the police-station, laid down on the table the things he was carrying, and produced from his collection the envelopes containing the fatal bullets and also some sticks of plasticine, at which the sergeant stared uncomprehendingly.

"This is only a rough trial," Rufford explained. "If we have to go into the business thoroughly, we'll have to send the things to a real fire-arms expert. But this ought to give us something to go on with. You know what the inside of a pistol-barrel's like? Have a look through this one, to make sure."

He picked up the borrowed pistol, removed the magazine from the butt, pulled back the slide to eject the cartridge left in the barrel, and then, slipping the safety-catch into the second notch to hold the breech open, he handed the weapon to Quilter.

"Look down the muzzle and get some light into the breech," he directed.

Quilter obeyed, manœuvring the pistol until he got the lighting in the proper position.

"You see those projections sticking up from the sides—lands they call them? And the spaces between the lands; what they call grooves?"

"Yes, sir," confirmed Quilter.

He knew what lands and grooves were, just as well as the inspector, but if it pleased Rufford to explain such elementary points, it was all the same to the sergeant. "Never seem too clever or get too big for your boots" was one of his guiding principles in life.

"Now look at this," said the inspector, handing him one of the bullets fired from the borrowed pistol. "You see six well-marked furrows running from nose to base? These are cut by the lands in the barrel. Notice that they don't run straight from nose to base. They've got a slant on them. That's because the rifling puts a twist on the bullet, and it begins to spin as it travels up the barrel."

"I see, sir."

"Now take this lens and look between the furrows. See some striations on the bullet casing?"

"Yes, sir," said the sergeant with more interest, since this was fresh ground to him.

"These are made by the tool-marks at the bottom of the grooves in the barrel; and since the tools used in making the barrel vary a bit, these striations are never the same in any two pistols."

"I see, sir. Like finger-prints. Very interesting."

"Right! Now we'll try something else."

Rufford took some of his plasticine sticks and rolled them out with a ruler into slabs. Picking up a bullet which had been fired from the borrowed pistol, he rolled it lightly over the plasticine surface, thus producing a pattern of raised lines, like a series of parallel groynes on the sea-shore, each raised line corresponding to one of the furrows on the bullet casing. He repeated the process with a bullet fired from the fatal pistol, and then showed the results to Quilter.

"You see the two sets have the same slant, and there's the same number of lines to the inch in both cases? That proves they've both been fired from barrels of the same type. But not necessarily the same barrel, as you can see. Let's try again."

He picked up the two bullets and set them base to base, fixing them together with a dab of plasticine and turning one bullet until the furrows on the pair came into coincidence at the bases.

"See how they match, furrow for furrow?" he asked, turning the conjoined bullets round for Quilter's inspection. "Not much doubt that they were both fired from pistols of the same make, is there?"

"No, sir. They match perfectly, so far as I can see."

"Now we'll try the bullets that Dr. Fanthorpe found in the bodies," said the inspector. "They've both got a bit deformed in hitting the bones of the skulls; but they're fairly intact at the bases, where the rifling marks show clearest. Here's number one: the bullet from Barratt's head. Let's compare it with a bullet from the pistol found beside the bodies and also with another bullet I fired just now out of a borrowed Colt."

He rolled the three bullets in turn across three slabs of plasticine and then made a gesture inviting the sergeant to look closely at the results.

"You see the general type's the same in the lot: six grooves, a left-hand twist in the rifling, narrow lands and wide grooves. That goes to show that all these bullets were fired from pistols of the same make. Now we need to look for smaller details. See that scratch here, made by some tiny projection at the bottom of one of the grooves of the pistol? Look for it in the other two."

"It's in this one, but not in that one, sir, so far as I can see," said the sergeant, cautiously.

"That's to say, it's shown by the bullet from Barratt's skull and also on the bullet from the pistol we found beside the bodies. But it isn't shown by the bullet from the other automatic, the one I borrowed from a gunsmith. Pretty conclusive proof, this, that Barratt was killed by a shot from the pistol that lay beside his hand."

"Yes, sir," agreed Quilter, though his own opinion was that the inspector was making a lot of fuss about nothing. Man found shot; pistol beside him; obviously it was the pistol that killed him. And that was all that Rufford had managed to prove, with all this tomfoolery of his.

"Now we'll have a shy at the bullet from Mrs. Callis's skull," said the inspector, suiting the action to the word.

The results here were the same as before. Obviously Mrs. Callis also had been shot by the automatic which had killed Barratt.

"Well, that's that!" said Rufford in a satisfied tone. "Nothing like putting the thing beyond doubt for a coroner's jury. They can't pick any holes in this evidence, that's sure."

"No, sir," Quilter agreed perfunctorily, before broaching a subject which he thought of more importance. "I want to report, sir, that we got the information you wanted from the Alcazar people."

"Good!" said the inspector. "What have they got to say?"

"They turned up their files, sir, when we asked them about the matter. It seems that they got a wire signed 'Barratt' exactly a fortnight ago, asking them to book a double room from last night. It was a reply-paid wire and they sent the answer to Barratt's address, confirming the booking of the room."

"You have to book well ahead if you want to get into the Alcazar at all," Rufford explained from his experience. "A double room, you say?"

"A double room it was, sir."

"That seems to put the lid on the can and solder it down tight, doesn't it? Not much doubt, after that, about the two of them meaning to make a bolt. Everything nicely pre-arranged, evidently."

"Then why didn't they, sir?"

As this was precisely the question which Rufford was least able to answer, he was relieved when the door opened and a constable came in with a message.

"Abbot's Park Station ringing up, sir," he announced. "That missing car's been found. It was in Granby Holt, standing on a forest track away near the centre of the Holt, they say; and that's why it hasn't been found before. No one thought of looking for it off the roads."

"Then how did they find it?" demanded Rufford.

"Some children, playing in the Holt, came across it by accident, sir, and reported it. Abbot's Park Station reports that it's badly smashed up. A tree had fallen across the track, and the car must have gone into it, full tilt, for the radiator's all crumpled."

"Did they say anything about that black bag that Barratt was carrying?"

"Yes, sir. They found the bag on the floor of the car, just thrown down there. But it was empty. No money in it when they found it."

"Had these children been helping themselves, by any chance?"

"No, sir. The Abbot's Park people happen to know all about them. One of them's the daughter of an Abbot's Park constable and a strictly honest little girl. She says nothing was touched by them."

"That sounds O.K.," admitted the inspector. "Anything further?"

"In the pocket of the door on the driving-seat side they found two driving licences: Callis's and his wife's one, sir. And the insurance certificate for the car. That was all they found, so they say."

Rufford nodded impassively, but to himself he allowed himself a comment:

"Damnation! It looks as if this affair is going to keep me on the run for twenty-four hours on end."

Even the most zealous official has his human side.

"All right!" he said aloud. "Get me a car round as quick as you can. I suppose I must go and look at this wreck."

CHAPTER IX

THE CAR

At Abbot's Park police station, Rufford made fuller inquiries about the discovery of Callis's car and picked up a constable as a guide to the spot where it still lay. He learned that the track along which the missing car had gone was so rough that he would be risking his springs if he attempted to follow it; so he and the constable left their own motor on the public road and entered the wood on foot.

Granby Holt was a fair-sized pine-wood in which some felling had been done in the previous year. Its forest tracks were deeply scored by the wheels of timber-carts; desolate clearings dotted with stumps and strewn with bark, showed where the work had been done; and, here and there, the roots of storm-stricken trees reared up in the moonlight like the arms of uncouth decapods lying in wait for their prey.

"Nobody but a born fool would have brought a car here at all, sir," the constable pointed out, unnecessarily. "You see how rough this track is, and how it winds about amongst the trees. And yet the fellow must have been driving at a fair lick, to judge by the smash he came when he did hit something. The car's just round this bend, sir, at the bottom of a slope."

When they came to the top of a steep incline in the track, Rufford could see the damaged vehicle. A pair of long deep scores cutting through the skin of fallen leaves and deep into the soft soil below spoke plainly of a frantic application of the brakes as the danger below had come in sight of the driver. Evidently the wheels had locked and the car had slid headlong to the crash. Followed by the constable, Rufford advanced to the scene of the disaster.

In the shock between the car and the fallen tree, the bumper had been useless as a protection. It had been driven in; the radiator shield was crumpled like pasteboard; and the radiator itself had suffered badly. One wing, with the head-light and side-lamp, had been twisted free. The bonnet had been distorted and the glass was gone from the windscreen frame.

"That looks a bit of a mess," said Rufford, sardonically, as he ran his flashlight beam over the injuries.

"There's some blood on the floor of the driving-seat, sir," the constable pointed out enthusiastically. "If you'll bring your flashlamp you'll be able to see it. There isn't much; but it's blood, all right."

"Not much wonder, after a smash like this," commented the inspector as he moved round to the side of the car.

He examined the stains, dipped the tip of his finger into the blood to satisfy himself, and then ran his flashlamp beam over the dashboard of the car. The clock had stopped at eleven-ten, evidently as the result of the collision. Rufford reached over to the winding-rod and very carefully began to wind up the spring, counting the clicks as he did so. When he had made half a dozen turns, the clock was fully wound up. He noted the number in his pocket-book before turning again to the constable.

"You've read Sherlock Holmes?" he asked. "No? Well, that was one of his tricks. But all I really wanted to know was whether the clock was going when the smash happened. It might have been run down, you see? Some people forget all about winding up their dashboard clocks."

He examined the dial of the speedometer. The trip recorder stood at seven miles; but it was one of those which run from zero to one hundred and then repeat themselves, so that evidently it had not been set at the beginning of the day, and it threw no light on how far the car had actually gone.

"What ages were the children who spotted this car first?" Rufford demanded from the constable.

"The youngest would be about nine, sir, and the oldest one's thirteen, I believe. She's the daughter of one of my mates."

"Nobody else been about, except some of you Abbot's Park people?"

"Not so far as we know, sir. We've kept our thumb on this business for the present."

"Quite right. That *makes it possible to get something out of the footprints, hereabouts, in this soft soil. I'll ask your inspector to go into that for me.*"

"There's one thing I was told to explain to you, sir. Last night, about ten-fifty-five, one of our men was on patrol along Rickman's Lane. A car passed him, going all out, doing about seventy, he said. The tail-lamp was out and he whistled them to stop; but no notice was taken of him. The car was coming in this direction. When he got to the nearest phone post, he rang up; and orders to stop the car were given out. But no one seems to have seen it after that, at least not with its tail-lamp extinguished. When this smashed-up car came into our hands, we examined the tail-lamp bulb and found the filament gone. That might have happened in the smash, of course. But it might have been gone before that."

"In other words, this was the car that went along Rickman's Lane and when the driver heard the whistle, he got off the road and hid the car here? Likely enough. It wasn't his car—it's got Mr. Callis's number-plate—so even if the driver smashed it up, it wasn't going to cost him a penny for repairs. Furiously driven, you say, when it passed the constable?"

"Yes, sir, very carelessly driven, my mate said. He had to pick up his feet and jump out of the way, when it came along, for it was yawing about all over the road."

"Where's the nearest station?" demanded Rufford.

"Abbot's Park, sir."

"When does the last train pass through at night?"

Fortunately the constable seemed to be an expert in local communications.

"Five past eleven on the up line and a quarter past eleven on the down line, sir."

"What about bus services? Any of them running at that time of night in your area.?"

"The last one passes through Abbot's Park at eleven seven, sir, going away from here," explained the constable, catching Rufford's drift. "No bus route comes anywhere near Granby Holt, sir. That's a third-class road we came up by, and it leads nowhere that a bus would want to go. Not enough population, hereabouts, to make a service worth while."

"I see," said the inspector. "It amounts to this, then. The smash here occurred at eleven-ten, apparently. The last possible transport out of Abbot's Park was the eleven-fifteen down train; and nobody could have caught that, starting from here at ten past eleven. And I'm twelve miles from my happy home and bed. Very jolly, no doubt. It's lucky I had a square meal when I got the chance."

"Yes, sir," said the constable agreeably. "Would there be anything else you'd like to examine, before we go?"

Rufford stared at the wrecked car for a few seconds before answering.

"No, I don't think there's much to be learned from this scrap-iron just at present," he said. "Your people went over it carefully, I was told; and they found nothing of importance except the licences in the door-pocket and that blood on the floor. I think I'll get off home now. I'll drop you at Abbot's Park. Let's get back to my car."

The constable was nothing loath, and they set off through the pine wood towards the road. When they reached Abbot's Park police station, Rufford interviewed the officer in charge.

"I've had a look at the footprints round that car in Granby Holt," he explained. "Most of them were made by children,

I noticed. Four of them in all, I made out. Is that right?"

"That's correct, sir," said the sergeant in charge.

"There were two other sets of prints, constabulary boots unless I'm mistaken. These would be made by the men sent up from here after the children brought in the news?"

"Yes, sir. That's so."

"Then there was another set of prints—tennis-shoes with patterned rubber soles, not quite full size for a man. They might have been made by a woman or a boy, to judge from the size. Is there anyone here who could take plaster casts of some of these impressions? Someone who really knows how to do it, I mean, not somebody who merely thinks he knows all about it."

"I could do it myself, sir. I've had some experience over a case lately, when I had to make some casts."

"Then, if there's no objection, I'd like a few casts of these tennis-shoe prints," said Rufford. "But find out for certain, first of all, that none of the children were wearing rubber shoes."

"Very good, sir. I'll see to it."

The inspector bade him good night and got into his car again. As he drove homeward, he let his mind run over the evidence which he had accumulated since the morning, trying to fit it together into a consistent scheme.

In the first place, there was this intrigue between Barratt and Mrs. Callis. On the face of the evidence, that wasn't an affair of yesterday. The two love-letters which he had pieced together were not isolated documents; their tenor proved them to be parts of a longer ardent correspondence. Why they in particular should have been picked out from the rest, he could not guess; for there was nothing in either letter which suggested that it was of especial importance. But then, as he reflected, unless one knew the ins and outs of the affair, one was bound to miss some point which had a special meaning for a pair of lovers, but which meant nothing to an outsider. He had tested them for finger-prints as part of the routine, but had found only a few hopelessly blurred marks.

Another datum was the anonymous letter which he had secured from Callis. Somebody had spotted this hankey-pankey between Barratt and Mrs. Callis. But the principals in any illicit attachment are pretty sure to be very circumspect in their behaviour at the start. It's only after the intrigue has gone undetected for a while that they grow careless. Since somebody *had* spotted that there was a screw loose, it was plain that the liasion was far beyond its initial stages. And they must have been clever enough in their proceedings, since Callis had not had the slightest suspicion of what was going on under his nose. True enough, the man most concerned in these affairs was usually the last one to notice anything wrong, since he, of all people, was the person who had to be hoodwinked by the guilty couple. But even when Callis had been put on the alert by that anonymous scribbler, he had persisted in his belief that his wife was innocent. Rufford prided himself on knowing the ring of truth when he heard it; and Callis's asseverations of his wife's irreproachability had sounded genuine beyond cavil. On the face of things, those two turtle-doves had been remarkably clever in throwing dust into Callis's eyes. And that was a point worth remembering in connection with later events.

The inspector passed on to consider the problem of the actual elopement. It had not been decided upon on the spur of the moment. That was plain enough. The room at the Alcazar had been booked a fortnight ahead; so the decision to cut and run must have been taken even longer ago than that. Then there was that fake wedding-ring found on Mrs. Callis's hand. Obviously they needed a wedding-ring to show, or there would have been difficulties at hotels and elsewhere. Mrs. Callis's real wedding-ring was of a conspicuous type, apt to draw attention, from Callis's account of it. That would be a sound enough reason for discarding it. Besides, a married woman eloping with a paramour might well have sentimental notions about wearing her proper wedding-ring. It would have been a reminder of her true position, which might make her feel at least slightly uncomfortable every time she happened to glance at her hand. Sentimental idea, no doubt. But then she obviously was sentimental in some ways, or they would not have had her initials and Barratt's put on the new ring. And, as Peter Diamond said: "Some people can persuade themselves that anything's straight, so long as they want it badly enough." The new ring probably helped her to believe that her new venture was a marriage of sorts "contracted in heaven without the intervention of mere registrars and such-like." The main point here was that one can't walk into a jeweller's shop and come out in five minutes with an engraved ring. The lettering takes time. So the existence of that ring went to confirm the Alcazar evidence that this elopement had been planned well ahead.

Passing on to the affairs of the previous day, the inspector saw his way through them easily enough. Barratt and his wife occupied separate rooms; so it would be easy enough for him to pack that cane suit-case without her knowledge. The Barratts kept no maid, and after breakfast Mrs. Barratt would be in the scullery, busy with washing up the dishes. That would give Barratt an opportunity to take the suit-case out of the house unobserved, when he told his wife he was going round to the church to meet the organist. Mrs. Callis must have joined him at some rendezvous in town, after smuggling her own suit-case out of her house without attracting the notice of her maid. When they met, Barratt evidently took charge of both suit-cases, handed them in at the left-luggage office and took the tickets for London, while Mrs. Callis sent off the telegram which was supposed to come from Mrs. Longnor. That would finish the morning's work for the pair of them. In the afternoon, Mrs. Callis probably took her car into town, parked it, went to some picture-house and then had dinner at a restaurant, thus passing the time until she could pick up Barratt after his meeting at the church hall. He had to attend that meeting; for if he absented himself, immediate inquiries might be made at his home, and the hunt would be up before he and his lady-love had got away from the town. And with a scent as fresh as that, it would not have been long before the pair of them were run down at the Alcazar.

That was all plain sailing. But now, once more, Rufford came up against the psychological difficulty which had baffled both himself and Peter Diamond earlier in the day. Why, with everything cut and dried, had these two suddenly changed their minds at the eleventh hour? It was not because of any hitch in their arrangements. They had enough ready cash for emergencies; the residue from that £25 cheque would suffice there. Mrs. Callis had her cheque-book, which would provide further sinews of war when they were needed. They had their London tickets, their luggage was at the station, the room at the Alcazar was booked and waiting for them . . . and, at the very last moment, they turned their backs on the future they had planned and went off to die amongst the bracken. As the inspector himself had said, it was like paying for something and not taking delivery of the goods.

A suicide pact? The more Rufford considered this hypothesis, the less it satisfied him. And yet, even there, preparation had been made in advance. Mrs. Callis had taken the automatic pistol from her husband's armoury and brought it with her when she left the house. Somehow or other, that incident had to be interleaved into the story, with an adequate motive attached to it. And there was no getting over the facts which the inspector himself had established. Barratt's finger-prints were on the fatal pistol; and the bullets extracted from the bodies bore the sign-manual of the weapon in those striations which he had detected on their casings. Barratt's hand had fired those shots, beyond all doubt. . . .

And then, suddenly, the inspector's mind was lit by a

flash of illumination which seemed to make the whole puzzle plain to him. He recalled those books on hypnotism which he had noticed in Barratt's study.

Rufford's knowledge of hypnotism and its effects was sketchy at the best, but now he tried to recollect what he had read about the subject. You could hypnotise a patient, and if he was well under your control, you could make him believe all sorts of things and force him to play pranks of one sort and another. But only on one condition: that your orders did not run counter to his normal character. Post-hypnotic suggestion had its limits. You could make a man buy a book of stamps at eleven o'clock on the following day, or write his name on a piece of paper ten minutes after he had come out of the hypnotic trance. But you could not compel him to carry out an action which would be foreign to his nature as shown in ordinary life. The patient would refuse to perform acts which were normally abhorrent to his character. Hypnotism could make play with unimportant sides of human affairs, but it left unaffected the deeper springs in the nature of men.

There was the key to the mystery, Rufford reflected, triumphantly. Barratt had been successful in hypnotising Mrs. Callis. No doubt he had found her a good subject, easily amenable to post-hypnotic suggestion. He could make her perform all sorts of minor actions. Now suppose that he came to desire her. Easy enough to make her buy a new ring. That would not go against any woman's nature. Simple enough to order her to pack a suit-case and bring it to the station. That lay well within the limits of her normal life; she had packed suit-cases often enough before that. Easy, too, to make her send a telegram with a dictated content. The securing of the pistol would hardly revolt her; it was not plain theft, or anything like that. But when it came to embarking on an elopement with a man who had no passionate attraction for her—then the citadel would be attacked and the attack would inevitably fail. When he tried to compel her to join him in the London train, his power would over-reach itself and come to nothing. What then? Barratt could hardly hypnotise her again on the railway platform. No, his plan would be to persuade her to go with him to some unfrequented spot, and there he would strive afresh to bring her under his control. That would account well enough for their visit to the bracken-slope. But what if he failed there? Brute passion had queer effects on disappointed men. The shooting was just the kind of thing which often happened in such cases. And then, once the fatal shot had been fired, the cool fit might come on. Reflection would show only one way out—suicide.

"*That* fits!" Rufford assured himself, in high glee at his own ingenuity. "It accounts for the change in their plans—and that's been the sticker all along. Lucky I spotted those books on the shelf."

But very soon he was forced to recognise that his explanation, satisfactory enough in one respect, did not by any means cover the whole of the facts.

First and foremost, there was that unfinished sermon against slanderers. If all this elopement scheme had been elaborated to the last detail a fortnight earlier—as the booking of the Alcazar room established—why had Barratt troubled to begin the preparation of a sermon which he would never preach? A snag there, apparently. But then a man capable of such careful scheming would be just the fellow to provide for all emergencies, even the break-down of his plans. If the elopement failed to come off, he would have to preach a sermon on the following Sunday; and therefore a clever plotter would make sure that he had one in reserve, ready for use.

"I wouldn't put it past him," Rufford reflected. "He was a fellow who looked well ahead."

Second point, the number of trails in the bracken leading up to the site of the crime. Three people had gone up to it; two had remained there, dead. What about the maker of the third trail? How had he got away? But the inspector dismissed this problem quickly enough. Anyone can walk down a double-width trail without leaving much sign of his passage. But that implied that number three had come there first and had left after the shooting, following the ready-made double track of the other two. But that, in its turn, implied . . .

"Oh, damn!" muttered the inspector. "Leave that aside for the moment. I'll think it out clearly later on."

Third point, the four empty cartridge cases. Why, four of them, when there had been only two fatal shots?

"Let's get on further, first, before tackling that," Rufford suggested to himself. "It'll be clearer, perhaps, if it's taken along with some other things."

And then he had a second flash of illumination.

"The car, of course! And the blood by the driving-seat! That's how the third party got away and the blood came from some flesh-wound he got up among the bracken. Somebody fired the extra two shots at number three, and winged him slightly. That fits in neatly enough."

But further consideration left him less satisfied. If blood had dripped from a wound on to the floor of the car, why had Loman found no blood-trail among the bracken on the way down to the car? Rufford pondered over this problem for some seconds before he found a solution.

"Why, of course!" he assured himself. "The fellow may have been wounded in the left arm, say. He'd do his best with his handkerchief as a temporary bandage. That would keep the blood from dripping on to the leaves as he was passing through the bracken. But once he started to drive, he'd be using his left arm for gear-changing and that might make the bandage work loose and allow some blood to drip on to the car floor. There wasn't over-much blood. Just what one might expect if my notion's true. That fits as well as one can expect."

Fourth point, the car smash.

Easy enough to see one's way through that, Rufford believed. No. 3 had escaped from the scene of death in the waiting car. Naturally he would be shaken by what he had seen, and especially by being shot at. Then, when he heard a police whistle summoning him to halt, he would take to the forest road through Granby Holt to escape from detection. And going through the wood, all out, he went full tilt into the fallen tree at eleven-ten, smashed the car, and left himself stranded. What happened to him then?

"I'll bet he didn't get back to town till long after midnight, anyhow," said Rufford to himself. "No trains, no buses, and twelve miles to cover."

Who, then, was this mysterious No. 3? Obviously the first question to ask was: Who had any interest in the doings of Barratt and Mrs. Callis? And Callis's name suggested itself immediately. Whether he knew it or not, Callis was the man most directly concerned, apart from the two principals. But Callis had been seen by his maid through his sitting-room window at twenty past eleven. Short of a miracle, he could not have gone from Granby Holt to Fern Bank, twelve miles or more, in ten minutes. And that maid of his had her wits about her, as Rufford had seen when she was giving him her evidence. She was a perfectly sound witness, and Rufford was prepared to take her word for the time. Besides, Rufford had seen no signs that Callis had been wounded.

Mrs. Barratt was another person interested to the same extent as Callis. She certainly had shown no signs of having been hurt; she had used both hands in opening drawers during the search for Barratt's belongings, and she had walked without the slightest indication of a limp. Callis had been with her until 10.15 p.m. and as she had no car, it was out of the question that she could have got to the bracken-slope in a reasonable time. Besides, and this applied to Callis as well, how could she know where the guilty pair were to be found? They had gone to the bracken-slope on the spur of the moment and not according to any pre-arranged plan. Nobody could have followed them up. . . .

Once more the inspector had an illuminating flash. Suppose No. 3 had not encountered them on the bracken-slope in the first place. Suppose the pair had been overtaken at the station by No. 3 and that the trio had then gone in the Callis car out to the slope among the bracken?

But this was only a flash which died out as soon as Rufford reconsidered the rest of the evidence. If all three had gone together to the death site, then they would have walked up through the bracken in a group. There would have been one broad trail, instead of the broad one and the single-track. He dismissed this idea, though with some regret.

Who else had an interest in Barratt or Mrs. Callis? Possibly some people unknown to him at the moment; but Alvington's name suggested itself as a "possible." Alvington was fond of money, as the whole trend of his tale had made clear to Rufford during their interview. Alvington had let slip the fact that Barratt was influencing that old dame, Alvington's mother, to leave her fortune to the Awakened Israelites instead of to her family. Irritating for Arthur Alvington, that. But immediately Rufford dismissed Alvington from consideration. Old Mrs. Alvington was strait-laced in the extreme. She had cut Edward Alvington out of her will for his irregular conduct. If Barratt had eloped with Mrs. Callis, it would have been the end of his influence with the old lady. On that basis, Arthur Alvington's interest was to stand aside and let the elopement succeed. Certainly he had nothing to gain by hampering it. And he was hardly the man to risk his skin to avenge his niece's honour. Alvington could safely be ruled out.

The only remaining person in that circle, of whom Rufford had knowledge, was Stephen Kerrison. His house was close to the bracken-slope. He had possession of an automatic pistol at the crucial period. And, according to Peter Diamond, he was next door to a religious maniac, with a special hatred of marital infidelity. But these facts hardly made a hanging case of it.

The inspector's thoughts went back to the motor smash, and one of the facts about it loomed rather larger in his mind as he reconsidered the matter. That black bag, which Barratt had taken with him, had been emptied of its contents when it was found in the car. Barratt had not transferred the cash to his pockets, as a search of the body had shown. Someone else had taken the money. It could hardly have been a vast sum, Rufford reflected, for the Awakened Israelites did not seem, on the whole, to be the sort of people who had much money to spare, though one or two of the congregation appeared to be wealthy, like old Mrs. Alvington. None of the people whose names he had run through his mind was likely to have stolen a pound or two, especially in such circumstances. One had to add that indication to the rest when one was trying to get a picture of this No. 3, who now seemed to be at least one of the keys to the whole enigma.

CHAPTER X

THE TWENTY-ONE CLUES

Peter Diamond's family were old friends of Sir Clinton Driffield, and this gave Peter a slight advantage over his confrères in constabulary business. Not that the Chief Constable favoured Peter unduly. But knowing him personally, and being sure that he would betray no confidences, Sir Clinton could discuss cases more freely with him than he would have done with an unknown journalist. Peter, on his side, seldom intruded unless he had a sound reason for his visit. So when he sent in his name on the evening of Sir Clinton's return from leave, he was shown into the smoking-room without delay.

"Come in, Dwarf," the Chief Constable welcomed him. "You know Wendover, of course. There's whisky and soda over yonder. Help yourself. The cigars are in that box."

"The brand you keep for visitors, eh?" said Peter, doubtfully. "They might make me yellower than Donnington would like. I'll stick to a pipe, thanks."

He pulled out his pipe and pouch, settled himself in a low chair, and busied himself with preparations for a smoke. When he had got his pipe alight, he turned to his host.

"Had a good holiday?" he demanded.

"Oh, very fair," Sir Clinton answered. "We had some golf to start with. Then we went for a week to a place on the West Coast of Scotland, where there was a good loch and a river."

"Catch much?"

"Eighty-five trout from the loch, averaging half a pound to two pounds, mostly on a Gold Butcher. The river was in spate, and one day I got a couple of salmon out of it, a ten-pounder and a twelve-pounder on a Jock Scot."

"No complaints, then," said Peter. "And what about *your* record?"

"Not quite so good," Wendover admitted cautiously.

"Hotel comfortable?" demanded Peter sceptically.

"Very fair," Wendover assured him.

"I know these fishing inns," said Peter, who was no angler. "Rod racks in the passages. Gillies hanging about the doors in the morning. The stark corpses of the day's catch laid out, side by side in a neat row, on the stone floor outside the bar, as you go in to dinner. The bar full of my namesake's successors in the evening, swapping lies, and talking their lingo about Greenwell's Glory, Water Hen Bloa, Wickham's Fancy, Peter Ross, and Bloody Butcher. And a lot of piscine monstrosities in glass cases on the walls, looking down with that sneering expression that all stuffed fish seem to take on. And if it's near the sea, somebody goes down and catches a six-stone skate. It's brought up in a wheel-barrow and everyone goes out to look at it. Then it's smuggled away and buried by dusk in the back-garden, because no one at a fishing hotel would eat skate if you offered it to 'em on a gold plate. Not that I blame 'em. Far from it."

"Spoke very feelingly, Peter," said Sir Clinton, lazily. "We know you never soared higher than the 'prentice level, with liberty to practise on tadpoles and tiddlers. Suppose now, for a change, that you talk about something that interests you. I leave the subject to you."

"Then I'll choose something I know more about than you do," said Peter, amicably, "and that's the Barratt-Callis affair. But perhaps you know something about it already?"

"I do," Sir Clinton retorted. "I've read Rufford's report

up to date. It's on my desk over there. But don't let that hamper you."

"I shan't," Peter assured him. "You haven't read the stop press news on it. I bring the glad tidings myself. I wish I'd brought my pulsimeter and my electrocardiograph with me to register your reactions to the news, which is sensational—or will be, when I've written it up."

"We are all ears," Sir Clinton assured him, politely.

"That's as it should be," said Peter, unabashed. "I give you the headings first—force of habit, you know. 'The Jubilee Double-Florin Clue' and 'Message in Hymnbook.' That's just to whet your curiosity. We've a good bit to go before we come to them."

"Then suppose we get started," suggested Sir Clinton.

"Right! One, two, three . . . bang! Now we're off. Partly for my own satisfaction, and partly as a favour to Rufford, I've spent some of my spare time interviewing various Awakened Israelites who congregated under the late Barratt. I made a few notes, which I shall now consult."

He took out a note-book and placed it open on his knee.

"Here are some specimens of public opinion. Sample One. A nice old lady, mother of a grown-up family, strong on the wing in the matter of sewing-meetings, etc. 'Mr. Barratt was *such* a nice man and I don't believe a word against him. He was very kind when I had an illness, and came to see me regularly. I'm quite sure all this in the papers is a pack of lies and will soon be cleared up. All nonsense, I think. As for Mrs. Callis, I never saw her do anything she oughtn't to have done. If she saw much of Mr. Barratt, it's quite understandable, because she took a lot to do with church work. I won't hear a word against either of them.'"

"Well, she knows her own mind, at any rate," commented Sir Clinton. "The question is, does she know anything else?"

"Sample Two," continued Peter, taking no notice of the interjection. "An angular old maid, churchy, thin-lipped and censorious-looking. 'I've nothing to say against Mr.

Barratt, except that he was careless in some ways and that his wife didn't take her proper part in church work. I never liked Mrs. Callis. She was far too pushful and managing in her ways, and she did her best to monopolise Mr. Barratt whenever she could. As to what has happened, I know nothing about it; but you can count on it that there's never smoke without a fire. I'm surprised at Mr. Barratt. He ought to have had more sense than get entangled with a woman like that. But one step aside . . . and down you go. Wait for more evidence? Oh, certainly, if you want to. My mind's made up already. I never liked that young woman. Her husband was a good man and looked well after all the money affairs of the church. If he'd kept as strict an eye on his wife, it would have been better.'

"Sample Three: the organist of Barratt's church. Decent little fellow, rather hard put to it to make a living, between organ-playing and teaching music. Depones thuswise: 'I didn't like Mr. Barratt, but I respected him. He was always high-principled, but very obstinate; and he generally got his own way by wearing down opposition. As to Mrs. Callis, I never saw anything between her and Mr. Barratt; but I don't take much interest in church affairs except when the organ's concerned. She was inclined to be bossy, people told me; but she'd nothing to do with the organ or the choir, so I hardly ever came across her. I was most surprised by the whole affair and I hardly know what to make of it.'

"Sample Four: a hard-working, cheery little grocer. Spoke thus: 'I'm all upside-down about this business. I'd a great admiration for Mr. Barratt: as honest a man as you'd wish to meet. Once I got into difficulties—but thanks be, that's all past now—and he helped me over the stile by getting friends to subscribe a guarantee fund so that I could get an overdraft at the bank. It was the saving of me, that was. After that, I wouldn't hear a word against Mr. Barratt. It'll all come out in the end, and you'll find his character won't be touched, black as it may look. He was a fine man and I can't tell you how sorry I am that he's gone. I've lost a real friend in him. As to Mrs. Callis, I didn't much like her. Nor did my wife. But she's dead now, poor thing, and I'm not the one to say anything against her. If there was any fault in the business, it wasn't Mr. Barratt's. I'll say that, and I'll say no more.'

"Sample Five: a well-meaning, rather flustered, middle-aged, stout lady, mother of five. 'It's all stuff and nonsense, this talk about him and her, and nothing will persuade me different. Mr. Barratt was a powerful preacher and a good abstainer and a man one could look up to. I've no patience with people who're ready to believe the worst of everybody. Mrs. Callis was far too above-board to do anything of the sort, even if she had got tired of her husband a bit. I haven't read the stuff printed in the newspapers about it. I don't need newspapers to tell me what I ought to think about people I know.'

"Then there's Sample Six," Peter continued. "She's a Miss Jessica Legard, a nice little old lady who does a bit of dressmaking and finds the church a great help in adversity. She liked Barratt. Mrs. Callis didn't get such a good mark. She smoked, for one thing. Miss Legard doesn't hold with these modern girls' ways. No other complaints to speak of. But she was more worried about something else. It seems she was a child in 1887, the year of the first Jubilee. You remember they put out a special coinage then?"

"Before you were born, Diamond, if you will allow me to get a word in edgeways," interrupted Wendover. "They issued a five-pound piece and a two-pound piece in gold and a double-florin in silver. People didn't like the look of the Jubilee coinage, and about five years later Boehm's designs were replaced by a new one by Brock, and the issue of the double-florin was discontinued. Double-florins are pretty rare nowadays. Numismatists have snapped them up."

"I've heard all that already—or most of it—from Miss

Legard," Peter explained. "Point is, her daddy in 1887 presented her with one of these double-florins. She's preserved it religiously and it's come to be a sort of mascot to her. She carries it about with her everywhere. Now when they came to gather up the loaves and fishes at that last meeting where Barratt presided, the old lady discovered with horror that she'd left her purse at home, or forgot to put any cash in her bag before coming out. So when the collecting-plate came round, the only coin she had on her was this double-florin. You know the sort of old lady; the kind that would die rather than let the plate go by without putting in something. So she hawked out her double-florin and dumped it in, bravely. What she meant to do was to see Barratt after the meeting and ask for her mascot back in exchange for four bob in current coin, which seemed to her fair enough in the circs. Unfortunately, she missed Barratt. So the double-florin went off in that black bag with the rest of the dibs. And now she's very distressed about it. So I thought I'd mention the point. If the dibs turn up, you'll see she gets it back again, won't you? It has a hole in it to hang it up by, so you'll recognise it."

"I'll see what can be done," said Sir Clinton, who seldom promised anything. "What was the figure of the collection, Peter? Any idea?"

"Well, there were about fifty people present," Peter explained. "I happened to ask that. I've attended services at the Awakened Israelite church—on business, I may say. They're not the sort that roll in rhino. Coppers mainly. The rest was tanners, with an occasional bob or half-dollar from the few plutocrats in the congregation. I doubt if the total would rise above thirty bob in the case of this meeting."

"Any more? Or have you exhausted your material?" asked Sir Clinton.

"Not quite. Just one more sample of opinion. Miss C. R. Maldon. Like a fat pussy-cat with a harsh voice and

—I imagine—a nasty mind. Age uncertain. Perhaps forty-five, but looks more. Obviously jealous of Mrs. Callis and the part she took in church work. As a result, the good lady had a grudge against Barratt also. Or so it sounded. I condense her statement. There was a lot of it, mostly irrelevant. Boiled down, it came to this. She'd had her eye on the pair of them for quite a while. And what she'd spied out had been far from pleasing her. She was quite sure they'd been 'carrying on' on the sly. Of course, if you start out with a spite against people, you're bound to notice a lot of trifles which other folk would overlook; and by putting the worst interpretation on them, you can build up quite a solid-looking case. That seems to have been her method. Looks, and behaviour, and little private jokes, and the cold-shouldering of a bore—for the good lady *is* a bore, and no error—all point the same way when it happens to be the way you want to go. She seems to have spied on them pretty efficiently. Once, just to catch them, she'd gone back into the hall after a meeting had dispersed and there she found Barrett with Mrs. Callis, and he'd got his arm round her neck."

"That didn't look well," commented Wendover. "I don't wonder your friend was surprised."

"There's nothing in it, really," Peter explained. "Barratt put his arm round *my* neck when I interviewed him about the prospects of the Awakened Israelites. It was just one of his less agreeable mannerisms and meant nothing whatever. I saw him once, after a service, festooning himself round the neck of a pretty young girl in the face of all the congregation. No one seemed to mind. It was just his little way. So I discount that."

"And a good deal of the rest too, I suppose," Wendover interjected.

"A good deal of the rest, too, as you say. In fact, almost all of it. And I told her so. But she would have none of my apologetic. She knew what she knew, and that was a damned sight more than I did, for all my cleverness. And then, just as I was leaving her, she brought out something really fresh."

"Suppose you do the same," suggested Sir Clinton, as Peter made an orator's pause for effect. "This is pretty dull, if you don't mind my saying so."

Peter fished a wallet from his pocket, extracted a paper, and spread it out impressively before continuing.

"Miss Maldon's what you might term a confirmed snooper," he went on. "No pains spared, as you can infer from my previous anecdote. When she heard about these torn-up love-letters, the news acted on her like trinitrin on a crocked race-horse. In the distant past, it seems, she'd read a novel which described how the hero and heroine, separated by stern parents, managed to communicate with each other by notes left inside hymn-books in their pews. . . ."

"That's common ground," said Wendover. "Mark Twain used it in *Huck Finn*."

"Perhaps she got it there," Peter conceded. "Anyhow, it set her on the snoop. And more to the purpose than you'd think. She got into the church. Borrowed the key on the excuse that she'd left her bag behind, after that meeting. She clawed through the books in the Callis pew, and in one of them she found a scrap of paper. I got it from her to give to you. She seemed to shrink from handing it over to you herself."

"It's curious to see what people will boggle at, especially after doing Paul Pry work like that," said Wendover contemptuously. "Did she ask you to keep her name out of it?"

"She did. But I refused—after I'd got the paper out of her. I gave her a sound lecture on the danger of suppressing evidence. Put her in a blue funk, if no worse. So that's all right. Now here's the document, Driffield. The writing is Barratt's, identified by Miss Maldon, who states that she knew his fist well. Besides, there's an embossed heading on the paper, with Barratt's address. Contents as follows:

'Wait for me after the service to-night, darling. Fondest love. J.' Which sounds fairly affectionate to an amateur like me."

"No date on it?" inquired Sir Clinton, holding out his hand for the document.

"No. No need for any, seeing it was left in her hymn-book," Peter pointed out as he handed over the billet-doux.

Wendover saw that it was a half-sheet of white note-paper with an embossed heading.

"I'll keep this," said the Chief Constable. "I suppose you've taken a copy of it?"

"Yes, I've got one," said Peter. "You can keep the thing. It's a sprat thrown out to catch a herring, if you take my meaning. Where's my herring?"

"Meaning that you expect me to dole out some exclusive information in return for that document? I'll have to think over that proposal, I'm afraid."

"Meaning that you've got none to dole?" asked the journalist sceptically. "Ha! That strikes homes, does it? Chief Constable Confused. Driffield Detects Damn All."

"You ought to enter for the jumping match at our police sports, Dwarf. You leap to a conclusion quicker than most people, I'll say that for you. Unfortunately, it's sometimes the wrong conclusion. As in this case. But while I'm turning the matter over in my mind, suppose we play a small parlour game invented by myself on the spur of the moment. I call it: 'Choose your clue.' We take turn about, and each of us mentions what he thinks is an interesting clue in this business. When you come to the end of your stock of clues, you drop out. The last man left in is the winner. You may have the honour of starting, Dwarf. What's your choice?"

Peter reflected for a few seconds before taking his plunge.

"This is where I become subtle," he announced at last. "My first clue is the hue-and-cry that the late Barratt raised against Edward Alvington at the time of that divorce case.

And I'll just ask you, Driffield, if you know anything about Ted Alvington's movements on the night that Barratt was put on the spot."

"That's ingenious, Dwarf," Sir Clinton admitted frankly. "I've no secret information about that particular Alvington, though, so your subtlety's been wasted if you were hoping to elicit any by this move. Your turn to play, Squire."

Wendover had his answer ready.

"I'm not subtle like Diamond," he admitted with a smile. "Plain facts are all I can think about. So my clue is the four empty cartridge-cases found near the two bodies. That's twice as many as were needed. I think that's interesting. Now it's your turn, Clinton."

"Oh, I play the packing and labelling of the suit-cases," the Chief Constable volunteered.

"Because that shows premeditation?" queried Wendover.

"Obviously it shows premeditation," said the Chief Constable. "Your shot now, Dwarf."

"I play that missing twenty-five pounds," said Peter, thoughtfully. "Barratt had that in his pocket, evidently for initial expenses. But it wasn't in his pocket when his body was found. Was it stolen from him, dead or alive? Or had he found an unexpected use for it? Squaring somebody, for instance?"

"That's a bright idea, Diamond," said Wendover with hearty approval. "It looks as if you might have hit something, there. That extra trail through the bracken certainly suggests that some third person was on the spot; and Barratt may have parted with the twenty-five pounds to buy him off. A blackmailing Peeping Tom might fit the case. But," he added with less assurance in his tone, "if Barratt paid over the twenty-five pounds then, it would leave him with next to nothing to foot his hotel bill in London."

"No good, that objection of yours," said Peter definitely. "First and foremost, they'd probably dropped the idea of going to London at all, when they retired to the bracken-slope. So the twenty-five pounds wouldn't be needed. Secondly, the Alcazar isn't as expensive as the Carlton or wherever it is that you put up when you go up to town. The extra notes Barratt had in his pocket would easily cover the cost of bed-and-breakfast for two at the Alcazar. And Mrs. Callis had her cheque-book in her suit-case. She could cash a cheque next day at a London branch of her bank. They might have to make inquiries, but she'd get the dibs, eventually. It's your turn, now."

"Very well," said Wendover, "since I've mentioned the trails in the bracken, I'll take them as my next contribution. There should be either one broad trail or two single trails, if it was a suicide pact business. Actually, there's a broad double trail and a single track. There's no getting away from the fact that there was someone else on the spot beside the two victims. It may have been a suicide pact all the same; but it may just as easily have been murder, so far as I can see."

"So the murderer first blackmailed them and then shot them. Or else they were shot first and the twenty-five pounds lifted from Barratt's body," commented Peter. "There's no evidence either way, so far. Let it go at that. What's your next, Driffield?"

"Oh, those love-letters, I think," said the Chief Constable.

"Hot stuff, are they?" asked Peter. "Rufford didn't show them to me."

"I don't know what precise meaning you attach to 'hot stuff,' Dwarf," said Sir Clinton. "If you mean 'obscene,' they certainly aren't. Wendover's seen them. I brought home Rufford's complete dossier and let him glance through it, seeing that he's a magistrate. He could perhaps find the right word for you."

"A gentle hint that they're too sacred—or is it secret?—for the eyes of a mere newspaper man," said Peter, in a tone of annoyance. "Well, what would you call them, Wendover?"

"Passionate, I think," said Wendover in a judicial tone. "That would fit them. Very passionate, in fact. But rather touching; though perhaps you wouldn't think so, Diamond. At least, one could see that the writers were in earnest and were deeply in love. The language wasn't anything special. They were very ordinary love-letters, I'd say."

"As between bachelors, I'll take your word for that," declared Peter. "Personally I'm no judge. Nobody writes love-letters to me. I read 'em in the newspapers—in the reports of breach-of-promise cases. Usually they're funny."

"These weren't," said Wendover, rather nettled. "It's your turn again, Diamond."

"He's anxious to shut me up," explained Peter, unnecessarily. "So be it. And I play the anonymous letter which Callis handed over to Rufford, the one that warned Callis that he was blind if he didn't see what was happening under his nose. That shows there's someone in the offing who knew there was some funny business afoot. If you could lay hands on him, Driffield, you might extract something of interest."

'No doubt," admitted the Chief Constable, drily. "First catch your hare. . . . But I don't know the hare's name and address, unfortunately. So we can leave that aside for the moment. Your turn, Squire."

"Second in hand plays low," said Wendover. "I'll content myself with the text and unfinished sermon that Rufford found on Barratt's desk. That suggests to me that Barratt knew quite well that someone had been gossiping about his doings and that he meant to get a bit of his own back from the pulpit. He'd planned his elopement long before that."

"Which suggests my next contribution," interrupted the Chief Constable. "I'll pitch on the booking of the room at the Alcazar, since it follows naturally upon your clue, Squire."

"It's certainly hard to bring those two into line," said Wendover musingly. "If Barratt had everything ready for a bolt, I do not see what need there was for him preparing a sermon which he'd never preach."

"Force of habit, perhaps," Peter suggested flippantly.

"Now it's my turn. I play the Clue of the Jubilee Double-Florin. No one has more right to it than I have, seeing that I spotted it myself."

"Seeing that it hasn't led to anything yet, and may never do so," said Wendover acidly, "I don't think you need look so pleased with it. My turn now? Then I'll mention the accident to Callis's car. That will have to be fitted in, somehow."

"He's jealous," declared Peter, with a pretence of pique. "Not having discovered any clue by his own exertions, he runs down more able practitioners. Let's get on with the game. What's yours, Driffield?"

Sir Clinton lit a fresh cigarette before answering.

"The rifling marks on the two fatal bullets and the finger-prints of Barratt on the pistol," he said, as he put down the spent match. "These really ought to count as two points, but I'll make one of them just to give you a chance of winning, Peter. What's your next?"

"Another of my own discoveries," declared the journalist. "The rendezvous letter found in the hymn-book. That's a good 'un."

He turned to Wendover expectantly, but at this stage Wendover was evidently running dry of material. He thought for a few seconds before producing his choice.

"I'll mention the wedding-ring found on Mrs. Callis's hand, with her initials and Barratt's inside it."

"And now you, Driffield?" queried Peter, hopefully.

"Oh, I think the disinheriting of Edward Alvington will serve my turn," said Sir Clinton.

"Ah!" exclaimed Peter. "The revenge motive, eh? Might be something in that," he added, more thoughtfully. "I'd forgotten about that side of Ted's troubles. He certainly owed Barratt something over that business. . . . Hum! Suggestive. In fact, it suggests something entirely different to me, which I now proceed to play. I've made a few inquiries on the strict Q.T., Driffield. And the result of them was that I found the firm of E. and A. Alvington's not regarded as a rock of finance, down town. Some of their recent building specs. haven't shown the hard-headed acumen so necessary in speculative builders. They're not broke, or even on the edge of it. But some people are beginning to say: 'Oh, well, old Mrs. A. is bound to die soon, and then Arthur'll come into something.' And that suggests to me that if anything happened to make the old lady change her will again, Arthur's credit might suffer when people discovered that he *wasn't* going to come into money. And if his credit suffered at this juncture, that firm very might well go B U S T—bust. So, quite without any ill-feeling or after-thoughts, I play the Alvingtons' financial position as my next clue. Now what about you, Wendover?"

Wendover sat silent, evidently thinking hard. Peter shifted up his coat-sleeve and inspected his watch.

"You've had half a minute," he said at length. "I think there ought to be a time-limit, otherwise we'll be sitting here all night, waiting for the great brain to work. Come on! Spit it out."

"I resign," said Wendover, reluctantly. "I can't think of anything else."

"Say you so? Then it's between us, now, Driffield. *À nous deux!* Your turn."

"Mine, is it?" said Sir Clinton. "Oh, well, then, I suggest the brush and comb that Mrs. Callis forgot to take with her."

"Thrilling!" said Peter, ironically. "Then, just to put us square I'll suggest the pistol which she *didn't* forget to take with her."

"Variation of the same theme," said Sir Clinton. "I suggest the wire which Mrs. Longnor didn't send. And you, Peter?"

But Peter, like Wendover, seemed to have come to the end of his resources. He lay back in his chair, ruffled his hair, glared at Sir Clinton who was ostentatiously taking the time.

"Oh, I give up," he growled, at last. "I can't think of anything else just at this moment. You win, all right. But I bet you couldn't go any further yourself, if you tried."

"Think so?" retorted the Chief Constable. "I'm not so sure about that. Let's try. What about this fellow Kerrison and his cat-shooting exploits?"

The expressions of Wendover and Peter betrayed that to them this was a wholly unexpected idea.

"You're not hinting that these two people were killed by stray shots, surely?" Wendover demanded. "That's a nonsensical notion, Clinton. The cartridge-cases were found close to the bodies."

"They were. Too many of them, in fact. No, I was thinking of something quite different, Squire. I'm going to interview Kerrison to-morrow. That's what brought his cat-shooting into my mind. As he lives close to the bracken-slope, he may have heard something that night."

"Oh, is that all?" said Peter, rather contemptuously. "I don't think that should count, then. It isn't a clue. Not in the proper sense, anyhow."

"Very well, then, I'll give you another instead," said Sir Clinton amiably. "You were allowed to spring a fresh one on us; I'll give you a new one myself, to balance the account. I've seen Dr. Fanthorpe's report on the results of his P.M. examination of the bodies. He found that Barratt's last meal had been made up, partly at any rate, from bread, boiled eggs, and cheese, which fits in well enough with what we know of the Barratt ménage. Dr. Fanthorpe's always cautious, and he won't tie himself down to anything definite beyond a surmise that Barratt's death occurred probably three hours after his supper. That's more or less of a guess. You can't gauge the rate of digestion accurately. It varies from individual to individual and the process often goes on even after death has taken place."

Wendover got up, walked across to a book-case, took down

a volume of Taylor's *Medical Jurisprudence* and came back with it to his chair.

"Your library's handy, Clinton," he said, turning over the pages. "Ah! here it is. Bread: time for digestion, two hours. Soft-boiled eggs: time, three hours; hard-boiled eggs, half an hour longer. Cheese: three hours and a half. What did he find in the case of Mrs. Callis?"

"Cooked apples, fowl, boiled potatoes, and bread," explained the Chief Constable. "It looks like a cold meal, with potato salad, perhaps."

"Apples: an hour and a half; fowl: four hours; boiled potatoes: three hours and a half; bread: two hours," Wendover read from the table which he was consulting. "As you say, Clinton, there's a pretty wide margin of error. I don't know that one could lay too much stress on the point. But what guess did he make in her case?"

"He put the death roughly about a couple of hours after her last meal," Sir Clinton explained. "But neither he nor I attach over-much importance to the figure. It's all guesswork, really."

Wendover walked across the room and restored the volume to its place on the shelf.

"What about the inquest?" he asked, as he came back to his chair. "It was adjourned, wasn't it, after evidence of identification had been given?"

"Yes," said Sir Clinton. "I've seen the coroner. To-morrow he's going to take Fanthorpe's evidence and then adjourn further."

"Are you bringing a definite charge of murder against anyone?" Wendover inquired. "That would mean an adjournment until the criminal case is finished."

"Oh, no," Sir Clinton explained. "It is merely that the coroner and I agree that it's best to adjourn the inquest until more evidence is available. There's no charge against anyone."

"Twenty-one clues, if I've kept an accurate tally, and our

able Chief Constable makes nothing out of them," said Peter, sarcastically. "I see. Mountain Manufactures Mouse. You're not much help to a poor journalist, I'll say that gladly. But when the well's dry, it's not much use wasting energy in pumping, is it? I'll just have to say that the police have an important clue. But the public are getting tired of that remark. It cuts no ice with them."

"Then tell them the plain truth," suggested Sir Clinton helpfully. "Say we've got more clues than we know what to do with, and that we're throwing them out in pairs, as in 'Old Maid'."

"Donnington would never pass that," said Peter, with obvious regret. "He'd say it was flippant and unsuitable for his readers. I wish I could meet one of these readers he talks about, just to see what it looks like. A dreary article, I can't help but think. No snap, vim, or yip about it. Now if I were editor . . ."

"The circulation would grow like bindweed in a garden. Quite so. Pushful Peter Paralyses Population, as you would say. Really, Dwarf, I think things are better as they are."

"That began like praise," complained Peter, "but it didn't somehow seem to keep on the right note. Perhaps you haven't a good ear for music. But let that pass. Tell me about your paulo-post-future doings. The next step, in fact."

"I don't mind telling you, if you promise not to hang on to my coat-tails. I've various calls in view, to be paid personally or by deputy. First of all, I'm going to make the acquaintance of one Kerrison the Cat-shooter. (This alliteration of yours is infectious, apparently.) Rufford summarised your opinion of Kerrison in his report, and I yearn to hear all about the Lost Tribes and the Great Pyramid. . . ."

"And this is what we pay you for?" interjected Peter in high contempt. "To run round and complete your education? Well, I . . ."

"Calm yourself, Peter. You live in rooms, so you aren't a ratepayer; therefore you needn't use the editorial We when you talk about my salary. I'm going to see Kerrison because the bodies were found near his house and he may be able to recall something useful, if we give him a chance. Then I'm going to have some inquiries made among the railwaymen. Probably I'll see Alvington, if I can. And possibly I may drop in and have a chat with Mrs. Barratt, just to form impressions of her at first hand and extract any odds and ends of information which suggest themselves as time goes on."

"Quite the social butterfly, you'll be," said Peter caustically. "I shan't dog your heels. My legs aren't as long as yours and it would keep me on the run if I followed you on that trail. Well, my love to them all. Anything further in view?"

"I may have a little digging done. It's said to be good exercise; and it's part of my duty to look after the health of my constables. Now I see you're burning to get away, Peter. Don't let us detain you."

CHAPTER XI

THE SHOOTER OF CATS

Accompanied by Rufford, the Chief Constable set out next morning in his car to pay his proposed visit to Kerrison, whom he had forewarned by telephone.

"First of all," said Sir Clinton, "we'll drive round to the place where you found the bodies. I want to have a look at it. We can turn back, after that, and visit the Hermitage."

"You could walk straight up the hill to it, if you like, sir, after you've seen the bracken-slope," suggested the inspector. "It's no distance. We could leave your car on the road and go back for it after you've had your talk with Kerrison."

"No," the Chief Constable decided, after a moment's consideration. "We'd probably have to climb a fence if we went that way. It would look too much like sneaking in by a back way. This is an official visit. We must be dignified, so we'll go in by the front door, if you don't mind. You'd better con me when we get outside the town. I don't profess to know this by-road to the place; I've never gone that way."

Twenty minutes' driving brought them to the turn-off into the lane. Sir Clinton pulled up his car at a signal from Rufford, and they both got out.

"This is the place, is it?' asked the Chief Constable. "That's the bridge down there, and this is the home signal on the line that you mentioned in your report? The bodies were up there, where Loman & Co. cut down the bracken? Well, let's go up and have a look round. Not that there's much to look at, I suppose. The bracken seems to have been trampled down all over the place. Sightseers, no doubt."

"We couldn't keep them off it, sir, once we'd finished our own work on the ground. There's no use your trying to look for the tracks I mentioned in my report. The whole place has been trodden down by these rubber-necks since then."

"Evidently," Sir Clinton agreed, after a casual glance at the slope. "I really wanted to get the general lie of the land into my mind. Who owns that little wood, further along the slope, just above the distant signal?"

"It's part of the farm over yonder, sir, I believe. Full of rabbits, they say, and the farmer's only too glad to let anyone go and shoot them if they care to, just to have them kept down. They do a lot of damage to some of his crops."

"Likely enough. Kerrison's house is up above us, isn't it, beyond the crest of the slope?"

"Yes, sir. A hundred or a hundred and fifty yards back."

"Just let me see exactly where you found the bodies. Then we can go. There's nothing to be seen, after all that multitude has trodden everything flat."

The inspector was able to show him exactly where the bodies had been found. Then they returned to the car and drove round to the Hermitage. It had a short, ill-tended drive leading to the front door; and the whole place had the appearance of having seen better days. The whitewash on the walls needed freshening; the small garden was neglected; and a hen and some chickens were scratching the gravel at the side of the house. An ancient maid, with a forbidding countenance, admitted them suspiciously.

Lewis Carroll was one of the Chief Constable's favourite authors, and he was irresistibly reminded of Tenniel's drawing of the Frog Gardener when Stephen Kerrison entered the room and confronted his visitors. The big splay feet, the large hands, the general aspect of ill-kemptness, the air of portentous solemnity: all were there. Kerrison did not wait to be addressed.

"You want to see me about a pistol that I borrowed from Callis, I believe?" he began, without any preliminary greeting.

"Yes," Sir Clinton admitted pleasantly. "You see, Mr. Kerrison, you haven't got a certificate. So I found, when I looked the matter up."

Kerrison's eyes kindled angrily at this.

"Do I need a certificate?" he demanded, staring at his visitors with barely-concealed hostility. "I've only been using that pistol inside my own garden and for killing vermin. No licence is needed for that. I looked it up in the encyclopœdia."

"No gun licence, perhaps," agreed Sir Clinton. "But you've forgotten the Fire-arms Act, 1920. You can't have in your possession, use, or carry any fire-arm or ammunition, unless you hold a special certificate from me."

"Oh, indeed? I didn't know that," said Kerrison, rather less truculently. "I'm in the wrong, am I? It was quite unconsciously, then. No one's more of a stickler than I am in the matter of right and wrong. What's to be done about it?"

"It depends on whether you want to go on using the pistol," said Sir Clinton. "If you don't, then if you hand it back to its owner, we'll say no more about it. But if you wish to retain it, you'll have to apply to me for the proper certificate and pay the stipulated fee. You have to show good reason for requiring the certificate. I suppose you want the pistol for destroying vermin about your premises?"

"Yes, I do," declared Kerrison, evidently surprised to find the Chief Constable so ready to oblige him. "I've been losing a lot of fowls lately with stray cats. I've settled the hash of some of them," he added, with a gleam of satisfaction on his face. "but there are a lot more of them still bothering me. They get into my runs, no matter what I do to protect them; and I don't raise chickens for the benefit of stray cats."

"They are strays, are they? Not neighbours' pets?"

"No, they're half-wild beasts—gone back to nature. They live in that spinney over yonder, I believe, killing rabbits when they can get them; but lately they've discovered my chickens, and my losses are quite considerable."

"I'd have thought a shot-gun would have served your purpose better," Sir Clinton suggested.

"It wasn't worth while to buy a shot-gun for the sake of killing a cat or two," Kerrison pointed out. "I borrowed the pistol from Callis. He was quite ready to lend it to me. That saved the price of a gun."

"Ah, quite so. I see your point. But unless you're a good pistol-shot, it might be expensive in the matter of ammunition."

"I've managed to kill two of the beasts," Kerrison explained, with evident gratification. "They won't give any further trouble to my chickens."

"What did you do with the remains?" asked Sir Clinton. "Burn them, or bury them?'

"I buried them out in the garden, over yonder," Kerrison explained, indicating the spot through the window.

"Well, if you wish to use that pistol in future, you must get a certificate, Mr. Kerrison. And now I want to ask you a question about something else. Were you at home here on the night when this tragedy happened just down below your garden?"

Kerrison considered carefully for a moment or two before answering the question.

"Yes, I was at home," he admitted. "I had a sore throat, and my mother was against my going out that day. Otherwise I'd have been at a meeting at the church that evening."

"That's a fair distance to go to church," Sir Clinton commented. "But I suppose you have a car."

Kerrison shook his head.

"I don't keep a car," he said. "We're not so isolated as you think. There's a bus route quite near us, only a matter of seven minutes' walk, and there's a ten-minute service on it. I can get into town in under half an hour, if I leave here just in time to catch a particular bus. As a matter of fact, I don't go into town much, except to church and occasional visits to the public library to look up references. I'm engaged in research," he added, rather pompously.

"I've heard of your work on the Great Pyramid," said the Chief Constable tactfully.

"It didn't get the attention it deserved," Kerrison declared in a resentful tone. "I spent years of study on that book. And the subject is one of the utmost importance for the proper understanding of history. The problem of the Inch, in itself, is of the most fundamental character for a true realisation of the course of events during the last three thousand years. The adoption of this new-fangled metric system on the Continent ranks almost with the Noachian Deluge in historical significance. It divides the sheep from the goats in the most decisive manner, making a clean cut between the British race and the rest of the world. And what's very significant, too, is the fact that Inch meant an island in the older British languages. Inchkeith, Inchcomb. It runs through Welsh, Cornish, Irish, Gaelic, with trivial modifications. And the British are an island race, the Race of the Inch, obviously. It's much more than a mere coincidence that we not only live on an Inch but we use the Inch as the basis of all our measurements. I'll give you a copy of my book. It's a work that every thinking man ought to read."

"That's very kind of you," said Sir Clinton, "but let's finish our present business first, if you don't mind. You were at home all that evening? Did you hear any unusual sounds?"

"You mean reports of firing, I suppose?" said Kerrison. "I did hear something—like two shots coming one after the other—but I'm just a shade hard of hearing and I didn't pay much attention to them."

"What time was that?" demanded Sir Clinton.

"I can tell you, almost exactly, as it happens," Kerrison answered. "It was just about ten o'clock, when my mother always goes to bed. I'd gone out to see that my chickens were all safely shut up for the night. I usually go out about that time after she's gone upstairs, and I walk round the back premises and see that everything's secured for the night and to make sure that none of these cats are lurking about. I heard two . . . thuds or claps, you might call them."

"They didn't surprise you?" inquired the Chief Constable.

"No, not particularly," Kerrison explained. "We hear gunshots quite often here, in the evenings about dusk. That spinney over yonder is full of rabbits, and the farmer who owns the place often sends someone across to shoot them as they come out in the dusk to feed. He finds them very destructive, I understand."

"When did you shoot these cats?" inquired Sir Clinton, harking back to a previous subject.

"I can't remember what day I shot the first one on," Kerrison replied, after a short pause for consideration. "But I shot the last one four days ago. I can remember that quite well."

"Did you clean your pistol after using it?"

"No, I don't know much about pistols except how to load and fire them. I took it to Callis and he cleaned it each time after I'd used it. He said it was an old pistol and it didn't much matter when it was cleaned; but he'd told me, once, that pistols ought to be cleaned as soon as possible after use, for they deteriorated if this wasn't done, so I felt that I ought to give him the opportunity of cleaning it."

"You won't shoot any more cats until you get your certificate, of course?" said Sir Clinton. "I'm stretching a point, you know, Mr. Kerrison, in not saying anything about the past. But now the matter has become official, so to speak, I rely on you not to go on with your vermin-killing until everything's shipshape."

"Oh, certainly, if you wish it," Kerrison agreed.

"Now there's another point I want to ask you about. I gather that this bracken-slope down yonder is a favourite resort of couples in the evenings. They don't come up near your garden and disturb you?"

Here he evidently touched one of Kerrison's sore spots.

"The place is a plague-spot," he said, vehemently. "Things go on there which are a disgrace to a decent community, let me tell you; and it's high time that something was done about it by the police. I've done what I could, as a private citizen; but I had to give it up in despair. I used to go down and protest to couples that I found there, lying about in the bracken; but all that I got in reply was insolence. Finally, when I spoke my mind to one couple who were embracing there—I used the language of the Bible in rebuking them—the man, a big burly fellow, was very abusive because, he alleged, I'd insulted his fiancée, who was 'a perfectly decent girl' and he threatened me with physical violence on account of what I had said. As if any decent girl would come and sit among that bracken in the dusk. The thing's absurd."

"Then you didn't see any actual impropriety?" asked Sir Clinton.

"I saw them embracing each other and kissing in what I can only describe as a very passionate manner," said Kerrison. "One has a very fair idea of what that kind of conduct leads on to."

"Marriage, not infrequently," said Sir Clinton, with a smile.

"You make a joke of it, sir," said Kerrison angrily. "But it's no joking matter. Far from that, indeed. If there's one thing which ought to be sternly dealt with, it's this laxity in morals which one sees all about one."

"I've had some experience," said Sir Clinton, soothingly, "and I really think you're exaggerating a little, Mr. Kerrison. Personally, I find young people a very decent lot, take them all in all."

"Indeed?" retorted Kerrison, heatedly. "Then I can only congratulate you on your simple mind, sir. Or perhaps it's wilful blindness on your part. Why, to go no further back than the present week, we've seen, down in that very patch of bracken, a man and his paramour come to a well-deserved end. I was very much mistaken, in that matter, and I frankly admit it. I judged too hastily. The man Barratt seemed to me a person of unblemished character; and although I found Mrs. Callis frivolous in many ways, I certainly never suspected that she and he were carrying on a base intrigue, until the truth was unveiled to me. Well," he added sombrely, "the instrument of the Lord smote them and they perished."

"By the instrument of the Lord, do you mean a Colt .38?" asked Sir Clinton irascibly. "I think you might leave the Lord out of it."

"I mean the agent who executed those two shameless hypocrites," declared Kerrison in an uplifted tone. "He did a good deed when he shot them there, in the midst of their sins."

"H'm!" commented the Chief Constable. "It's to be hoped that the Boy Scouts don't include that kind of good deed in their list. I've heard of Murder as a Fine Art; but Murder as a Good Deed is new to me. We'll have to differ on the point, Mr. Kerrison, I'm afraid. Let's change the subject. Do you know anything about hypnotism?"

"No, I don't," said Kerrison. "If you want my opinion of it, I think it's an unholy art."

"Have you ever seen it practised?" asked the Chief Constable.

Kerrison's dark eyes lighted up with the flame of fanaticism, and his voice was harsh as he answered:

"I have—once. I allowed an unsanctified curiosity to overbear my better judgment. I forgot the injunction against enchanters in the eighteenth chapter of Deuteronomy and the passage in Exodus: '*Thou shalt not suffer a witch to live.*' I witnessed how this man Barratt exercised his uncanny power over the woman Callis and bent her to his will."

"Where was that?" demanded Sir Clinton in a matter-of-fact tone.

"In his own house," Kerrison replied. "Some of us had gone there to spend the evening, and the talk fell upon mesmerism and odylic force. Someone—I think it was a man Alvington—pressed Barratt to give us a demonstration, since he had claimed to possess some powers of that kind. I made no protest; I did not believe that there was any truth in these tales about mesmeric influence, and I was quite glad to see the thing tried, since I expected it to fail. Barratt began with the man Alvington, and succeeded in making him do certain things to order. But my impression was that Alvington was merely playing the fool with Barratt and making a jest of the whole matter. Then Barratt tried to mesmerise his wife, but she very properly treated it all with contempt, and his efforts failed in her case. Callis offered himself for the experiment, and Barratt had some success with him; but at the time I imagined that he was following Alvington's example, and laughing in his sleeve at Barratt. It was only in talking to Callis, later on, that I found some of the effects were genuine. After Callis, Barratt tried Mrs. Callis. He told her that her powder-puff was a rose, and made her sniff its perfume and describe its petals. Then he suddenly told her that it was a toad she had in her hand, and she flung it down with disgust. He ordered her to take off her shoes and then persuaded her that they were two kittens, which she fondled and stroked. And he did other things with her as well. She was obviously completely in his power and amenable to any suggestion he made. After that he tried his powers on a Miss Spencer, with even more striking results. I refused to have anything to do with it."

"Just a little parlour magic, with some of the people acting as confederates?" suggested Sir Clinton, sceptically.

"No," declared Kerrison morosely, "it was Black Magic, the forbidden knowledge."

"Let it go at that, then," said Sir Clinton with a slight shrug. "I'd like to make a note of the names of these people. May I have a sheet of note-paper, please?"

Kerrison moved across the room to an escritoire from a drawer of which he took a sheet of note-paper. He handed it to the Chief Constable without a word. Evidently he was deeply vexed by the reception of his story.

"Let's see," said Sir Clinton, as he jotted down the names. "Alvington . . . Which of them was it? Arthur or the other one?"

"Arthur Alvington," said Kerrison. "I would not go anywhere if there was a chance of meeting Edward Alvington, that loose liver and hypocrite who has been expelled from our congregation for his sins. And when I think that the man Barratt played a chief part in excluding him, I am amazed at the duplicity of human nature. Satan rebuking sin. But evil-doers reap their reward in due course. They were cut off in their prime, in the midst of their transgressions. Judgment is sure."

"Quite so," agreed the Chief Constable. "At least, we do our best. Alvington, I've got. Mrs. Barratt—she was not a good subject, you said? Then Callis, a partial success. Mrs. Callis, very susceptible to the treatment. And a Miss Spencer. . . . What's her Christian name, and her address?"

"Julia Spencer, I think," said Kerrison. "And the address is 35 Basingstoke Crescent."

"Thanks. Then that finishes my business for the present, I think. You'll apply for that certificate in due course? I'll send you a form. And, by the way, please write your name and address in block letters. We have to make that rule because some people write such an illegible fist."

Kerrison accompanied them to the front door, where Sir Clinton paused for a moment.

"Where did you say you buried these cats?" he asked, as if in idle curiosity.

"Over there," explained Kerrison, pointing, "at the foot of that cypress."

"Ah, very appropriate," said Sir Clinton suavely. "Now, I must say thanks and good-bye."

As the car passed out of the garden, Sir Clinton turned to the inspector.

"Well, well," he said with a straight face, "I clean forgot to remind him to give me that book he promised me."

"You can always turn and go back for it, sir," Rufford suggested helpfully.

"I think it will keep," answered Sir Clinton with an unconcealed smile. "If it's like his conversation, I'm not sure that I yearn to read it."

"Clean off his rocker, I'd say," said Rufford contemptuously. "Do you think it's safe, sir, to give a pistol certificate to a man like that? I'm not sure about it myself. That look in his eyes when he gets excited. . . ."

"Oh, we can spin out the time a little, if necessary. You know what red tape is, when one has a use for it. You needn't hurry over the business to please me, remember. But send him a form by next post. You can dawdle in the later stages if you choose."

"Well, sir, it's for you to say," grumbled the inspector. "But for my own part, I'd give him no certificate. He's not right in his head, with all that stuff about the Inch and all that."

"He's a fanatic, I admit," said Sir Clinton, in a serious tone. "But he's not a lunatic. So I judge, at least, from the fact that he confessed that he'd been 'mistook in his jedgements' —like Disko Troop on a well-known occasion. No lunatic would ever have said that."

"That may be so, sir," admitted the inspector. "But that man's got a bad mind. He's just running round looking for nastiness where likely enough there's nothing going on beyond a little courting, hugging and squeezing, like all engaged young folks do, and some that isn't engaged. It would have served him right if that young fellow had kicked him all the way home. I wouldn't have blamed him, if he had."

"Yes," agreed Sir Clinton, thoughtfully. "He seems to have his feelings on a hair-trigger when it comes to sex. And I'd say that he has a mind like a cess-pool. I liked him no more than you did. By the way, is he the Kerrison who figured in the civil courts twice in the last eighteen months?"

"That's the man, sir. Two actions against him for defamation of character; and he had to pay up both times—pretty stiffly in the second case. He's got a slanderous tongue, and he can't keep it quiet. I suppose he'll break out again, though he ought to have learned his lesson by this time, one would think."

Sir Clinton stopped the car and then took from his pocket the sheet of note-paper which Kerrison had given to him. He held it up to the sky and then passed it to the inspector.

"Have a look at the water-mark," he directed. "AVIAN WOVE and a bird of sorts. Manufactured by A. Vian & Co., Liverpool. You see it? I've an idea that we'll come across it again."

He took back the paper, stowed it in his pocket, and set the car in motion again, after a glance at his watch.

"We've another call or two on the list," he explained. "We may as well hear what that organist can tell us about the meeting between Barratt, the contractor, Callis, and himself, at the church. Not much, I expect. Still, one never knows what may transpire. If we hurry up a little, we'll catch him between two music lessons. I've made an appointment with him."

"And who else do you want to see, sir?"

"Mrs. Barratt," the Chief Constable explained. "I want to ask her a question or two. Nothing that will worry her. And after that, we'd better drop in on Messrs. E. & A.

Alvington, Ltd. I've fixed an appointment with them also. I'd like to have a look at the pair of them. And we may pick up a tip or two about the building trade while we're there. General knowledge is always useful in our line of business, and I know very little about building except that one should always lay one brick on top of two others. What sort of person is Arthur?"

The inspector rubbed the side of his nose, as though that might help him to collect his impressions of Arthur Alvington.

"He's a thin-lipped fellow, sir. Suave way of talking—I mean his tone of voice. When he speaks about anyone, he always starts with a bit of faint praise; but I noticed that he generally ends up by giving a dig at them. Money seems to bulk fairly large in his outlook, sir."

"That's hardly to be wondered at, if his firm's in deep water," Sir Clinton pointed out. "Finance must be a worry to him in these days, if all I hear about him is true. You haven't seen the other partner: the hero of this recent divorce case?"

"Not yet, sir."

"A pleasure in store," said the Chief Constable. "Happy Families, No. 1, Buggins the Builders. It's a long time since I played Happy Families. The kind of family I come across professionally doesn't seem to merit the adjective. We'll hope for the best."

CHAPTER XII

AN ORGANIST AND SOME OTHERS

Tudor Quixley, a depressed-looking little man with a slight cast in one eye, was the organist of the Church of Awakened Israel. He was at first obviously perturbed by the descent of the police upon his home; but he regained composure when he learned the object of their visit.

"Of course I shall be only too happy to do anything which can forward the cause of justice," he declared, in a resonant bass voice which contrasted strangely with his feeble physique. "I have nothing to conceal, Sir Clinton, and if anything I can do will serve to throw light upon this mysterious, this most mysterious tragedy, I shall be only too glad to help. You desire some information with regard to a meeting which took place at the church, in connection with alterations in the organ?"

"Exactly," said the Chief Constable, wishing that Quixley would copy his own brevity.

"Then I had better begin by telling you who were present," Quixley went on. "There was Mr. Rastell from London, representing the firm of organ builders which has been chosen to carry out the work. Shall I give you his address?"

"Do, please," said Sir Clinton; and Rufford jotted down the address as Quixley gave it.

"Then there was an employee whom he brought with him—a practical man—of the name of Vowler. And there was Mr. Callis, representing the finance committee of the church, of which he is treasurer. There was the Rev. Mr. Barratt, our late minister, the grounds for whose presence are obvious,

I think. And, last but not least, there was myself, as the expert on the church side."

"What time did this meeting begin?" asked Sir Clinton.

"At ten o'clock, Sir Clinton. The contractors had sent us a detailed estimate some days earlier, and I had gone over it item by item, in readiness for this meeting. I had also consulted the Rev. Mr. Barratt and found him in agreement with myself as to what should be done."

"What sort of man was Mr. Barratt?" demanded Sir Clinton. "Easy to get on with?"

Quixley hesitated for a moment before answering.

"Not altogether," he said, reluctantly. "In some ways, he was rather inclined to be overbearing. He held very definite opinions on most subjects: and once he had taken up a position, it was hard—if not impossible—to get him to change his mind. That was why I consulted with him beforehand," he added, artlessly.

"A wise precaution," commented the Chief Constable, with a faint smile. "What happened at the meeting?"

"We discussed the estimate, item by item," Quixley explained. "Mr. Callis being—as one might say—the watch dog of the church finances, was inclined to question the necessity for one or two of them. I was, I admit, rather put out by this. Mr. Callis has no knowledge of organs and could, naturally enough, not understand the necessity of sundry items in the estimate. He and I had a slight argument which I regretted at the time but which was unavoidable, since his objections, if upheld, would have necessitated a complete recasting of some other sections of the estimate."

Obviously poor little Quixley had been fighting hard for his ideas about the organ repairs against Callis's determination to cut expenses down to a minimum. It was a case of a weak expert against a business man resolved to show a satisfactory balance-sheet. But it seemed that Quixley had not been left to struggle alone.

"The Rev. Mr. Barratt listened to us both," Quixley went

on. "I could see that he was displeased by this argument going on in the presence of these outsiders from the organ firm. Finally, he intervened and took my side of the matter. He spoke very decidedly in favour of my point of view. Mr. Callis continued to argue in favour of economy. I tried to show him that his suggested cuts were really false economy and likely to cost us more in the long run. Finally, the Rev. Mr. Barratt said that the matter must be settled as I wanted. He spoke very plainly—not exactly rudely, you understand, but with a sort of finality in his tone that showed he had made up his mind. We all knew that tone in his voice. Mr. Callis was rather huffed, I think, at having his contentions brushed aside. He said something like: 'I wash my hands of the business.' These were not his exact words, of course. They were more polite, really, if I could remember them; but that was the sense of what he said. He was quite evidently piqued by the Rev. Mr. Barratt's manner, and he left our group and wandered about the church for a few minutes, taking no further part in our discussions for the moment. I was very sorry to have seemed to go against him, as you can understand, Sir Clinton. I like to be on good terms with everyone: and in this case my position was, I felt, a very awkward one. I was quite relieved when Mr. Callis rejoined us, having apparently got over his little display of hot temper. I think that on reflection he had found that I was really quite reasonable in my contentions. At the termination of our proceedings, he quite frankly admitted that, as a layman, he had perhaps failed on the spur of the moment to see the force of my arguments. He said he would think over it further and let Mr. Barratt know his final decision in the course of the afternoon, because, if possible, he thought we should be unanimous. Of course I bore no malice; and Mr. Barratt clapped him on the shoulder in that friendly way he had. I was relieved, I confess. I was afraid there might be ill-feeling; and once that starts, one never knows where it may end."

"How long did the meeting last?" inquired Sir Clinton casually.

"About an hour, I think," said Quixley. "I stayed behind for some further discussion with the two experts. Mr. Barratt also stayed with us; but I think he was content to leave the matter in my hands, since he knew nothing about organ construction. Mr. Callis shook hands with me before he left; and he also nodded in a friendly way to the Rev. Mr. Barratt, who was standing beside me at the moment. I am quite sure he bore me no grudge whatever over the slight disagreement, none at all; for he very kindly offered me a lift in his car if I was going his way. But I was going in the opposite direction, and in any case I wished to discuss some details with Mr. Rastell. That took us about half an hour, and then Mr. Rastell and the man Vowler went away. The Rev. Mr. Barratt kept me a little while longer, to discuss some points about choir practices. It really hardly concerned him, but he liked to have his finger on everything connected with the church. Then he shut up the church and I hurried away, because I had a pupil coming for a lesson at noon, and I had just time to get home to receive her."

"How long does it take you to walk to the church on Sundays?" asked Sir Clinton.

"Just under a quarter of an hour," the organist informed him. "I can do it in twelve minutes, but I generally allow the full fifteen."

"You have a good many private pupils?" queried the Chief Constable.

"Quite a number," answered Quixley, evidently not anxious to give too definite an estimate. "If you were thinking of arranging for a pupil, Sir Clinton, I dare say that I could find time. I'm always glad to be of assistance, and no doubt I could manage to squeeze in one more on to my list."

"Thanks. I'll bear it in mind if anyone applies to me," Sir Clinton answered. "But I see you looking at your watch, and we mustn't keep you late for an appointment, if you have one. Thanks for your assistance."

He and Rufford took their leave of the organist. When they got back into the car, the inspector evidently expected his Chief to make some comments on the evidence which Quixley had furnished; but Sir Clinton's only remark was:

"We'll try Mrs. Barratt, next."

When they reached 38 Granville Road, Mrs. Barratt opened the door to them. She recognised the inspector, showing no surprise at this second visit from him; and when he introduced the Chief Constable, she invited them both into the house as naturally as if they had been two of her acquaintances come to pay a friendly call. Even in an awkward situation she had the talent for seeming perfectly at ease.

"Can I help any further?" she asked, when she had shown them into Barratt's study. "I suppose you want to ask more questions, or you would not have come back. I'm quite ready to tell you anything you want to know."

Sir Clinton took her at her word, and put his first question without further preliminaries.

"Did you or Mr. Barratt ever stay at the Alcazar Hotel in London?"

Mrs. Barratt seemed rather surprised by this opening, but obviously she was in no way perturbed.

"Yes, we did," she replied without hesitation. "Last month, my husband had to go to London to attend some general meetings in connection with church affairs. I took the opportunity of going with him. I had not been in town for a good while, and that visit gave me the chance of seeing the shops and other places, while he was busy with his meetings. It was a little change for both of us; and I was glad to get away from housekeeping for even a few days."

"Could you, without too much trouble, give me the date of that visit?" Sir Clinton inquired.

"Oh, easily enough, if you'll just wait for a moment."

Mrs. Barratt went across to a cupboard, searched for a few seconds, and then came back with a packet of neatly-docketed papers, evidently a series of receipted accounts. She leafed through them rapidly, extracted one, and handed it over to the Chief Constable.

"That's our bill for the hotel," she explained. Then, seeing the expression on Sir Clinton's face, she added, "I was trained as a girl to keep receipts for three years. My uncles taught me that. Something about people being able to sue you for a small account so long as it hasn't been standing for longer than three years, I think. Anyhow, I've always preserved receipts."

"Quite a sound practice," Sir Clinton agreed. "I see this bill is for your stay from the twentieth to the twenty-third. Had you any difficulty in getting them to reserve a room for you? I've never stayed at the Alcazar myself, but I believe they are always pretty full."

"No, we had no trouble," Mrs. Barratt explained. "I wrote to them a fortnight ahead to book the room. Somebody told me I ought to do that. They made no difficulties. I think I could show you their reply, if you would like to see it. I was trained to keep all business documents, you see, and I could probably find it for you if you want it."

"Don't trouble," said Sir Clinton hastily, as she made a movement to rise from her seat. "Now there's another question I want to ask about the Alcazar. You didn't book a room there lately, I suppose?"

"No, of course not," retorted Mrs. Barratt in a tone of surprise. "I had no idea of going there."

She got up, went to a small table at one of the windows, and came back with a pocket diary.

"Here's my engagement-book," she said, handing it to the Chief Constable. "If you glance over it you'll see that all my time has been filled up with one thing and another. I couldn't have got away just now without cancelling a whole lot of engagements."

To satisfy her, Sir Clinton opened the little volume and glanced over some of the pages. Then he handed the book back to her without comment, and turned to a fresh topic.

"Do you get many telegrams?"

"Telegrams?" Mrs. Barratt's tone showed her surprise at this jump to an unexpected subject. "No, I can't say we get many. A telegram always suggests bad news, doesn't it? So few people think of wiring good news to one; a letter's quick enough for that. But they're always ready to spend a shilling if it's bad news they have to send. So I can't say I'm sorry that we don't get many wires."

"Then it will be easier to recall if you've had any lately," Sir Clinton suggested.

"Obviously," agreed Mrs. Barratt, with a faint smile of amusement. "As it happens, my husband did get a wire about a fortnight ago. It was from Mr. Callis, apologising for not being able to attend some meeting or other on church business. I don't know whether you'd say that was good or bad news. I kept that telegram, if you'd like to see it."

"I should," said Sir Clinton, somewhat to Rufford's surprise. "If it wouldn't trouble you too much to find it."

"It's easy enough," Mrs. Callis explained. "It's a 'business' document, so it should be amongst my collection. You see how strong a habit becomes, when it's been acquired when one was young. I'll get it for you in a moment or two."

She went again to the cupboard, hunted for a few seconds amongst packets of documents, and came back again with the telegram which she handed to Sir Clinton in passing.

"Why did Mr. Callis go to the trouble of wiring?" asked the Chief Constable, as he glanced at the contents of the telegram. "You are on the phone, aren't you? Surely he could have rung up."

"I believe he did ring up, more than once," Mrs. Barratt explained. "But both my husband and I were out for the whole afternoon, that day; and as we keep no maid, there was no one to answer Mr. Callis when he rang up. That was probably why he was driven to sending a wire. You might look up that date in my engagement book. I'd like to be sure that I'm right in this."

Sir Clinton turned over the pages of the engagement book as she asked him to do, found the date, and put the book down again.

"It says: 'Classic, 2.45 p.m., Mrs. Sidworth,'" he reported.

"Yes, that's right. I remembered it, but I want to be quite sure. I went to see a news-reel with Mrs. Sidworth, and had tea with her in town, afterwards. My husband had a meeting to go to, which kept him rather late in the afternoon. I found the wire lying in the letter-box when I got home and gave it to him when he came in."

"You'd opened it, I suppose?"

"Oh, yes, of course. It came addressed to 'Barratt' and it might have been meant for me, for all I knew. One generally opens any wire when it arrives, doesn't one? In case it needs an immediate answer."

Sir Clinton agreed with a nod and then turned to another fresh topic.

"You don't keep a car, I understand.?"

"Oh, no," said Mrs. Barratt, rather scornfully. "Cars are luxuries beyond my husband's means. Very occasionally, if I happen to need one, I borrow it from one of my uncles; I have a key of his garage. But that's a rare treat."

"When did you last borrow one?"

"About three weeks ago," Mrs. Barratt answered promptly. "If you'll look up my engagement book there, you'll find I went out to see the gardens of Rockingham House. They throw them open to the public once a week in the summer. I'm very fond of flowers; and I went there one afternoon. My uncle, Mr. Arthur Alvington, lent me his car so that I could get there comfortably."

Sir Clinton verified this by referring to the engagement book.

"Yes, that's quite correct," he said with a smile. "You have a wonderfully good memory, Mrs. Barratt. Now, another point. I believe Mr. Barratt was interested in hypnotism. I gather from Mr. Rufford that you did not share his enthusiasm for the subject."

"No, I didn't," Mrs. Barratt admitted frankly. "I know very little about hypnotism, but it seems to me either too silly or too dangerous to dabble in, as an amusement. My husband tried to hypnotise me several times, but he never had the slightest success. Whether he succeeded with other people or not, I can't say. It's so easy to pretend that you've been hypnotised, if you want to flatter the vanity of the hypnotist."

She hardly troubled to conceal the sneer which flitted across her features as she made this last suggestion. Obviously she believed that people had played up to Barratt when he attempted to hypnotise them.

"Evidently you and I are in the same boat," commented Sir Clinton. "No one ever succeeded in hypnotising me, and consequently I've no real proof of these things. I don't deny that the phenomena occur; but I've had no convincing experience of them, personally."

He paused for a moment or two, as if reflecting, and then turned to yet another subject:

"You remember telling Inspector Rufford that your husband took a small black bag with him when he went away? (Just open that parcel, inspector, please.) Is this the bag?"

Mrs. Barratt examined the bag which Rufford extracted from its wrappings.

"Yes, that's the one," she confirmed. "I recognise it because a bit of the lining is beginning to fray—here."

"You've no doubt about it?"

"None whatever."

"He always used it to carry money in, didn't he, if he had to bring church collections home?"

"Yes, it was just about the right size. We had nothing else suitable."

"Thanks," said Sir Clinton, with a gesture which gave Rufford permission to wrap up the bag again. "Now, another point. At what time had you dinner on the night that he went away?"

This time, Mrs. Barratt made no attempt to mask the derision in her smile.

"Dinner?" she echoed. "You must remember that my husband often had to attend evening meetings at the hour when civilised people are sitting down to dinner. He insisted on having his principal meal in the middle of the day. I'm afraid you don't realise how simply we live. The meal he had before he went out that evening was what we called supper."

Sir Clinton made a gesture admitting his blunder.

"Well, perhaps you can tell me what he had for supper," he answered accepting the correction without comment. "And at what time he had it."

"Tea, bread and butter, boiled eggs, and some cheese," Mrs. Barratt explained. "Seven o'clock is our usual supper-time. Really, Sir Clinton you do ask curious questions, if I may say so."

The Chief Constable conceded this with a smile.

"They must seem queer to you," he admitted, "but they're really mere routine inquiries. Now, here's something else that I want to ask. Do you know if your husband has been having any disagreements with people recently? Just tell us, even if they were only slight disputes."

Mrs. Barratt seemed to give this question a certain amount of consideration before she answered it.

"I'm afraid that my husband was in some ways not very easy to get on with," she admitted. "He liked his own way, and generally got it because he didn't realise how much he was rubbing people up the wrong way. You mustn't think that he went out of his way to pick quarrels. He really regarded himself as a very peaceable person, and I am sure he meant to be that. But he hadn't much imagination and couldn't see how he hurt many people without meaning to do so. I want to make that perfectly clear, so that you'll understand that he wasn't deliberately quarrelsome."

"I quite understand," Sir Clinton assurred her. "You needn't give us a catalogue of minor grievances. What I want are instances of real disagreements, if you can give me any."

"Well, quite recently he seems to have had a squabble—I think that's probably the best word for it—with Mr. Callis, about some repairs to the church organ. My husband gave me his side of it when he came home to his dinner, after the meeting. Mr. Callis gave me his version when he called to see my husband that evening. It seemed to me a very trivial affair altogether. Evidently, after consideration, Mr. Callis felt that himself, and he came round here meaning to smooth things over. So I gathered, at any rate. But I don't think you need attach much importance to the business, in any case. There was a much more awkward affair over my uncle's divorce case. You've heard of that? My husband had very strong views about it, and he made things difficult for my family. There's no use my trying to conceal that from you; it's common knowledge and every loose tongue in that congregation has gossiped about it to the full, My Uncle Edward and my husband had a definite quarrel over it, a really bitter affair. And my other uncle, Mr. Arthur Alvington, got dragged in also to some extent. And of course I myself got mixed up in it, with an uncle on one side and a husband on the other. I'd rather not discuss it, unless it's really necessary."

"I quite understand," said Sir Clinton in a sympathetic tone. "I don't think we need go into it. Can you think of any friction with other people?"

Mrs. Barratt evidently had difficulty in adding to the examples which she had already adduced; but after a moment or two for consideration, she produced a final one, though she gave it with unconcealed contempt for its pettiness.

"My husband got into hot water not long ago with a Mr. Kerrison," she explained, rather disdainfully. "Mr. Kerrison has ideas about the Book of Revelation, and he took exception to a sermon which my husband happened to preach. I really paid no attention to the matter. That kind of thing doesn't interest me. But I know that my husband was very cross about it all, and no doubt Mr. Kerrison felt the same. Neither of them was very tactful, so . . ."

She shrugged her shoulders instead of completing the sentence.

"Thanks," said Sir Clinton, stifling a smile. "I quite understand. Now just a final question. I suppose you know that the coroner may want you to give some evidence, when he resumes his inquest?"

This seemed to take Mrs. Barratt rather aback.

"Will he?" she asked. "I'd no idea that he'd want me as a witness."

"Oh, it will be nothing very serious," Sir Clinton hastened to assure her. "He'll merely want to ask you the same kind of thing as Inspector Rufford and I have asked you already; and probably he'll not be half so inquisitive."

"That isn't what I was thinking about," explained Mrs. Barratt. "This house belongs to the church, and they'll want it for my husband's successor, so I shall have to leave it, perhaps in a week or two. In any case, I couldn't afford to go on living in it. Probably I shall go to London. It's not very pleasant, living here now, after what has happened."

"So long as you leave an address where we can find you," said Sir Clinton, "that will be all right. I didn't know that the house was church property. And now, I think, that's all I need trouble you with just now. Thanks for giving us this information. I realise how much you must be disturbed by the whole thing."

He and Rufford took their leave and went back to the car. As they drove away, Sir Clinton turned to the inspector.

"She's rather deceptive," he commented unexpectedly.

"Deceptive?" echoed the inspector. "What do you mean, sir? She seemed to tell a plain tale."

"I mean 'apt to deceive'," Sir Clinton explained, with a smile at the inspector's surprise. "What age would you reckon her? I think you put it under thirty, didn't you? Well, I took the trouble to ring up the registrar's office to find out when she was born. She's thirty-five. Obviously she's deceptive, if she looks at least five years younger than she really is."

"Oh, indeed," muttered Rufford, annoyed at having been caught by the Chief Constable's equivocations.

Sir Clinton seemed to drop that subject and started another which surprised the inspector just as much.

"Did you ever read a book called *The Dangerous Age*, by Karin Michaelis?"

"I never even heard of it, sir."

Inspector Rufford had a certain contempt for works of fiction, and he was also suspicious that the Chief Constable was trying to pull his leg a second time.

"Before your time, perhaps," said Sir Clinton. "It had a vogue in its day. Curious that the title should cross my mind just now. As a matter of fact, I'd say that any age is 'the dangerous age' for some women. It just depends on the particular woman. . . . But I see I'm boring you. Sorry. We'll now intrude on the labours of Buggins the Builder, I think. That Happy Family is busy at its temporary offices on the new estate that it's developing—rather unsuccessfully, I'm afraid."

It did not take them long to reach the tract on the outskirts of the town where E. and A. Alvington were operating. It had all the ugliness and rawness of building ground in course of development: the grass trampled down, heaps of soil thrown here and there in the course of levelling operations, gaps torn in the old hedges to give easy access to working points, and trenches dug for drainage purposes. Two roads had been laid down, metalled, and finished; but the rest of the lay-out was indicated merely by lines of granite kerbs, or even by the removal of turf. Wooden pegs marked the boundaries of what would in future be gardens. Here and there, the ground was scarred by the digging-out of tree-stumps and roots. At vantage-points on the completed roads stood three decoy houses, fresh and attractive-looking with their green-tiled roofs. A fourth decoy was under construction, its grid of rafters still uncovered, and its unglazed windows showing dark on its frontage. Heaps of bricks, piles of drain-pipes, and a mound of old mortar gave an untidy aspect to its neighbourhood. Near at hand was a temporary wooden hut which formed the office of the firm.

"They're nice decoys," commented Sir Clinton as he drove past them. "But not one of them's been taken, evidently. The white patches are still on the window-panes and the notice-boards are still there, offering them for sale. There must be a fair amount of unremunerative capital locked up in the ground and these decoys. The Alvingtons are having no luck, it seems. Well, I can't help their troubles. But I can add to them, and I'll do it now," he ended, unsympathetically, as he pulled up his car before the wooden office building.

Both the partners were on the premises, and the inspector introduced his Chief to them. Edward Alvington had a strong family likeness to his brother; but whilst Arthur's lips were thin and compressed, Edward's were slacker and suggested a weaker and more self-indulgent nature.

"You're busy people, I suspect," Sir Clinton began without preliminaries, "and I'm fairly busy myself. Shall we get to business straight away?"

Arthur Alvington nodded, examining the Chief Constable rather distrustfully. His brother fumbled with a pencil which he had in his hand and avoided the Chief Constable's eye.

"Very well, then," said Sir Clinton, addressing himself to Arthur, "I think you told Mr. Rufford that on the night of Mr. John Barratt's death, you were at home after dining at a restaurant down town. Your brother came in, later, and you passed the evening in going over your accounts. That's correct?"

"Yes, that's correct," echoed Arthur. "But seeing that I told this to the inspector, I don't see why you come here to ask it again."

"Merely a matter of routine," said the Chief Constable suavely. "In cases of this sort, we have to begin by eliminating from consideration a lot of unlikely people, and an alibi's the simplest step in ruling anyone out." He turned to Edward Alvington. "You can confirm what your brother said?"

"Yes, yes, of course," Edward asserted with rather unnecessary eagerness. "I dropped in at my brother's house that night, some time about nine o'clock. We'd arranged to go over our accounts together. There were one or two points that needed looking into, you understand? Some decisions we had to take, and we had to see just how matters stood before we could make up our minds. The bank . . ."

He broke off abruptly, evidently realising that he was giving away unnecessary information. Sir Clinton had little difficulty in guessing that "overdraft" might have been in the rest of the sentence.

"Who let you into the house?" he inquired.

"Nobody," said Edward, seemingly surprised by the question. "My brother's housekeeper was out. There was no one to open the door to me. I just walked in. As a matter of fact, I always do walk straight in. I'm living with my brother since my divorce, so there was nothing in that."

"What had you been doing before you went to your brother's house?"

Edward Alvington passed his hand over his brow as if perplexed.

"What was I doing?" he echoed, apparently in the hope that this action would stimulate his memory. "I was busy here until nearly seven o'clock in the evening. Then I had dinner at my club—it's the Colnbrook in Chandos Street. I talked to some friends there. Then I went on to my brother's house; I've been staying with him since my divorce. I got there about nine o'clock and we spent the rest of the evening going into our accounts. We stopped about half-past eleven, didn't we, Arthur?"

Arthur Alvington confirmed this with a nod.

"Go back a little earlier," said Sir Clinton, addressing both brothers. "Had either of you any occasion to visit the railway station that day? About delivery of building material, or anything of that sort?"

The Alvingtons exchanged a glance which suggested that they were surprised by the question.

"No," said Arthur. "There was nothing to take us to the station. I certainly didn't go there."

"Nor did I," Edward chimed in. "I haven't been there for weeks; not since I went to London on business, and that was two months ago."

"Very good," said the Chief Constable, turning to Arthur Alvington. "Now I want to ask you something about these hypnotic experiments which Mrs. Barratt mentioned to Inspector Rufford. Do you remember an evening when Mr. Barratt tried some experiments with Mr. and Mrs. Callis, a Miss Spencer, and yourself?"

A faint smile flitted momentarily across Arthur Alvington's face but vanished almost at once.

"Yes, I do remember that affair," he admitted. "What do you want to know about it?"

"I'd like to know what led up to the hypnotic experiments,' said Sir Clinton. "Perhaps you can remember how the subject came up."

"I think I can," said Arthur, rather doubtfully. "Oh, yes, it was like this. We happened to be at my niece's house for the evening. These affairs were always very dull. Barratt disapproved of card-playing. He generally took charge and gave us an hour of nice clean fun—the sort of thing which would have kept an eight-year-old juvenile in fits of laughter, but just a shade boring to more mature minds. He was rather childish in some ways. A case of arrested development in the sense of humour, one might call it. But I admit that he enjoyed himself immensely with that kind of thing, and it was always something to know that one of the party was brimming with cheerfulness and gaiety. He got Callis to do a little parlour conjuring, which was some relief; for Callis is quite a good hand at leger-de-main. And then Callis proposed these hypnotic experiments. I expect he was as bored as the rest of us by the Barratt amusement programme and welcomed any substitute. And he knew that Barratt dabbled in mesmerism a bit. Anyhow, that's how it started."

"How much of the results was genuine?" asked Sir Clinton, with an unconcealed smile. "Take your own part, for example. Were you genuinely hypnotised?"

"Not a bit," confessed Arthur Alvington frankly. "I was just pulling his leg and pretending to be under his control. It was easy enough. He gave me a glass of water and pretended to put a Seidlitz powder into it and told me to drink it while it was fizzing. Anyone can imitate a man drinking a Seidlitz powder. You don't need to be much of an actor for that."

"Did he ask you to do anything else?"

"He ordered me to count the money in my pockets. That was easy enough. Then he told me that one of the pictures was a mirror and that I was to look at myself in it and put my tie straight. I'd no objection to humouring him up to that point. After that, I showed signs of coming out of my trance. That finished my turn. He was quite proud of his results with me."

"After that, he tried his hand with the other guests?"

"Oh, yes. Callis, I think, was pulling his leg, just as I'd done. Mrs. Callis I'm not so sure about."

"Why?" asked Sir Clinton, with obvious interest.

"Well, she was a girl who took a lot of pains with her make-up. Quite an artist in that way, always beautifully turned out, from the tip of her nails to the last wave in her hair. Well, that fool Barratt, among other things, ordered her to wash her face—rub it with her hands, as a boy would do. You can imagine the result, when the black stuff from her eyes got smeared all over her cheeks. My niece was horrified, and took her off at once out of the room to repair damages. Quite time, too. Now I doubt if a girl like her would have gone that length—making a sight of herself—merely to carry on a joke. No, it looks to me more as if Barratt was really able to hypnotise her. And I believe the results he got with Miss Spencer may have been the genuine article also. She's got about as much personality as a rabbit or a hen, and anyone can hypnotise a hen."

"Thanks," said Sir Clinton. "That seems to make the matter as clear as we are likely to get it. Now about Mr. Barratt himself. I couldn't very well ask his wife about him. But you knew him intimately. What kind of man was he?"

"A hypocritical blackguard," Edward Alvington declared, vehemently. Then, seeing Sir Clinton raise his eyebrows slightly, he continued in self-justification. "Oh, yes, he's dead, I know. *Nil nisi bonum*, you think? I don't agree with you, where he's concerned. Look at him! He hounded me over this divorce case, nothing was too bad to say about my doings. Did he feel restrained because I was his wife's uncle? Not a rap, not a rap! He let himself go, all out. He denounced me in public and in private. Nothing was too bad to say about me. Nothing! He turned my mother against me and persuaded her to change her will so as to cut me off. Nice forgiving fellow, wasn't he? And all the while he himself was in tow with this Callis woman.

There wasn't a pin-point's difference between us—except that I was found out and he wasn't. Is that enough to justify what he did to me? You may think so; I don't. I didn't mind his chucking me out of his church. That's all in the day's work, a mere matter of professional etiquette, one might say. But to come crawling and sneaking into my family and using his position to undermine me and do me out of my inheritance . . . That takes more forgiving than I feel up to, and I don't mind saying so."

He stopped abruptly, either through lack of breath or because he caught a warning glance from his brother. Then he added a few more words.

"You'd better ask my brother what his opinion is. He's not actually suffered a cash loss, as I've done. But he can tell you that Barratt was trying to get round our mother and persuade her to leave *all* her money to that wretched little sect. Oh, yes, Arthur. Your turn was coming next, yours and Helen's. Neither of you would have seen a stiver of the old lady's money, if Barratt had had his way. You'd have been in the same boat with me, if he'd lived much longer. Lucky for you that he didn't."

Arthur Alvington evidently felt that this kind of talk was injudicious, for he intervened swiftly.

"My brother's naturally prejudiced," he said coolly. "My sympathies are on his side, of course. I didn't like Barratt's methods, though no doubt he was acting according to his lights. Until these recent revelations, I always looked on him as an upright man, a trifle narrow in his views, perhaps, and very obstinate when he had got a notion into his head. He seemed to have many good points. . . ."

Here Edward Alvington sniffed audibly and contemptuously, but Arthur continued without changing his tone:

" . . . but he had a queer indifference—a personal indifference, I mean—to money, which possibly accounts for some of his curious views and their results. There must be a defect somewhere in any man who lacks the money-sense so completely. And, of course, as this affair shows, he was hardly the man with the right to treat my brother as he did treat him. I'm afraid he must have had a strong streak of hypocrisy in his make-up. I won't say more than that, but I can't say less."

"He had a queer mentality, certainly," Sir Clinton agreed. "But we're all rather curious, aren't we? In some way or other. Well, we are all pretty busy people, so I mustn't waste any more of your time."

As they drove away, Rufford turned to the Chief Constable.

"You didn't get much out of them, sir," he opined, evidently comparing his own methods with those of Sir Clinton.

"Think so?" said Sir Clinton, indifferently. "I got what I wanted, which seems the main thing."

"What did you want, sir?" persisted Rufford.

"Just another piece or two of the jig-saw," retorted the Chief Constable with a glimmer of a smile about the corners of his mouth. "Mr. Edward Alvington is fresh to both of us. And I picked up a point or two about Mrs. Callis which might be useful. Oh, it wasn't time wasted. That reminds me. Will you get hold of the lawyers who are handling Mrs. Callis's estate and ask them two things: if she was insured, and who profits under her will, if she made one. She had a fair amount of capital, apparently; and we may as well know who gets it."

"Very good, sir," said Rufford.

"The next port of call will be the post office in Silver Street," Sir Clinton decided. "That's where Callis's wire came from—the one Mrs. Barratt told us about. You can do the talking for a change, inspector. I've done my share for the present. Ask to see the record of that message; and when you've got it, make sure that you see any other wire that went to the Barratt's house on that day."

"You're expecting to find a wire from the Alcazar, sir,

confirming the booking of that room for Barratt and Mrs. Callis?"

"There may be none," pointed out Sir Clinton. "The Alcazar may have sent a postcard of acknowledgment, which has disappeared. All I want is to check whatever we can."

It turned out, however, that the hotel had sent a wire. Rufford had little difficulty in tracking it down; and he took copies of both it and the wire from Callis to Barratt.

"We'll try the bank, next," Sir Clinton proposed, when the inspector returned to the car. "You'd better let me take a turn, now. Banks are apt to be sticky when it's a question of giving away their clients' affairs. But in this case the client's dead, which makes a difference. And if they're reluctant, I can say that I'll get an indemnity for them from Barratt's executors, whoever they may be. We can't allow banking etiquette to stand in our way in a case of this kind."

The bank manager showed some scruples, as Sir Clinton had foreseen; but these were overcome without too much discussion, and Barratt's account was thrown open to the Chief Constable's inspection.

"It's this twenty-five pounds I want to know about," he explained, putting his finger on the item. "It was drawn out over the counter, I believe. Can you let me see the cheque itself? You haven't returned it to the drawer, obviously, since it was cashed only a day or two ago."

The manager went out of the room for a few moments and came back with the cancelled cheque in his hand. Sir Clinton took it and gave a glance at each side.

"Drawn to 'Self,' signed by J. Barratt, and endorsed by him. The signatures are all right? I wonder if I could see the paying-out clerk who dealt with this?"

The manager retired and returned in a few minutes with his subordinate.

"Have a look at this cheque," said the Chief Constable, handing it across. "Do you remember dealing with it?"

The clerk examined the cheque carefully, thought for a

moment or two, and then, after a glance which asked permission from his chief, he gave his information.

"I remember it quite well, because Mr. Barratt was an old client of ours and he always made a little conversation when he came into the bank. He asked for notes, and I gave him it in new Bank of England pound notes. I offered him fives, but he took one-pound notes. I've looking up my jottings, and I find that I gave him a consecutive series of numbers: E 50 A 900829 onwards."

"Thanks," said Sir Clinton. "There was nothing unusual in that transaction?"

"Oh, no, nothing," said the clerk, rather surprised by the question. "He used to draw a cheque for about that figure once a month—to pay tradesmen's bills, I expect. There's nothing wrong, is there, sir?" he asked, anxiously, turning to the manager. "The signature's all right I know, and I saw him write the endorsement myself. Besides, I couldn't have mistaken Mr. Barratt. I was perfectly well acquainted with him. No one could have personated him."

"It's all right," said Sir Clinton, reassuringly. "We only wished to know how he took the payment, and you've given us that. Thanks for your help."

The clerk, evidently relieved in his mind, went out of the room. When he had gone, Sir Clinton turned to the manager.

"We may want this cheque, later on. Don't send it to the executors with the rest of his cancelled cheques. Better put it in your safe. I'll take the responsibility."

"Oh, if you make yourself responsible, Sir Clinton, then it's all right," said the manager. "I don't care to divulge anything about a client's account. You know our etiquette. . . ."

"When subpœnas come in, etiquette has to take a back seat," Sir Clinton pointed out. "You'll probably be ordered to produce this cheque by and by. That's why I'm suggesting that you should take care of it."

He returned to his car, where Rufford was waiting for him.

"That seems to finish our round," he said, as he pressed the self-starter. "Now there's another thing. What luck have you had in the matter of that Jubilee double-florin? Any news of it?"

Rufford shook his head.

"No, sir, not so far. We've warned the banks, of course; but it's a curiosity, and no one would be likely to use it as current coin. It hasn't been seen at any of the local pawnshops, either. None of the jewellers have seen it, either. We tried the bric-à-brac shops, too, Southcote's and Whitefoot's and Springs, but none of them has seen it. We'll just have to wait, I'm afraid, sir."

"Have you tried an old fellow Wilmot?" asked Sir Clinton. "He's just started in the business a week or two ago. Japanese and Chinese stuff is his main line, but he does a little in numismatics too. I paid him a call the other day to look at some netsukés he sent me a message about, but he hadn't been offered a double-florin at that time. Try him again, will you? He's an absent-minded old creature, I gathered, and he may have forgotten all about my inquiry."

"I'll see to it, sir," the inspector assured him.

CHAPTER XIII

THE DOUBLE-FLORIN

"MATE in three moves, Squire," Sir Clinton announced. "Your mind doesn't seem to be on this game. What's wrong with you?"

"I've been thinking about this Barratt case," Wendover confessed. "You've shown me the evidence, but it all seems so disjointed that I can't make a single pattern out of it. It looks like two or three independent crimes superimposed on each other. A puzzling affair."

Sir Clinton glanced at his watch before answering.

"We needn't start a fresh game, then," he decided. "It's no fun playing with you when you're in that state. Too much like taking toffee from a child, for my taste."

He swept the pieces into a drawer of the chess-table as he spoke.

"Besides," he went on, "I'm expecting a young visitor—perhaps two young visitors."

"Not Peter Diamond?" queried Wendover, apprehensively.

"Calm yourself, Squire. No, it's not Peter. Though why you have such a dislike of the Dwarf I can't make out. The worst you can say about him is that he's young and therefore a bit cocksure. You'll be sorry to hear that my expected visitor's even younger and not half so nice. Rather a bad lot, I'm afraid."

"Who is he?" asked Wendover. "Anybody I know?"

"No, you don't know him. You weren't on the Bench when his case came up. That was a little while ago. But we've got a few minutes in hand, so I'd better begin at the beginning. You may remember, among the evidence in the Barratt case, the matter of a Jubilee double-florin, the property of a Miss Legard. Peter unearthed that for us, so Peter has his uses, you must admit. Miss Legard put that double-florin into the collection the night of the Barratt-Callis tragedy; and Barratt carried it off in his black bag with the rest of the money. The collection cash disappeared from Callis's car, though the bag was left behind. We've been on the hunt for that Jubilee double-florin since then; and now we've got it. Old Wilmot—a fellow who set up in town a few weeks ago as a curiosity-dealer—had it offered to him, and through him we got on the track."

"He could describe his client well enough for that?" interjected Wendover in a sceptical tone.

"No," admitted Sir Clinton. "All he could tell us was that it was a red-haired boy about sixteen or so, with a rather cheeky manner. But we had other evidence to help us. Callis's car had obviously been snatched by someone who took it away from the lovers' nook and after driving about the country for a while, wrecked it in Granby Holt while escaping from the police patrol. We get epidemics of this car-snatching from time to time, unfortunately. So we looked back in our records for any red-haired youngster who'd been caught in a prank of that kind and we were lucky enough to find one. Rufford picked him up, and old Wilmot identified him as the boy who offered him the double-florin. Simple enough. Rufford's bringing him up here now, and possibly we shall have a second person to interview, later. I don't feel sympathetic towards the young man. He's been in trouble before, as I told you; and he's been mixed up in other misdeeds as well."

"Some young guttersnipe?" asked Wendover.

"No, and that makes it worse. He's the only child of quite decent middle-class people. I'm sorry for them, if not for the boy himself. But he's a wholly useless creature, bitten with the idea that he's rather a daredevil. I'd like to come down on him—hard. But unfortunately we'll need his evidence; and if we get that, I suppose we'll have to overlook his present peccadillo. I must ask him questions, and I can't do that if we're going to bring a charge against him which is covered by the questions. You're a magistrate, Squire, and can see fair play. That's one reason why I've had him brought here this evening."

"He doesn't sound very attractive," Wendover commented.

"You'll like him even less, I expect, when you hear more about him," Sir Clinton affirmed. "But that's someone at the front door. Rufford and his captive, no doubt. It's as well we didn't start a fresh game."

In a few seconds, Inspector Rufford and his prisoner were ushered into the room.

"H'm! This is the boy, is it?" said Sir Clinton in no friendly tone. "Stand over there. You'd better sit down, inspector, and take notes—shorthand ones, I think. You'll find paper over yonder on the writing-desk."

While the inspector was making his preparations, Wendover examined the boy. He was, as Sir Clinton had said, no guttersnipe. Rufford would have put him in the £1,000 per annum class of society. Tall for his age, wearing a good plus-four suit, with the cap of one of the best schools in the town crumpled up in his hand, he stared sullenly at the carpet, with an occasional swift side-glance at the officials who had got him in their grip. Wendover disliked his heavy features and the irregular teeth which showed occasionally in an uneasy smile of defiance.

"What's your name?" demanded Sir Clinton sharply, as soon as he saw that Rufford was ready to take notes.

"Oley," muttered the boy, without looking at his interrogator.

"Speak up," ordered the Chief Constable. "What's your full name?"

"Patrick Turnbull Oley."

"Where do you live?"

"At 35 Airedale Avenue."

The boy seemed to be plucking up his courage, since the preliminary questions were so simple. He lifted his head and stared curiously at Wendover, whom he evidently could not recognise.

"You, and a few other little boys, have got up some sort of society, haven't you? What do you call it?"

"The Wrecking Club."

"What are the objects of this precious club?"

Oley shuffled his feet and stared at the carpet without answering.

"Don't take that line with me," warned the Chief Constable. "This is going to be serious for you, Oley, if you give us trouble."

The boy evidently gathered from the Chief Constable's tone that he would stand no nonsense. With marked reluctance, he gave his answer.

"We used to go into newly-built houses and cut some of the lead pipes; or else we broke window-panes; and sometimes we lit a fire on the floor and then rang up the fire brigade to see the fun. And we used to go out with a pot of black paint and paint over the tail-lamps of any cars we found parked by the roadside. Things like that."

"Not very amusing," commented Sir Clinton. "Some of your friends were caught I think, but we didn't lay hands on you, unfortunately. Another of your pastimes was car snatching, wasn't it? You were caught in the act in that."

Oley nodded sullenly, with an angry look in his eye.

"You got off then, as a first offender," Sir Clinton continued. "He promised to reform, didn't he, inspector?"

Rufford confirmed this with a nod.

"Instead of reforming, you went from bad to worse," the Chief Constable pursued. "You took to associating with a girl. What's her name?"

"Polly Quickett," said Olley, surlily.

"Her parents complained about your doings in that affair," Sir Clinton went on. "You were had up in Court, weren't you for stealing money to buy things for her and take her to the pictures? And you were sentenced to six strokes with the birch for your behaviour. You got off lightly, Oley. And you gave your promise not to see that girl again, didn't you? Have you kept that promise?"

Oley shuffled from one foot to the other, avoided the eyes of his audience, and at last admitted sulkily:

"No."

"Your father promised to see that you were indoors by nine o'clock in the evening. What about that, inspector?"

"Mr. Oley saw to that, sir. But he and Mrs. Oley are away from home at present. The boy's been on his own since they went off."

"H'm! And as soon as their backs were turned, you took up with this girl again? What age is she?"

"About fifteen," Oley admitted.

"You've been with her frequently since your parents went away? On one occasion you and she went to a spot between the Hermitage and the railway. Tell us exactly what happened that evening."

"I won't tell you anything about it," snarled Oley. "You've no right to ask me questions like that. It's up to you to prove anything you can against me. Our solicitor told me that, when you had me up last time. So there!"

Sir Clinton looked him over coldly, and under that steady inspection the fight began to ooze out of Oley.

"I don't see why you should be so down on me," he complained, twisting his school cap in his hands. "I can't help it. I've tried to keep away from her—I really have. But I can't manage it, when I get a chance."

"If we send you to a reformatory or an industrial school, you'll be out of temptation," Sir Clinton said, reflectively. "You don't like the idea? But that's what it's coming to, if you go on like this, Oley. That's fair warning. You understand?"

Oley evidently realised that there was some possibility of escape offered to him. The threat of the reformatory had shaken him badly. He seemed to feel that anything was better than that.

"If you don't do anything to me this time, sir, I'll try to go straight. And I'll tell you anything you want to know; I will, really. I'll do anything you want, sir, if you'll let me off this time."

Sir Clinton examined him again in silence for a second or two, as if making up his mind.

"You haven't given us much satisfaction in the past, have you? No. Still, we'll give you this last chance, if you make a clean breast of things. Tell us exactly what happened that night."

Oley took out his handkerchief and blew his nose. Evidently he had been on the brink of tears, despite his obstinate front.

"I'll tell you what happened, sir. That evening, I said to our maids that I'd got a headache and was going to bed to try and sleep it off. I'd arranged to meet Polly Quickett at eight. When I heard the maids shut up in the back premises, I sneaked downstairs again and got out of the front door. I had tennis-shoes on, so I made no noise. I've got a latch-key and I could shut the front door without making any noise by slamming it; and the kitchen windows look out to the back, so the maids couldn't see me getting out. I met Polly where we'd fixed up to meet, at the drinking-fountain in Mapesbury Road. We'd arranged what we were going to do, take a bus out to the Half Way House and go to that bracken-patch that runs down from the Hermitage garden. We'd been there before once or twice, because nobody can see you there, amongst the bracken. So we took the tram, got off at the stage at the Half Way House and walked along the lane there, towards the railway. There was nobody in sight when we got there, so we cut up the slope and lay down amongst the bracken. . . ."

To Oley's evident relief, the Chief Constable had no immediate interest in the peccadillos of adolescents. He interrupted the boy's tale with a curt question:

"While you were there, did you see anybody in the neighbourhood?"

Oley hardly hesitated before answering:

"Just after we'd sat down, we saw two people—a man and a woman—drive up in a car on the lane below. They stopped the car and got out, but they didn't lock the doors or take away the ignition key."

"What time was that, do you know?" demanded the Chief Constable.

Oley, by this time, had recovered his courage, since he apparently realised that something more important was in view than his own escapade. He was evidently taking pains to give what evidence he could, with the hope of placating the Chief Constable by frankness.

"It was just a little after nine o'clock, sir. I know that, because we had to keep an eye on the time. I'd promised Polly that she'd be home before half-past ten at the very latest, so I was taking a look at my watch now and again."

"Was it still light enough to see things clearly?"

"Well, it was getting on for dusk, sir, but I could see fairly clearly."

"You could see that they didn't take the ignition key with them when they left the car?"

Oley hesitated before answering.

"Perhaps I was wrong about seeing that, sir. I think I must be thinking about what I found, later on. No, I didn't actually see that. But it was light enough to see that they didn't lock the car door. They stood beside the car for a little while, talking, and then they came up towards us. They didn't see us amongst the bracken, and they sat down quite close to us—about twenty yards or so away from us."

"Could you recognise them if you saw them again?" asked the Chief Constable.

"No, sir, I don't think I could. When they came near enough for that, Polly and I lay down amongst the bracken so as not to show ourselves, and so I didn't get a look at the two of them close at hand. The woman was wearing a dark dress, not black, but some dark stuff; and the man had a dark suit and was wearing a soft black felt hat—the kind that clergymen sometimes wear."

Sir Clinton was obviously not satisfied with this account.

"You've heard, of course, that the Rev. Mr. Barratt was found dead at that place," he said. "Now, be careful, Oley. Aren't you letting your memory get muddled up with what you've read in the newspapers? Wasn't it from them that you got this notion about a clergyman's hat?"

"No, sir, it wasn't," Oley declared definitely. "He was wearing a black hat, right enough. I'm dead sure of that."

Sir Clinton seemed satisfied by this.

"How were they walking, as they came up towards you? In Indian file?"

"Yes, sir. The bracken's very stiff. You have to force your way through it. I expect he went first to clear a path for her."

"Perhaps. Now what happened next?"

"I didn't like the two of them being so near us," Oley confessed, looking down at the carpet again and flushing. "I whispered to Polly that we'd better get out of that and go over to the spinney—you know the spinney, there, sir? So I told her to wait where she was for a minute or two, till I could be sure the coast was clear; and I set off, crawling through the bracken so as not to show myself."

"What did you do that for?" demanded Sir Clinton. "Why didn't you and the girl go together?"

"Because there's often a couple or two up there amongst the bracken and I didn't want to run any risk of blundering on top of them with Polly. You never know who may be in a place like that, and I didn't want to run any risk of Polly and me being recognised there together."

"Pity you don't use these wits of yours in a better cause," Sir Clinton commented drily. "What happened next."

Oley had by this time completely recovered his control and had evidently made up his mind that he was safeguarding himself by complete frankness.

"I crawled through the bracken, sir, keeping well under cover and making for the edge of the spinney. Once, behind me, I heard that woman cry out as if she was startled or frightened; but I didn't pay much attention to that, because one often hears girls squealing up there in the bracken when they go there along with men. I just thought they were having some fun."

"You didn't hear what she said?"

"No, I didn't. The bracken was rustling in my ears and by that time I was a good distance away. Then I heard a couple of thuds, but I took them for shots fired by somebody shooting rabbits, likely, and I paid no attention to them but just crawled on."

"You didn't come across any other couples in this exploration of yours?"

"No, sir. I was keeping a sharp look-out for that, of course. But there didn't seem to be anybody about. I was afraid the noise might bring old Kerrison down to investigate. He sometimes comes down and pokes about amongst the bracken in the dusk. Once he nearly caught Polly and me; and that gave us a fright, because he'd have been sure to report us, if he'd found us. But luckily he came across another couple and they nearly had a stand-up fight over some things he said, and after that he went away and I haven't seen him down in the bracken since then. But he might take it into his head to start his snooping again, so I was a bit anxious on that score."

"Well, go on," the Chief Constable ordered.

"When I got through the bracken without coming across

anyone, I gave Polly a whistle, so that she could follow along the track I'd left and be sure of not running into anyone. Then we went into the spinney. . . ."

"I'm not interested in your doings in the spinney," said Sir Clinton, "unless you heard anything more from the couple in the bracken."

"No, I didn't," said Oley, eagerly, "I didn't pay any attention to what they were doing."

"Then go on to the time you came out of the spinney," Sir Clinton ordered.

"I forgot to look at my watch," Oley confessed shamefacedly. "And when Polly looked at hers, later on, it was later than we thought. It was too late for us to get back to her house by bus and be there by half-past ten. And if she was later than that, there would have been a row, and we didn't want that at any price, of course. We didn't want her people starting to ask questions about where she'd been. She was in an awful state about it, and I didn't know what to do until I remembered about the car that the couple had left in the lane. When it came into my mind, I told Polly I'd get her home all right, and she was quite ready to do anything that would keep her out of a row. So we went down into the lane from the spinney, and we found the car standing there, just as I'd hoped."

"What time was that?"

"Just about ten o'clock, sir. I know that, because Polly had looked at her watch, as I told you. So we got into the car and I drove off, back to town. I had to hurry a bit, but I got Polly back before half-past ten all right. I dropped her quite close to her home. She stumbled over something as she got out. When she'd gone away, I looked to see what had caught her foot, and I found a small black bag on the floor of the car. It was heavy, and when I opened it I found a lot of money in it, mostly coppers. I wanted to buy some things, so I took the money and put it into my pockets and left the bag in the car."

"You don't seem to have stuck at much," said Sir Clinton, in no amiable tone. "Broken your word of honour, snatched a car, and gone in for petty theft. This has been a narrow squeak for you, Oley, and you'd better bear that in mind. But go on with your story."

"Well, sir," Oley continued, losing his assurance completely, "I'd snatched the car, so I thought I might as well get some fun out of it while I had it. Besides, I didn't want to go home till I was sure the maids had gone to bed and wouldn't hear me coming in. So I started driving about the country a bit to amuse myself and to pass the time. And then somewhere in Rickman's Lane a policeman whistled, and I thought I was for it. I didn't want to be caught, so when I got to Granby Holt, I ran the car into the wood a bit, meaning to leave it there. But there was an accident. I hit a fallen tree, somehow, and bled my nose in the smash-up. So after that I just left the car where it was and went home. It took me till well on in the morning to walk the distance, and I was dog-tired when I got home, for I didn't dare to ask anyone for a lift in case they began asking questions about what I was doing on the road at that time in the morning."

Oley paused, as if he imagined that he had given Sir Clinton all that was necessary.

"What became of the money you stole?" demanded the Chief Constable.

"Oh, the money? There wasn't much, sir, Under two pounds. I spent it buying some things for myself and things for Polly. It went in no time, and all I had left was a funny big silver coin, a thing I'd never seen before, with Victoria's head on it. I knew it was no use trying to pass it in the ordinary way. Nobody would know what it was, and they'd ask questions. I didn't like to take it to any of the curiosity shops for fear I might run across some shopman who happened to know me. And then I remembered a new man who'd opened a shop of that sort, a stranger who'd just come here to set up in business, and I thought he wasn't likely to know anything about me. So I sold it to him. Wilmot's his name, sir, I wish I hadn't; but I'd spent all the money I had, and I wanted money for the pictures, so I risked it."

Sir Clinton said nothing for several minutes. Oley, under the strain of this silence, shuffled slightly from one foot to the other and gazed hopelessly about the room, avoiding the glances of Wendover and the inspector. At last the Chief Constable seemed to make up his mind.

"You knew that Mrs. Callis had been murdered among the bracken that evening, Oley. It was in all the papers, and you couldn't have helped hearing about it. Why didn't you come forward and tell the police what you knew?"

Oley broke down completely at this renewal of the attack which he had imagined was over.

"How could I?" he retorted in an anguished voice, broken by gulps of terror. "I'd stolen that money I'd gone off in the car, I'd been with Polly. That would all have come out if I'd said a word about it. My father and mother would have known about me. And you said yourself that I'd have caught it from the police. I just *couldn't* do it. I did think about it, once or twice. I got Polly to swear that she wouldn't give us away. I've had the birch once, and I don't want it again. I simply wasn't going to run the risk."

"If you'd said you kept your mouth shut because of the girl, I might sympathise with you," said Sir Clinton. "But apparently your own skin was all you cared about. Not much need to waste words over you, Oley. Now the inspector will take you into another room and read you the notes he's made. You'll sign them. And, as we'll probably want you to give evidence, at the inquest, anyhow, you'd better see that none of these details slip out of your memory before then. Understand? Then perhaps we may not think it necessary to lay our hands on you over this stealing, and so on."

Oley listened to this with deepening anxiety.

"But, sir, does that mean that I'll have to tell all this before people? In public, I mean. I don't want to do that. It would mean that my father would get to know...."

"What does that matter to me?" asked Sir Clinton unsympathetically. "If you don't like your doings to come out in public, then mend your manners in future and you won't need to worry. You'll have to give evidence now, whether you like it or not. And, before I let you go, get it quite clear in your mind that if you ever so much as speak to Polly Quickett after this, you'll smart for it. Understand that? You'll get no further chance. Take him into the dining-room, inspector, please, and get rid of him as soon as possible."

When Rufford had gone out with the boy, Wendover turned to Sir Clinton.

"You let that unlicked cub off rather lightly, Clinton," he declared in a censorious tone. "He needs another dose of the birch. And the girl's younger still, isn't she?"

"Juliet was just under fourteen," Sir Clinton reminded him. "Romeo wasn't much older; and yet he managed to kill his man and commit suicide on account of his girl. Master Oley seems quite moderate in his doings, by comparison. A trifle sordid, I agree. Stealing pennies is a poor business. But we've got his evidence, which is the important matter."

Wendover shrugged his shoulders and decided not to continue the argument. The front door bell rang, and he expected to see someone ushered into the room.

"That's probably a constable in charge of young Miss Quickett," Sir Clinton surmised. "The inspector will bring her in, once he has done with her boy-friend. Shall I unleash the thunders on her, Squire, just to please you?"

"No, a girl's different," Wendover declared, true to his code.

"Well, we'll see what she's like," Sir Clinton conceded.

When, a few minutes later, Rufford ushered Polly Quickett

into their presence, Wendover summed her up at a glance. "A congenital *hetaira*," was his verdict, for even in his unspoken thoughts he preferred euphemisms to plainer but coarser expressions in some cases.

Polly Quickett looked older than her age. Wendover would have put her down as between seventeen and eighteen if he had not been forewarned. She was an obviously attractive girl; trim-figured, straight-backed, neat-legged, with a mass of naturally-curling brown hair and large brown eyes. But to Wendover's mind, she would have been better without the over-lavish application of rouge and lipstick at her age. In contrast to Oley, she seemed perfectly at her ease and showed not the slightest trace of timidity. She waited in silence, filling in the time by examining each man in turn with a steady, cataloguing gaze which ran slowly from head to heel.

"This is Polly Quickett, sir," explained Rufford, unnecessarily.

"What's your age?" asked Sir Clinton.

Polly seemed faintly surprised by this beginning. She opened her eyes more widely as she answered.

"I'll be sixteen in January."

"You arranged to meet young Oley the other night at the drinking-fountain in Mapesbury Road. What time did you meet him?"

"About eight o'clock, it was," Polly replied, composedly.

"You spent the rest of the evening in his company. Where did you go with him?"

"We took a bus to the Half Way House and after we got off, we went to a place down the lane, just below a house called the Hermitage."

"What happened after that?"

"We went up among the bracken."

Wendover could not refrain from giving Polly a good mark as a witness. She volunteered nothing, but she answered the questions promptly and concisely.

"Shortly after that, a car came along the lane," continued Sir Clinton. "What happened then?"

"A couple got out of it and stood for a moment or two on the road, a man and a woman."

"Did you notice how they were dressed?"

"It was coming on to twilight," Polly explained carefully. "I didn't see them as clearly as I see you, of course. The man had on a dark lounge suit and he was wearing a soft black felt hat. I noticed that, because most men wear the same kind of hat, only in fawn or grey. It was the kind of hat that clergymen sometimes wear."

"You're not saying that because you've heard about the Rev. Mr. Barratt having been there that night?"

"Oh, no," Polly declared definitely. "I saw it quite well at the time. The woman wasn't old—she seemed to be about twenty-five, I'd say, but it's only a guess—and she walked lightly, as if she'd plenty of go in her. She was wearing a dark coat and skirt, and light stockings. It was too dusky to tell exactly what colour her clothes really were, but I thought they were dark green. She wasn't wearing a fur or anything like that; the night was quite warm. Her hat probably matched her dress, but I couldn't see it clearly at that distance."

"What happened after they got out of the car?" asked Sir Clinton, evidently satisfied that Polly was a good witness who needed no prompting.

"They came up amongst the bracken and seemed to be making for where we were; but they stopped about twenty yards off, and sat down. Pat didn't like them being there, and he whispered to me that we'd better go off into the spinney. I was to wait a minute or two and then follow along his track. He went away and I sat there, waiting till he whistled to let me know it was all right. As I was waiting, I got such a fright. I heard the woman saying: 'No, no! Don't, John, *please* don't. . . . Oh!' And then came a couple of sounds like shots, one immediately after the other."

"You didn't hear any cry after the shots?" demanded Sir Clinton.

"No, nothing at all."

"You're sure you heard two shots? Only two?"

"Quite sure," said Polly, definitely. "And just then Pat whistled, and I began to creep through the bracken to join him. I didn't look back. It never entered my head that anyone had been shot, of course. All I thought was that somebody was letting off a pistol and that a bullet might come in my direction. I just wanted to get away to a safe place as quick as I could."

"Why didn't you stand up and let them see you, if you thought the pistol was just fired for fun?"

"Because Pat and I weren't supposed to be seeing each other, and if I'd stood up, these people might have wanted to know what I was doing there, and who was with me."

"You were in that spinney for a while. Then you came out again. What time was that?"

"I looked at my watch just before that, and it was a minute or two to ten. I'm quite sure of that, because I wanted to be home by half-past ten at the latest, and we couldn't have managed it by walking and taking the bus back. I was very worried about the time. That's why I remember it."

"What did you do then?"

"Pat saw I was anxious, and he said the only thing to do was to snatch that car the couple had left in the lane and use it to get me home in. He's mad about driving cars, and of course he's too young to have a licence except for a motor-cycle. He's done car-snatching before, and he can drive well enough, though he goes far too fast sometimes and takes risks. There didn't seem anything else for it, so we went down and took away the car. And that's a funny thing. I was almost sure that when we saw the couple leave the car, it was left just as they drove up; I mean it faced the bridge under the railway. But when we got to it, they'd turned it round so that it faced towards the Half Way House. They must have done that while we were in the spinney, I expect. We kept a sharp look-out as we were getting in; but by that time it was pretty dark and probably they didn't see us until the car had got started, and Pat drove off as hard as he could."

"They didn't call after you? You didn't hear any sound, while you were at the car?"

Polly shook her head decidedly.

"Not a sound. I'd have noticed it, because I was in a bit of a state lest they'd catch us before we got away."

"You got home again in time?"

"Yes, Pat drove pretty fast into town. He dropped me near our house, and went off by himself in the car."

"You learned, later on, that Mrs. Callis had been shot, up in the bracken? Why didn't you come forward at once and tell this story?"

"I wanted to; but Pat got into a blue funk about it and persuaded me to keep quiet. You see, he'd promised that he wouldn't go about with me, and he went on and went on about how he'd get into terrible trouble if I said anything to anyone. I didn't like it. I knew I ought to own up about the whole affair. But I couldn't very well let Pat down, and he insisted on my keeping quiet. We had long arguments about it, for I felt miserable over the business. I knew I ought to own up. So at last I gave in and promised that I wouldn't say anything off my own bat; but if the police got to know about our being there, then I'd tell the truth about it all when I was questioned. I don't think he'd the least fear that the police would find out about us, so he seemed quite satisfied with that arrangement."

"And that's the whole story, is it?"

"Everything I can remember just now; and if anything else comes back to me, I'll be sure to tell you about it. I only want to be quite straight, now that it's all come out. And . . . you won't do anything to Pat, will you? I know we oughtn't to have been going about together, after what he promised. But he's keen on me, and perhaps it isn't really his fault. I wanted to see him as much as he wanted to see me. I put myself in his way. It wasn't really his blame, altogether."

"You'll have to repeat this evidence in public," Sir Clinton warned her.

"That'll be beastly," Polly confessed, ruefully, but looking him straight in the eyes. "But I don't mind, if only you'll not be hard on Pat."

"You see how this sort of thing ends up," Sir Clinton pointed out. "Now, Polly, will you promise to see nothing more of Oley in future? If you do, and if you give your evidence when it's wanted, I'll do my best for you. It's a bit hard on your parents, though, isn't it?"

"Oh, I've been a little beast, I know I have," Polly admitted with a gulp. "But if you'll not be hard on Pat, I'll take my share of the blame. And I promise I won't see him again —I mean I won't have anything more to do with him after this."

"Not till the parents of both of you agree, anyhow," suggested Sir Clinton. "Now, Inspector Rufford's been taking notes. He'll read them over to you and you'll sign them. After that, he'll see you get safe home. I'm not going to say I admire your doings, Polly, but I wish you luck, if you keep that promise."

CHAPTER XIV

DEATH CALLS AGAIN

"THAT boy Oley's a rank bad lot, without a redeeming characteristic," declared Wendover, when Inspector Rufford had retired with his charge. "But I couldn't help liking that little girl. In some ways, she's a bad lot, too; but she gave me the impression that she was very straight in others. She was obviously out to tell the truth, cost what it might; and that's a good trait. And she seemed anxious to shield the boy, so far as she could, which is more than he thought of doing for her. You showed more consideration than I expected, Clinton, when you started in to question her."

"I'm sorry for her, in a way," Sir Clinton admitted, lightly. "She's a physiological misfit. She's developed quicker on one side than on the other, and our system frowns on that kind of lop-sidedness. She'll make a better witness than that hangdog companion of hers; and that's what counts, so far as I'm concerned."

He took a fresh cigarette from the box near him.

"Now, Squire," he continued, "you've got the whole evidence up to the stop press news. What do you make of it all? I'd like to hear your views."

"I'd like to hear yours," retorted Wendover.

"You'll hear 'em in good time," the Chief Constable assured him. "But remember that I'm paid, in part, to keep my mouth shut until the right time comes. Besides, I got in first with my request."

"I suppose you're going to treat this Barratt affair in the same way as you handled that business of Hassendean and

Mrs. Silverdale," said Wendover. "Given two deaths which might be due to accident, or suicide, or murder. Take all the possible combinations, and there are nine possible solutions. Eliminate the wrong 'uns, *à la* Sherlock Holmes, and the last remaining one must be correct. Is that what you're doing in this Barratt affair?"

Sir Clinton lit his cigarette before answering.

"No," he explained, as he put the spent match in his ash-tray. "I think we could do better by falling back on a little rhyme that you've heard before. I'll repeat it, just to get our minds clear:

"What was the crime? Who did it?
When was it done? And where?
How done? And with what motive?
Who in the deed did share?"

"That puts the trouble in a nutshell, Squire. It ought to be the Manhunter's Manual or Criminologist's Constant Companion, as Peter would say. That mannerism of his is infectious, evidently; for I don't talk alliteratively, as a general rule. Well, now, Squire. There are seven simple questions to answer."

"Before I heard the evidence of these two youngsters," Wendover admitted, "I thought it was a very complex affair. But from what they told us, it seems much simpler than I supposed. The wrecked car, the blood on its floor, the disappearance of the cash from the bag: these things all worried me. But now they're out of the picture. One doesn't need to bother about them. That clears the board considerably."

"No doubt," Sir Clinton acquiesced, gravely. "But it leaves a good deal still cumbering the ground. Don't evade the issue, Squire. Question number one: 'What was the crime?' Speak up promptly, since you're so sure about it all."

"There were *two* crimes," Wendover pointed out. "Barratt and Mrs. Callis were both found dead."

"True, Squire. But let's take them one at a time, if you don't mind. Ladies first. How did Mrs. Callis come by her end?"

"Murder," Wendover declared without hesitation. "She was shot; the bullet that killed her had the rifling-marks of a certain pistol; that pistol was found close to Barratt's hand; and the only finger-prints showing on it were Barratt's."

"H'm!" said Sir Clinton in a reflective tone. "Closely reasoned from your premises, Squire. And on that basis you've given your answer to the second question also. 'What was the crime?' The killing of Mrs.Callis. 'Who did it?' Barratt. As you say, it's a simple matter; there are really no difficulties. Now what about the third question: 'When was it done?'"

Wendover did not hesitate for more than a second before replying.

"A little after nine o'clock," he said, confidently. "The boy Oley gave us the time almost exactly; and he'd just looked at his watch, you remember. It obviously happened when the girl heard Mrs. Callis cry out: 'Don't, please don't!' Clearly she'd seen Barratt aiming the pistol at her; and the two shots followed immediately after that cry of hers. That was Polly Quickett's evidence; and she was telling the truth, I'm quite convinced of that. Besides, Oley confirmed what she said. He heard the woman's voice, though he didn't catch her words; and he heard the two shots, though he said he took them for rabbit-shooting. That's two witnesses, supporting each other. And I don't think there was any collusion between them about the kind of tale they were going to tell."

"No," agreed Sir Clinton. "I believe the girl was telling the plain truth, anyhow; and the boy's story fits in well enough."

"One shot killed Mrs. Callis," Wendover went on, "and

the second shot was the one when Barratt committed suicide."

"M'yes," said Sir Clinton in the tone of a man not wholly convinced. "But you're missing out Kerrison's evidence. He heard a couple of shots—or he said he did, anyhow—about ten o'clock. What about them?"

"Kerrison himself said—or so you told me, at any rate—that he thought they came from someone shooting rabbits in the spinny," objected Wendover rather testily.

"I'm struggling to keep an open mind about the existence of that convenient rabbit-shooter," said Sir Clinton slyly. "But despite all my efforts, I can't help feeling that he's like Mrs. Harris. 'There ain't no sich a person livin'.'"

"Oh, that's quite unwarranted, quite unwarranted," declared Wendover, heatedly. "After all, Kerrison's an uncorroborated witness. No one else heard these shots at ten o'clock."

"We've unearthed no one who heard them," rectified Sir Clinton, with the glimmer of a smile. "But having myself seen four cartridge-cases, collected from the ground beside the bodies, I'm inclined to think that four shots were fired there. To fill the bill, according to your hypothesis, Barratt must have sat up after he was dead and given two extra pulls on his trigger. And the resulting shots made no noise, since Polly Quickett, close at hand, heard only two reports. It doesn't sound wholly convincing to me, Squire. My sceptical mind, and all that. I prefer to believe that two and two make four, as I was taught at school."

"I'd forgotten these cartridge-cases, for the moment," Wendover confessed, with a crestfallen air. "Four shots, eh? I suppose one can't get over that."

"One can't," Sir Clinton assured him, with mock sympathy.

Wendover, through sheer obstinacy, was still bent on backing his own hypothesis.

"Well, here's a possibility," he said, after a few seconds reconsideration. "We're dealing with the murder of Mrs.

Callis, aren't we? and not Barratt's death. It was a lonely place, but there was always the chance of some people being about—as that boy and girl actually were. Barratt may have fired two shots at random, just to see if they brought anyone down on him. Nobody came. That showed the coast was clear. After that he could shoot Mrs. Callis without fear of interruption."

"I hate to say it," said Sir Clinton, "but really that's hardly one of your best efforts, Squire. In fact, it's a dud. First of all, what about the words that Polly Quickett heard."

"You mean her exclamation to Barratt: 'No! Don't John, please don't.' Obviously that was just a protest against his firing at random. Polly Quickett took that view, remember, and she actually heard the words spoken."

"She imitated the voice," Sir Clinton pointed out, "and I got the impression that she was mimicking somebody in a state of terror. But there's another objection. If these two shots were fired merely to make sure that the coast was clear, why fire a couple. One would have been sufficient. And if he fired the two shots for that purpose, why didn't he fire the two fatal shots almost immediately afterwards? On your assumptions, he waited almost an hour; and the fatal shots were those heard by Kerrison at ten o'clock. But between nine and ten, a whole host of fresh visitors might have swarmed into that vicinity, for all he could tell. There was no point whatever in firing two shots and then waiting for an hour before firing the second pair. And he didn't fire four shots close together, or Polly Quickett would certainly have heard more than the couple that she did hear. Finally, if Barratt meant to commit suicide immediately after he'd shot Mrs. Callis, what did it matter to him whether anyone heard the first shot and came down upon him? He'd be dead himself by that time, and past caring. No, it won't do, Squire. You don't get full marks for that question. But let's go on to the next one: 'Where was it done?' That's an easier one."

"It was done amongst the bracken in that lovers' nook," said Wendover, sure of his ground. "That's as clear as can be. The positions of the bodies, the pistol, the empty cartridge-cases, the fact that they had a car to take them there—it all points to the one conclusion."

"Don't let's quarrel over it," said the Chief Constable. "Now, the fifth question: 'How done?'"

"With that pistol that Rufford found near Barratt's body, of course," said Wendover, rather contemptuously. "The bullet that killed her had its rifling-marks on the casing. You're not going to deny that, are you?"

"A pistol," said the Chief Constable, with wilful pedantry, "is a complicated mechanism actuated by a trigger. When the trigger is pulled, a spring is released which drives a striker-pin against the percussion-cap of a cartridge. An explosion follows, which propels a bullet along a barrel; and in its passage through this barrel the casing of the bullet is engraved with marks scored upon it by the lands and grooves of the barrel. Unless some intelligent or unintelligent agent moves the trigger, the mechanism of the pistol remains inactive...."

"Oh, if you want to refine down to that extent," Wendover interrupted impatiently, "I'll say it was done by Barratt pulling the trigger of the pistol found beside his body. Will *that* satisfy you?"

"If it satisfies you, we'll let it go at that," said Sir Clinton, with a twinkle in his eye. "There's nothing like being contented. So few people are, in this world. But now, Squire, we come to the crux, nub, or teaser. Question number six. 'With what motive?' Answer me that, if you please."

But here Wendover obviously felt at a loss.

"There are several possible motives," he said dubitatively. "It's just here that I feel things don't fit neatly together."

"Well, mention one or two motives," said Sir Clinton encouragingly. "They can't all be correct, you know. Some of your collection must have a screw loose in them, if one looks carefully. Produce them, and we'll put them under the magnifying glass."

"It's very complicated," complained Wendover. "And yet some things seem beyond doubt. It couldn't be money at stake. Killing Mrs. Callis wouldn't put a penny into Barratt's pocket; that certain."

"Unless she'd made a will in his favour," Sir Clinton pointed out. "We'll need to look into that, by and by. But Barratt, from all I've heard about him, was hardly mercenary. Even his uncle-in-law, who had no love for him, declared that he was devoid of the money-sense. And friend Alvington was a good judge of that, I'd say. No, Barratt wasn't the man to commit a murder merely to fill his own pocket. I'll do him that amount of justice. Now, what else can you suggest, Squire?"

"I can't see how it could have been done as a matter of revenge for anything," Wendover continued, "unless you couple that with jealousy, and then it would point to her husband. But Callis wasn't jealous. Rufford made a point of it that Callis believes strongly in his wife's innocence, even in the face of the facts."

"I'm inclined to accept Rufford's ideas, so far as that goes," said the Chief Constable. "He's not a bad judge of such things, I've noticed; and I could infer something of the sort from one or two bits in the evidence as well."

"But Callis wasn't the only man in the world," Wendover pursued, evidently growing more pleased with his idea. "Is it possible that while she was philandering with Barratt, she fell in love with somebody else? You've got to account for that sudden change in the elopement plans. Suppose that, at the last moment, when she was faced with the choice between Barratt and this other man, she decided to give Barratt the go-by."

"And Barratt, in a rage, murdered her? It's possible. But on that basis it's difficult to see why she was so thoughtful as to bring the pistol with her," Sir Clinton pointed out with owlish solemnity. "That would indicate a combination of foresight and indulgence which, really, I find incredible, Squire."

"She may have meant to break off with Barratt at the last moment, and been afraid of his turning nasty," said Wendover, fighting hard for his hypothesis. "The pistol was taken to be used for self-defence if he cut up rusty when she gave him his dismissal. All we know about him indicates that he was a man who was set on having his own way."

"No good," said Sir Clinton flatly. "If she'd been afraid of anything of the kind, she'd never have gone with him to a lonely place like the lover's nook. She'd have had it out with him at the station, with plenty of people ready to protect her if he cut up rough on being dismissed. From all I can gather, she was no fool. You're on the wrong track there, Squire, I'm quite certain of that. Any further suggestions?"

"I suppose that disposes of jealousy, revenge, and diasppointed passion, then, as motives," said Wendover reluctantly. "Mind, Clinton, I'm not sure I agree with you in what you say. But even so, I'm not at the end of my tether yet. What about an attack of religious mania brought on by long brooding over their affairs? A sense of guilt becoming overpowering at the last moment, I mean. Originally, they were both churchy people; and religious feeling and sex get queerly mixed up at times. At the eleventh hour she may have come to her senses, if you like to put it so, and decided that she was too wicked to live any longer. Hence the pistol. And if Barratt was suffering from the same kind of qualms, a murder and a suicide wouldn't be so very improbable."

"Now, Squire, that's damned ingenious," admitted Sir Clinton without reserve. "I give you full marks for that notion. In fact, I rather wish I'd thought of it myself, it's so good. Almost thou persuadest me . . . but not quite. Sorry, but it won't do."

"Why not?" demanded Wendover, in a tone which showed clearly his disappointment at this cavalier dismissal of his idea. "Psychologically there's nothing against it. Things do sometimes work out like that in some minds."

"See Sunday papers, *passim*," retorted the Chief Constable. "I'm not denying that it's an ingenious notion, Squire. But did you ever read Huxley? Remember his definition of the tragedy of science: a beautiful theory killed by an ugly fact. Well, your beautiful theory has to die the death; and the ugly fact is the discovery of those four empty cartridge-cases. You can't fit them into this pretty notion about a psychological catastrophe. Sad, I admit. But there it is. Any other suggestions?"

Wendover was nettled, seeing his theory so summarily discarded. He pondered for a full minute before speaking. Then he hit upon the idea which Rufford had evolved at an earlier period.

"What about all this hypnotic stuff?" he asked, though with no great assurance in his tone. "Could Barratt have hypnotised her and used his control of her to make her fall in with this elopement plan? And then, perhaps, she broke free from his control and he saw himself faced with a fearful scandal unless he silenced her. And once he'd shot her, in a storm of rage, he'd find that suicide was the only way out. He *could* hypnotise her, according to the evidence of wholly independent witnesses."

Sir Clinton shook his head at once.

"No use, Squire. Same old fact: the four cartridge-cases. They don't square with this notion any better than they did with your other ones."

"Then I give it up," admitted Wendover disconsolately.

"I'll tell you where you went off the rails," said the Chief Constable, putting away the stub of his cigarette and helping himself from the box beside him. "You confessed, a few minutes ago, that you thought this was a complex affair, but you'd changed your mind after hearing the evidence of

Oley and Polly Quickett. They convinced you that it was just a plain case of suicide pact, didn't they? And I believe their evidence was accurate enough. But your interpretation of it has brought you into a blind alley. Well, now, as in the Ludo of our nursery days, you've got to go back four squares and start afresh. It's a plain case of murder. I knew that as soon as I went through the evidence Rufford collected in his initial burst of energy. I'm not going into details about that just now. But suppose you begin on the assumption of murder committed, and let's hear what you make of it."

"Very well," agreed Wendover. "Take your questions as before. 'What was the crime?' Murder, you say. Pass that, then. 'Who did it?' is the next question. You want to make out that *both* of them were murdered?"

"If you please," said the Chief Constable equivocally, though Wendover failed to notice the ambiguity of the phrase.

"That means the intervention of a third party," Wendover proceeded with rising interest as he found himself tackling a fresh problem.

"If you please," repeated Sir Clinton.

"That limits me down to certain known persons," Wendover declared, with some satisfaction at the manner in which he was developing the theme. "It's a short list: the two Alvingtons, Mrs. Barratt, Callis, Kerrison, young Oley, Polly Quickett, Mrs. Longnor, that organist—I forget his name—Maud Endell, the Callis's maid, Miss Legard of the Jubilee double-florin, and some other people who obviously have only the remotest connection with the affair. Now we can safely eliminate all but seven of these."

"Do so, then," suggested Sir Clinton, encouragingly. "Just give me the residual names to save time."

"The Alvingtons, Mrs. Barratt, Callis, Kerrison, Mrs. Longnor, and Maud Endell," said Wendover, ticking them off on his fingers.

"Why leave Maud Endell on the list?" inquired the Chief Constable.

"Because she might have had access to Callis's little armoury and got hold of the pistol," retorted Wendover. "I'm including everybody who might have been interested."

"Why Mrs. Longnor?"

"Because we've only got her word for it that . . ." began Wendover. "Oh, no, I forgot. She wasn't in town that day. Leave her out, then."

"Now, take them in turn and let's hear what you have against each of them."

"Very well." Wendover settled himself comfortably in his chair. "Arthur Alvington. He disliked Barratt, personally. He was evidently perturbed lest Barratt should wangle old Mrs. Alvington into leaving her money to the Awakened Israelites instead of to her own kin. And from what I've heard about Mr. Arthur, that seems to be a pretty strong incentive. I don't say he did it. I'm just taking the facts as we know them. Finally, he has an alibi; but it depends on his brother's word."

"Correct," agreed Sir Clinton. "Now what about the said brother?"

"He obviously hated Barratt, who'd persuaded Mrs. Alvington to alter her will and to cut out Edward Alvington from it. Also, Barratt had hounded him out of the church and caused him annoyance by that. The Alvingtons' sensitive spot is cash, and it's very sensitive. Edward has an alibi; but it depends on his brother's word. Either of them might be shielding the other for all we can tell."

"Pass that," conceded Sir Clinton. "Now what about Mrs. Barratt? She, being a woman, you'll be tempted to let her down lightly, Squire. Play fair."

"Well, she and Barratt were entirely unsuited to each other," said Wendover. "She was obviously tired of him, to put it mildly. Also, the Alvingtons seem a rather clannish crew, and no doubt she disliked the part Barratt had played in the matter of her uncle. And if Barratt wangled the old lady's will, Mrs. Barratt was going to be a sufferer just as much as her Uncle Arthur. But she has an alibi outside the family. Callis was with her, waiting for Barratt, on the night of the crime."

"You've forgotten two other bits of evidence," Sir Clinton volunteered. "At shortly before nine o'clock that night, Mrs. Barratt rang up a Mrs. Stacey about some bridge engagement. There's no doubt about that call; we've checked it by asking Mrs. Stacey. And at ten-fifteen, Miss Legard rang up Barratt's house, trying to get hold of Barratt and tell him about her precious Jubilee double-florin, since she'd missed him after the meeting in the church hall. Mrs. Barratt answered the phone. Miss Legard recognised her voice. We've checked that also."

"So you suspected Mrs. Barratt of telling lies?" said Wendover, with a sharp glance at the Chief Constable.

"We check everything that we possibly can, as well you know, Squire. There's nothing in that except routine. And, as you see, our checking proved that Mrs. Barratt was actually at home that evening; so I don't see what objection you can take."

"Oh, none," admitted Wendover. "It seems quite satisfactory."

"It is," said Sir Clinton. "Now, let's see who's left. Callis is next on your list, isn't he?"

"Callis is a doubtful character," said Wendover, with a certain amount of hesitation. "The pistol came from his collection. He called Rufford's attention to that himself, quite voluntarily. And that's a point in his favour; for without his doing so, it would have taken a lot of trouble to identify that weapon as his property. You might not have managed it, if you'd been left to yourselves."

"Pass that," Sir Clinton agreed.

"Well, on the face of it, Callis is the man with the strongest motive amongst the lot, if he knew that his wife was philandering with Barratt."

"I don't think he knew that," said Sir Clinton, promptly, rather to Wendover's surprise. "But go on; don't let's get led up side trails for the present, Squire. What else have you to say about him?"

"He didn't get on with Barratt, that's plain. There was that organist's story about their squabbling."

"But Callis made that up, as the organist told me. And Callis went round that night to see Barratt, according to Mrs. Barratt's evidence. I'd rule that disagreement out as a murder-motive, Squire, or else I shall have to go armed every time you and I don't see eye to eye. I often see a nasty look on your face when I happen to disagree with you. Anything further about Callis?"

"Well, he has an alibi. He was at Barratt's house when the murder was done."

"That's Mrs. Barratt's evidence. So she gives him an alibi and he gives her one. In fact, it's just the case of Messrs. E. and A. Alvington over again, so far as that goes. Except, as you pointed out, that in the Alvington case it's all in the family. That leaves you with Maud Endell. What about her?"

"She had access to the pistol," said Wendover. "And you haven't proved an alibi for her yet."

"Ah! No alibi, therefore guilty, eh? There are about forty-five million people in this country. How many of them could prove an alibi for that particular stretch of time? Could you establish one for yourself, Squire? Really, you must be growing desperate. Anything else against her? Remember," he added, impishly, "she's a pretty girl. Rufford mentioned that to me, and Rufford's quite a good judge of beauty, I'm told."

"If you're suggesting that she and Callis were having an intrigue and that it furnishes a motive . . ." began Wendover, indignantly.

"I'm not suggesting anything of the sort. I don't know. But I dare say we can find out," said the Chief Constable in an ominous tone. "But you've still got one name on your list, haven't you?"

"Kerrison?" said Wendover. "Oh, I've nothing much to say about him. He's got a slate off, from all I can see; and he's apt to get into a passion over any sweethearting he comes across, to judge by the evidence."

"And he's got no alibi," Sir Clinton reminded him.

"You've just been poking fun at the lack of an alibi," said Wendover tartly. "You can't expect to have it both ways, Clinton. But seriously, Kerrison's of no importance, really."

"Think so?" Sir Clinton retorted, lazily. "Have it your own way. Personally, I attach a good deal of importance to Kerrison. It's not often that one meets a man who'll own up to a mistake without being pressed to do it. And besides, look at his researches on the Great Pyramid and the Lost Tribes and the Inch. Say what you like, he's got more originality than all the rest of them put together."

"Lunacy and originality aren't quite the same thing," commented Wendover, in a testy tone.

"Oh, it's too late to start arguing about philology at this time of night," protested Sir Clinton. "Let's go back two squares. 'Who did it?' You've dragged a lot of red herrings across the trail, Squire, but what I want is the fox's brush and mask as a guarantee of good faith. Have you the foggiest notion who did it?"

"Have you?" retorted Wendover, restively.

"A glimmering, perhaps."

"Moonshine, probably," said Wendover scornfully. "That's why you're so pleased with Kerrison, I suppose. They call lunatics Minions of the Moon, don't they?"

"Then I shall pay a special visit to one of the moon's minions to-morrow, Squire. I won't tease you any more, honour bright. But just look at three of our exhibits."

He went across to his desk, extracted from a drawer the

large folder containing the evidence in the Barratt case, and returned to his chair with three sheets of paper.

"Here's number one," he said, handing a sheet to Wendover. "It's an anonymous letter which Callis gave Rufford. The usual kind of thing: '*Watch your wife and you'll see what other people have seen long ago. A preacher ought to set a better example. There's a plain hint for you. . . .*' and so on."

"Some dirty dog at work," commented Wendover with a grimace of disgust. "I see you've been trying to develop finger-prints on it."

"You needn't trouble about them; they're nothing but blurs," Sir Clinton explained. "We couldn't find a clear impression amongst the lot. What I want you to look at is the watermark on the paper."

"Picture of some bird," Wendover reported, after holding the sheet up to the light for examination. "And the lettering is AVIAN WOVE, manufactured by A. Vian & Co., Liverpool."

"Compare this one," directed Sir Clinton, handing over a similar sheet.

"Same watermark," Wendover reported, after examining the two sheets side by side. "What's this second sheet?"

"It's one I got from Kerrison on the excuse of making him write down a list of the people who were present at a hypnotic display that Barratt gave. Now here's a third specimen. It's an official form of application for a fire-arms certificate, and I asked Kerrison specially to fill in his name and address in block letters, because I wanted to compare his capital lettering with the block letters in this anonymous '*Watch your wife . . .*' production. Have a look at the two of them, side by side, Squire."

Wendover made the comparison with some care.

"He's given himself away completely," he declared in a tone of satisfaction. "A schoolboy could spot that these were both written by the same man."

"Pretty obvious," agreed Sir Clinton. "Of course he was hardly likely to remember about the capital letters in the anonymous letter when he was filling in an innocent-looking official form where it's usual to insist on block lettering for the name and address."

"So Kerrison wrote that anonymous letter, evidently?"

"No doubt about it. After that, Squire, don't you think he's worth a call? I certainly do. And while I'm at his house, I think we'll try to unearth something further."

"What?" asked Wendover, eagerly.

"Two dead cats," returned Sir Clinton with an unconcealed grin.

"What on earth do you want to dig up dead cats for?" demanded Wendover in amazement. "A filthy job; and I don't see what it can lead to."

"Neither do I," admitted the Chief Constable, with disarming frankness. "But Rufford prides himself on his expertise in the matter of bullets, so it will please him to have another specimen or two to play with. And by that time, he and a constable will have got into nice practice for digging, so I'll find them another job in the same line, I think. If one goes on digging long enough, one's almost sure to discover something interesting. Australia, perhaps."

"You seem to be planning a busy morning," said Wendover sardonically. "Sure you haven't forgotten anything?"

"I have," said Sir Clinton. "I ought to have mentioned that I'm going to have a look at the stationers' shops in town. I'm running a bit short of note-paper. You must have been writing a lot of letters while you've been here, Squire. . . . Hello! There's the phone!"

He went over to the instrument, picked up the receiver, listened almost without comment to the message. Then putting down the instrument, he turned to Wendover.

"I'll have to change and go out, Squire. No. It's no use your coming; and you needn't sit up. I've no notion when

I can get back. And if I don't see you at breakfast, I'll tell you all about it after dinner to-morrow."

"What's happened?" demanded Wendover, noticing the intentness of the Chief Constable's expression.

"Kerrison's been killed—a motor accident. I was a fool not to have tackled him before this, but it's no use crying over spilt milk now. See you at dinner to-morrow, if not before."

CHAPTER XV

JUGGERNAUT

THROUGH all the next day, Wendover had to bridle his curiosity as best he could. Sir Clinton, he learned, had returned early in the morning, had taken a hasty breakfast before his guest was afoot, and had gone out again at once. And in the evening he appeared only in time to dress for dinner. During that meal, Wendover did not venture to draw his host, knowing that he would say nothing of importance before the waiting servants. It was only after he and the Chief Constable had settled down in the smoking-room that he ventured to put the questions which were burning his tongue.

"Well?" he demanded. "What's happened to Kerrison?"

"Kerrison? I really don't know," said Sir Clinton callously. "It depends on what view one takes of our post-mortem condition. Perhaps he's joined the choir of the immortal dead and is busy telling them all about the Great Pyramid. Or he may be giving Charon a tip or two about the Inch while they paddle on the Styx and Acheron. Don't ask me. He's dead, and I told you that last night, Squire."

"No need to be so unfeeling about it," Wendover commented in a tone of disapproval.

"I don't pretend to like white slavers, blackmailers, murderers, or the writers of anonymous letters," retorted Sir Clinton cheerfully. "And, as you saw last night, Kerrison sent off at least one anonymous letter with the plain object of stirring up trouble. I shan't bother my florist over *his* funeral. Now if you care to ask me how he came by his end, that's another matter, and I'll tell you with pleasure. It's quite simple, so I'll make a plain tale of it."

He took a cigarette and lighted it before continuing.

"Last night, after dinner, the late Kerrison had some business which took him into town. His house, you may remember, stands just above that bracken-patch we've heard so much about lately; but there's no road down from it on that side, so he doesn't use the lane to the Half-Way House when he wants to take a bus. Instead, he has to go by the road on the other side of his house, which takes him to the bus-route in seven minutes, as he explained to me once. I've been along that road in daylight. It's lonely, no houses about, no foot-path; and steep turf banks topped by hedges cut it off from the fields on either side. It lands you out at a bus-stop further away from town than the one at the Half-Way house. We've got hold of various bus-drivers and conductors on that route, and two of them remember seeing a dark-blue car standing at the kerb, just short of the bus-stop, with its headlights on. As there's a ten-minutes service on that route, you'll perceive immediately that this car must have been waiting for at least ten minutes, since two buses came up while it was there. Kerrison got off the second bus. The conductor recognised him, as Kerrison travels fairly regularly by that line. That was about 10.30 p.m. or a shade later. The driver of the next bus didn't see any blue car waiting there."

"Did Kerrison get into the blue car?" interjected Wendover.

Sir Clinton shook his head.

"No, the bus conductor noticed that he didn't. He turned out of the main road into the side one just as the bus started. He was the only passenger to get off the bus at that stop."

"Well, go on," said Wendover.

"The next witnesses are a young fellow and his fiancée. They're quite respectable people, Curious, in this case,

Squire, how often we seem to find the actors running in couples. These two had been for a walk along this side-road—it goes a good way past Kerrison's house—and had sat down by the road-side for a few minutes before going back to the bus route. 'Parting is such sweet sorrow, etc.' as Juliet said. They heard someone coming along the road from the bus route. It was pretty gloomy by that time; but this passer-by had the courtesy to stop and call out to them: 'Haven't you anything better to do at this time of night than to sit there? Get away home with you!' Which I recognise at once, Squire, as the true Kerrison touch. They ignored him, which was the best thing to do; and he lumbered off, muttering to himself.

"Just at that moment, they heard a car start up and, after turning into the by-road, accelerate like fury. You know some cars can get up to fifty in a few seconds from a standing start. This was one of them. It came flying along the road, headlights on, and passed them like a flash. It had no tail-light burning, so they couldn't have seen its number even if they'd wanted to. They heard a yell of dismay, then a thud, and the car went tearing on without so much as slowing down."

"Did they see the driver at all?" queried Wendover.

"No, not enough even to say whether it was a man or a woman at the wheel. Young Loraine—that's the man's name—realised that there had been a bad smash, and very wisely he told his fiancée to stay where she was, while he went to investigate. He found Kerrison dead in a pool of blood. Or rather, he found a stranger, since he didn't know Kerrison. One look by the light of a match was about all that young Loraine wanted; but he was lucky enough to spot a side-lamp which had evidently been wrenched off in the collision. Then he bolted back to his fiancée and the two of them legged it for the bus route where there's a public telephone kiosk not far down the road. Young Loraine phoned up the police. Then he put his girl aboard the next town-going bus and waited at the kiosk until one of our squads arrived in a car. They took over."

"Evidently a young man with his head well screwed on," commended Wendover. "And what happened after that?"

"A routine all-stations call warning everyone to look out for a car minus a side-lamp, obviously," said Sir Clinton. "Unfortunately, it didn't reach all our patrols until a little time had elapsed, or we'd have caught the driver *en route*. Still, we can't complain of our luck. One constable spotted a car driving with headlights on but no second side-light. He couldn't stop it; but its tail-lamp was lit up and he got the number; and as soon as he got the all-stations' message he guessed that this was probably the car we wanted. So he got on to us at once from the nearest phone-box and gave us the number he'd noted. It was the number of Arthur Alvington's car, as we found on looking it up."

"Ah!" said Wendover, with satisfaction. "That looks like business."

"It depends on what you call business," retorted the Chief Constable. "We wasted no time, anyhow. I descended on Arthur Alvington instanter, and found him at home along with his brother. I asked to see his car, a request which seemed to take him by surprise. However, there was nothing for it; and he took us round to his garage in the garden. The door was locked, as I was careful to ascertain by trying it before he could put a paw on it. He produced his key, opened the door, switched on the lights—and there was a dark-blue car with one of the side-lamps torn away. Friend Alvington gave an excellent display of amazement. He seemed quite taken aback by this state of affairs. The car had been all right when he put it into the garage on coming home. He couldn't understand it, and so on and so forth. Very natural behaviour, in the circumstances, one imagines."

"Very natural," echoed Wendover, sceptically. "And what next?"

"We got down to dots," continued Sir Clinton. "I need

hardly say that he denied having had the car out. He knew nothing about the affair at all, nothing whatever. His maid had gone out after dinner. About 8 p.m. Callis rang up on business. But friend Arthur had an alibi. His dear brother and he had spent the evening in the same room. They'd not heard anything amiss. Each of them was prepared to swear hard that the other hadn't been out of his sight for five minutes since dinner-time."

"Did you detain them?" demanded Wendover.

"What could I detain them for?" asked the Chief Constable. "We've had one car-snatching episode in this case already and that's enough to make one think a bit before one acts."

"But in the Alvington case the car was in a locked garage," objected Wendover. "That's entirely different from a car lifted from the roadside, the way young Oley did."

"Have it your own way, Squire," said Sir Clinton acidly. "No doubt you'd have lodged the two brothers Alvington under lock and key and landed yourself in for an action for wrongful arrest, if things went askew."

"But you've left them in a position to make a get-away," protested Wendover. "They could get off in that car, once your back was turned."

"I don't think so," Sir Clinton said, soothingly. "Not after I'd taken out the distributor arm. And I left a man on duty to watch the car—and the brothers, if they happened to be seized with wanderlust. They're quite safe."

"H'm!" said Wendover doubtfully. "I suppose you know best, but . . ."

"We needn't argue the point," said the Chief Constable. "They're still on hand to-day. We've kept an eye on them."

"Oh, well," said Wendover, finding the ground cut from under his feet, "what happened after that?"

"We paid a visit to the Hermitage. One of our men had broken the news to the old lady, and she'd retired to her room, overcome with sorrow. I didn't bother her at the moment. The maid gave me all I wanted. I'll put it concisely. About six o'clock, there was a ring at the phone. She answered it, and Callis gave his name and asked to speak to Kerrison. Kerrison answered the phone and she didn't hear his side of the conversation. But at the dinner-table, she heard him tell his mother that he would have to go out that night to see Callis. She's a doting mother, and she made him promise that he wouldn't be out late. He said he'd be back shortly after ten. And about a quarter-past eight the maid heard him leaving the house."

"Did he seem perturbed at dinner-time? I suppose you asked about that."

"I did. The maid said he was quite as usual. No doubt he was full of the latest gossip about the Great Pyramid and the Lost Ten Tribes."

"So I suppose you went off to see Callis?" asked Wendover.

"Not just then," Sir Clinton explained. "We searched the house pretty thoroughly, first, except the old lady's room."

"And you found nothing?"

"Nothing. Not even a pistol," said the Chief Constable, with a faint emphasis on the phrase.

Wendover was surprised, but he refused to fall into what he imagined was a trap.

"And what then?" he inquired.

"I gave orders for exhuming those cats I've heard so much about and for the extraction of the bullets from them. A grisly job. But we'll talk about that later on."

"You got hold of Callis, after that?" asked Wendover.

"We did. Though it was rather late—or a bit early, whichever you like. However, he was still afoot, buried in a thriller and not wanting to go to bed till he'd wrested its secret from the last page."

"Well, what had he to say?" demanded Wendover, anxious to get to something definite.

"Oh, he told a plain unvarnished tale," said the Chief

Constable. "He'd an engagement to spend the evening with the Alvingtons. He made it clear that their affairs are growing rather complicated, and he was to go as a friend and put his accountant's experience at their disposal. I've checked that. It's quite true. However, during the day he got a letter from Kerrison about some church business; and it struck him that he'd seen note-paper like that before. He must have his wits about him, to judge by the fact that he remembered the watermark on that anonymous letter and found an identical one on Kerrison's letter. In fact, he followed on our heels in identifying Kerrison as the author of that 'Watch your wife' epistle."

"Why was he so sure about Kerrison?" demanded Wendover, in a sceptical tone. "Plenty of other people must be using similar paper."

"Kerrison had already got into trouble over slander," Sir Clinton reminded him. "The other users hadn't, so far as one knows. Anyhow, Callis felt sure enough of his ground to tax Kerrison with the job; and he told me that he was so angry that he meant to have it out with Kerrison at once. He meant to take precautions against any further libels or slanders on his wife's name, which seems very natural. So he rang up Kerrison and asked him to call that evening, using Kerrison's letter about church affairs as his excuse."

"Did you see this letter about church business?" interjected Wendover.

"Oh, of course. I have it here, if you want to see it. There's nothing in it of any importance from our point of view. Well, Kerrison never guessed that he'd been spotted. He agreed to visit Callis about nine o'clock, which fits in with what we learned at the Hermitage. Meanwhile Callis rang up the Alvingtons and explained that Kerrison was coming to see him on urgent business, so that he wouldn't be able to drop in on them that night and lend his accountancy expertise to untangling their affairs. He arranged another evening instead."

"So the Alvingtons knew that Kerrison would be at Callis's house that evening," interrupted Wendover. "Ah!"

"'Ah!' as you, say Squire," Sir Clinton went on. "But let's proceed with this unvarnished tale, if you please. I gather that when Kerrison arrived, Callis talked to him like a Dutch uncle and spared his feelings in no way. He must have been clever enough to jar the fellow completely off the rails by bluster, for Kerrison admitted that he was the author of the 'Watch your wife' masterpiece. Callis got quite hot when he was telling the tale to me. One may infer that he was probably even more heated in the original version. Anyhow, the upshot was that he dictated a letter to Kerrison and Kerrison was so cowed that he took it down. Here it is. I brought it away with me."

He took from his pocket a sheet of note-paper and handed it to Wendover, who examined it.

FERN LODGE
HAYDOCK AVENUE

"I confess that I wrote an anonymous letter reflecting on the character of one of my friends and I unreservedly withdraw the statements which I made in that document, knowing them to be false. I express my deepest and most sincere regret for what I did.

"S. KERRISON."

"Is this actually in Kerrison's handwriting?" demanded Wendover.

"I've compared it with specimens of Kerrison's MS.," Sir Clinton answered definitely, "and I haven't the slightest doubt that Kerrison actually did write that apology. The ink's quite fresh, as you see. It must have been written last night."

"H'm!" said Wendover. "Well, go on."

"The next stage was that Callis, keeping Kerrison waiting, went and rang Mrs. Barratt up to tell her about the state of affairs. He meant to take Kerrison round to her house and make him apologise to her personally for the reference to Barratt in that anonymous letter: '*A preacher ought to set a better example . . .*' and so forth. He's still harping on the string that his own wife was completely innocent, you see; and he wanted a second witness to clinch the authorship of the anonymous letter, if Kerrison dared to deny it later on. He'd got Kerrison into a blue funk—remember those two slander actions—and he meant to put the screw on while the funk lasted. But Mrs. Barratt was out, and he got no answer to his phone call. I think that's sound enough. Mrs. Barratt *was* out at that time. We checked up her evidence, by inquiries. She went out at eight o'clock to visit some old friends in Windsor Drive—people called Mallard. She reached there at eight-thirty, stayed for about an hour, and was home again about five past ten. We know she was home then, because she found that she had run out of tea, and she went out and borrowed a quarter of a pound from a neighbour. We've checked that up also. There's no doubt that Mrs. Barratt was home at Granville Road at ten-fifteen, as she stated."

"Why all this checking up in her case?" asked Wendover.

"We're checking everything we can, naturally," said the Chief Constable, "and, as it happens, we can check her statements easily. But now I'd better go back a bit and give you the rest of Callis's evidence. Having failed to get hold of Mrs. Barratt, Callis had no further use for Kerrison, and dismissed him with very little ceremony. That was about a quarter to ten. Callis, feeling a bit worked up by the interview, then settled down to his thriller to divert his mind from the recent scene. His maid came in at eleven-twenty and saw that he was still downstairs. In fact, he gave her some orders about breakfast. We've checked that also; and she confirms his story."

Wendover opened his mouth to make some comment, but Sir Clinton hurried on to complete his story.

"There were one or two questions I wanted to ask Callis, after he'd finished his tale. The first was about Mrs. Callis's will. There was no difficulty there. Callis was one of the executors, and knew all about it. Her father left her a life-interest in his estate; that's where her private income came from. If she died without issue, then that capital went to her aunt and some other members of her family. All that she had to leave in her own will were a few personal possessions, jewellery and so forth, which she left to her husband. We've checked that by her solicitors—Callis gave me their address—and they reckon that these chattels may be worth a couple of hundred pounds or so—not more. Nobody else was mentioned in her will."

"So Callis gets next to nothing by her death—financially?" said Wendover.

Sir Clinton gave a confirmatory nod.

"I'm suspicious of everyone, in a case of this sort," he admitted, "so I questioned the solicitor rigidly. It's quite all right. There are no concealed assets or anything of that kind. Actually, Callis is worse off financially, since her income disappears and he won't have it to help out his housekeeping expenses. I don't think that matters to him. He's making a moderate income from his business."

"She wasn't insured?" demanded Wendover.

Again Sir Clinton shook his head.

"No, there's no policy on her life, none of any sort. There are no concealed assets, as I told you. It's all square and above-board."

"What else did you ask Callis?"

"I asked him if Kerrison had returned that pistol which Callis lent him for his cat-shooting. He hadn't, Callis told me."

"Then where's it gone?"

"Where we'll never find it, I expect," said the Chief Constable in a regretful tone. "I've no notion what's become of it. All I know is that we didn't find it at the

Hermitage, though we searched for it everywhere. And now Squire, I've given you the whole of Callis's evidence. Let's turn to a fresh field. This morning, these victims of Kerrison's pistol were dug up and the bullets extracted from the corpses. Rufford and I had a look at the bullets. And the rifling marks on those bullets out of the dead cats are identical with the rifling marks that Rufford found in the bullets which killed Barratt and Mrs. Callis. Sensation! Won't Peter Diamond be pleased when he gets that bone to gnaw? But perhaps you'd like to try your teeth on it first, before he rushes into print."

Sir Clinton had meant to surprise Wendover, and he succeeded completely.

"What's that you say? Are you quite sure there's no mistake?"

"Oh, quite," Sir Clinton assured him definitely.

"So *that's* why you found no pistol when you searched Kerrison's house after the motor smash," said Wendover, in the tone of one who at last sees his way through something which has puzzled him. "Of course if that pistol was found beside the bodies, it never went back to the Hermitage at all, after . . ."

"After Kerrison shot the pair of them?" Sir Clinton completed the sentence. "Very ingenious, Squire. Very convincing—to you, at any rate. But if Kerrison shot them with that pistol, how do you account for Rufford finding Barratt's finger-prints on the weapon instead of Kerrison's? Surely there's a screw loose in the reasoning."

"H'm! that's true," Wendover admitted. "But he may have shot them and then, after cleaning his own prints off the pistol, taken Barratt's hand and made the prints from his fingers."

"Your guess may be right," the Chief Constable conceded. "It's yours, not mine; and you can have full credit for it if you turn out to be right, Squire. But my own notion's different."

"What is it, then?" demanded Wendover.

"I hate repeating myself," said Sir Clinton, "and I gave you a tip on the subject a while ago. If you can't remember it, there's no harm done. Besides, what we're immediately concerned with just now is the matter of Kerrison's death. Suppose we stick to that, Squire. 'What was the crime?' The murder of Kerrison. 'Who did it?' It's your turn to play, Squire. Go ahead."

"Who did it?" echoed Wendover. "The Juggernaut gentleman who drove that blue car over him, obviously. And if you want to identify driver——"

"Wait, wait, wait," interrupted the Chief Constable. "You've started off with an unproved assumption. What evidence have you that it was a male driver? Nobody can swear to that, so far as we've been able to ascertain."

"Well, the driver, then," said Wendover, rather snappishly, as the interruption had thrown him off his line of thought. "The driver must have been someone who could get the use of Arthur Alvington's car. Unless you're prepared to deny that Alvington's car was the one that did the trick."

"I'm not prepared to deny it, Squire, so you may proceed."

"But you won't assert it? Cautious fellow, you are."

"I won't assert it till the time comes, Squire. But I did find some blood on the radiator shield, as well as observing that the side-lamp was missing from the mudguard, so I'm not prepared to deny you your assumption that Alvington's car did kill Kerrison. So go on."

"Then the driver must have been somebody who had access to that car at the right time," Wendover proceeded. "What kind of lock was on the garage door? A Yale, which snaps by pulling the door shut? Or an ordinary lock which needs the turn of a key to lock it?"

"It was an ordinary lock, not a Yale," said Sir Clinton. "Alvington had to fish his key out of his pocket before he could open it. And, to make all definite, he assured me that when he brought his car in before dinner, he locked the garage before going into his house. That may help to clear your way for you. Go ahead."

"Then it must have been one of the Alvingtons who drove the car," Wendover asserted flatly. "They were the only two people who could open the garage."

"Oh, no," Sir Clinton retorted with dangerous suavity. "There was another key that we know about. Mrs. Barratt told me that she had a key of her uncle's garage. He allows her to use his car now and again. You've been too quick in making your list of possibles, Squire. Not only so, but we know that she was within a stone's throw of her uncle's house that night between eight-thirty and nine-thirty, for she was paying a visit to her friends the Mallards, who live only a few doors from Alvington's house in Windsor Drive. What have you to say to that?"

"You're trying to pull my leg, Clinton; but it doesn't come off this time," retorted Wendover, obviously pleased to be able to score off the Chief Constable. "I've got a better memory than you think. Mrs. Barratt did *not* kill Kerrison. Why? Because Kerrison was killed at ten-fifteen whilst Mrs. Barratt was in Granville Road, miles away from the Hermitage, at five-past ten. She borrowed tea from her neighbour, then. That's your own evidence, Clinton."

"I give you best, Squire," admitted the Chief Constable. "I really thought I'd catch you, though."

"So that limits us down to the two Alvingtons, just as I said," Wendover continued. "And they haven't a credible alibi, since the maid was out. Either of them would swear an alibi for the other, no doubt; but would you believe them if they did?"

"Not whole-heartedly, I'll confess," Sir Clinton conceded. "I don't care much for these family alibis. We see too many of them break down in practice. But I'd feel happier about your ideas, Squire, if you'd suggest a motive for either of the Alvingtons murdering Kerrison."

Wendover evidently had his solution ready.

"By your own account of them," he pointed out, "the Alvingtons put a lot of weight on money. That's the tender point with both of them. Now Edward Alvington's divorce case resulted in his losing his expectations under his mother's will. Who was the main agent in that business? Barratt, from all we've heard. And what's happened to Barratt? He's dead. But Kerrison was also an actor in that affair. He backed up Barratt strongly in the matter of ostracising Edward Alvington from their church; and that move may have a good deal to do with old Mrs. Alvington's decision to change her will."

"Ah! So you're narrowing it down still further?" asked Sir Clinton. "It's *Edward* Alvington you've got your eye on for this murder? I'm not going to put limitations to the vagaries of human nature, but don't you think that the provocation here is comparatively small when you weigh it against the risk of a hanging? Would Edward Alvington have reckoned the game worth the candle?"

"My point is that he wouldn't be risking a hanging," explained Wendover. "Has anyone been hanged yet for a road accident? I can't remember any case of it. Manslaughter at the worst, that's all Edward Alvington could be charged with; and he'd get off with imprisonment, and not a long one, either. On that basis, it might be quite worth his while to give himself the satisfaction of knocking Kerrison out."

"I suppose that's true," Sir Clinton admitted in a thoughtful tone. "Very suggestive, Squire, and no irony intended. I'll have to think over things carefully, now that you've put that idea forward. On the face of it, I frankly admit, we couldn't prove that Kerrison was deliberately run down. But if I'd been the man who did it, I think I'd have loaded myself up with whisky immediately afterwards, just to give ground for the defence that I wasn't quite myself when the 'accident' happened. And both the Alvingtons were dead sober when I called on them. Perhaps they're not really so very clever."

He reached over for a fresh cigarette from the box, lighted it, and then turned back to Wendover.

"You can't say I haven't led a busy life to-day, Squire. Rather a hectic time, now I look back on it. And I forgot to mention that I dropped in at a stationer's shop and ordered fresh note-paper, so you can continue your epistolary exertion without fear of running short. That's by the way. I've kept one tit-bit to the last."

"What's that?" demanded Wendover, as Sir Clinton irritatingly broke off his explanation.

"I interviewed another railwayman," the Chief Constable pursued. "He's the guard of a goods train, and he's been on the sick list for some days, too busy with his own troubles to bother about ours, I gather. Anyhow, he's now come up to the scratch and produced his evidence. I can put it in a nutshell. On the night of the lovers' nook affair, his train passed the bracken-slope at nine-twenty-five. It was dusk by that time, but one could still see largish objects at a fair distance. This fellow—Judkins is his name—knows that bracken-patch well. He takes a friendly interest in it; and gets some amusement out of some things he sees happening there at times. So when his van came opposite to it that night, he was all alert for his evening fun. He saw something on the spot where Rufford found the bodies. But he was slightly disappointed to observe that there was only one person present. He saw a woman lying amongst the bracken. I took him in hand myself and examined him most carefully, but he stuck to it that all he saw was a woman lying down and that there was no other figure near."

"What about young Oley and the Quickett girl?" Wendover demanded. "If he can see things so clearly, why didn't he notice them?"

"Because they crept away very soon after nine o'clock.

They told us that. Your memory's not so good as you make out, Squire, or you'd remember that."

Wendover was obviously perplexed in his attempt to fit this new fact into the chain of evidence already in his mind.

"It seems to muddle things up, more than a little," he admitted in a puzzled tone. "What do you make of it, Clinton?"

"Baffling, at first sight," Sir Clinton agreed cheerfully. "But it's best never to admit that you're baffled. I seldom do."

"And since it baffled you at first sight, what did you do next?" sneered Wendover.

"I took another glance at it," explained Sir Clinton. "That's the most natural thing to do, I think. But now, Squire, I've had a busy day and I've talked more than I wanted to. Suppose we play one game before going to bed. I've got enough breath left to say 'Mate' when the proper time comes."

CHAPTER XVI

THE FOUR CARTRIDGE-CASES

EARLY on the following morning, Sir Clinton summoned Rufford to his office at the police headquarters. The inspector's eyebrows lifted slightly when he found Wendover installed beside the Chief Constable. Sir Clinton noticed his surprise.

"I've brought Mr. Wendover along," he explained. "We may need a magistrate before we're through with this business."

"To sign a warrant?" queried the inspector, evidently satisfied by this pretext for Wendover's presence during an official interview.

Sir Clinton refused to rise to the bait.

"He's been an onlooker at the game," he explained, "while you and the rest of us have been struggling with this Barratt case. I think we're in the last lap, now, and he may as well see the finish."

"Certainly, sir," agreed Rufford, making a fairly successful effort to conceal his surprise at the chance of such a speedy termination of the affair.

"I've got the dossier of the case here," Sir Clinton went on, taking from a drawer the folder which Wendover had seen several times before. "Just let Mr. Wendover see the extra exhibits, inspector. We'll put all our cards on the table for him. Then he can't say that we've kept him in the dark about any bit of evidence."

"Very good, sir," agreed the inspector, placing a number of envelopes of various sizes on the Chief Constable's desk.

"I've got all the stuff here, as you told me to have it handy. The envelopes are labelled, if you want to pick any of them out as we go along."

"Thanks," said Sir Clinton.

He turned over the various envelopes, glancing at the inscriptions, and finally selected two small ones from the series.

"We'd better begin with these," he said, turning to Wendover. "This one contains four empty cartridge-cases which the inspector discovered beside the bodies of Barratt and Mrs. Callis; this other one contains four empty cartridge-cases obtained by firing four shots out of the pistol which was lying beside Barratt's hand. I don't want to get them mixed up, so I'll pour out the one lot at this end of my desk. That will keep them apart."

He suited the action to the word, and Wendover examined the four little objects cursorily.

"You may have to look more closely than that," said Sir Clinton. "Here's a watchmaker's lens. Now, inspector, you're a fire-arms expert. Just explain to Mr. Wendover how the cartridge-case is removed from an automatic after the shot's fired."

Rufford seemed pleased that his Chief had delegated this task to him.

"It works this way, Mr. Wendover," he explained. "In these automatics, the firing of the cartridge drives back a sliding breech-block. Attached to that breech-block is an extractor-claw which slips over the rim of the cartridge during the loading process. So when the breech-block jerks back, it carries the cartridge-case with it, gripped by the extractor-claw. The breech-block is stopped suddenly at the end of its 'travel,' whereupon the cartridge-case flies on and is jerked clean out through the opening left by the retreat of the slide. Now if you left the design like that, most likely—if you fired straight to your front—the cartridge-case would hit you in the face, since it's travelling backward in line with the barrel of the pistol. So a small piece of metal is put on the pistol—it's called the ejector-block—and when the back-travelling cartridge-case strikes this, it's diverted to one side, and the cartridge-case usually flies over your shoulder safely. That's what you wanted, sir, isn't it? I've got a spare pistol with me. Here's the extractor, Mr. Wendover, and here's the extractor-block.

"Thanks, I see what you mean," said Wendover, with a pleasant courtesy.

He knew a good deal more about fire-arms than Rufford; but he was too kind to rob the inspector of his feeling of superior knowledge.

"Now just take the magnifier," said Sir Clinton, "and examine the end of this cartridge-case. You see the mark of the extractor, where it slipped over the rim of the case during loading: a slight flattening of the rim's metal. Turn the thing round until that's at the top. Then, at about the seven o'clock position, you'll see the ejector mark: a slight straight cut in the brass. Got it?"

"Yes, I can make it out all right," Wendover agreed.

"Good! Now you see the depression punched by the striker-pin which fired the cap of the cartridge? About half-way between it and the rim, you'll see another feature on the brass."

"A sort of island of metal, it looks like," said Wendover, examining the object through the magnifier. "About the five o'clock position, isn't it?"

"Yes, that's the thing I meant," Sir Clinton confirmed. "It's a mark made by a particular chance tool-marking on the breech-block of the pistol out of which that cartridge was fired. Now turn that case on its side and look for a scratch on the metal, running straight along, parallel to the axis of the cartridge. See it? You may have to turn the thing about a bit till you get the light falling just right."

"I've got it," Wendover reported after a few failures.

"Then just note its position relative to the ejector mark,"

Sir Clinton advised. "And then you might let the inspector have a look. He hasn't seen it before."

When Rufford had made his examination, Sir Clinton produced the three other cartridge-cases from the same envelope for their inspection. In each case they were able to identify the same types of marks in the same relative positions.

"That set," Sir Clinton explained, "is the four which were found beside the bodies."

He put them back in the proper envelope, and then poured out the remaining quartette from the second envelope.

"Have a look at these," he suggested, "and see if you find the same set of marks on them."

Wendover took precedence of the inspector. He examined the little objects first with his naked eye, then with the lens, taking each cartridge-case in turn and making no comment until he had completed his survey.

"Something wrong here, surely," he said at last, putting down the magnifying glass. "Each of them has got the flattening of the rim produced by the extractor. But the ejector mark's not quite in the same relative position. And I can't see any scratch on the side of any of them, nor can I see that little island that I noticed in the last set. Perhaps Mr. Rufford has better eyes."

Rufford had hardly troubled to conceal his contempt for the "amateur" while Wendover was making his investigation. He now picked up the little objects in turn. As his examination proceeded, surprise and annoyance showed on his features and deepened as each cartridge-case failed to reveal the indications he was seeking.

"You don't see 'em?" asked Sir Clinton. "I'd be surprised if you did, because they aren't there."

"But they *must* be," asserted the inspector. "It must be some trick of the light, or something. All these shots came out of the same pistol, sir. And I've compared the bullets very carefully. They all have the same rifling marks. Let me have another try."

"Don't bother too much with the scrape on the side of the case," Sir Clinton advised. "These scrapes are not altogether to be relied on as proofs. But the other three points are sound."

Rufford set himself again to his examination of the cases; but it was evident that he was making no better progress than he had done before. At last, baffled, he put them back on the desk with a certain pettishness in his gesture.

"No, they aren't there," he confessed, crossly. "I don't understand it, sir. All of these shots were fired from the same pistol. That's plain, since the rifling-marks are the same on the two bullets from the bodies and the four bullets I've fired myself. These are identical; I'll swear to that in the box."

"The same pistol," repeated Sir Clinton, though with a fresh intonation. "What is a pistol? Before we go any further, we'd better be quite sure what we're talking about. I had the same trouble when Mr. Wendover and I were discussing the subject. You people seem to think that when you say 'pistol,' you've covered the whole ground. So you may have, in the dictionary sense. But a pistol is a complicated bit of mechanism, remember."

The inspector scented a trap.

"I know you've got something up your sleeve, sir. You're just pulling our legs. I admit I've got tangled up. Put it to us straight."

The Chief Constable, instead of answering, began a search among the papers in the dossier, from which he finally extracted the rough sketch which Rufford had made to indicate the places where the four cartridge-cases had been discovered. (See diagram opposite.)

"Now," he said, spreading the paper out on the desk so that both his hearers could examine it. "Here are the relative positions of the bodies and the four cartridge-cases. You reminded us, inspector, that an automatic pistol ejects its cartridge backwards and towards the side; and if I'm not mistaken, the Colt automatic pitches the empty shell over one's right shoulder, more or less. Now look at the diagram. Mrs. Callis, facing south, was shot by someone standing on her left side—which is the same thing as saying that the shooter must have been somewhere near B in the diagram, standing with his face towards the west. Now on that basis, I reckon that the case of the cartridge which killed her must have been the one which landed at the star marked 3 in the diagram. Barratt was shot in the right temple, but he was apparently facing north at the moment (to judge

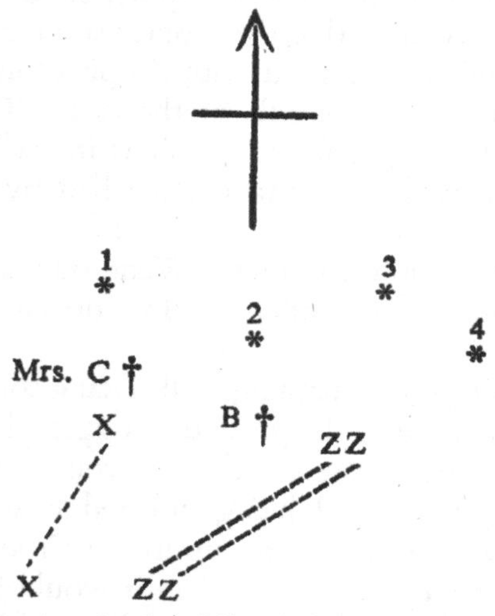

from the way his body fell). If you allow that he was standing a few feet south of Mrs. Callis's position, then the cartridge-case found at 3 gives you almost exactly the same range of travel as the one found at 4."

"And the northward distance between 4 and 3 is roughly the same as the northward distance between where Mrs. Callis was sitting and the spot Barratt was standing when he was shot," said the inspector, alertly. "That seems sound enough, sir. But we more or less knew all that already, didn't we?"

"I admit it. But what you didn't know was where the other pair of empty cartridge-cases came into the business, the ones marked 1 and 2. Let's take them now. I'll admit at once that they might have come from shots fired from any point over a fair zone and in any direction. But that can be narrowed down a bit in practice. The two shots heard by Polly Quickett came fairly close together. There wasn't much time for the shooter to shift his position. One may reasonably assume that Mrs. Callis cried out 'Don't!' when she saw the pistol pointing at her; then came the fatal shot; and then came the second report, fired from almost the same spot. Assume that the shooter stood at about B in the diagram, and that he fired with his pistol in the normal position, neither 1 nor 2 will fit the case. The range of travel from pistol to ground is too short in each case, when one compares it with the distance travelled by the cases 3 and 4."

"That seems sound enough," Wendover agreed, after scrutinising the sketch carefully. "How do you account for it?"

"Imagine that you're standing at B, facing south, and that you fire your pistol into the ground," suggested Sir Clinton. "The empty cartridge-case recoils over your right shoulder; but owing to your pistol being directed downwards, the ejected case goes almost straight up in the air and falls back in the bracken far nearer to you than it would have done if you'd held your pistol level. Now the position 1 seems to me to be just about where the empty case might fall, under these conditions. And the case which fell at 2, on the same reasoning, might have been fired by a shooter standing near ZZ and facing south. Have a good look at the sketch. I think you'll agree with me."

Rufford and Wendover bent over the desk. The inspector made one or two rough measurements on the diagram and then looked up.

"That's sound enough, sir," he admitted, "and of course I

know you're right; because we dug up those extra two bullets exactly where you told us to look for them, at B and at ZZ. That was a very neat bit of prophesying, sir, and until you explained it, I didn't see how you'd managed to do it."

"Satisfied?" asked Sir Clinton, glancing at Wendover.

"Oh, quite, quite. One can't get over the actual bullets," Wendover admitted. "And, of course, they've got the same rifling-marks as the two fatal ones. Have they?" he ended, suspiciously.

"They have," Sir Clinton assured him.

"But that makes four shots," objected Wendover. "Polly Quickett heard only two. She was positive about that."

"Two and two make four," Sir Clinton pointed out. "Two reports were heard by Polly Quickett shortly after nine o'clock, and two were heard by the late Kerrison at ten o'clock or thereabouts."

"Stop a bit," objected Wendover in a critical tone. "Your theory goes a bit further. It implies that an hour elapsed between the two deaths—three-quarters of an hour, at any rate."

"Exactly," agreed the Chief Constable.

"Then it may have been a suicide pact after all," Wendover pointed out. "Barratt may have shot Mrs. Callis at nine-fifteen and then sat hesitating for three-quarters of an hour before he could screw himself up to keeping his bargain by shooting himself."

Rufford had listened to the "amateur" with a faint smile of superiority.

"If you're right, sir, then Barratt must have gone for a little stroll, after murdering the girl. To collect his thoughts, perhaps. That railway guard, Judkins, saw her body lying there at nine-twenty-five, and he's spot-certain that there was no other figure in the bracken-patch at that time."

"Let's finish with the cartridge-cases before we start a fresh hare," suggested Sir Clinton, coming to Wendover's rescue. "We've got four bullets, and four cartridge-cases connected with this affair. Unfortunately, these two sets don't correspond in their markings, as we've just seen."

"That's true enough," said Wendover, not ill-pleased to see the inspector at a loss. "On the face of things, the bullets were fired from the pistol you found, whereas the cartridge-cases were fired from another pistol entirely. So you people ought to be able to produce four more cartridge-cases corresponding to the shots from that pistol which Barratt had."

"Not necessarily," said Sir Clinton with a faint smile. "I think a practical demonstration is what's wanted here. Did you bring those two automatics with you, inspector?"

Rufford dipped his hands into his jacket pockets and produced a pair of Colts.

"I borrowed them from a gunsmith," he explained. "They're identical with the .38 pistol that I found beside the bodies."

He put them down on the desk before the Chief Constable, who looked at them rather fastidiously.

"They're rather oily," he complained, pulling out his handkerchief and giving each of them a rub with it before going further. "That's better. I wonder if they've been cleaned since they were fired last—if they have been fired."

He twisted a piece of paper into a screw and inserted it into the barrel of one pistol; but he pushed it too far in and gave an exclamation of vexation.

"It's stuck inside the barrel. Never mind, we'll get it out by and by. Meanwhile, we'll put it into this drawer, to keep it quite separate from the other one."

As he pulled open the drawer in his desk, somebody passed the window of the room in which they were, and an expression of annoyance flashed over the Chief Constable's face.

"Was that Arthur Alvington?" he asked. "Looked like him. I don't want him shown in here while we're busy. Will you see that he's kept waiting till we have time to deal with him, inspector, please."

Rufford turned to leave the room. Sir Clinton dropped

the pistol into the drawer, which he then closed with a slight slam. Wendover had stepped to the window to look into the street. In a moment or two, Rufford returned and explained that Alvington had not entered the police station.

"Well, we can go on, then," said Sir Clinton, with relief in his tone. "I'd no particular desire to have Master Arthur popping in at this particular moment. Just hold this pistol, will you?"

He picked the second pistol from the desk and handed it to Wendover, who took it, looking rather puzzled.

"H'm!" said the Chief Constable ruminatively. "We've got six bullets in all: two from the heads of the bodies; two from the turf; and two from the dead cats that Kerrison shot. All of these bear the same rifling-marks. That's right, I think? And we've four empty cartridge-cases, which don't correspond to the pistol found beside the bodies. That's the state of affairs. Not so very difficult, after all. Just put that pistol down on the desk, Wendover, please."

Wendover did so, and Sir Clinton picked it up, holding it so that they could see exactly what he did.

"I told you that a pistol was a complicated piece of mechanism," he reminded Wendover. "Now, we'll dismount this one a bit. I'll take out the magazine, first."

He suited the action to the words and laid the empty magazine on the desk before him. Then, holding the pistol well in view, he made two swift and simple movements of his hands, after which he put down separately on the desk the barrel of the pistol and the remainder of the weapon.

"Quite simple, isn't it?" he commented. "You see how easy it is to remove the barrel from an automatic of this type. These weapons are all practically standardised. Now I'll assemble this one."

He did so, while they watched him carefully. When he had finished, he put the assembled automatic down on the desk with a gesture warning them not to touch it.

"Now I come to the gist of the demonstration," he said,

with a sardonic smile. "Thanks for your attention, so far. Observe that when I handed this pistol to Mr. Wendover, I held it by the butt, which is roughened and does not take finger-prints of any value. Mr. Wendover took it from me, naturally, by catching the slide, which is smooth and takes finger-print impressions excellently. Result, the only clear finger-prints on it are Mr. Wendover's."

He pointed to the pistol and Rufford bent over it to examine the prints which were quite visible on the black metal surface.

"That seems right," the inspector admitted. "And I suppose you were careful not to touch anything but the roughened parts when you picked it up after Mr. Wendover had laid it down on the desk?"

"Just so," Sir Clinton confirmed. "Well, now that you're satisfied so far, will you just pick it up, inspector, and have a look down the barrel? If you pull back the slide to the half-way catch you'll get enough light at the breech end. Is the barrel clear?"

"No it isn't," reported Rufford. "There's a bit of paper or something stuck in it. But you put the paper into the barrel of the other pistol, sir, the one that's in the drawer. I watched you doing that."

Sir Clinton laughed at the sight of the expressions on his hearers' faces.

"Try the one in the drawer, then," he adviced.

Rufford pulled open the drawer, picked up the pistol which lay there, and seemed still further amazed.

"Why, this thing hasn't got a barrel in it at all!" he ejaculated . "I don't see how that comes about, sir."

"No? Well, here's a spare barrel if you want one," the Chief Constable returned, opening his hand and showing it. "It's rather oily."

He put it down on the desk and wiped his fingers with his handkerchief.

"I ought to have been on the watch for your tricks," said Wendover, "but you did it so naturally that you took me in.

You see, Mr. Rufford, Sir Clinton used to be a good amateur conjuror. It's clear how he bamboozled us. When he picked up that first pistol to drop it into the drawer, he distracted our attention by pretending to see Alvington passing the window. Just the ordinary conjuror's patter, but it took both of us in. While our attention was diverted, and under cover of the desk, he took the barrel with the paper in it out of the first pistol, and palmed it. When he dismounted the second pistol he put down the first barrel and palmed the second one. Then, when he reassembled all the stuff on the desk, the barrel with the paper in it went into the stock of the second pistol, and he was left with the other barrel palmed in his hand. That was how it was done, wasn't it?" he demanded, turning to the Chief Constable.

"That was how it was done," Sir Clinton admitted. "And if I could do it in front of a critical and alert audience, no doubt somebody else could manage it with an audience that wasn't on its guard. You can see from that business how little stress we can lay on Barratt's finger-prints."

Wendover pondered for a moment or two.

"I see my way through it, now," he declared. "The same barrel was evidently used by Kerrison in his cat-shooting and in the killing of Mrs. Callis and Barratt. That's right, isn't it?"

"It's obvious," corrected Sir Clinton with a touch of irony, "seeing that all the bullets involved bore the rifling-marks of one barrel."

"And that barrel was finally transferred to a stock which had Barratt's finger-prints on it," continued Wendover, working out his ideas aloud.

"It looks like Kerrison to me," hazarded the inspector. "Kerrison had the right barrel. That's proved by the bullets in the cats."

"I bet on Callis," said Wendover. "Callis was a bit of an expert at legerdemain. That came out in the evidence about Barratt's hypnotic experiments."

"If Kerrison did it, no conjuring was needed," the inspector pointed out. "What do you say, sir?"

"I think you're both simplifying things rather too much," said the Chief Constable. "Besides, there's more evidence to come. Suppose we take it now."

He opened a drawer in his desk and took out further exhibits. Some of them were new to Wendover, but he recognised two items at once; the torn fragments of love-letters which had been found beside the bodies. The pieces had been carefully fitted together and clipped for safety between sheets of glass. Sir Clinton put these aside for the moment and picked out some other sheets of paper.

"Here's a sheet of note-paper which the inspector secured from Barratt's desk," he began. "It's inexpensive stuff with nothing to identify it specially. On a cursory examination, it seems very much like the paper on which that torn love-letter was written. I doubt if it's worth while pursuing the matter further, though no doubt we could find out more about it if we wanted to. For the present, all I want to point out is that it hasn't any printed heading. The inspector noticed that the Barratts used an embossing press to stamp their note-paper as they needed it."

He picked up the glass-protected reconstitution of Barratt's love-letter.

"The paper's just like the other, so far as casual inspection goes," he pointed out, holding the two side by side. "No watermark on either specimen. The only curious point about the torn letter is that the whole document is complete except for the top right-hand corner of the first page."

"I see what you're after," said Wendover. "That's the place where the date would be. I ought to have thought of that before."

"But you omitted to do so," said Sir Clinton. "Quite so. It does seem suggestive, doesn't it? But let's go on to something more amusing."

He produced several sheets of note-paper of a bluish tint

and laid them out on his desk along with the glass-protected letter in Mrs. Callis's handwriting.

"I've been chaffing you about buying note-paper," he said to Wendover, "but it's a fact that I've been in touch with some of the local stationers in the last day or two. As a result, I've identified the firm that Mrs. Callis dealt with. You know that when you go into a stationer's shop to choose note-paper, they often haul out a vast volume with samples of paper and headings stuck down on the pages, so that you can turn the thing over and make your choice. By a bit of good luck, Millman & Co. have preserved these tomes from year to year. They've got a perfect library of them. I showed them the sheet of bluish paper which the inspector got from Callis: a list of names in Mrs. Callis's handwriting. The address heading is in Roman type, you see, identical with the Roman heading on this love-letter under the glass. Have a look at them both. There's no deception."

Wendover and the inspector gave the two sheets a cursory examination; but being eager to hear what more the Chief Constable had to say, they did not waste much time.

"I asked Millman & Co. for particulars about purchases of note-paper with that address on it; and I chivvied them back through a number of years in their accounts. Mrs. Callis, it seemed, had a special liking for that particular shade of paper. She always asked for it when she bought a fresh supply, and she generally bought a good big lot at one time. Now here's a sample removed from the 1931 scrap book. Have a good look at it. Roman type heading, you see, just like the love-letter. Hold it up to the light and look at the watermark. FINLANDIA, isn't it? See anything else of interest?"

"It has parallel lines across it, watermarked," Wendover reported. "They run vertically, about an inch apart; and there's a set of horizontal lines, too, but fainter and closer-ruled, made in the watermarking. Is that what you mean?"

"Yes," the Chief Constable explained. "That distinguishes the kind of paper that's called 'wove.' If there are no lines of that sort, it's a 'laid' paper. Now just hold that love-letter up to the light. What do you find there?"

"Just the same," Wendover reported, passing the specimen to Rufford when he had finished his examination. "Heading in Roman type, FINLANDIA watermark on what you call 'wove' paper of the same bluish shade."

"Try again," suggested the Chief Constable, handing over a fresh sheet. "This one was bought from Millman & Co. in 1935. What do you make of it?"

"The *Fern Lodge* heading is in Gothic type this time," Wendover pointed out to the inspector. "Apart from that, everything's the same: wove paper with FINLANDIA watermark. The tint seems to be identical with those of the other samples."

"That's what I wanted," Sir Clinton declared. "Now here's one more sample. It's the list of some church committee written by Mrs. Callis only a few days ago."

Wendover examined it carefully, with the inspector looking over his shoulder.

"I see no difference from the last one," he announced. "Heading in Gothic type, wove paper, FINLANDIA watermark, and tint identical with the others. Have I missed anything?"

"No, I believe it's a sheet from the 1935 batch," said Sir Clinton. "Here's the last sample."

He passed over yet another sheet of note-paper which resembled the others; but when Wendover held it up to the light he showed some surprise.

"This isn't the same as the rest," he declared. "The heading is in Roman type, like the one on the earlier samples you showed me. And it's laid paper, not wove. And the watermark's a new one: ZEBRA CREST. The tint's the same, or nearly so. See for yourself, Mr. Rufford."

He handed the sheet of paper to the inspector who examined

it with care and then nodded a confirmation of Wendover's observations.

"That last sample is part of a purchase made by Callis just a month ago. Millman & Co. tell me that the FINLANDIA stuff hasn't been manufactured for over a year; and they've replaced it in stock by this ZEBRA CREST paper, which is almost identical in tint. Now you've got the evidence that's needed to settle the business. Most of it was collected by the inspector before I came on the scene at all, so the credit's mainly his. Oh, there is one point more, though it's not essential. Neither of those letters under the glass has any clear finger-prints on it; some faint smudges are all that came up with the powder."

"Have you got the solution of the business?" Wendover asked, turning to the inspector.

"No, I don't see my way through, even yet," Rufford confessed frankly.

"It's not often that one comes across such a painstaking bit of crime," said Sir Clinton, intervening to shield his subordinate as far as possible. "Quite a pleasure to unravel a case of this sort. But actually, in some ways, it was easier than it looked. The desire for perfection is the worst disease that ever afflicted the human mind. This affair would have been harder if it hadn't been contrived by someone suffering from that trouble."

CHAPTER XVII

"THEY ARE SO GRATEFUL"

THE Chief Constable had not liked Wendover's blunt question to the inspector. Now he gave Rufford the satisfaction of seeing the Squire himself at fault.

"One of the keys to this affair is the sentence: '*They are so grateful*'," he said, turning to Wendover. "You're a student of criminological literature. Can you place it?"

Wendover pondered for a few seconds and then shook his head.

"It seems to stir something in my memory, but I can't recall the context," he confessed. "Where does it occur?"

"We'll come to it, by and by," said Sir Clinton. "Our immediate business is to pave the way for your signing an official document."

"Then the sooner we start, the better," said Wendover. "It's high time you put your cards on the table, I think."

"Very well, then, since you wish it," said Sir Clinton. He turned to Rufford and continued: "If you hadn't taken such full notes of all the evidence, we might have been left high and dry. Congratulations. Now when I saw the evidence you'd collected before I came upon the scene, one or two points in your notes caught my eye at once. Probably they struck you, too. The first of them was the list of things you found in the suit-cases; and that coupled up with some other facts you'd jotted down. One thing we know definitely about Mrs. Callis. She took a pride in her appearance. She was an artist in that line, as Arthur Alvington told us; and you yourself noticed that her hands were carefully manicured. And when you found her body, you jotted down in your notes that you detected a faint odour of verbena bath salts. Now, on the face of things, Mrs. Callis packed her suit-case in order to elope with Barratt. On a trip of that kind, a woman would want to be at her best. And yet, in the packing, her beauty-box got left behind, and she took no manicure set with her. Nor did she pack any bath-salts, although bath-cubes were there in her bath-room, ready to hand."

"Perhaps she packed in a deuce of a hurry, sir," objected the inspector. "She forgot some other things as well: tooth-brush, nail-brush and sponge-bag. That certainly looks like a bit of a rush."

"And yet she remembered to take her jewellery, curiously enough," Sir Clinton reminded him. "And her cheque-book. And, to continue my line of thought, she deliberately picked out a dress which she seldom wore, one which her maid thought she didn't like very much. Not only so, but she left behind her the belt corresponding to that particular dress. I'm not laying too much stress on these things at the moment; all I say is that they caught my attention. There were other omissions from that list of the suit-case contents, but I needn't bother you with them. Now turn to Barratt's packing. His suit-case contained a bath-gown and a bath-sponge; but he forgot his shaving tackle."

"I've done that myself once, sir," objected the inspector. "It might have slipped his memory."

"And I suppose you've also forgotten your hair-brush, tooth-brush, nail-brush and slippers simultaneously? I'll admit that one may forget one article, or even a couple, but surely not the whole of that collection. Only amnesia would account for it. And did you remember your omissions on the way to the station and drop into a shop or two to buy substitutes, as Barratt apparently must have done, since he had new hair-brushes, a new tooth-brush, and a fresh tube of tooth-paste in his suit-case."

"You mean. . . ." interjected Wendover.

"I mean that it all struck me as peculiar," said Sir Clinton. "So perhaps I approached the rest of the case from a different point of view to the one that you preferred. Take the next queer business: those torn-up love-letters. . . ."

"They were genuine enough, surely," interrupted Wendover. "I compared the handwriting in them with other specimens of Barratt's writing and Mrs. Callis's, and no mistake was possible. They weren't forgeries, if that's what you're hinting at."

"Quite true," agreed the Chief Constable. "But can you suggest why they were torn up?"

Wendover had his explanation cut and dried.

"On the face of things," he pointed out, "they'd decided to relinquish this elopement. Perhaps they'd made up their minds to turn over a new leaf and go straight in future. In that case, the tearing up of old love-letters might be a kind of symbolic gesture."

"Curious that they should have the letters there to hand," said Sir Clinton drily. "I think you're missing out a point, though. The letter in Mrs. Callis's writing was complete, you remember. It was an undated letter. Perhaps she was one of these people who never put the date on their epistles. But a piece of the Barratt letter was missing; and that missing bit was exactly where the date would normally be put. That struck me immediately. Why was that bit of it the only one that Constable Loman couldn't find? And further, why were all the finger-prints on both letters mere blurs? Finger-prints are made by the natural grease of the body. It's soluble in alcohol or chloroform to some extent, and you can destroy finger-prints almost completely by soaking the paper in one of these solvents—which don't affect old ink—and brushing the surface with cotton-wool or something soft. Whoever it was that scattered the letter-fragments about, had taken care to remove that date and any finger-prints before throwing them down. That struck me as strange."

"It does sound very rum when you put it together like that," the inspector agreed. "So I see now, sir. Was there anything else?"

"The initials on the new wedding-ring," answered the Chief Constable. "Here's a woman who's throwing off her old life, leaving her husband, won't wear the wedding-ring that he gave her but gets a new one made and engraved specially. Would she put the initial of her *married* name, Callis, on the new ring? 'Esther and John,' I could have understood; or even 'E.P.' for her maiden name; but not 'E.C.' for Esther Callis. It doesn't ring true, psychologically."

"There's something in that, sir," confessed Rufford. "I ought to have thought of that point. But it never occurred to me."

"Even murderers can't think of everything, thank goodness," said the Chief Constable. "And now, another thing struck me, and I've harped on it all through this business: Why did Loman find four empty cartridge-cases when two shots did the killing?"

"These two youngsters heard two shots at nine o'clock, sir, and Kerrison heard two shots at ten o'clock; that makes the four," Rufford pointed out.

"That's a fact, inspector, if you accept Kerrison's unconfirmed story. But a fact isn't an explanation, and it's an explanation that's wanted. Why were four shots fired instead of two? And, yet another point, why were there two trails through the bracken, a single one and a double-width one. When I looked at all these oddities, the only explanation I could find for them was a bizarre one."

" And that was?" demanded Wendover.

"That the whole affair was a case of ingenious substitution," said the Chief Constable. "It almost deserved to come off."

"Substitution?" echoed Wendover, with a blank expression. "What are you talking about? There's no question as to the identity of the bodies. Where's the substitution?"

"It runs through the whole case," said Sir Clinton, "once you've got the key."

"No doubt," said Wendover, restively. "But I haven't got the key. What is it?"

"Unless I'm mistaken," said the Chief Constable, "the key to the affair was Barratt's marriage. I think the simplest thing I can do is to reconstruct the whole business for you, as I see it. Some of it will be guesswork, obviously; but there's enough in the way of facts to set the Director of Public Prosecutions in action and to make the result satisfactory. If you see any weak spots, don't hesitate to point them out."

He took a cigarette from his case and lighted it before proceeding.

"We know how Mrs. Barratt was brought up by her grandmother, a domineering old lady, ruling her family by the power of the purse, and with a strong bias towards one particular obscure little religious sect. Some girls, in their teens, 'take' to religion fervently, and the really earnest ones stick to it. Mrs. Barratt at that age was evidently fascinated by some sides of religious affairs; so much so, that when Barratt came along, he was able to capture her, although he obviously did not belong to her class of society at all.

"We've heard various opinions about Barratt; and we can discount a good many of the adverse criticisms, because every cleric is a cock-shy for disgruntled individuals in his congregation, and one ought not to take that kind of thing too seriously. But even when one puts him in the best light, he was a tactless man, apt to rub people up the wrong way without meaning it, very set on having his own way, and rather narrow and rigid in some of his ideas.

"If he had married some mouse of a woman, she would probably have adored him for the rest of their joint lives. Unfortunately, he married Helen Alvington. You haven't seen her, Wendover. She's a handsome woman, round about thirty-five, nowadays; but she doesn't look more than twenty-six or twenty-seven. She's clever, attractive, not easily perturbed, and she has a very natural leaning towards her own class and its ways. She's by no means the mouse who would have been the ideal mate for Barratt.

"It's easy to imagine the reactions of that marriage. Once the original glamour faded a bit, she found herself tied to a man who was unfitted by temperament and upbringing to mix easily with friends of her own social status. He despised their amusements, I expect, and looked askance at their whole manner of living. She couldn't entertain people of her own circle, with Barratt glooming and disapproving in the background. And, in any case, Barratt's salary was so small that it can have left little margin for even the simplest entertaining. Year by year, she must have seen the strands between herself and her old life snapping one by one. That was inevitable. And, on the other side, she couldn't feel much at home among the church people, mainly drawn from a lower class and with interests wholly different from hers. Some women might have managed it; but she wasn't the type that could do it. We know the result. She neglected church affairs almost ostentatiously.

"Barratt himself, as a personality, must have jarred on her more than a little. She has a strong character, he was stubborn and peremptory. Between them they were not likely to smooth over any roughnesses which were bound to show themselves in such a situation. I can't give you chapter and verse for every bit of that fancy picture; but I think it's a fairly truthful one."

"It fits everything I was able to pick up from all the people who gave me evidence about Barratt's affairs," confirmed Rufford. "You've put the whole thing quite fairly, sir."

"Remember my mentioning a book to you?" said Sir Clinton, turning to the inspector. "Karen Michaelis's *The Dangerous Age*. The dangerous age is the age when a woman feels that she hasn't got all out of love that she expected and when she finds that her own attractiveness is threatened with a decline in the near future. It doesn't take much acumen to see that Mrs. Barratt had probably reached her 'dangerous age.' She'd lost all interest in Barratt, as she told you very plainly. And that false youth of hers wasn't likely to last for much longer. If she wanted to make a fresh start in love-affairs, it was now or never."

"But did she want to make a fresh start?" queried Wendover, sceptically.

"Assuredly," retorted Sir Clinton with certainty in his tone. "And the man she fixed on was Callis. What did you make of Callis?" he asked, swinging round to Rufford.

"Callis, sir? Good-looking young fellow, nice manners, social position about the eight hundred or nine hundred pound a year mark, I'd say, speaks well with a good accent. About the same class as Mrs. Barratt and the Alvingtons, as near as makes no difference. But . . . Oh, yes, I see. . . ."

"Thinking about alibis?" interrupted Sir Clinton, with a slight lift of his eyebrows. "We'll come to them in due course. Meanwhile, let's assume that young Callis and Mrs. Barratt became lovers. After the first step, they'd plenty of opportunities. The Barratts kept no maid. When Barratt was at his church meetings, Mrs. Barratt had the house to herself. And Callis's wife was keenly interested in church affairs and went regularly to these meetings too, thus leaving Callis free to pay visits to Mrs. Barratt. In fact, everything favoured an intrigue running with clockwork smoothness."

"That's guesswork," objected Wendover. "You haven't a scrap of proof for it."

"The proof's implicit in the whole of the facts," said Sir Clinton, undisturbed. "Wait till we get them all fitted together. I've no doubt that, when we set about it, we shall be able to fish up more direct evidence on that point. For the present, all I'm assuming is that this intrigue had been going on for a while. It hadn't passed wholly unobserved. Kerrison, for one, had his suspicions about it, as you'll see by and by."

Wendover evidently was about to interrupt here, but altered his mind.

"What changed the whole face of affairs," Sir Clinton went on, "was the Alvington divorce case and its consequences. That revealed starkly that old Mrs. Alvington had very decided views about marital misdeeds and also that she didn't hesitate to put on the financial screw when anything of that kind happened in her own family. But Mrs. Barratt, like all the Alvington clan, has a strongly developed respect for cash. If news of her own intrigue leaked out, she knew—after her uncle's affair—that she would never see a penny of her grandmother's money. And even short of that, Barratt—according to Edward Alvington— had some scheme for persuading the old lady to leave all her money to the Awakened Israelites. Helen Barratt might have been glad enough to be rid of Barratt, even at the cost of a divorce action; but when that divorce meant being cut out of the old lady's will and having to live on nothing a year, I don't think the prospect attracted her. And by that time, I surmise, she was madly in love with young Callis and Mrs. Callis stood in the way of her marrying him, even if Barratt divorced his wife. So the two of them began to lay plans which would obviate a divorce and eliminate the hindrances to their marrying each other. What they hit upon was a most ingenious scheme of substitution, as I told you before."

"Substitution?" queried the inspector, doubtfully. "I'm afraid I don't quite get you, sir."

"This is what they did," explained Sir Clinton. "They fabricated an imaginary love-affair between Barratt and Mrs. Callis, paralleling their own one. Barratt was a substitute for the real Callis, and Mrs. Callis was the substitute for Helen Barratt. Then they buttressed this shadow-intrigue with evidence drawn from their own liaison, and they filled in gaps with materials in their possession, until they had lent the shadow an apparent solidity. In practice, they substituted so much that in the end they overdid the business."

"It would sound more convincing if you would show us how it worked out in detail," said Wendover, critically. "As you've put it, I can't say I think much of it."

"Very well," agreed the Chief Constable. "I'll start on the assumption I've made, and take the affair chronologically. They must have spent a lot of hard thinking over the details before they actually launched out; but we can omit that and begin with the visit which Barratt and his wife made to the Alcazar Hotel, a few weeks ago. Barratt wrote the labels for their luggage. Mrs. Barratt secured those labels when they got to the Alcazar. That accounts for the labels in Barratt's handwriting which were tied to the two suit-cases recovered from the left-luggage office by Sergeant Quilter. They were just the labels of the previous visit."

"Well, I'm damned!" ejaculated Rufford, in a tone of extreme vexation. "I never thought of that! And there it was, staring me in the face. I see now what you meant by substitution, sir."

"Take another example of it, then," went on Sir Clinton. "As I told you, these two hadn't managed to conceal their intrigue completely. At least one person had suspicions about it. That person wrote an anonymous letter. Here it is. '*You must be very blind if you don't see what goes on under your nose. Watch your wife and you'll see what other people have seen long ago. A preacher ought to set a better example. There's a plain hint to you. And read Proverbs, VII.*' When Callis handed over that letter to you, inspector, you naturally assumed that *he* had received it from the writer, and that the wife referred to in it was Mrs. Callis. But read it as addressed to Barratt and you'll see it in a fresh light. '*Watch your wife . . . A preacher ought to set a better example*' by stopping the immorality which was going on under his own roof. Remember, too, Mrs. Barratt volunteered that she also had received an anonymous letter which she had put into the fire I imagine that it denounced her conduct, so she destroyed it."

"But how could Callis get hold of a letter written to Barratt?" demanded Wendover, sceptically.

"Barratt was the sort of man who'd show it to his wife; and no doubt she managed to retain it and pass it on to Callis," said the Chief Constable. "I don't profess to know precisely how it was done. I'm merely showing you how the substitution-hypothesis fits the facts. The wording satisfies me that it was written to Barratt and not to Callis."

"Kerrison wrote it, of course?" interjected Wendover.

"Yes, and if Kerrison had lived, we'd have definite proof from him that he sent it to Barratt and not to Callis. Which was one reason why Kerrison came to a bad end and didn't live to tell his tale," Sir Clinton pointed out. "You remember I was going to visit him next day, but that was too late."

"Please go on, sir," urged Rufford, who was now seeing the whole case from a fresh standpoint and was eager to see it fitted together.

"The next episode is the fake elopement and the deaths of Mrs. Callis and Barratt," the Chief Constable continued. "The idea was to suggest suicide as the result of a suicide pact. But a suicide pact by itself might have roused suspicions. There wasn't enough evidence of a long intrigue between Barratt and Mrs. Callis. But supply evidence of a planned elopement and it goes to prove that the intrigue has been going on for a while. That strengthens the shadow-case markedly, doesn't it? And, what's more, by superimposing a suicide pact affair on the elopement preparations, you tend to make people spend their energy on wondering why the pair of them suicided at all, instead of examining the facts for another explanation."

This described Rufford's own doings so well that he grew rather red in the face and refrained from any comment.

"Now look at these elopement preparations," Sir Clinton continued. "Take the two suit-cases that Quilter extracted from the left-luggage office. When I saw the lists of contents, it seemed to be a rummy sort of packing. Take Barratt's suit-case first. No shaving-tackle, a new tooth-brush and new hair-brushes. Why had his hair-brushes and tooth-brush been left out? Well, most of us brush our teeth and our hair more than once a day. But that suit-case was dumped in the left-luggage office in the morning. Suppose that Mrs. Barratt had packed it surreptitiously. She couldn't risk packing these brushes, because Barratt, when he came home for luncheon—dinner, in his case—might want to brush his teeth or his hair; and then he would miss his brushes and want to know what had become of them. So new brushes were bought and put into the suit-case instead. As to the shaving-tackle, it's possible that a woman might forget that altogether. But as it stood in the Barratt bath-room in plain sight—you noticed it yourself, inspector—it's likely that it was left out of the packing lest Barratt should notice that it had gone amissing."

"That was one of the first things that made you suspicious, wasn't it?" asked Wendover.

"Yes, and my suspicions got a good deal deeper when I ran over the things missing from the Callis suit-case. No tooth-brush, tooth-paste, nail-brush, face-cloth or sponge; and no brush and comb, although they were lying quite handy on the dressing-table. The same reasoning applies to the lot; they might be missed during the day if they were packed up. A black dress, but no corresponding belt, although it was an essential part of the outfit. That's a man's blunder. A woman wouldn't have made it. No manicure set or beauty-box. That might be forgetfulness or perhaps it wasn't safe to risk removing them, as Mrs. Callis might take a fancy to use them during the day. One might have expected to find a hair cap and a dressing-gown or dressing-jacket. I'm inclined to put their absence down as a masculine oversight. Put the two lists together, and one can't help a suspicion that a woman packed the Barratt suit-case whilst a man packed the suit-case supposed to belong to Mrs. Callis. Certainly one can't account for the various brush omissions except on the assumption I've made. By the time I'd run over these two lists, I was well on my way to the notion of substitution, and that without having to press the facts too far, either."

"And the next point?" asked Wendover, as Sir Clinton paused.

"Well, there's that telegram to the Alcazar, booking a double room for the night of the murder and so supplying further evidence that the sham elopement had been carefully planned in advance. And, just in case Barratt got wind of the reply telegram without actually seeing it, we have the wire from Callis which Mrs. Barratt could produce if Barratt asked about a wire being delivered. He might have spotted the telegraph boy at the door, you see; so it was advisable to have something to show him in that case. Really, this affair was very creditably planned, apart from the inevitable blunders."

"You make it sound damned plausible," Wendover conceded in a rather aggrieved tone. "But then you always do sound damned plausible when you start in with your explanations. What comes next?"

"Another bit of substitution. That fake wedding-ring had to be ordered and engraved, ready to slip on to Mrs. Callis's finger instead of her real one. Again, you see, the idea was to suggest a fairly longstanding intrigue between her and Barratt."

"And after that?" asked Wendover.

"Callis had to persuade Kerrison to borrow a Colt automatic for shooting cats. Obviously the barrel in that pistol when it was lent to Kerrison was the barrel eventually used in the murders. I suppose the idea was to provide a stalking-horse if things got too hot. It would be easy enough to get those cats dug up and the bullets in them examined. Their rifling-marks would implicate Kerrison, if one chose to look on the affair from that point of view. Once the cats were shot Callis recovered the barrel under pretence of cleaning the pistol, as I demonstrated to you is possible. After that, if the borrowed pistol disappeared—as it did—the obvious explanation would be that Kerrison left it beside the bodies, where Inspector Rufford found it."

"Substitution again," commented Wendover. "Certainly it does seem to run through the whole business, as you said. Go on."

"We can go on now to the actual day of the tragedy," Sir Clinton proceeded. "After breakfast, Barratt went out to the meeting of that organ committee. Callis was there from ten-fifteen to eleven-fifteen. Note what he did, according to the organist's evidence. He got up a squabble with Barratt—which was an easy enough matter, considering Barratt's character—and under pretence of pique he left the group and stalked about the church. Nobody would notice what he was doing. In a case like that, one doesn't stare after a man. So while he was unobserved, he slipped that appointment note—'*Wait for me after the service,*'—etc. into one of Mrs. Callis's books in her pew. Nothing very *outré* in a man wandering to his own pew in the church and fingering the books, is there?"

"No, sir. That's quite clever on his part," said Rufford. "But where did that note come from originally, I'd like to know. It's in Barratt's own fist; there's no question of forgery. And it had Barratt's address on the paper, too."

"Curious thing, inspector," said Sir Clinton. "That address convinced you that it was a genuine document. It convinced me that it was a fake. I put it to you. If you were conducting an intrigue and meant to leave a message for your paramour in her hymn-book where it might be discovered if anyone happened to sit in that pew and use the books on the desk, would you go out of your way to stamp your address on the paper? I'm a simple fellow myself, but I don't think I'd be quite such a zany as to do that. It's the old substitution business again. That was a genuine document."

"Genuine?" said the inspector, startled. "Then you mean there *was* some game on between Barratt and Mrs. Callis?"

"Just think it over," suggested Sir Clinton. "What sort of a woman was Mrs. Barratt? Didn't she produced one document after another when we asked for them? She keeps ordinary papers carefully, obviously. Wouldn't she preserve the love-letters she got from Barratt in her day with equal care? Most people keep love-letters and when the first burst of enthusiasm is over, they still keep them—perhaps because they're too lazy to destroy them. Mrs. Barratt, I think, was the kind of person who would preserve every scrap of a note that she got from Barratt during their courtship. This appointment letter was one of them."

"But it had their married address on it..." began Rufford. "Oh, I see, sir. The embossing press I saw on his desk! She stamped the address on the paper with that and so brought the thing up to date. That was it?"

"I expect it was," said Sir Clinton. "It sounds likely enough, doesn't it? Now we'll go on with the tale, if you want more. Callis left that organ committee meeting at eleven-fifteen. He had his car with him, and in his car, I imagine, the suit-case with the Strathpeffer label on it and its rather peculiar contents. He picked up Mrs. Barratt at some prearranged place to which she had brought the second suit-case. Callis, I believe, had a dark soft felt hat with him, the semi-clerical kind, which he wore when he was taking the London single tickets and dumping the suit-cases in the left-luggage office. The hat, of course, was intended to make the officials think they remembered a clergyman, if they were questioned later on. Meanwhile, Mrs. Barratt had gone to send off the faked Longnor wire of invitation from the G.P.O., where her appearance would not be noticed, as it might have been if she'd gone to some small district office. And, just to complete the story of that morning, Barratt seems to have gone to the bank and cashed the twenty-five-pound cheque we heard about. That was intended to suggest that he had enough cash in hand to start his elopement with. My impression is that we may find these notes in Mrs. Barratt's possession, which would account for their disappearance from Barratt's note-case. I bank a little on her not having destroyed them. That would go against the grain in the Alvington family, with its highly-developed money-sense. She's probably thought it safe to hold on to them, so long as she doesn't use them for a year or two. If we find them in her possession, it's always an extra bit of evidence. If we don't, it's a small matter. Make a note of it, please, inspector."

"Very good, sir," said Rufford. "But will you please go on? You're coming to the real business now."

"We'll take the Barratt side of things first, then," Sir Clinton continued. "In the afternoon, Barratt went out to call on some of his congregation. Mrs. Barratt tells us that she went to a picture-house and did some shopping. She was home first, and he followed soon afterwards. They had supper at seven. Then, while Mrs. Barratt was washing up the dishes, Barratt went off to the meeting in the church hall, taking his black bag with him. Mrs. Barratt did not go to that meeting. Just before nine o'clock, she rang up Mrs. Stacey; so we know that she was at home then, because that call has been checked by Mrs. Stacey's evidence. She was still at home at ten-fifteen, because Miss Legard rang her up then about the loss of the Jubilee double-florin. That was a thing which could not have been foreseen, so it seems clear that Mrs. Barratt really spent that evening at home."

Sir Clinton took out his case and lighted a cigarette before continuing. Wendover followed his example; but the inspector, being a pipe-smoker, refused the cigarette which was offered to him.

"Now let's turn to the doings of the Callis family," the Chief Constable went on. "This is guesswork, very largely;

but you'll find it fits neatly enough into the definite evidence which we have in our hands. We know from the evidence of the maid that Callis came home for luncheon rather earlier than usual, in advance of his wife. That was to make sure that he could secure the faked Longnor wire before Mrs. Callis saw it. He pocketed it, and next morning he told the maid its contents and explained that Mrs. Callis was at Mrs. Longnor's on a short visit. That accounted for the maid finding only one set of supper-dishes used, when she came to wash up, and it kept her from asking questions about her mistress's absence. So you see that the Longnor telegram served more than one purpose."

"A clever devil, evidently," said Wendover, reluctantly.

"My impression is that Mrs. Callis stayed in the house that afternoon," Sir Clinton continued. "She took a bath, probably just before supper-time."

"How do you know that, sir?" interrupted the inspector.

"Because the maid noticed a second cube of bath-salts had disappeared, as she told the inspector. Also because when he found the body next morning he detected a fairly marked odour of the verbena bath-salts. That suggests that she'd had a bath within the last twenty-four hours."

"We'll pass that," said Wendover. "I don't suppose it's important, anyhow."

"It helps to suggest that Callis was lying when he said that his wife went off during the afternoon," Sir Clinton pointed out. "The next probability is that he and his wife had supper together."

"Why 'probability'?" Wendover demanded. "You've no proof of that. No one saw them."

"No," admitted Sir Clinton, "but the maid gave us the supper menu: cold fowl, salad, and apple pie. And in Dr. Fanthorpe's P.M. report he mentioned that Mrs. Callis's last meal contained apples, fowl, potatoes, and bread. Say 'potato salad' and the two are identical. If Mrs. Callis had gone to a restaurant for that meal, is it likely that she'd have chosen precisely the same dishes as Callis was eating at home? It's much more probable that she had supper with him."

"I suppose so," conceded Wendover. "Pass that also. Go on."

"The next bit's pure guesswork," Sir Clinton admitted frankly. "I assume that Callis persuaded his wife to go out for a drive in their car after supper. He ran a certain risk there, if anyone had happened to notice them together in the car; but evidently he was lucky. He had taken the precaution to wear a darkish suit which could suggest a clerical garb, and he wore a dark felt hat to increase the likeness. In one pocket he had a loaded automatic with the barrel which he had extracted from Kerrison's pistol. In the other pocket he had a second automatic with two cartridges less than the full load, one being in the breech and the rest in the magazine. This represented a pistol from which two shots had been fired. He had carefully cleaned every vestige of a finger-print off its metal. And he took those love-letters with him also, as well as the railway tickets and the left-luggage receipt.

"I assume that he drove about a bit and then arrived at the bracken-patch. It would be easy enough to suggest that they should go up and look at the view. That was about nine. The two youngsters saw them arrive, coming up through the bracken in Indian file, and young Polly actually heard the murder of Mrs. Callis and her exclamation of dismay when Callis shot her."

"Wait a bit!" said Wendover, holding up his hand sharply. "What that girl heard was: 'Don't, John, *please* don't!' John? John Barratt surely. How do you make that fit?"

"John Callis, not John Barratt," Sir Clinton pointed out mildly. "You've forgotten that both men had the same Christian name."

"Oh, so they had. I'd forgotten that," mumbled Wendover, rather crestfallen. "But that girl Polly heard two shots at that time. Why the *two* shots?"

"Because Callis was faking a suicide pact, which implied a couple of shots close together," Sir Clinton pointed out. "There was no great risk in that. The only danger would have been if the same person heard the first pair and then, an hour later, the second pair: the pair that Kerrison heard at ten o'clock. But no one did hear both pairs."

"All right," said Wendover. "Go on."

"Callis shot his wife with the Kerrison barrel," Sir Clinton went on, forbearing even to smile at his friend's discomfiture. "That left the Kerrison barrel rifling-marks on the bullet, of course. Then he took the platinum wedding-ring from his dead wife's finger and replaced it by the faked gold ring with the initials on it. After that, he went down to his car, following the track he had made in coming up. And he drove off towards town."

"It seems a very risky affair," Wendover criticised. "What if some adult had seen the murder, instead of those two children? He might have been interrupted, if there had been a man on the spot."

"In that case, I'd be sorry for the man," Sir Clinton declared. "Callis is not a gentleman who sticks at much, apparently. I imagine that he'd have shot any interrupter out of hand, and he was a crack shot, remember. In that case, the thing would have worn a different aspect, and no doubt we'd have been on the hunt for a homicidal maniac as the likeliest murderer. But, if you don't mind, I've got my hands full in accounting for the real crime without dragging in imaginary ones as well."

"Well, go on with your reconstruction, then," said Wendover, tacitly admitting the justice of this.

"Just fit in here a bit of definite evidence to keep us in touch with reality," Sir Clinton suggested. "Callis left his wife dead among the bracken a few minutes after nine. At nine-twenty-five, the railway-guard Judkins noticed a woman's figure lying up there, with no one near her. Callis had gone, by that time. That fits, you see."

"Yes, sir, it does—and neatly too," said Rufford. "Your idea does seem to hang together, when it dovetails in with all these odd bits of evidence. Please go on."

"The next bit is pure guesswork again," admitted the Chief Constable frankly. "Callis knew roughly when that meeting in the church hall was likely to end; and he knew the route that Barratt would take in walking home from the hall. It's some little distance. I've no doubt he picked up Barratt on the road. Again he was running the risk of someone noticing the two of them together; but it wasn't a big risk, I think. Anyhow, he did pick up Barratt, I'm certain of that."

"I see, sir," interjected Rufford. "Because Barratt's black bag was found in the car later on?"

"Obviously," said the Chief Constable. "So Barratt was undoubtedly picked up somehow. Mrs. Callis couldn't do it. She was dead by that time. And it was Callis's car. Therefore Callis must have done it, if you want to square theory with facts. Assume that Barratt got into the car. Callis had to keep him there by talk until he could drive out to the bracken-patch again. If I had been in Callis's shoes, I'd have found one topic easily enough: the anonymous letter and the actual intrigue with Mrs. Barratt. Callis could make a fuss about the accusation in the letter; and say he had one of the same sort himself. All he wanted was a subject which would rivet Barratt's attention temporarily, and that topic would do the trick better than any other.

"Callis must have made some excuse to hand Barratt the unfingered automatic, so as to get the Barratt prints on it. That would not be difficult. Then when they came to the lane below the bracken-patch, Callis evidently turned his car before they got out. That would give him an opportunity of having a look at the bracken to see if there was anyone about the spot where his wife's body lay. Evidently he saw no one. It must have been darkish by that time, for they got there about ten o'clock. Callis had some excuse ready for going up into the bracken, obviously. When they got out of the car, Barratt left his black bag behind him, and they went into the bracken side by side, as the broad trail showed."

"And when he had led him up to his wife's body, Callis shot him with the pistol with the Kerrison barrel, I suppose?" said Wendover.

"Exactly," agreed the Chief Constable. "He fired two shots as before, the two shots which Kerrison heard at about ten o'clock. Since his wife's body was undisturbed, he probably reckoned that no one had heard the first pair of reports. After firing, he had several things to do. The first one was to transfer the Kerrison barrel from his own automatic to the pistol he had handed to Barratt."

"What about his own finger-prints, then?" demanded Wendover.

"What are gloves for?" retorted Sir Clinton. "Then he had to scatter the fragments of those two love-letters on the ground near the bodies. I expect he'd brought them, ready torn up, in an envelope so as to avoid finger-marking them as he threw them about. He had to stuff the railway tickets and the left-luggage receipt into Barratt's pocket. After that, he made his way, probably by a devious route, to the bus line, and so got home before his maid was likely to turn up. He had to leave his car, of course, since it was supposed to have been brought to the lovers' nook by Mrs. Callis; and she was dead."

"I don't quite see my way through that love-letter business, sir," objected Rufford, with a certain diffidence. "The one in Mrs. Callis's writing had the Fern Bank address on it, printed; and yet it sounded as if it had been written by a woman who was terribly keen on the man she was writing to."

"I thought I'd cleared that up already," said the Chief Constable. "I can't have been as lucid as I meant to be, evidently. The thing to remember is that Mrs. Callis was living at Fern Bank before she got engaged to Callis. When they married, he simply settled down in the same house."

"Ah, of course!" said Wendover, enlightened by this.

"It's another case of substitution," Sir Clinton explained to the inspector. "These were genuine love-letters: one written by Barratt to Helen Alvington during his courtship, and one written by Esther Prestage to Callis during their engagement. The Barratt one was on plain paper and he'd written no address on it. What was simpler than to put 35 *Granville Road* on it with the embossing press, thus bringing it neatly up to date? And the date on it, you remember, was on a missing fragment, which Callis destroyed before scattering the stuff about. That made it look quite genuine as a recent epistle from Barratt to Mrs. Callis. As to the one written by Mrs. Callis, there was a slip in the cogs from Callis's point of view. The original love-letter had a Roman type heading. That was the kind of paper that Mrs. Callis used in the days of her engagement. Later, she took a fancy to a Gothic type heading, so that the only note-paper of this kind in her house had this later heading on it. That was awkward for Callis, if we asked to see samples of current note-paper. So he provided against that by ordering a box or two of the same tinted paper with the old Roman heading at the top; and he handed out a sample without a qualm when he was asked for it. Unfortunately for him, he didn't notice that his new Roman type paper had a watermark different from the earlier stuff. The love-letter was on wove paper with the FINLANDIA watermark and a Roman heading. The sample he produced, purporting to come from the same batch, was tinted exactly like the other, but it was laid paper, ZEBRA CREST watermark, and a Roman heading. The FINLANDIA paper has been off the mark for a year and more, as I told you; and in recent times Mrs. Callis has favoured Gothic headings. Obviously, then, she hadn't written that love-letter in these days. In fact, it dated back to the Callis-Prestage engagement period. And I've no doubt that Callis selected that particular letter from his collection because it had no date on it beyond 'Tuesday,' which gave nothing away. When I put all these points together, I was pretty certain that my substitution theory was correct."

"And of course the 'Dearest John' on the love-letter was John Callis, wasn't he?" asked Rufford.

"Of course. If Barratt's name hadn't been the same as his own, Callis would no doubt have picked out some letter starting with 'Dearest' or 'Darling'; but the coincidence in the names made the thing look even more convincing."

"He's a clever brute," commented the inspector, in no very admiring tone.

"Now we can finish his doings that night," Sir Clinton went on. "He got home again unobserved and washed up the dishes which his wife had used at supper-time, leaving his own lot dirty. That was to make the maid believe that Mrs. Callis had not been there for supper, and so to furnish further evidence of the elopement idea. After that, all he had to do was to sit well in view with a book in his hand, to make sure that the maid noticed him when she came back at eleven-twenty. Mrs. Barratt was prepared to swear that he had been with her at Granville Road between nine and ten, which gave him an alibi for the times of both the murders."

"She was a good deal older than he was, I think you said," Wendover remarked after a pause. "And from your account she's a strong character. I suppose that it was she who led him into the whole business. From what you say about her family characteristics where money is concerned, she had every incentive to avoid either a scandal or even a divorce, since either of them would have led old Mrs. Alvington to cut her out of her will. She must have been a regular Delilah."

"I'm not sure I agree with you," said Sir Clinton, thoughtfully. "Did you ever come across a letter of Benjamin Franklin, giving advice to a young friend on the choice of a mistress? It was printed by Tennyson Jesse in the introduction to a volume in the Notable British Trials series."

"Is that the Franklin who flew a kite in a thunder-storm, sir?" inquired the inspector.

"The same," Sir Clinton assured him. "But he knew a lot about other things than electricity. Human nature, for one. His advice was that his young friend should get married. But if the young man insisted on taking a mistress, Franklin advised him to choose a mature one rather than a young girl, and he gave no less than eight reasons for this. The eighth one was: '*They are so grateful.*'"

"Oh, indeed?" said the inspector in a sceptical tone. "Do you agree with Franklin, sir?"

"Well, let's take Mrs. Barratt as an example," Sir Clinton suggested. "She was married young, probably before she'd gained enough experience of the world to make a suitable choice. Barratt was no doubt a decent enough man, but he came from a lower class and he was hardly a type that's capable of adapting itself to a fresh environment. Through no real fault on either side, those two could hardly run harmoniously in double harness, once the initial enthusiasm wore off. She said as much to you, didn't she, inspector?"

"Pretty plainly, sir. What struck me was that she really seemed quite indifferent in the matter. I mean, she hadn't any animus against Barratt for spoiling her life, or anything of that kind. I got the impression that he'd simply ceased to count, so far as she was concerned."

"So I inferred," Sir Clinton agreed. "But then Callis came along, and that must have roused a fresh interest in her. It's quite on the cards that she laid herself out to capture him, and succeeded. But once she'd secured him, things would take on a different aspect if she really fell in love with him. She was eight years or so older than he was. And she was just the age when age may begin to tell on a woman. See her in the street and you might take Mrs. Barratt for twenty-seven or twenty-eight. See her close at hand, and you'd perhaps notice these tiny betraying wrinkles about the mouth which destroy the illusion of fresh youth. She must have seen them herself in her mirror and understood that they were the fore-runners of further ravages to come. That's an awkward discovery for a woman who has captured a man younger than herself, and who means to keep him if she can. In the initiation of the affair, she may have been the dominant spirit; but once the intrigue started and she recognised that her physical charms were on the wane, the tables would be turned and it would be for her to go any length in order to retain Callis. She was 'so grateful,' I imagine. She wasn't prepared to give him up: that's plain. To keep him, she would have to marry him if possible. And I think one may assume that Callis was madly in love with her and wanted her for himself. Nothing else will fit the facts."

"That seems reasonable enough," Wendover conceded.

"Now bear in mind the Alvington money-sense," Sir Clinton pursued. "Suppose the intrigue leaked out and either Barratt or Mrs. Callis insisted on a divorce. If Mrs. Callis brought a case against Callis, she would retain her own private income and Callis would be no great catch financially. And if Mrs. Barratt came into court as either respondent or co-respondent, old Mrs. Alvington would change her will again and make sure that Mrs. Barratt never saw a penny of her money. Divorce, then, in any form, meant financial stringency for both Callis and Mrs. Barratt. And Mrs. Barratt had already had more than enough experience of that condition. But if you exclude divorce as a solution then the only other course open is the removal of both Barratt and Mrs. Callis. That course was the one that evidently recommended itself as the best way of cutting the knot."

"So they laid their heads together and evolved this scheme?" asked Wendover.

"They decided on murder," corrected Sir Clinton, "but when it came to planning the business, Callis was the leading spirit and Mrs. Barratt merely followed and took his orders."

"How do you make that out?" demanded Wendover in surprise.

"Look at the whole business of the substituted pistol barrels," said Sir Clinton. "That was the keystone of the affair. You must admit it was planned by a fire-arms expert. Callis was *au fait* with pistols. Mrs. Barratt knew nothing about their technique; she would never have hit on a notion like that. On the face of it, Callis was the planner of the murder episode, and he had the major part of the work to do in carrying it out. The woman merely helped him where necessary."

Rufford seemed to have been thinking of something else for a moment or two; and the trend of his thoughts betrayed itself when he spoke.

"Now, I see something that puzzled me, sir. All through the affair, when I happened to have a suspicion of Callis, one thing always put me off again, and that was the genuine way he protested about his wife's innocence. That rang absolutely true. Now, of course, I see that it *was* true. No one knew better than himself that there was no intrigue between his wife and Barratt. He could afford to be genuine there."

"Quite so," agreed Sir Clinton. "But to continue what I was saying before. The Kerrison murder furnishes another proof that Callis was the planner and Mrs. Barratt merely the helper. Not that it matters a rap, really. As an accessory before the fact in both cases, she's liable to the full penalty, even if she wasn't present when the actual murders were done. But I don't think that she was the dominant partner in any of them. Callis was the leading spirit."

"He must have been mad keen on the woman," said Rufford. "But even yet, I don't see how Kerrison's death came into the business. Why had they to put a finish to him?"

"The Kerrison case is easier than the other one," Sir Clinton explained. "Do you remember what happened when we interviewed him? He blurted out that the 'suicide pact' had surprised him. He'd never suspected Barratt of any intrigue.

In fact, he went the length of saying: 'I was very much mistaken and I frankly admit it. I judged too hastily.' Look back, now, and you see at once what this admitted mistake was. He'd suspected all along the intrigue between Callis and Mrs. Barratt; and he was thunderstruck to find that Barratt and Mrs. Callis were guilty, as the suicide pact business seemed to prove. I don't think I'd have noticed that point, but for two things. First, Kerrison was the last person to admit a mistake unless it was a glaring one. These fanatics never confess that they're wrong unless the evidence is incontrovertible, and not even then in some cases. Second, I'd already spotted the substitution business, and I was on the look-out for anything which fitted in with it, as Kerrison's remarks did."

"I never noticed that bit of his talk," Rufford confessed frankly. "He was obviously not quite in his right mind over the Great Pyramid and the rest of it, sir, and I didn't pay much attention to what he said. But I see the point now."

"The next thing is that Kerrison wrote to Callis about some church business, and Callis happened to spot that the watermark on Kerrison's note-paper was the same as the one on the anonymous letter: '*Watch your wife . . .*' It didn't take a smart lad like Callis very long to put two and two together and satisfy himself that these two letters on the AVIAN WOVE note-paper were written by the same person—Kerrison. And Kerrison was dangerous. He was a loose-tongued creature, as these two slander actions had proved up to the hilt. At any moment he might blab something about the Callis intrigue with Mrs. Barratt, which he obviously suspected when he wrote that anonymous letter to Barratt. And that would have brought down the whole house of cards at once, if we had got hold of it, as Callis saw immediately. So the only thing to do was to knock out Kerrison before he had a chance to let the cat out of the bag. I'll say this for Callis, he must be a quick thinker and a swift worker, for he managed to kill two birds with one stone that very night.

"He rang up Kerrison and asked him to come down that evening to Fern Bank, making some church business his excuse, no doubt. And, although I can't prove it, I'm certain that he asked Kerrison to bring back the pistol he'd borrowed to shoot those cats. Meanwhile, Callis had got in touch with Mrs. Barratt and completed the other half of his arrangements. She went off to visit the Mallards in Windsor Drive. When she left them, about nine-thirty, she walked along the road and, with the key she had, opened the Alvington garage and took out Arthur's blue car. As Callis had arranged to visit the Alvingtons that night and go through their books, both of the brothers would be at home and the car was sure to be in the garage. She got it out, and took it to a rendezvous close to Callis's house.

"Meanwhile Kerrison turned up at Fern Bank about nine o'clock. Callis told us that, and here I'm sure he stuck closely to the truth. He tackled Kerrison about the anonymous letter, just as he explained to us; and he put him into a blue funk by the threat of a third action—for libel over the anonymous letter. Then he dictated an apology which Kerrison was forced to write down. And here, once again, in comes the old substitution process. Here's the letter. You see it begins: 'I confess that I wrote an anonymous letter reflecting on the character of one of my friends . . ." Kerrison would understand that this meant Callis himself. But Callis represented to me that what he really wanted was to clear his wife's name and that 'one of my friends' was Mrs. Callis. That was meant to put us finally on the wrong track and to clinch the substitution hypothesis."

"Damned ingenious," Wendover admitted rather sourly.

"I told you he was a quick thinker," said Sir Clinton. "I've no doubt that he got the pistol from Kerrison before the row began. Not that he was afraid of trouble in that way, but for another reason. But let's go on. Having got the confession written to his dictation, he rang up Mrs. Barratt to make sure that she had gone off to play her part by securing the car; and also to support the yarn he was going to tell us. After that, he dismissed Kerrison, who went off to take his bus home. As soon as he was off the premises, Callis went hot-foot to the rendezvous. Mrs. Barratt handed over the blue car to him and went back to Granville Road to borrow that tea and so establish that she wasn't near the Hermitage when the smash took place.

"Callis drove hell-for-leather to the bus stop at the end of the road leading to the Hermitage; and he waited there in the blue car until Kerrison's bus came up and his victim got out. Then he did the trick and silenced Kerrison once and for all. After that, he drove back to the Alvingtons' place, put the car in quietly, locked the door with Mrs. Barratt's key, and got off home as quick as he could. He landed there in time to beat his maid by a short head, and he gave her some orders about breakfast, just to fix in her memory the fact that he was in the house when she arrived."

"He'd certainly tangled things up very neatly," Wendover admitted. "He'd no car of his own, just then, owing to the smash-up in Granby Holt; so on the face of things he'd lost the power of quick movement. That blocked out the possibility of his going to Windsor Drive and collecting the Alvington car himself. There wasn't time to do that and still get to the bus stop at the Hermitage in time to intercept Kerrison. On that basis, I'd ruled Callis out. And as Mrs. Barratt could prove she was in Granville Road just about the time of the motor-smash at the Hermitage, I ruled her out also. I was backing one of the Alvingtons as the criminal in that affair. He's a clever devil, as you say. But what was the point about the pistol?"

"I can't *prove* anything about the pistol," Sir Clinton pointed out. "But when we searched the Hermitage, we found no pistol. What Callis was driving at is fairly obvious. He meant to suggest that Kerrison had murdered those two in the bracken-patch and left the borrowed pistol beside the bodies. That was a possible line of defence for him if it came to a trial; and the rifling-marks on the bullets in the dead cats would support the argument, since these shots were undoubtedly fired by Kerrison and the marks were identical with those on the bullets used in the murders. With Kerrison dead and the pistol missing that would have been quite a good tale for his barrister to throw at a jury."

The Chief Constable took another cigarette from his case and lighted it before continuing. He turned to Wendover.

"Remember Peter Diamond's parlour game and the twenty-one clues?" he asked. "I think I've managed to weave every one of them into this reconstruction, and they all seem to fall neatly into place, don't they? I've even thrown in a solution of the Kerrison affair, for good measure. Now it's time we turned to business. I'll swear information formally now. You'll sign and seal two warrants, one for Callis and one for Mrs. Barratt. Then we'll hand the warrants over to someone to make the actual arrests. You'd like to see to that yourself, inspector, wouldn't you? It seems a fair division of labour amongst the three of us."

THE END

www.ingramcontent.com/pod-product-compliance
Ingram Content Group UK Ltd.
Pitfield, Milton Keynes, MK11 3LW, UK
UKHW022319280225
455674UK00004B/365